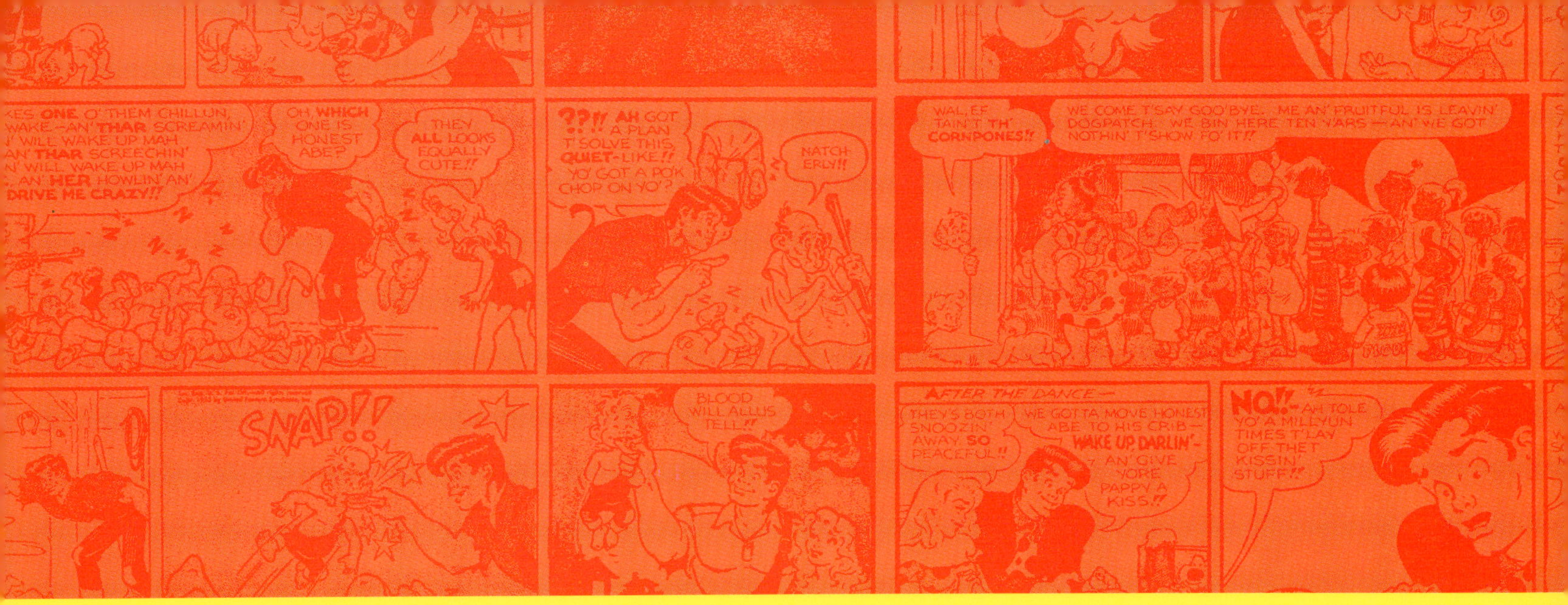
OH, WHICH ONE IS HONEST ABE?
THEY ALL LOOKS EQUALLY CUTE!!
??!! AH GOT A PLAN T'SOLVE THIS QUIET-LIKE!! YO' GOT A POK CHOP ON YO'?
NATCH-ERLY!!
WAL, EF TAIN'T TH' CORNPONES!!
WE COME T'SAY GOO'BYE. ME AN' FRUITFUL IS LEAVIN' DOGPATCH. WE BIN HERE TEN YARS—AN' WE GOT NOTHIN' T'SHOW FO' IT!!
SNAP!!
BLOOD WILL ALLUS TELL!!
AFTER THE DANCE—
THEY'S BOTH SNOOZIN' AWAY SO PEACEFUL!!
WE GOTTA MOVE HONEST ABE TO HIS CRIB— WAKE UP, DARLIN'— AN' GIVE YORE PAPPY A KISS!!
NO!!—AH TOLE YO' A MILLYUN TIMES T'LAY OFF THET KISSIN' STUFF!!

al Capp

LI'L ABNER®

THE FRAZETTA YEARS

VOLUME 1 1954-1955

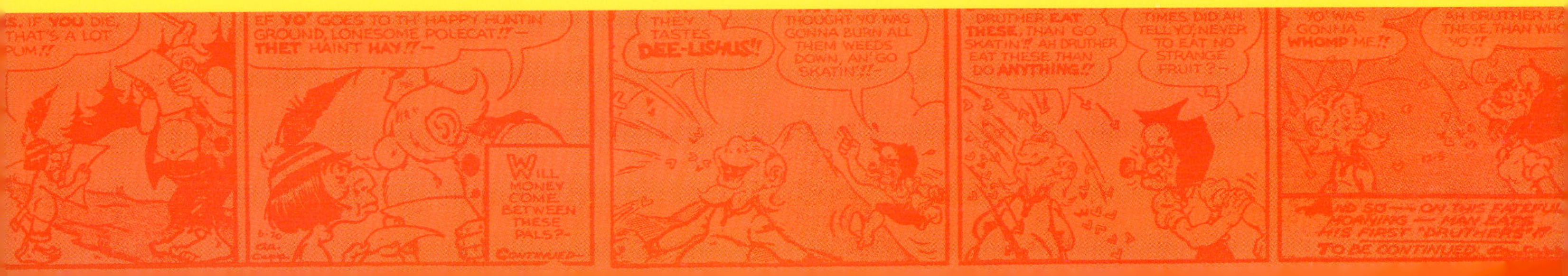
EF YO' GOES TO TH' HAPPY HUNTIN' GROUND, LONESOME POLECAT!!— THET HAIN'T HAY!!—
THEY TASTES DEE-LISHUS!!
THOUGHT YO' WAS GONNA BURN ALL THEM WEEDS DOWN, AN' GO SKATIN'!!—
WILL MONEY COME BETWEEN THESE PALS?
YO' WAS GONNA WHOMP ME!!

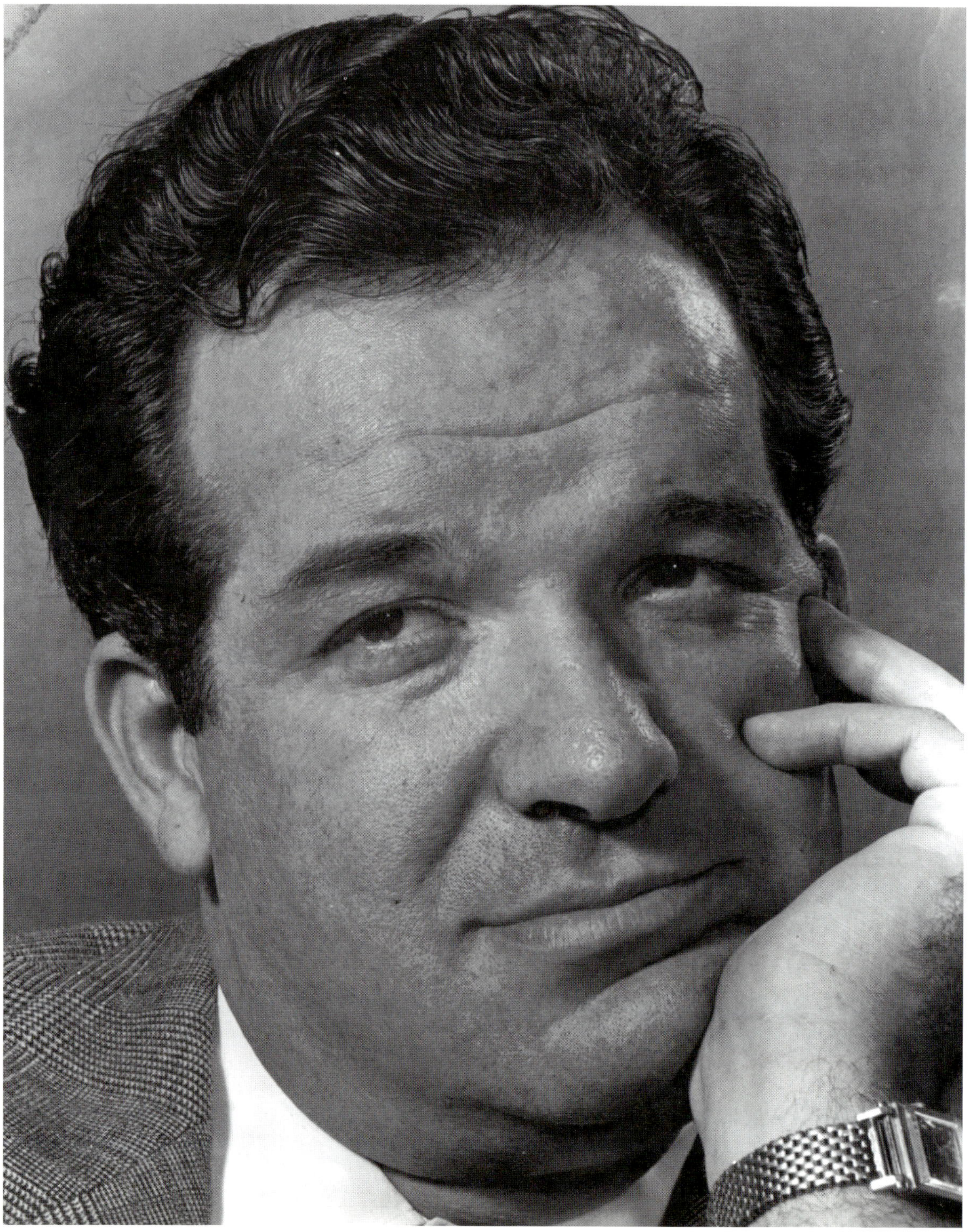

[AL CAPP
1909-1979]

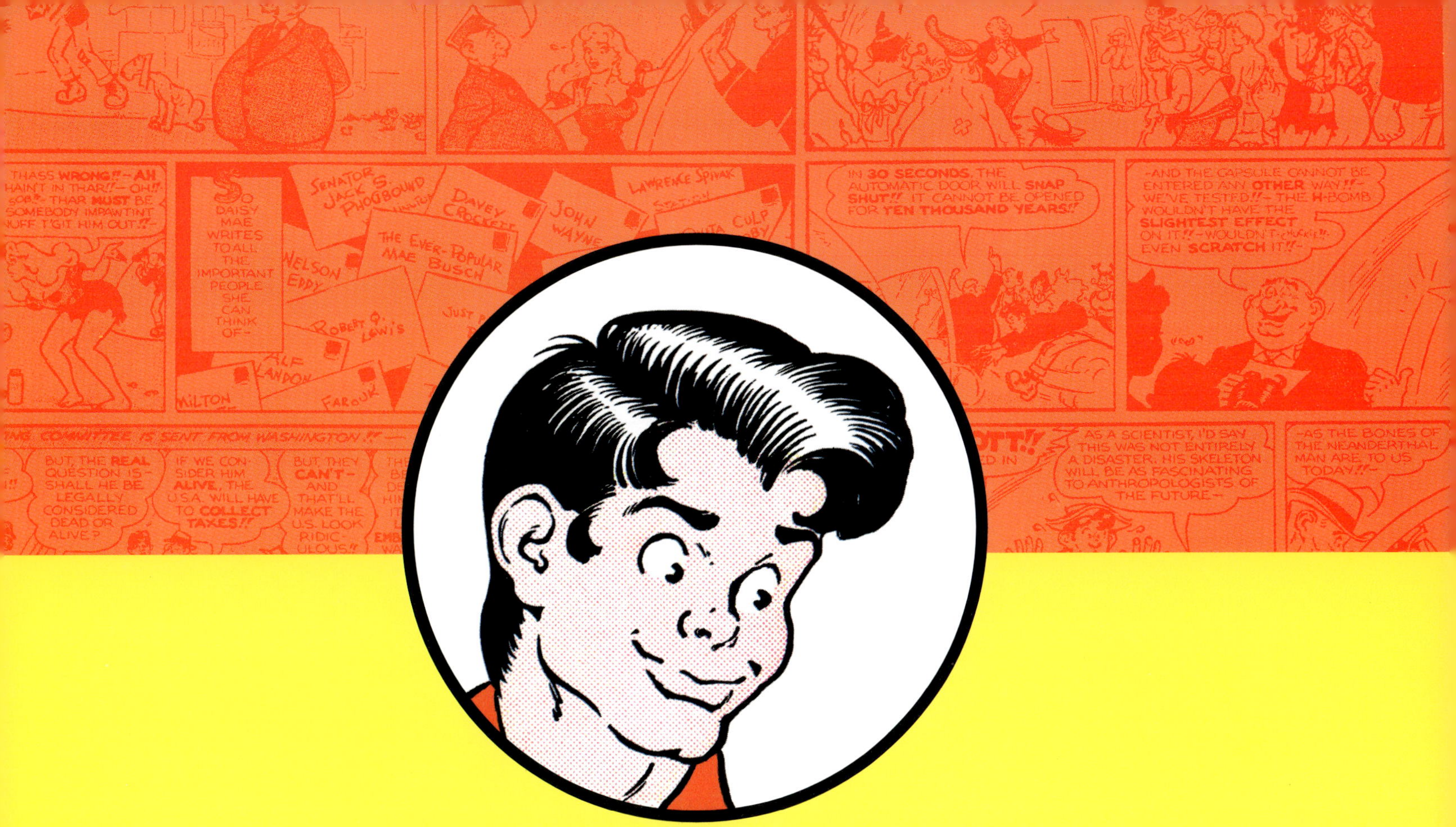
SO DAISY MAE WRITES TO ALL THE IMPORTANT PEOPLE SHE CAN THINK OF–
IN 30 SECONDS, THE AUTOMATIC DOOR WILL SNAP SHUT!! IT CANNOT BE OPENED FOR TEN THOUSAND YEARS!!
–AND THE CAPSULE CANNOT BE ENTERED ANY OTHER WAY!! –WE'VE TESTED!! –THE H-BOMB WOULDN'T HAVE THE SLIGHTEST EFFECT ON IT!! –WOULDN'T–CHUCKLE!!– EVEN SCRATCH IT!!–
BUT, THE REAL QUESTION IS– SHALL HE BE LEGALLY CONSIDERED DEAD OR ALIVE?
IF WE CONSIDER HIM ALIVE, THE U.S.A. WILL HAVE TO COLLECT TAXES!!
BUT THEY CAN'T– AND THAT'LL MAKE THE U.S. LOOK RIDICULOUS!!
AS A SCIENTIST, I'D SAY THIS WAS NOT ENTIRELY A DISASTER. HIS SKELETON WILL BE AS FASCINATING TO ANTHROPOLOGISTS OF THE FUTURE–
–AS THE BONES OF THE NEANDERTHAL MAN ARE, TO US TODAY!!–

AL CAPP

LI'L ABNER®

THE FRAZETTA YEARS

VOLUME 1 1954–1955

EDITED AND COMMENTARY BY

Denis Kitchen

DARK HORSE COMICS®

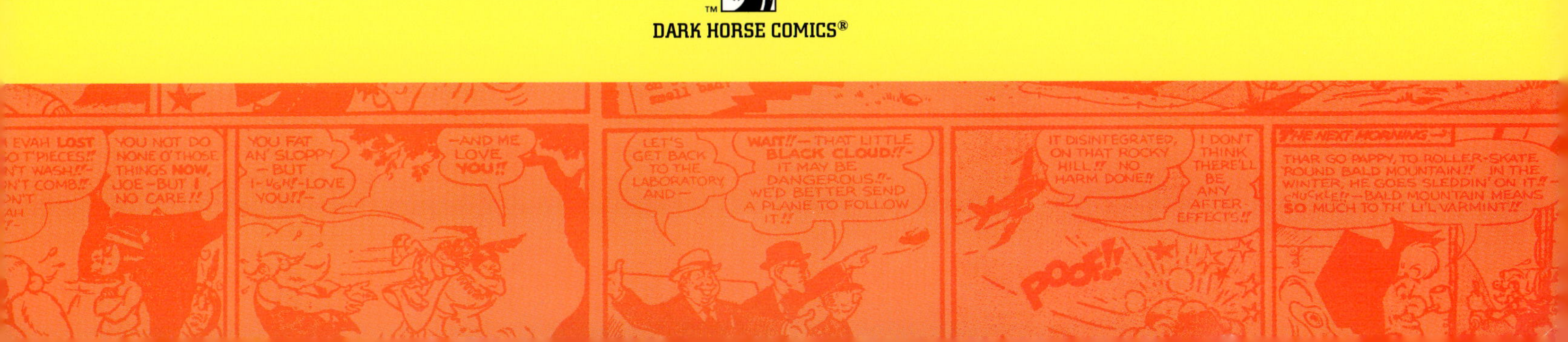
YOU NOT DO NONE O'THOSE THINGS NOW, JOE– BUT I NO CARE!!
YOU FAT AN' SLOPPY– BUT I-UGH!–LOVE YOU!!–
–AND ME LOVE YOU!!
LET'S GET BACK TO THE LABORATORY AND–
WAIT!!–THAT LITTLE BLACK CLOUD!!– IT MAY BE DANGEROUS!!– WE'D BETTER SEND A PLANE TO FOLLOW IT!!
IT DISINTEGRATED, ON THAT ROCKY HILL!! NO HARM DONE!!
I DON'T THINK THERE'LL BE ANY AFTER-EFFECTS!!
THAR GO PAPPY, TO ROLLER-SKATE 'ROUND BALD MOUNTAIN!! IN THE WINTER, HE GOES SLEDDIN' ON IT!! –CHUCKLE!!– BALD MOUNTAIN MEANS SO MUCH TO TH' LI'L VARMINT!!
POOF!!

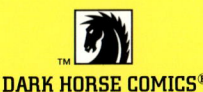

CONTRIBUTING ARTISTS
Frank Frazetta, Andy Amato, and Walter Johnson

DARK HORSE EDITOR
Dave Land

ART DIRECTOR
Mark Cox

DESIGNER
Lia Ribacchi

PUBLISHER
Mike Richardson

AL CAPP'S LI'L ABNER: THE FRAZETTA YEARS VOLUME 1

© 1953, 1954, 1955 and 2003 by Capp Enterprises, Inc. "Li'l Abner" and all other prominently featured characters are registered trademarks of Capp Enterprises, Inc. The Introduction and Annotations are copyright 2003 Denis Kitchen. Dark Horse Comics® is a trademark of Dark Horse Comics, Inc., registered in various categories and countries. All rights reserved. No portion of this publication may be reproduced or transmitted, in any form or by any means, without the express written permission of Dark Horse Comics, Inc. Names, characters, places, and incidents featured in this publication either are the product of the author's imagination or are used fictitiously. Any resemblance to actual persons (living or dead), events, institutions, or locales, without satiric intent, is coincidental.

Dark Horse Comics, Inc.,
10956 SE Main Street, Milwaukie, OR 97222

www.darkhorse.com

Sunday comic pages reproduced in this volume are from the collections of Bill Blackbeard and Denis Kitchen. Original artwork used in this volume came from the collections of Denis Kitchen and Joe & Nadia Mannarino (All-Star Auctions).

For more information about Li'l Abner, visit the official web site of Capp Enterprises, Inc. at www.lil-abner.com.

For out-of-print Li'l Abner books and related Al Capp memorabilia visit Steve Krupp's Gallery & Curio Shoppe at www.deniskitchen.com.

If you have an interest in licensing Li'l Abner, Shmoo, Fearless Fosdick, or related Dogpatch characters for merchandise, contact Denis Kitchen Art Agency, the licensing agent for Capp Enterprises, Inc. at agency@deniskitchen.com.

The editor of this series seeks old newspaper clippings, magazine articles, trade magazine ads, correspondence, memorabilia, artwork, and certain licensed merchandise related to Al Capp and the world of Li'l Abner. In addition, if you own original "Lil Abner" artwork that you would allow to be scanned for future volumes of this series, please contact us as well. E-mail denis@deniskitchen.com or write: DKAA, P.O. Box 9514, North Amherst MA 01054-9514.

Comic Shop Locator Service: (888) 266-4226

First edition: May 2003
ISBN: 1-56971-959-4

1 3 5 7 9 10 8 6 4 2

PRINTED IN CHINA

FAME AND ANONYMITY

Assistant Andy Amato, Al Capp (seated), and assistant Walter Johnson (far right) in Capp's Boston studio in the 1940s.

"Li'l Abner" ranks among the greatest comic strips ever created. Many devotees would argue that it is the greatest. What is indisputable is that Al Capp was the best known and most influential cartoonist of his era. "Li'l Abner," at its peak, appeared in more than 900 newspapers with a daily readership of 90,000,000. A handful of competing comic strips appeared in more newspapers, but Capp's exposure didn't end in the comics section. His personal celebrity transcended comics, reaching the public and influencing the culture in a variety of media. For a while he had his own syndicated newspaper column and his own syndicated radio program. In 1947, he earned a cover story in *Newsweek* and three years later got the same treatment from *Time*.

Other cartoonists were content to accept their share of any merchandising their syndicates

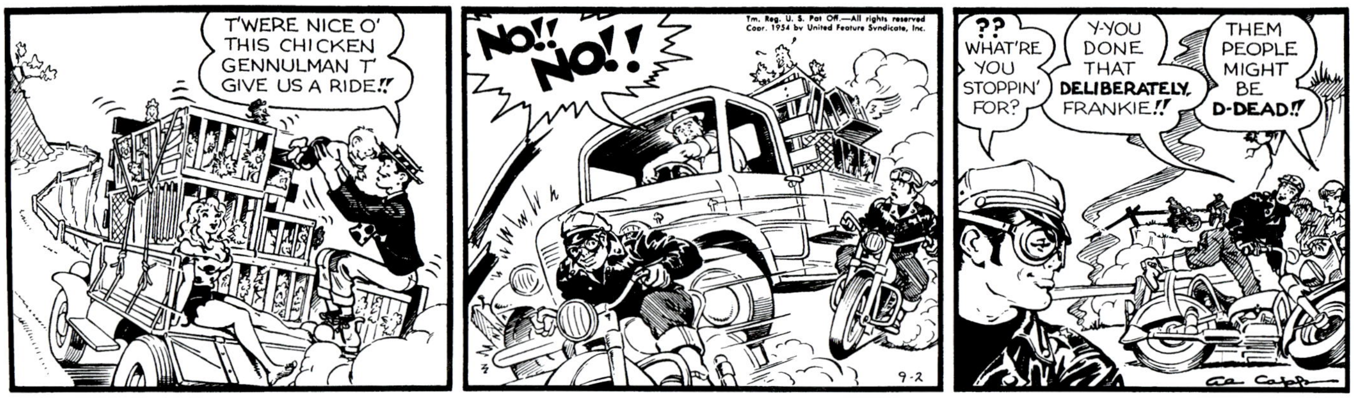
T'WERE NICE O' THIS CHICKEN GENNULMAN T' GIVE US A RIDE!!
NO!! NO!!
Tm. Reg. U. S. Pat. Off.—All rights reserved Copr. 1954 by United Feature Syndicate, Inc.
9-2
?? WHAT'RE YOU STOPPIN' FOR?
Y-YOU DONE THAT DELIBERATELY, FRANKIE!!
THEM PEOPLE MIGHT BE D-DEAD!!
Al Capp

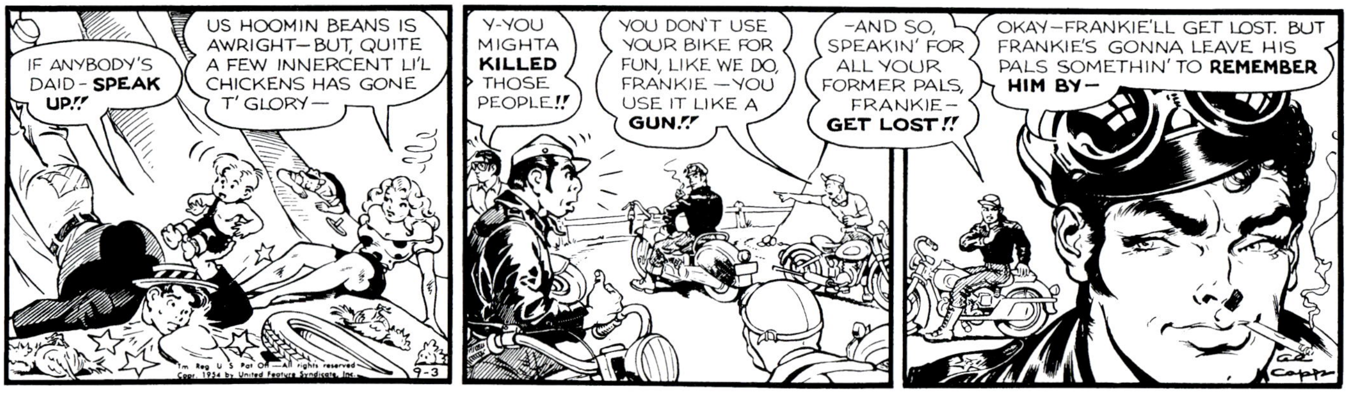
IF ANYBODY'S DAID - SPEAK UP!!
US HOOMIN BEANS IS AWRIGHT—BUT, QUITE A FEW INNERCENT LI'L CHICKENS HAS GONE T' GLORY—
Tm. Reg. U. S. Pat. Off.—All rights reserved Copr. 1954 by United Feature Syndicate, Inc.
9-3
Y-YOU MIGHTA KILLED THOSE PEOPLE!!
YOU DON'T USE YOUR BIKE FOR FUN, LIKE WE DO, FRANKIE —YOU USE IT LIKE A GUN!!
—AND SO, SPEAKIN' FOR ALL YOUR FORMER PALS, FRANKIE— GET LOST!!
OKAY—FRANKIE'LL GET LOST. BUT FRANKIE'S GONNA LEAVE HIS PALS SOMETHIN' TO REMEMBER HIM BY—
Al Capp

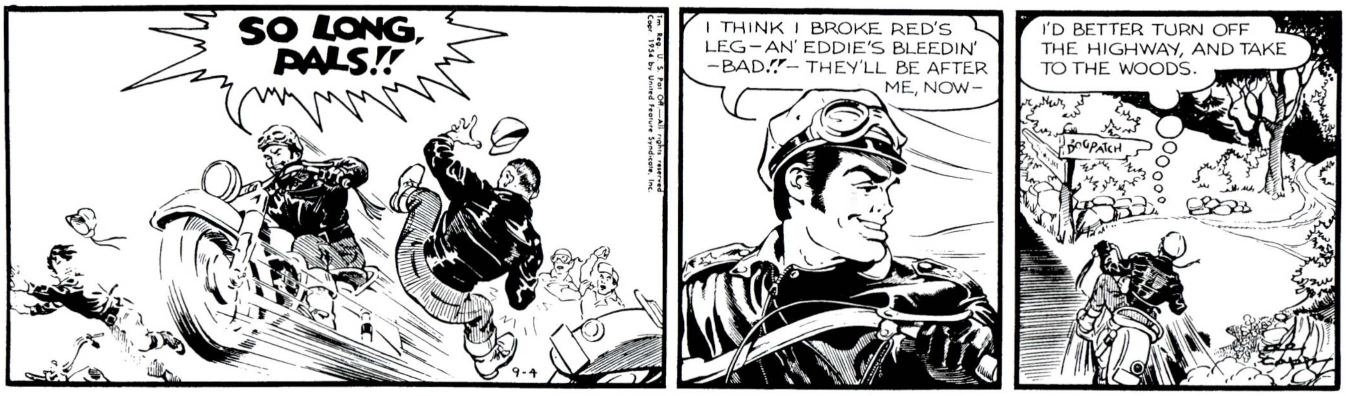
SO LONG, PALS!!
Tm. Reg. U. S. Pat. Off.—All rights reserved Copr. 1954 by United Feature Syndicate, Inc.
9-4
I THINK I BROKE RED'S LEG—AN' EDDIE'S BLEEDIN' —BAD.!!— THEY'LL BE AFTER ME, NOW—
I'D BETTER TURN OFF THE HIGHWAY, AND TAKE TO THE WOODS.
DOGPATCH
Al Capp

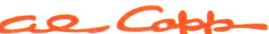

arranged on their behalf. Capp publicly embarrassed, sued, and wrested control of "Li'l Abner" from United Features Syndicate in time for his family-operated Capp Enterprises, Inc. to engineer the Shmoo merchandising phenomenon of 1948-49. Close to one hundred licensed Shmoo products from seventy-five different manufacturers were produced within the first year, some of which sold five million units each.

For decades it was difficult to look at a major periodical without seeing Al Capp's cast of characters in one prominent advertisement or another. Fearless Fosdick tirelessly moonlighted for Wild Root Cream Oil (a hair product) in countless black-and-white comic strip ads and on barbershop signage. Li'l Abner and other Dogpatchers pitched products as varied as Cream of Wheat and Grape Nuts cereals; Kraft caramels; Ivory, Oxydol, Duz, and

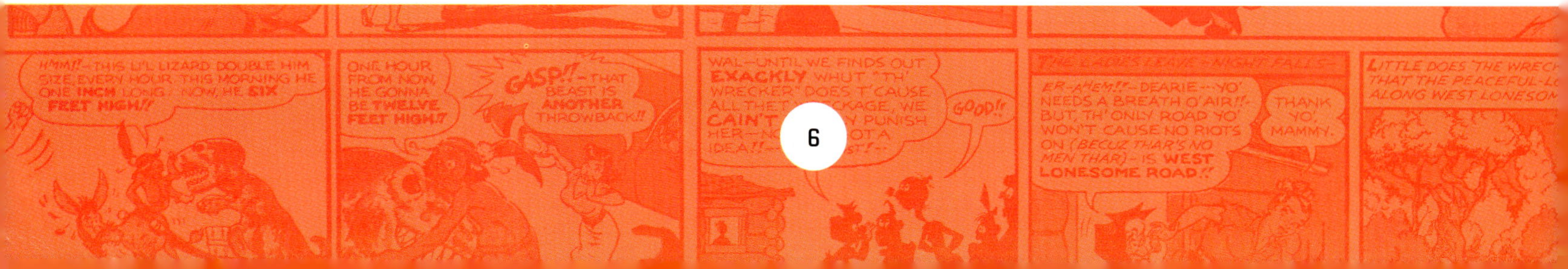

LI'L ABNER

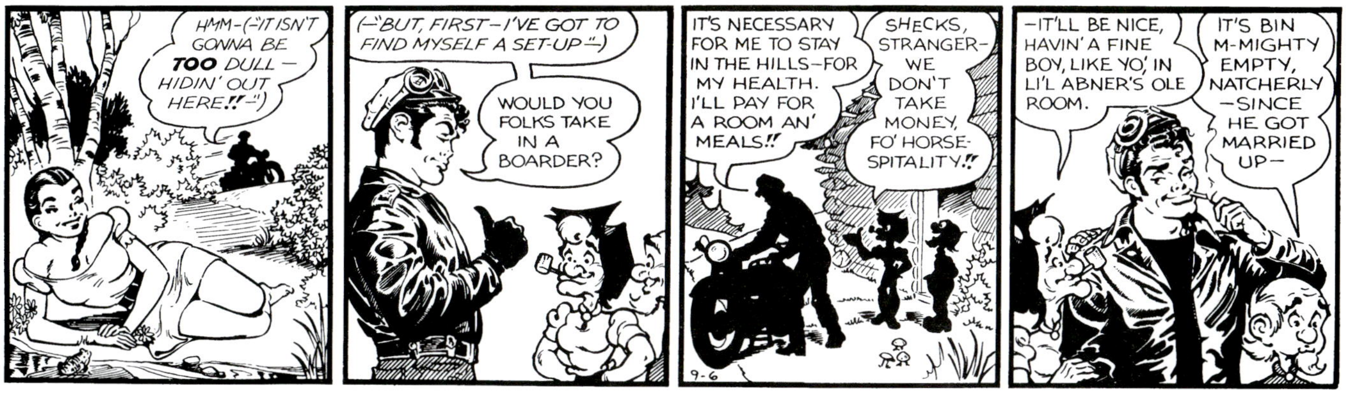

HMM–(–'IT ISN'T GONNA BE **TOO** DULL – HIDIN' OUT HERE!!–')
(–"BUT, FIRST–I'VE GOT TO FIND MYSELF A SET-UP"–)
WOULD YOU FOLKS TAKE IN A BOARDER?
IT'S NECESSARY FOR ME TO STAY IN THE HILLS–FOR MY HEALTH. I'LL PAY FOR A ROOM AN' MEALS!!
SHECKS, STRANGER– WE DON'T TAKE MONEY, FO' HORSE-SPITALITY!!
9-6
–IT'LL BE NICE, HAVIN' A FINE BOY, LIKE YO', IN LI'L ABNER'S OLE ROOM.
IT'S BIN M-MIGHTY EMPTY, NATCHERLY –SINCE HE GOT MARRIED UP–

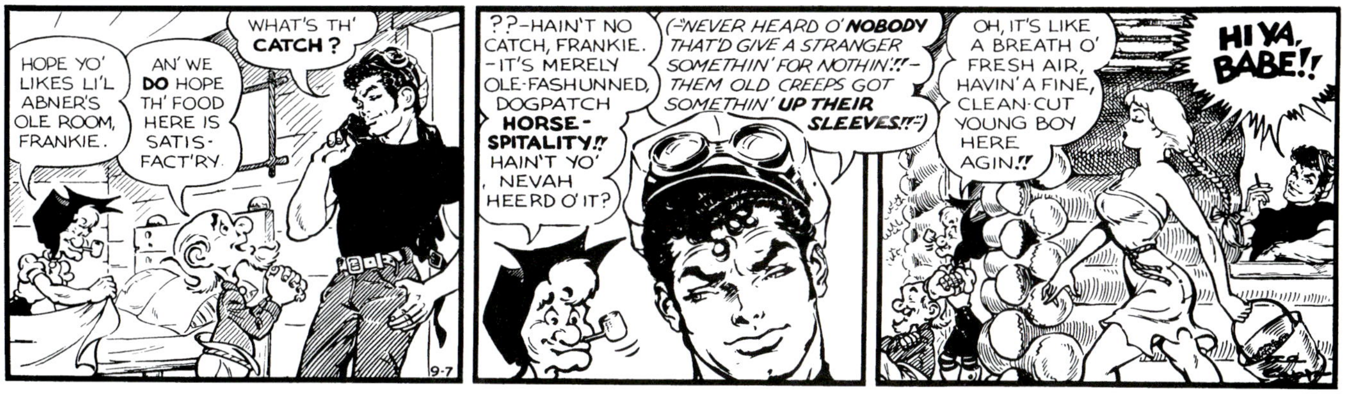

HOPE YO' LIKES LI'L ABNER'S OLE ROOM, FRANKIE.
AN' WE **DO** HOPE TH' FOOD HERE IS SATIS-FACT'RY.
WHAT'S TH' **CATCH?**
9-7
??–HAIN'T NO CATCH, FRANKIE. –IT'S MERELY OLE-FASHUNNED, DOGPATCH **HORSE-SPITALITY!!** HAIN'T YO' NEVAH HEERD O' IT?
(–"NEVER HEARD O' **NOBODY** THAT'D GIVE A STRANGER SOMETHIN' FOR NOTHIN'!!– THEM OLD CREEPS GOT SOMETHIN' **UP THEIR SLEEVES!!**"–)
OH, IT'S LIKE A BREATH O' FRESH AIR, HAVIN' A FINE, CLEAN-CUT YOUNG BOY HERE AGIN!!
HI YA, BABE!!

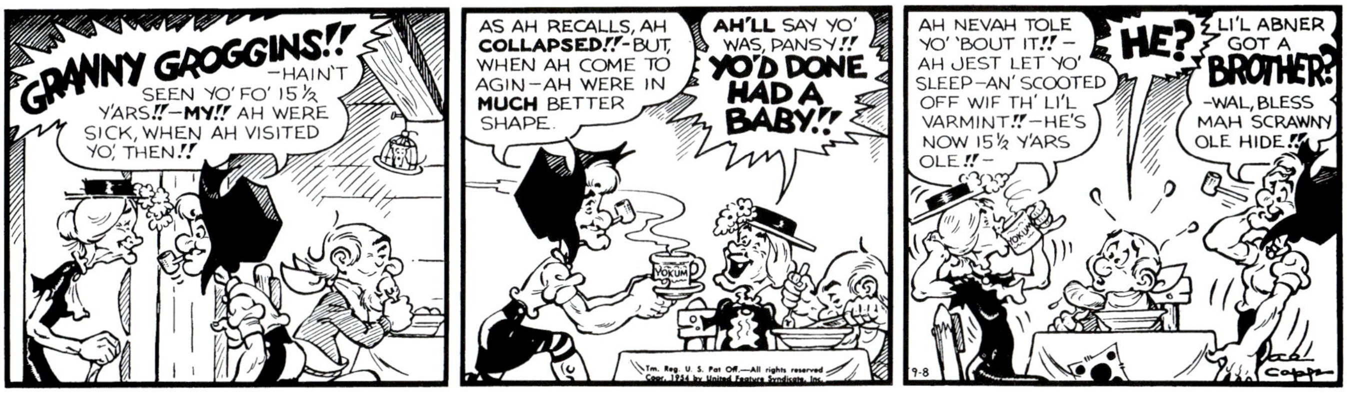

GRANNY GROGGINS!! –HAIN'T SEEN YO' FO' 15½ Y'ARS!!–**MY!!** AH WERE SICK, WHEN AH VISITED YO', THEN!!
AS AH RECALLS, AH **COLLAPSED!!**–BUT, WHEN AH COME TO AGIN–AH WERE IN **MUCH** BETTER SHAPE.
AH'LL SAY YO' WAS, PANSY!! YO'D DONE HAD A BABY!!
YOKUM
Tm. Reg. U. S. Pat Off.—All rights reserved Copr. 1954 by United Feature Syndicate, Inc.
AH NEVAH TOLE YO' 'BOUT IT!!– AH JEST LET YO' SLEEP–AN' SCOOTED OFF WIF TH' LI'L VARMINT!!–HE'S NOW 15½ Y'ARS OLE!!–
HE?
LI'L ABNER GOT A BROTHER?
–WAL, BLESS MAH SCRAWNY OLE HIDE!!
9-8
Capp

Dreft soap products; Fruit of the Loom underwear; Cheney neckties; Pedigree pencils; Strunk chain saws and General Electric light bulbs.

The advertising exposure (and revenue) did not end with his two-dimensional spokesmen. Al Capp himself appeared in numerous print ads. A chain-smoker, he happily plugged Chesterfield cigarettes; he appeared in Schaeffer fountain pens ads; pitched the Famous Artists School, in which he had a financial interest; showed his own hair slicked back by Wild Root Cream Oil; and, though a professed teetotaler, he endorsed Rheingold beer, among other products.

No medium could compete with the impact of television in the last half of the twentieth century, and Capp successfully integrated it as well. He was the only cartoonist to embrace and be embraced by

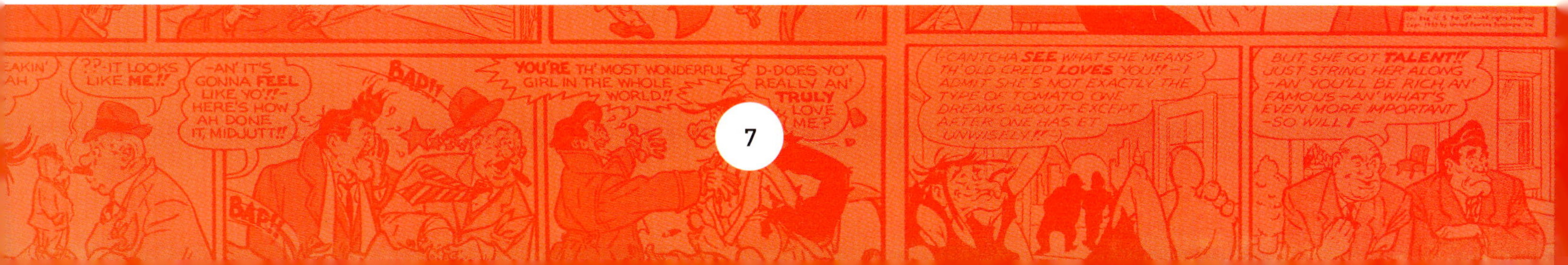

AH CALLS HIM "TINY"–ON ACCOUNT HE WERE SO TINY WHEN HE WERE BORN. IT **DO** SOUND FOOLISH, NOW, THOUGH–ON ACCOUNT HE'S NEARLY **7 FOOT TALL**–
THAT IS, HE **WAS**, WHEN AH LEFT HIM OUT THAR, 5 MINUTES AGO. HE'S PROB'LY **BIGGER**, NOW. HE'S ONLY 15½ Y'ARS OLE–AN' **STILL** GROWIN'.
NATCH-ERLY.
9-9
COME IN, TINY–

COME IN, TINY!!
AH IS **AFEERD** O' STRANGERS–
WHY, **THEY** HAIN'T STRANGERS, DEARIE. THEY IS YORE **MAMMY AN' PAPPY!!**
HAIN'T **YO'** MAH MAMMY AN' PAPPY, GRANNY GROGGINS?
SHECKS, NO, CHILE!! **AH** MERELY TOOK CARE O' YO', FO' 15½ Y'ARS. BUT, NOW AH IS (G'GGLE!!) GITTIN' MARRIED UP, MAHSELF!!
9-10
AN' MAH NEW HUSBIN DON'T WANT NO **STRANGERS** AROUND. MEANIN' **YO'**, TINY. GIT TH' HINT?
AH -GULP!!- SHORE DO, MRS. GROGGINS!!

C'MON, TINY!!
DO **YO'** SEE WHUT **AH** SEES, PANSY?– THET NEW CHILE O' OUR'N GOT A **TAIL!!**
WAL-GULP!!- EV'RYBODY GOT **SUMPTHIN'** PEE-KOOL-YAR 'BOUT 'EM–
BUT–HE'S **OUR** CHILE, IRREGARDLESS–AN' WE'LL TRY T'LOVE HIM, TAIL AN' ALL!!
9-11

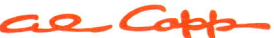

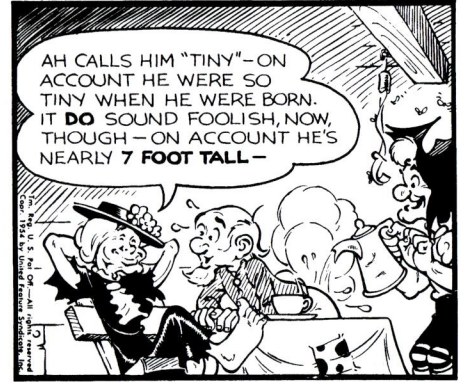

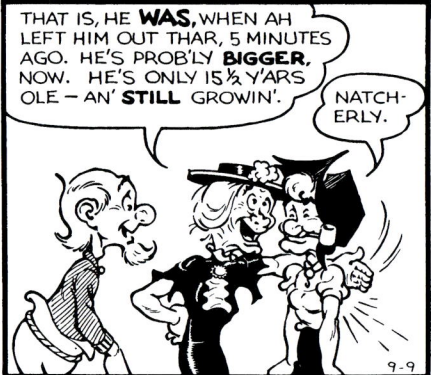

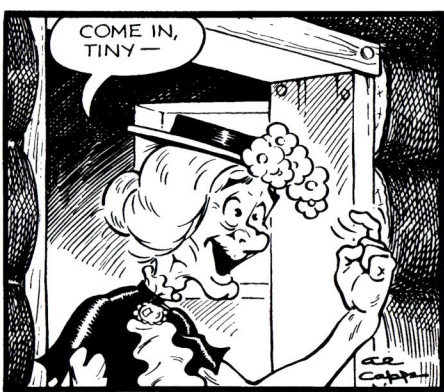

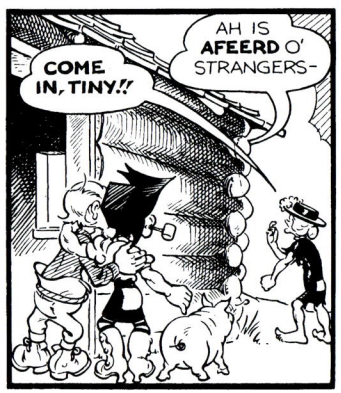

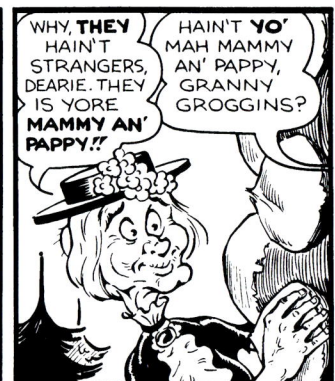

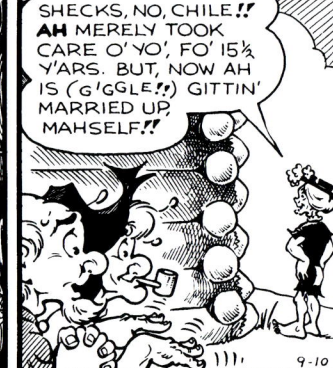

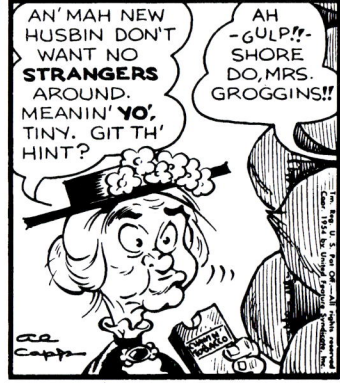

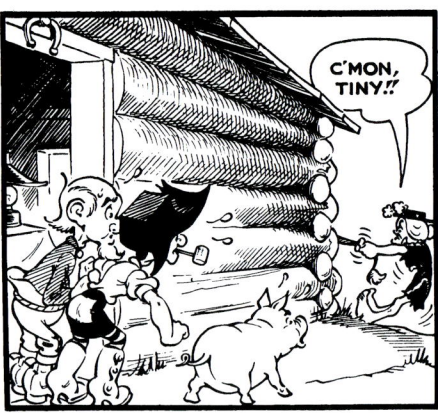

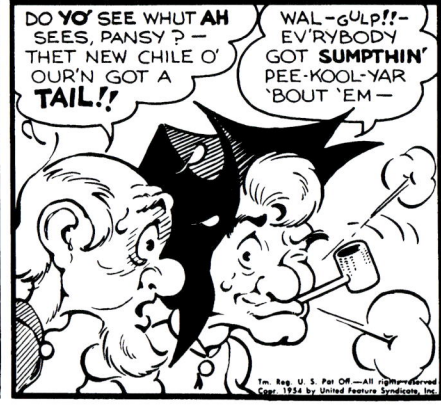

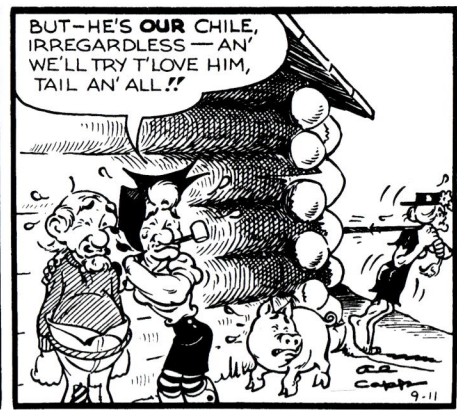

television. No other comic artist has come close to his televised exposure.

In TV's infancy, Capp appeared as a regular on *The Author Meets the Critics* (1947-54). He was a periodic panelist on ABC and NBC's *Who Said That?* (1948-55). In 1953 Capp moderated *What's the Story?* for the Dumont network. The same year he hosted *Anyone Can Win* for CBS (wherein one panelist regularly wore a Hairless Joe mask). He could appear as a celebrity guest on a kid show like *Rod Brown of the Rocket Rangers* as well as Sid Caesar's top-rated *Your Show of Shows*. For two decades the outspoken Capp entertained millions as a regular guest on NBC's *Tonight* show, spanning three hosts (Steve Allen, Jack Paar, and Johnny Carson). And no less than four different times he had his very own TV vehicle: *The Al Capp Show* (1952), *Al*

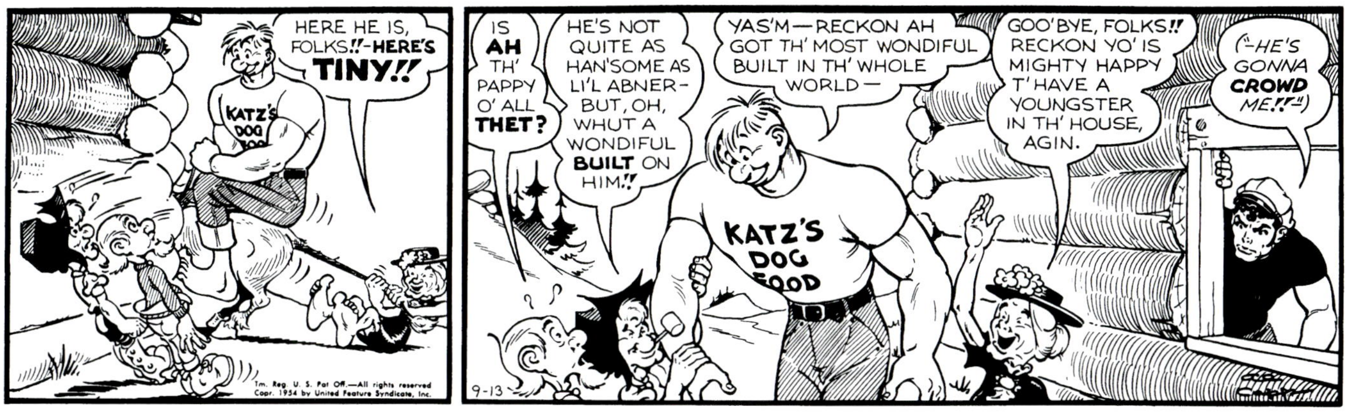
HERE HE IS, FOLKS!!-HERE'S TINY!!
KATZ'S DOG FOOD
Tm. Reg. U. S. Pat. Off.—All rights reserved Copr. 1954 by United Feature Syndicate, Inc.
IS AH TH' PAPPY O' ALL THET?
HE'S NOT QUITE AS HAN'SOME AS LI'L ABNER- BUT, OH, WHUT A WONDIFUL BUILT ON HIM!!
YAS'M—RECKON AH GOT TH' MOST WONDIFUL BUILT IN TH' WHOLE WORLD—
GOO'BYE, FOLKS!! RECKON YO' IS MIGHTY HAPPY T'HAVE A YOUNGSTER IN TH' HOUSE, AGIN.
("-HE'S GONNA CROWD ME!!"-)
KATZ'S DOG FOOD
9-13

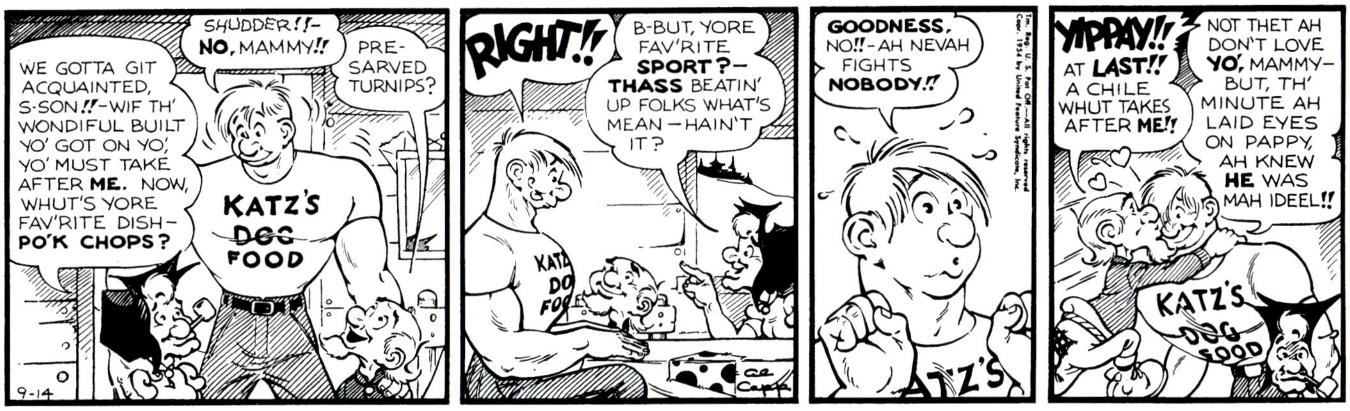
SHUDDER!!- NO, MAMMY!!
WE GOTTA GIT ACQUAINTED, S-SON!!-WIF TH' WONDIFUL BUILT YO' GOT ON YO', YO' MUST TAKE AFTER ME. NOW, WHUT'S YORE FAV'RITE DISH- PO'K CHOPS?
PRE-SARVED TURNIPS?
KATZ'S DOG FOOD
9-14
RIGHT!!
B-BUT, YORE FAV'RITE SPORT?- THASS BEATIN' UP FOLKS WHAT'S MEAN—HAIN'T IT?
GOODNESS, NO!!-AH NEVAH FIGHTS NOBODY!!
YIPPAY!! AT LAST!! A CHILE WHUT TAKES AFTER ME!!
NOT THET AH DON'T LOVE YO', MAMMY— BUT, TH' MINUTE AH LAID EYES ON PAPPY, AH KNEW HE WAS MAH IDEEL!!
KATZ'S DOG FOOD

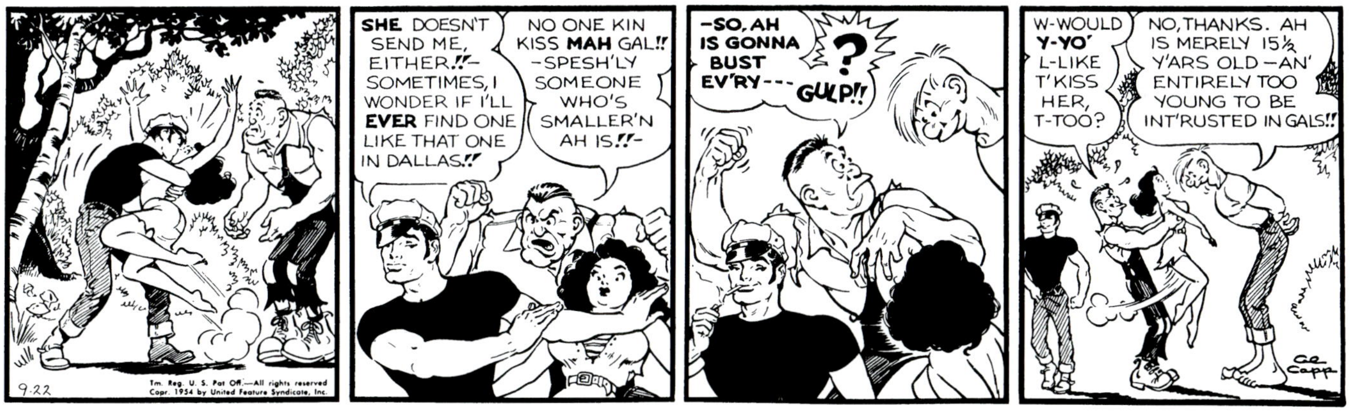
9-22
Tm. Reg. U. S. Pat. Off.—All rights reserved Copr. 1954 by United Feature Syndicate, Inc.
SHE DOESN'T SEND ME, EITHER!!— SOMETIMES, I WONDER IF I'LL EVER FIND ONE LIKE THAT ONE IN DALLAS!!
NO ONE KIN KISS MAH GAL!!-SPESH'LY SOMEONE WHO'S SMALLER'N AH IS!!-
-SO, AH IS GONNA BUST EV'RY--- GULP!!
?
W-WOULD Y-YO' L-LIKE T'KISS HER, T-TOO?
NO, THANKS. AH IS MERELY 15½ Y'ARS OLD—AN' ENTIRELY TOO YOUNG TO BE INT'RUSTED IN GALS!!

Capp's America (1954), *The Al Capp Show* (1968), and *Al Capp* (1971-72).

During Capp's high profile career over five decades, his assistants worked in virtual anonymity, as was industry practice. Capp was himself an "underpaid and unappreciated" assistant to Ham Fisher on "Joe Palooka" in 1933 before launching "Li'l Abner" in 1934. He regarded Fisher as an untalented and unsavory "monster," whose success was based on the crafty exploitation of talented assistants who often never met and whose contributions were carefully compartmentalized. The two engaged in a bitter and public feud for over twenty years. It ended only with Fisher's suicide, following his expulsion from the National Cartoonist Society for trying to expose Capp as a pornographer.

Capp evidently learned a valuable business

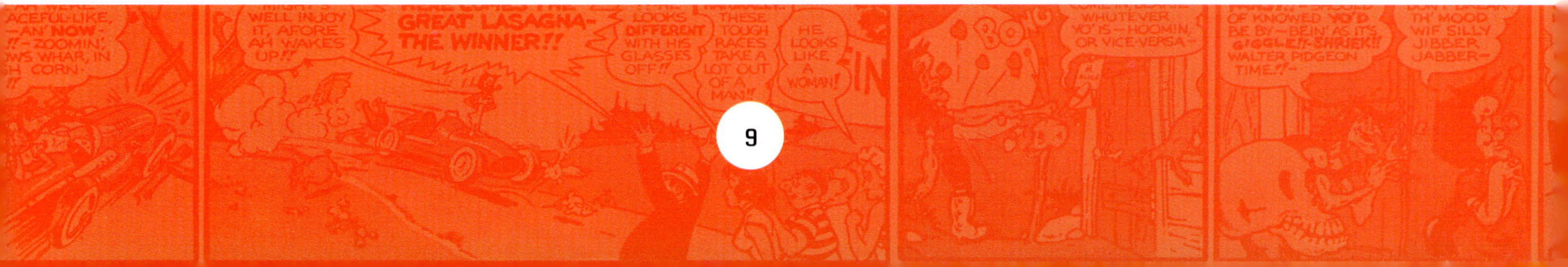

S'GH-H!!- I'VE KISSED DOZENS—BUT, NOT ONE OF 'EM SENDS ME, LIKE THAT ONE IN DALLAS USED TO.!!
AH S'POSE AH SHOULD WHOMP YO', FO' FRIGHTENIN' ALL THEM YOUNG LADIES—
KATZ'S DOG FOOD
Tm Reg. U. S. Pat Off.—All rights reserved Copr. 1954 by United Feature Syndicate, Inc.
BUT-S'GH!!-AH CAIN'T.!! —AH GOT TH' MOST WONDIFUL BUILT IN TH' WORLD —AN' TAIN'T FAIR T'USE IT AGAINST ANYONE WHUT HAIN'T GOT SUCH A WONDIFUL BUILT— AN'-NOBODY HAS.!!-
KATZ'S DOG FOOD
9-23
AH IS DOIN' RIGHT, HAIN'T AH?
SURE YOU ARE, KID.!!- YOU GOT BRAINS.!!-
WHO ARE THEY?

THAR HE IS.!!- TH' VARMINT WHAT KISSED OUR GALS.!!
WE IS ALL TOGETHER, NOW—AN' FULLY ARMED.!!
WE'LL SHOW HIM—BUT, FUST, LET'S GIT RID O' THET BIG ONE.!!—LET'S YO' GIT RID O' HIM.!!
KATZ'S DOG FOOD
AH'D LOVE TO-ONLY AH JEST REMEMBERED!! —AH LEFT TH' WATER RUNNIN', IN MAH BATHTUB.!!
AH LEFT TH' WATER RUNNIN', IN MAH BATHTUB, TOO.!!
ME, LIKE-WISE.!!
BUT- FELLAS—
9-24
THAR HAIN'T A BATHTUB IN ALL DOGPATCH!!- GULP!!-
RECKON AH BETTER SCOOT OFF AN' BUY ONE!! —THIS IS NO T-TIME T'BE WIFOUT A B-B-BATHTUB.!!-
Tm. Reg. U. S. Pat Off.—All rights reserved Copr. 1954 by United Feature Syndicate, Inc.

THE WOLF-GAL, SAVAGE QUEEN OF BEASTS—
(-"STRANGERS.!! -RUNNIN' UP FUM DOGPATCH.!!")
TAIN'T SAFE DOWN THAR—WIF THET F-FRANKIE AROUN'.!!
Tm Reg. U. S. Pat Off.—All rights reserved Copr. 1954 by United Feature Syndicate, Inc.
HE HAIN'T LIKE A HOOMIN BEAN.!!- WHEN HE GRABS YO'-HIS HANDS FEEL LIKE CLAWS.!!
AN'-WHEN HE KISSES—IT MAKES A GAL'S EYEBALLS POP.!!
THET FRANKIE'S A BEAST!!
(-"JEST MAH TYPE.!!")
9-25

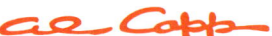

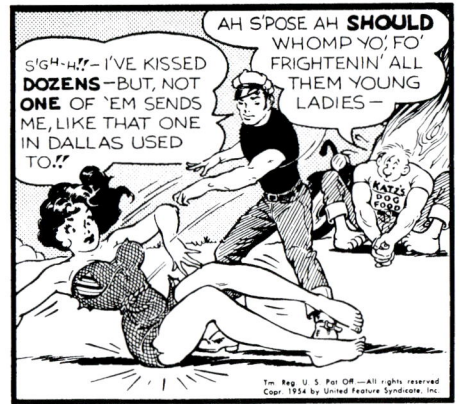

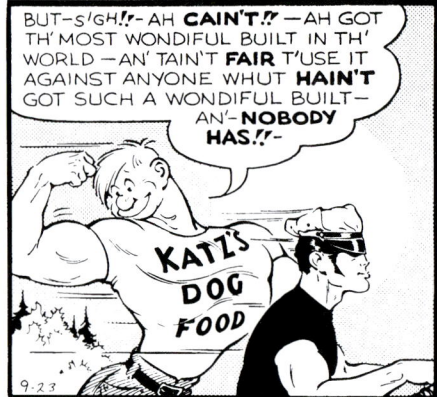

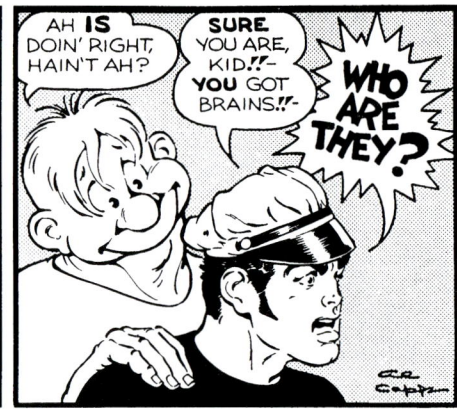

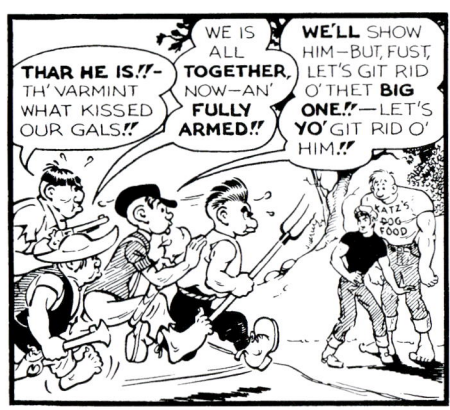

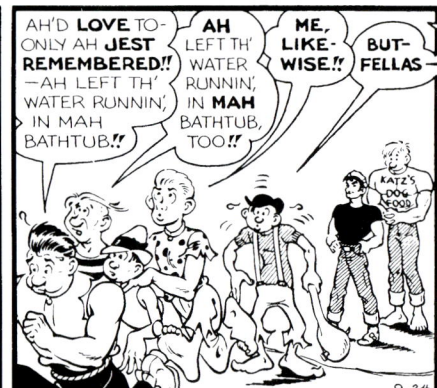

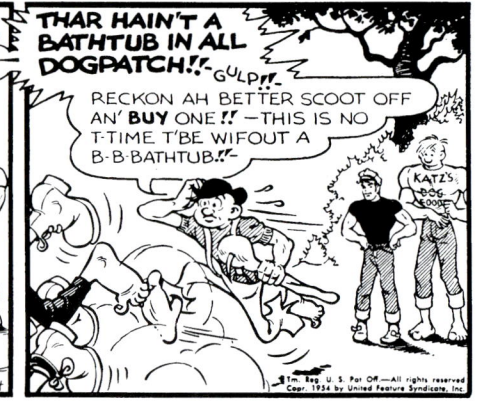

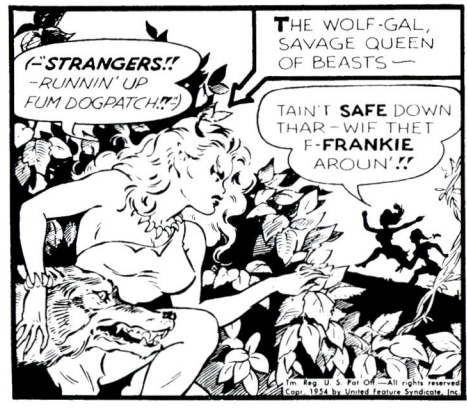

and life lesson from his early mistreatment under Fisher. When Capp was the subject of *Time*'s cover story in 1950, he didn't hide the collaborative nature of his studio. Capp encouraged raucous brainstorming sessions in his studio, gladly accepting ideas as well as drawing skills from his assistants. In the widely read *Time* feature his longtime assistants Walter Johnson and Andy Amato were both discussed and pictured. Capp also maintained liberal economic incentives, giving each primary assistant 10% of his annual profits. This translated to bonuses of about $30,000 a year (in 1950s dollars) on top of their salaries. Amato and Johnson in return were loyal, motivated, and productive employees.

Frank Frazetta joined Capp's studio in 1954 as opportunities in the declining comic book industry were diminishing. A New Yorker, he commuted to Boston for

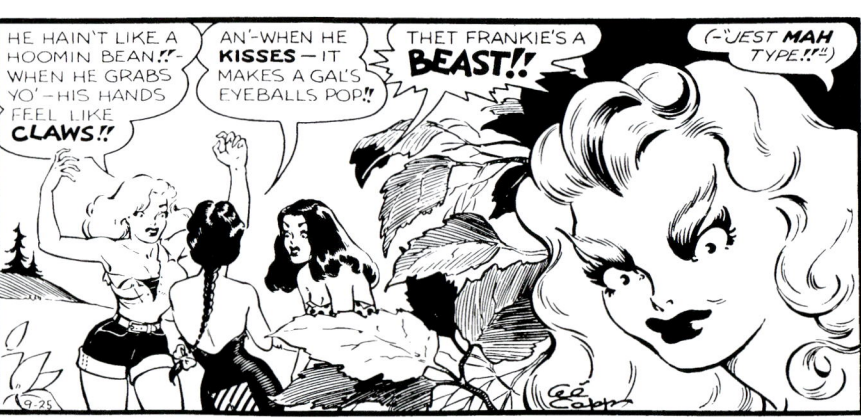

LI'L ABNER

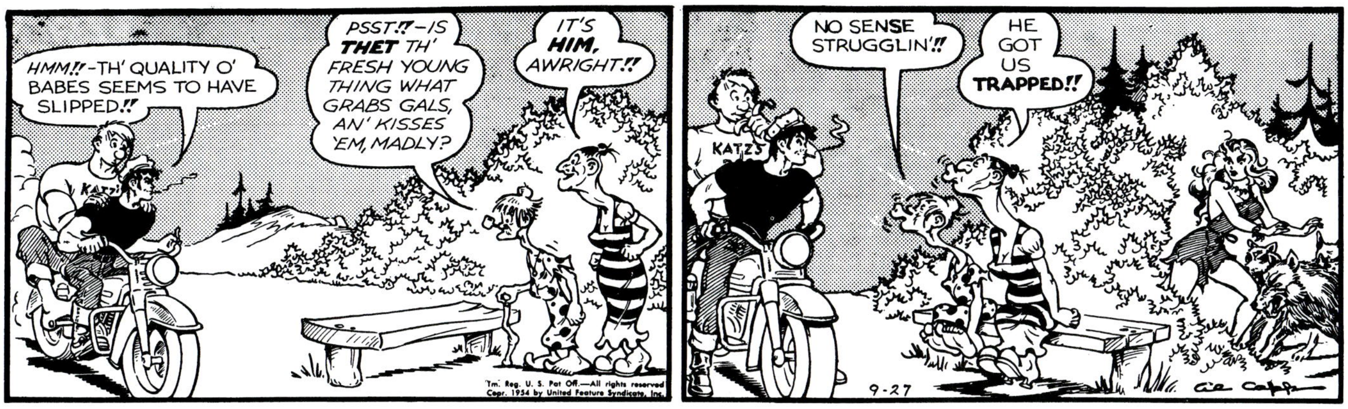

HMM!!-TH' QUALITY O' BABES SEEMS TO HAVE SLIPPED!!
PSST!!-IS THET TH' FRESH YOUNG THING WHAT GRABS GALS, AN' KISSES 'EM, MADLY?
IT'S HIM, AWRIGHT!!
NO SENSE STRUGGLIN'!!
HE GOT US TRAPPED!!
9-27
Tm. Reg. U. S. Pat Off.—All rights reserved Copr. 1954 by United Feature Syndicate, Inc.

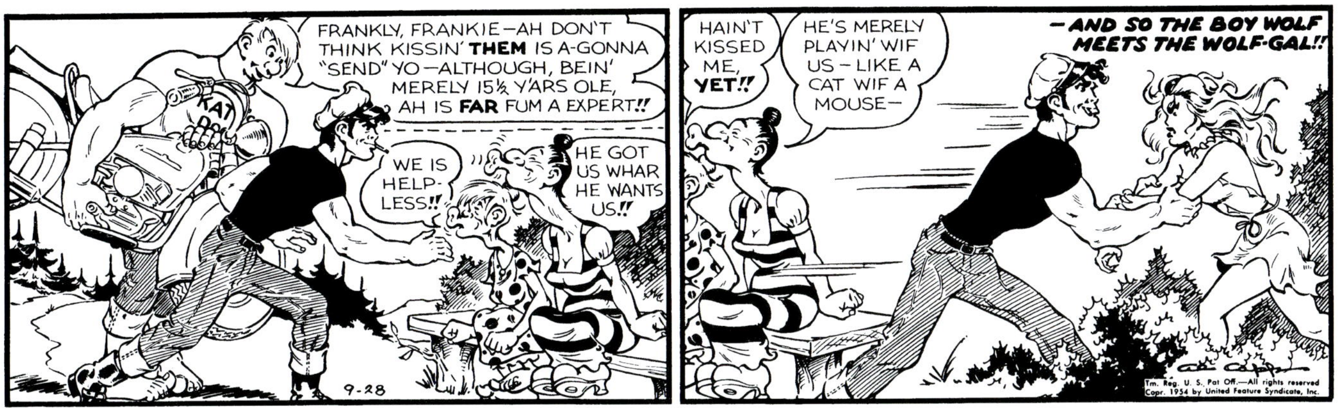

FRANKLY, FRANKIE—AH DON'T THINK KISSIN' THEM IS A-GONNA "SEND" YO—ALTHOUGH, BEIN' MERELY 15½ Y'ARS OLE, AH IS FAR FUM A EXPERT!!
WE IS HELP-LESS!!
HE GOT US WHAR HE WANTS US!!
9-28
HAIN'T KISSED ME, YET!!
HE'S MERELY PLAYIN' WIF US - LIKE A CAT WIF A MOUSE—
—AND SO THE BOY WOLF MEETS THE WOLF-GAL!!
Tm. Reg. U. S. Pat Off.—All rights reserved Copr. 1954 by United Feature Syndicate, Inc.

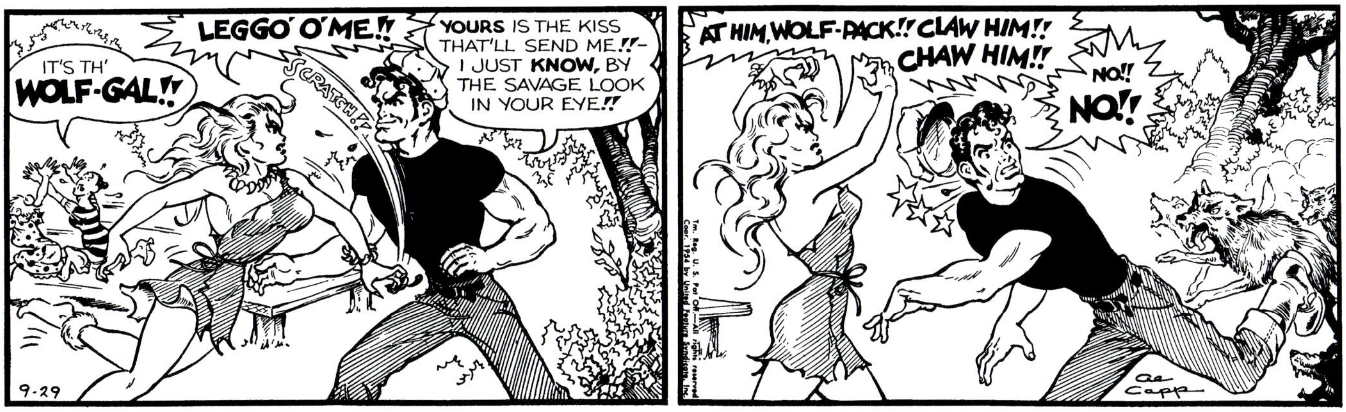

IT'S TH' WOLF-GAL!!
LEGGO' O'ME!!
YOURS IS THE KISS THAT'LL SEND ME!!—I JUST KNOW, BY THE SAVAGE LOOK IN YOUR EYE!!
SCRATCH!!
9-29
AT HIM, WOLF-PACK!! CLAW HIM!! CHAW HIM!!
NO!!
NO!!
Tm. Reg. U. S. Pat Off.—All rights reserved Copr. 1954 by United Feature Syndicate, Inc.

the first year or two, joining Amato, Johnson, and Harvey Curtis, all three of whom lived and worked full-time in Beantown. Frazetta initially worked on the daily "Li'l Abner." His distinctive pencilling and inking on *The Wild Ones* parody in the fall of 1954—featuring a motorcyclist named Frankie—is stylistically unique in the strip's forty-three-year run. After syndicate complaints that the strip was losing its familiar look, Frazetta was given fewer inking assignments and the strip returned to its earlier look. In 1955, Capp permitted Frazetta to work at home in Brooklyn. His primary responsibility from this point became pencilling the Sunday strips, a chore that he says often took him only one day a week and paid a then-handsome $500 weekly salary. He continued to work this way until the early '60s.

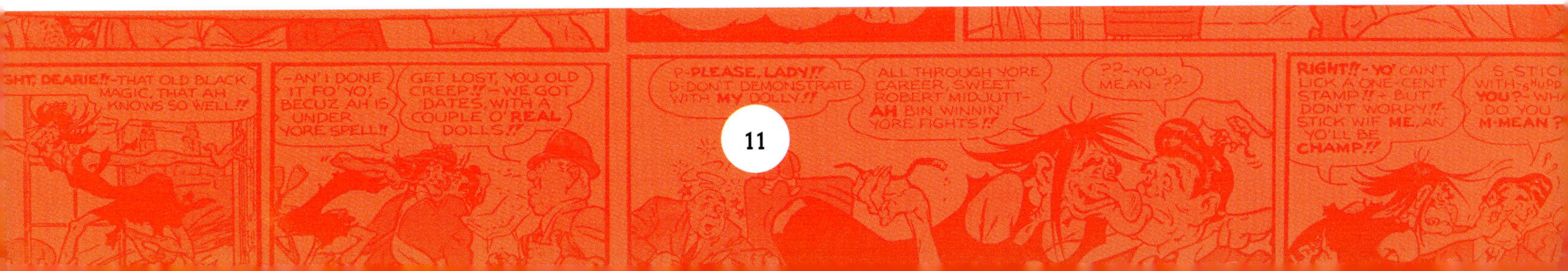

YO' SHOULD KEEP YORE PUPPIES ON A LEASH, MA'M!!
MY FIERCEST WOLVES!!-AN' HE HANDLES 'EM-LIKE THEY WAS RABBITS!!
KATZ'S DOG FOOD
YO' GOT GUTS, MAN!!
AH HAIN'T NO MAN, MA'M. AH IS MERELY 15½ Y'ARS OLD-
?
YOU THINK HE'S TOUGH-
WATCH!!
9-30
HE JUST DOES LI'L THINGS FOR ME-BUT I'M TH' BIG-SHOT!!-

??-AH IS TOO YOUNG T'UNDERSTAND SECH THINGS!!-
KATZ'S DOG FOOD
YOU SEND ME!! YOU'RE THE MOST!!
NEVAH DONE NOTHIN' LIKE THET, BEFO'-BUT-NOW-AH NEVAH WANTS T'DO NOTHIN' ELSE!!-
10-1
OH, KIN WE DO IT ALL TH' TIME?
SURE WE CAN, BABE- AFTER WE GET MARRIED!!- YOU'RE MY TYPE!!
BUT, FRANKIE- SHE'S TH' ANIMAL TYPE!!
KATZ'S DOG FOOD

AFTER MARRYIN' SAM MARRIES US UP, WE KIN LIVE IN MAH CAVE-
-ON TOP O' WOLF MOUNT'IN!!- IT LOOKS DOWN ON ALL DOGPATCH -AN' WHEN YO' SEES SOMEONE WIF SOMETHIN' YO' WANTS -
KATZ'S DOG FOOD
10-2
-YO' LOPES DOWN, AN' GRABS IT- AN' NOBODY DAST COME AFTER YO'- BECUZ TH' "WOLF-PACK STANDS GUARD!!"
IT'S THE LIFE I ALWAYS DREAMED OF!!-A BEAUTIFUL BABE!!-NO WORK!!-TAKIN' WHAT WE WANT!!- AN' A GANG TO HANDLE TH' ROUGH STUFF!!-

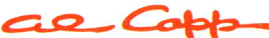

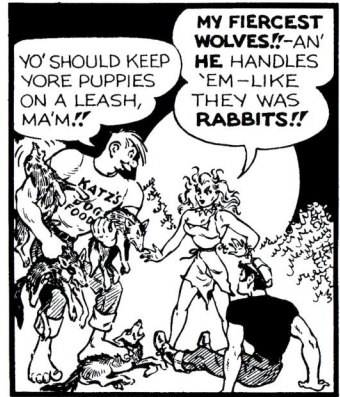

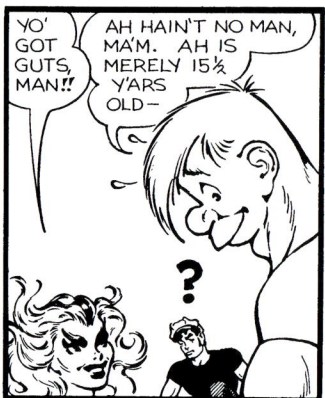

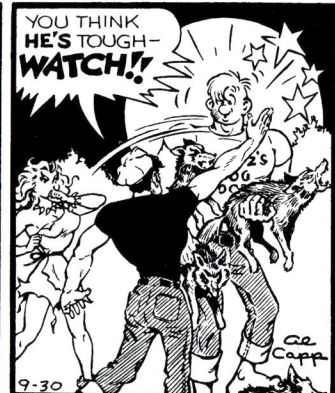

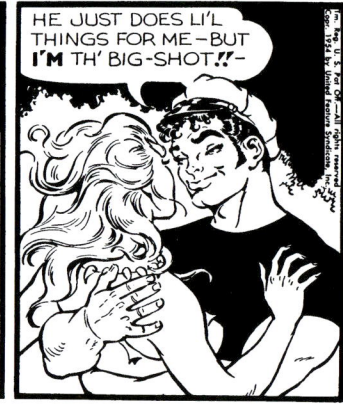

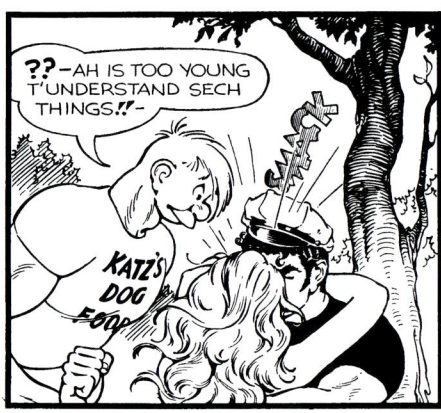

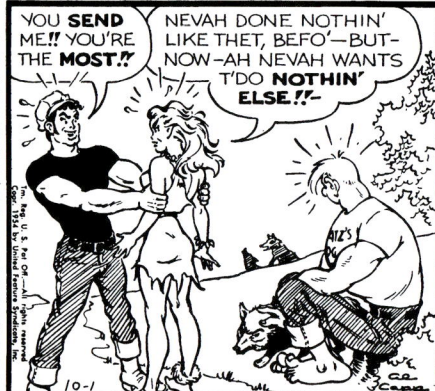

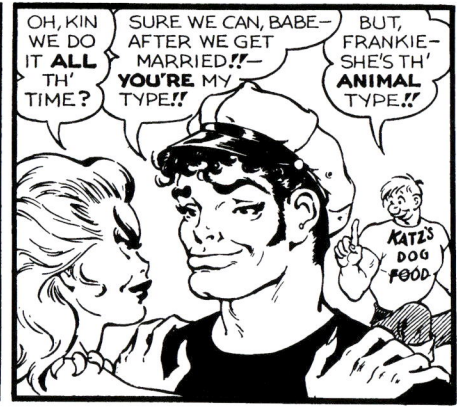

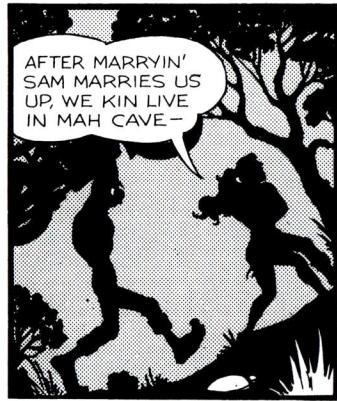

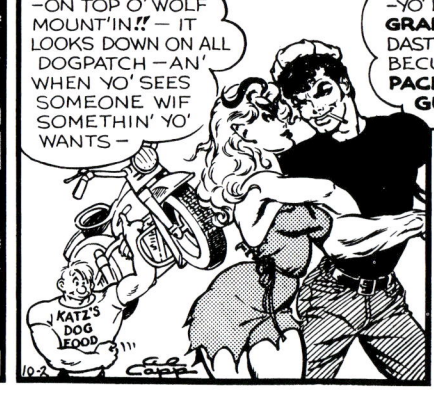

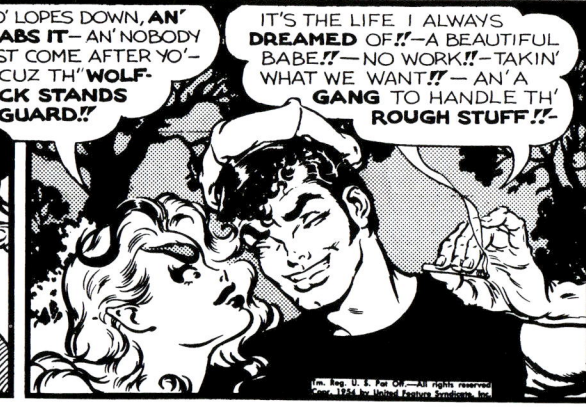

Frazetta had a love-hate relationship with Capp, telling his personal historian David Winiewicz that "it was an honor to be associated with a strip that was a central part of American life. Abner was a cultural institution of immense popularity and influence. Everyone read it; we entertained millions every day. On the other hand," Frazetta said, "those years were a complete waste in terms of my own art and vision. I was working in someone else's style, a style in direct contradiction to my own approach. But I was lazy; I should have left earlier."

Perhaps because he didn't participate in the everyday camaraderie of the Boston studio after 1955, Frazetta didn't feel the respect or enjoy the economic perks of Capp's other assistants. He admired Capp's talent but regarded him as "a miserable s.o.b." A breaking point came when he asked Capp for a raise in 1961. Capp

SIGH!!—ALLUS WONDERED WHUT IT FELT LIKE—T'FALL IN LOVE—NOW, AH KNOWS—
KATZ'S DOG FOOD
YO' FEELS LIKE YO' COULDN'T BEAR T'BE WIFOUT TH' ONE YO' LOVES!!—LIKE, IF HE LEFT YO', YO'D DIE—
GET LOST—
W-WHUT DO THET MEAN?
IT MEANS—TAKE A POWDER!!
FRANKIE'S EYES GLEAM — AT WHAT?

GET LOST!!
??-AH FEELS A PAIN!!-LIKE SOMETHIN' BREAKIN' -HERE!!
THAR?-OH, THASS WHAR YORE HEART IS, WOLF-GAL!!
KATZ'S DOG
THASS WHUT'S BREAKIN'. IT HAPPENS T' ORDINARY GALS, ALL TH' TIME!!
AH D-DON'T WANT T'FEEL LIKE A ORD'NARY GAL!!—IT H-HURTS!!
EVERY OTHER BABE I EVER SAW—I HAD TO KISS—TO KNOW IF SHE "SENT" ME!!—BUT—JUST LOOKING AT YOU - DOES IT!!—YOU'RE FOR ME!!-
WHO IS?

BABE!!—YOU SEND ME!!
OH, THANK YO'!!—AH NEEDED SOME-ONE, T'SEND AFTER LI'L ABNER AN' HONEST ABE—
THEY FELL ASLEEP IN TH' TRASHBERRY PATCH, PORE DEARS—BUT, AH WERE SO IMPAYSHUNT T'GIT HOME, AH---
CUT TH' JABBER—
—AN', KISS ME!!
NO!!
WAIT, FRANKIE!!—ALL T'OTHER GALS WHUT SAID "NO," DIDN'T REALLY MEAN IT—BUT, THIS ONE'S SINCERE!!—AH IS MERELY 15½ Y'ARS OLD, BUT AH IS A EXPERT ON SINCERITY, BECUZ AH IS SO CUSSED SINCERE, MAHSELF!!
KATZ'S DOG FOOD

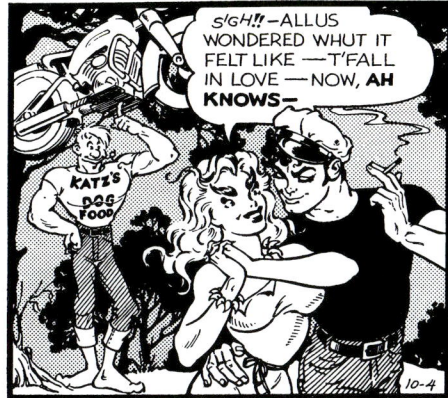

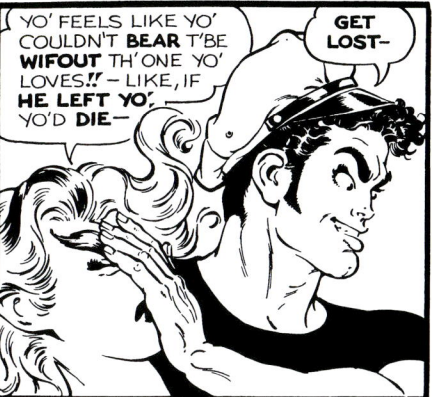

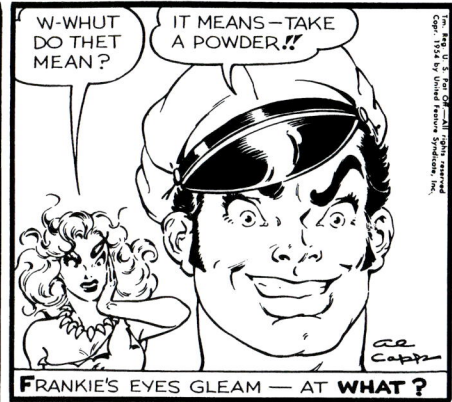

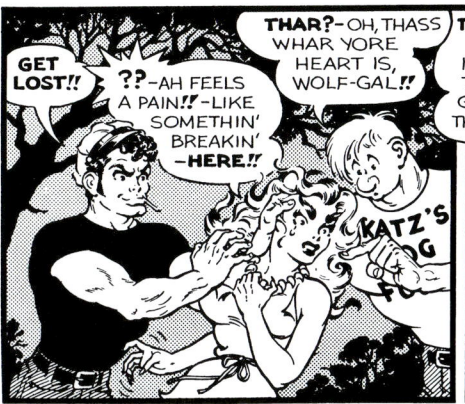

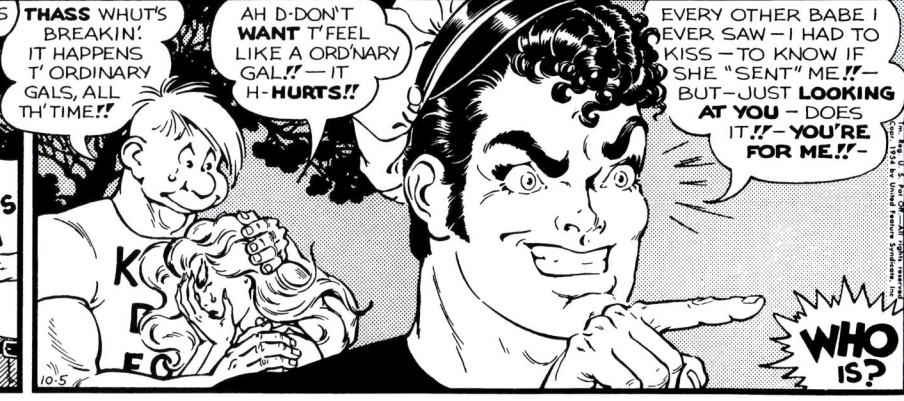

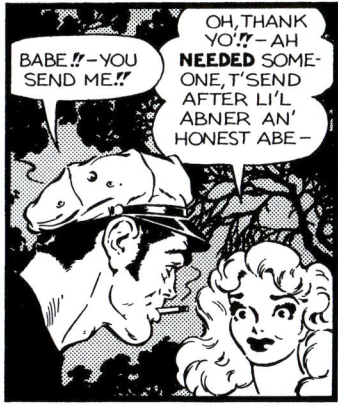

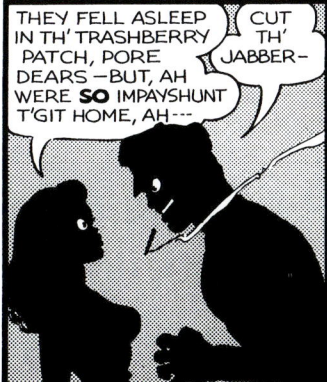

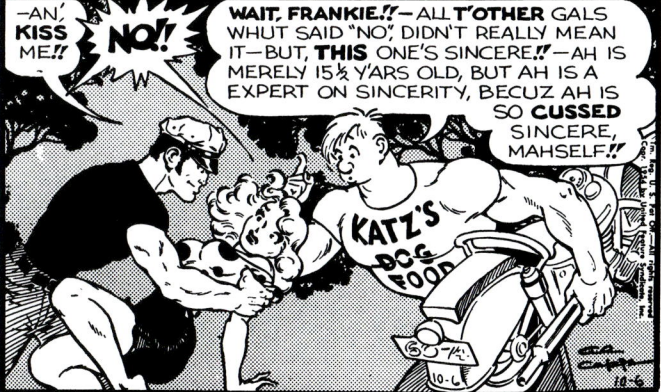

countered that he'd been losing newspapers and as a result his syndicate revenue was declining. "Instead of getting a raise," Capp suggested, "You should take a pay cut, like me." Frazetta unceremoniously quit and pursued his new career as an illustrator and painter, one that before long earned him international acclaim.

In the late '70s, with Frank Frazetta's fame growing and his own career clouded in controversy, a curmudgeonly Al Capp deflected questions about his former assistant. In some interviews he flatly rejected that Frazetta had ever worked for him. At least one interviewer, Bob Barrett, acknowledges that Capp was "in extreme pain and not thinking too clearly," during this period, but one is nonetheless left with the impression that Capp resented his once anonymous assistant eclipsing his own fading fame.

HEY, YO' THAR- YO' BIG LOUT!!-WHY DON'T YO' ACK LIKE A MAN -AN' PUNCH HIM IN TH' NOSE!!
AH HAIN'T NO MAN, MA'M!! — AH IS MERELY A OVER-GROWN CHILE—15½ Y'ARS OLE, T'BE EXACK!!
KATZ'S DOG FOOD
BUT, YO' GOT A WONDIFUL BUILT ON YO'!! YO' KIN LICK HIM!!-
THASS JEST IT, MA'M!! AH GOT SUCH A WONDIFUL BUILT ON ME—
-'TWOULDN'T BE FAIR FO' ME T'LICK ANYONE WHUT HAIN'T SO WONDIFULLY BUILT—AN' NOBODY IS!!— SO, AH- ??-GASP!!-CHOKE!!-
AN AMAZING CHANGE IS COMING OVER "TINY" — Al Capp
10-7

JUST ONE KISS!!
NO!! HALP!!
S-SOMETHIN' PEE-KOOL-YAR IS A-HAPPENIN', INSIDE ME!!
10-8
Scientific Explanation—
1 The sight of this ungallant behavior causes Tiny's Indignation Glands to pump blood, overtime.
2 But, since this is merely Pappy-blood, it doesn't count.
3 The Pappy-blood rushes madly through his huge body.
4 Until it collides with the single drop of Mammy-blood, which has been dozing in his big toe.
5 Once aroused, the fighting Mammy-blood zooms straight up ——
Takes a short cut to his heart—
6 Where it explodes into a flaming, fighting fury, that permeates every fibre of his wonderful built!!

??-B-BUT, TINY!!-YOU NEVER HIT NOBODY!!-
WAL- HARDLY EVER!!
RUSH OF MAMMY-BLOOD TO HEAD
KATZ'S DOG FOOD
DAISY MAE!! IS YO' SAFE?
10-9
("ANOTHER ONE!!"-TH' WOODS IS THICK WIF 'EM, TODAY!!"-) DEFEND YORESELF!!
MAMMY-BLOOD STILL BOILING
LI'L ABNER!! DON'T FIGHT HIM!!
DON'T WORRY, DAISY MAE!!-HE'S SOOPER-HOOMIN-BUT, AH HAIN'T SCARED!! NOBODY KIN LICK A YOKUM!!
Tm. Reg. U. S. Pat. Off.—All rights reserved Copr. 1954 by United Feature Syndicate, Inc.

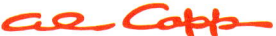

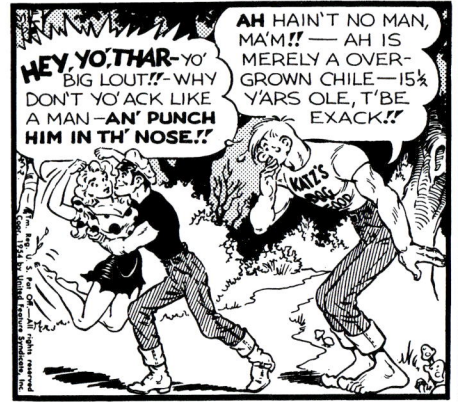

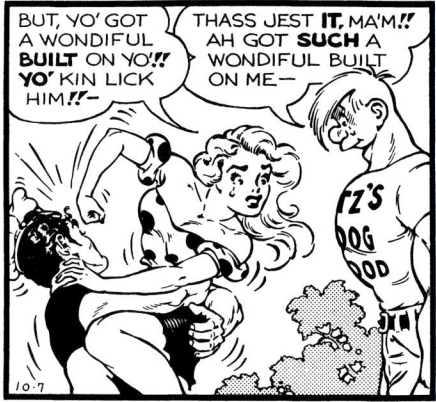

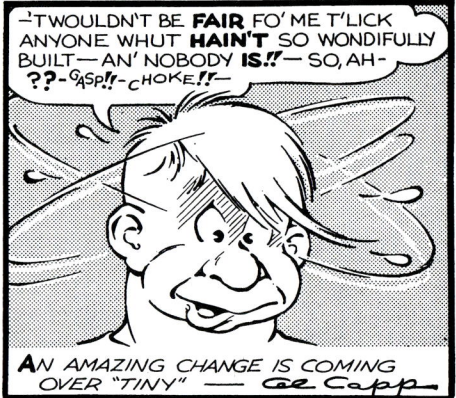

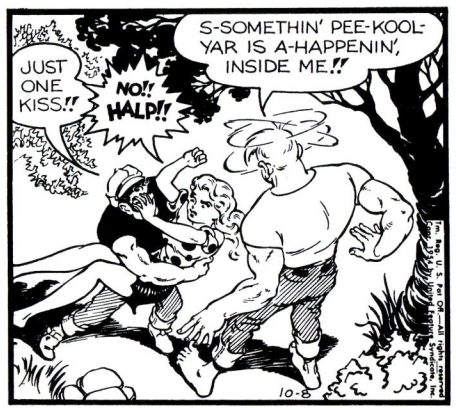

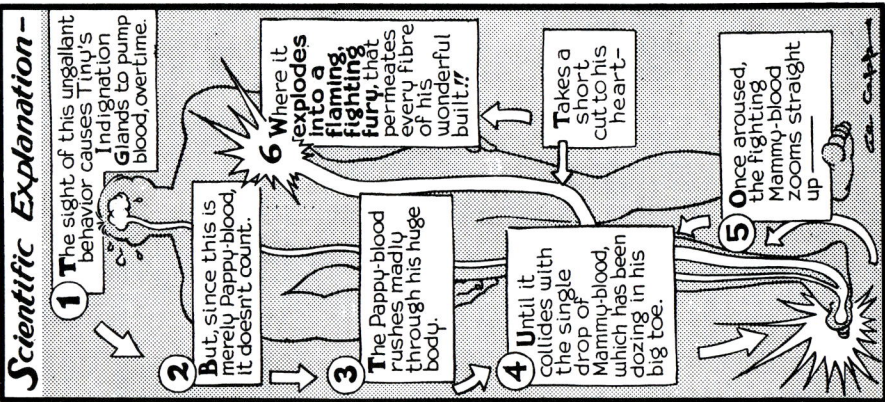

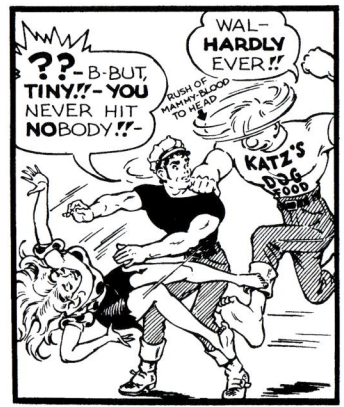

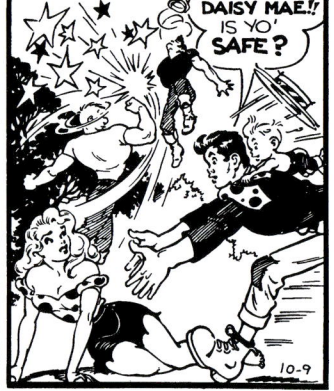

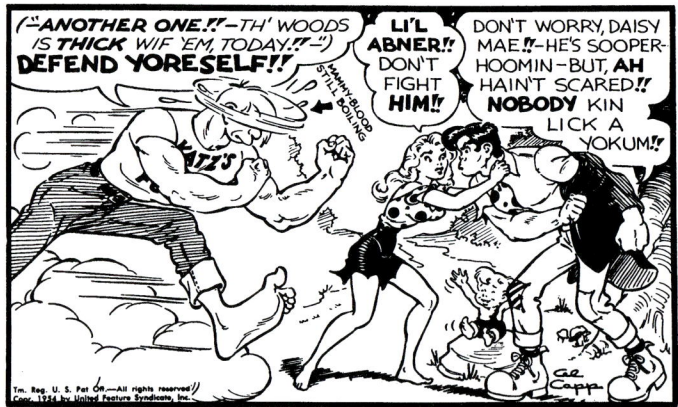

Since Capp's death, Frazetta has firmly established himself as the world's foremost fantasy artist. But at a time when Frazetta himself admits to being unemployable, it was Al Capp who recognized his deep talent and gave him a plum job. Capp's consummate talents as a satirist, cartoonist, and raconteur remain widely recognized. But in the context of these Dark Horse volumes, representing an artistic high point of "Li'l Abner," it is perhaps a less heralded Capp skill—his keen eye for talent—that we should particularly appreciate.

—Denis Kitchen

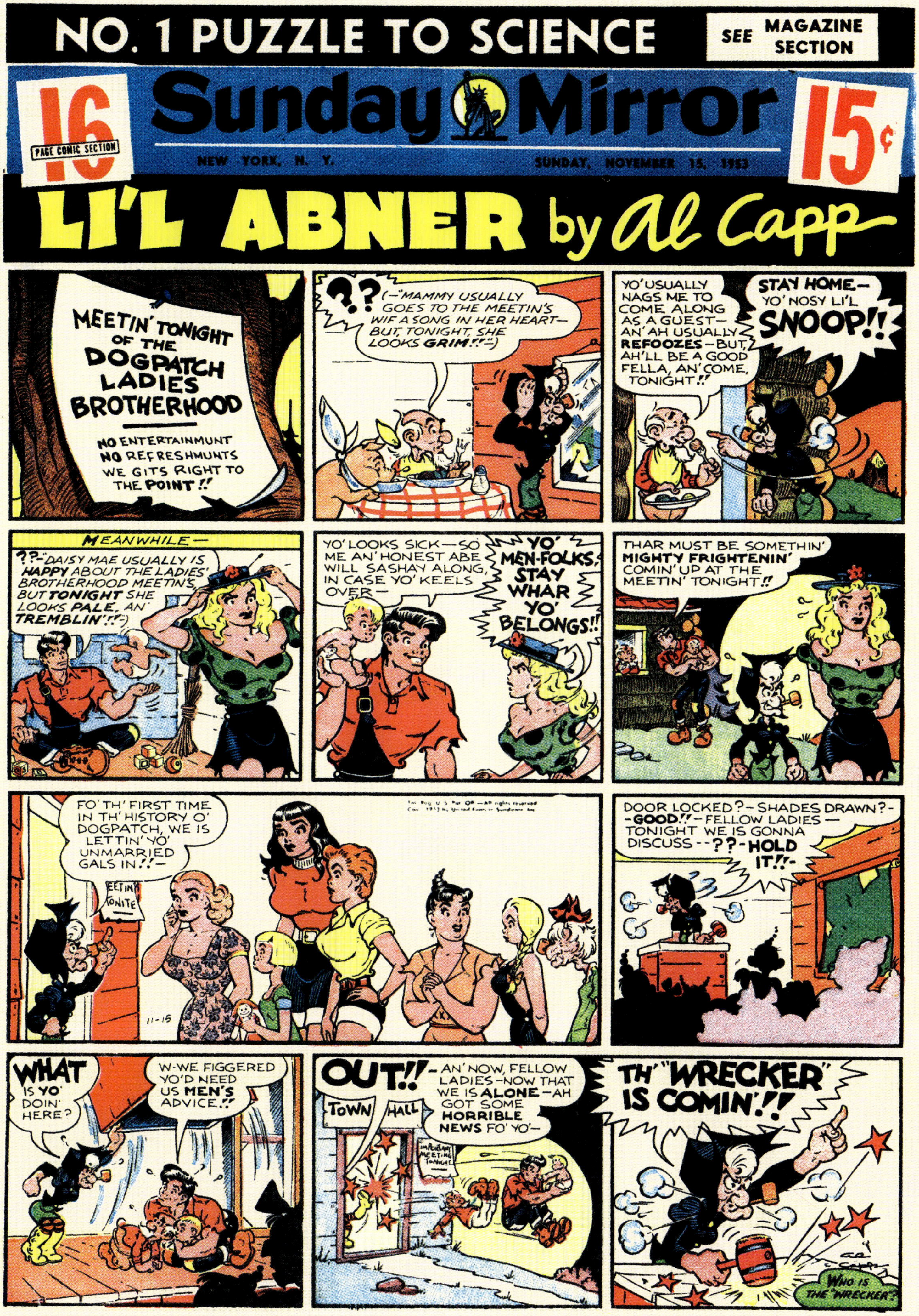

NO. 1 PUZZLE TO SCIENCE
SEE MAGAZINE SECTION
16
PAGE COMIC SECTION
Sunday Mirror
NEW YORK, N. Y.
SUNDAY, NOVEMBER 15, 1953
15¢
LI'L ABNER by Al Capp
MEETIN' TONIGHT OF THE DOGPATCH LADIES BROTHERHOOD
NO ENTERTAINMUNT NO REFRESHMUNTS WE GITS RIGHT TO THE POINT!!
??(-"MAMMY USUALLY GOES TO THE MEETIN'S WIF A SONG IN HER HEART— BUT, TONIGHT, SHE LOOKS GRIM!!"—)
YO'USUALLY NAGS ME TO COME ALONG AS A GUEST— AN' AH USUALLY REFOOZES—BUT, AH'LL BE A GOOD FELLA, AN' COME, TONIGHT!!
STAY HOME— YO' NOSY LI'L SNOOP!!
MEANWHILE—
??-"DAISY MAE USUALLY IS HAPPY ABOUT THE LADIES' BROTHERHOOD MEETIN'S, BUT TONIGHT SHE LOOKS PALE, AN' TREMBLIN'!!"-)
YO' LOOKS SICK—SO ME AN' HONEST ABE WILL SASHAY ALONG, IN CASE YO' KEELS OVER—
YO' MEN-FOLKS, STAY WHAR YO' BELONGS!!
THAR MUST BE SOMETHIN' MIGHTY FRIGHTENIN' COMIN' UP AT THE MEETIN' TONIGHT!!
FO' TH' FIRST TIME IN TH' HISTORY O' DOGPATCH, WE IS LETTIN' YO' UNMARRIED GALS IN!!—
EETIN' ONITE
11-15
DOOR LOCKED?—SHADES DRAWN?— -GOOD!!—FELLOW LADIES— TONIGHT WE IS GONNA DISCUSS--??-HOLD IT!!-
WHAT IS YO' DOIN' HERE?
W-WE FIGGERED YO'D NEED US MEN'S ADVICE!!
OUT!!-
AN' NOW, FELLOW LADIES—NOW THAT WE IS ALONE—AH GOT SOME HORRIBLE NEWS FO' YO'—
TOWN HALL
IMPORTANT MEETIN' TONIGHT
TH' "WRECKER" IS COMIN'!!
AL CAPP
WHO IS THE "WRECKER"?

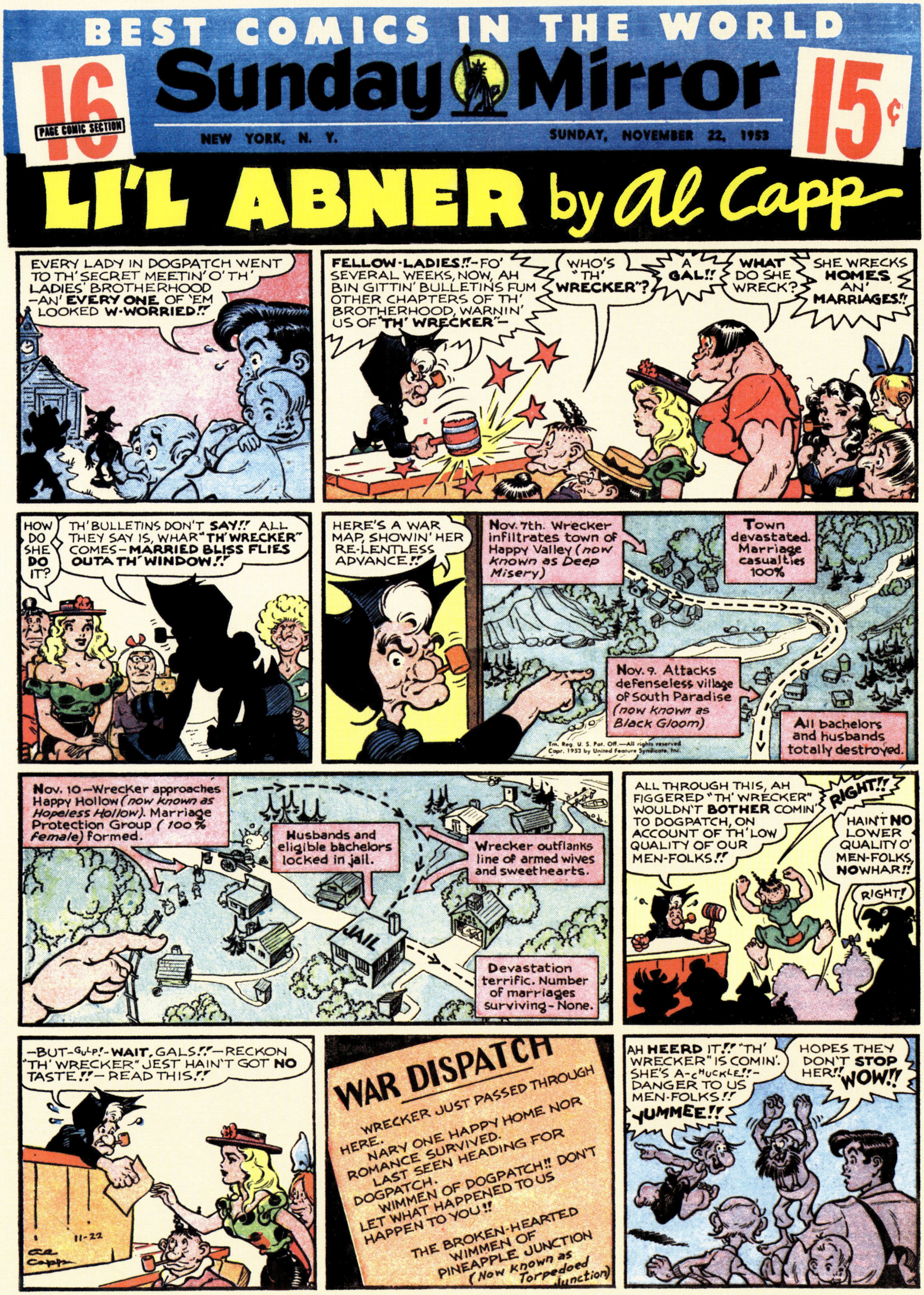

BEST COMICS IN THE WORLD
Sunday Mirror
16
PAGE COMIC SECTION
NEW YORK, N. Y.
SUNDAY, NOVEMBER 22, 1953
15¢
LI'L ABNER by Al Capp
EVERY LADY IN DOGPATCH WENT TO TH' SECRET MEETIN' O' TH' LADIES' BROTHERHOOD —AN' EVERY ONE OF 'EM LOOKED W-WORRIED!!
FELLOW-LADIES!!—FO' SEVERAL WEEKS, NOW, AH BIN GITTIN' BULLETINS FUM OTHER CHAPTERS OF TH' BROTHERHOOD, WARNIN' US OF "TH' WRECKER"—
WHO'S "TH' WRECKER"?
A GAL!!
WHAT DO SHE WRECK?
SHE WRECKS HOMES AN' MARRIAGES!!
HOW DO SHE DO IT?
TH' BULLETINS DON'T SAY!! ALL THEY SAY IS, WHAR "TH' WRECKER" COMES—MARRIED BLISS FLIES OUTA TH' WINDOW!!
HERE'S A WAR MAP, SHOWIN' HER RE-LENTLESS ADVANCE!!
Nov. 7th. Wrecker infiltrates town of Happy Valley (now known as Deep Misery)
Town devastated. Marriage casualties 100%
Nov. 9. Attacks defenseless village of South Paradise (now known as Black Gloom)
All bachelors and husbands totally destroyed.
Tm. Reg. U. S. Pat. Off.—All rights reserved
Copr. 1953 by United Feature Syndicate, Inc.
Nov. 10—Wrecker approaches Happy Hollow (now known as Hopeless Hollow). Marriage Protection Group (100% female) formed.
Husbands and eligible bachelors locked in jail.
Wrecker outflanks line of armed wives and sweethearts.
JAIL
Devastation terrific. Number of marriages surviving - None.
ALL THROUGH THIS, AH FIGGERED "TH' WRECKER" WOULDN'T BOTHER COMIN' TO DOGPATCH, ON ACCOUNT OF TH' LOW QUALITY OF OUR MEN-FOLKS!!
RIGHT!!
HAIN'T NO LOWER QUALITY O' MEN-FOLKS, NOWHAR!!
RIGHT!
—BUT—GULP!—WAIT, GALS!!—RECKON "TH' WRECKER" JEST HAIN'T GOT NO TASTE!!—READ THIS!!
WAR DISPATCH
WRECKER JUST PASSED THROUGH HERE.
NARY ONE HAPPY HOME NOR ROMANCE SURVIVED.
LAST SEEN HEADING FOR DOGPATCH.
WIMMEN OF DOGPATCH!! DON'T LET WHAT HAPPENED TO US HAPPEN TO YOU!!
THE BROKEN-HEARTED WIMMEN OF PINEAPPLE JUNCTION (Now known as Torpedoed Junction)
11-22
Al Capp
AH HEERD IT!!"TH' WRECKER" IS COMIN'. SHE'S A-CHUCKLE!!—DANGER TO US MEN-FOLKS!!
YUMMEE!!
HOPES THEY DON'T STOP HER!!
WOW!!

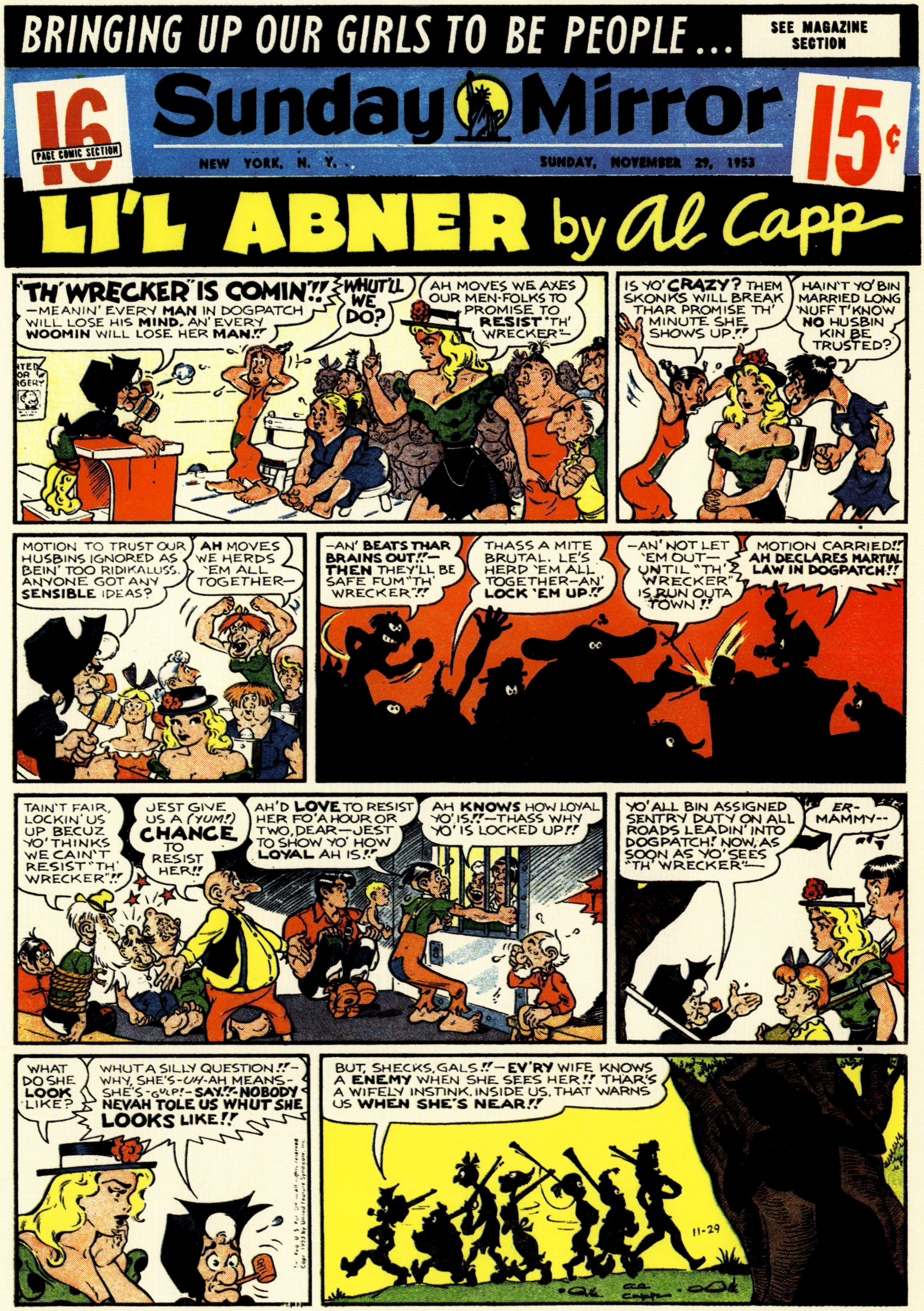

BRINGING UP OUR GIRLS TO BE PEOPLE...
SEE MAGAZINE SECTION
16 PAGE COMIC SECTION
Sunday Mirror
NEW YORK, N. Y.
SUNDAY, NOVEMBER 29, 1953
15¢
LI'L ABNER by Al Capp
"TH' WRECKER" IS COMIN'!!—MEANIN' EVERY MAN IN DOGPATCH WILL LOSE HIS MIND, AN' EVERY WOOMIN WILL LOSE HER MAN!!
WHUT'LL WE DO?
AH MOVES WE AXES OUR MEN-FOLKS TO PROMISE TO RESIST "TH' WRECKER"—
IS YO' CRAZY? THEM SKONKS WILL BREAK THAR PROMISE TH' MINUTE SHE SHOWS UP!!
HAIN'T YO' BIN MARRIED LONG 'NUFF T'KNOW NO HUSBIN KIN BE TRUSTED?
MOTION TO TRUST OUR HUSBINS IGNORED AS BEIN' TOO RIDIKALUSS. ANYONE GOT ANY SENSIBLE IDEAS?
AH MOVES WE HERDS 'EM ALL TOGETHER—
—AN' BEATS THAR BRAINS OUT!!—THEN THEY'LL BE SAFE FUM "TH' WRECKER"!!
THASS A MITE BRUTAL. LE'S HERD 'EM ALL TOGETHER—AN' LOCK 'EM UP!!
—AN' NOT LET 'EM OUT—UNTIL "TH' WRECKER" IS RUN OUTA TOWN!!
MOTION CARRIED!! AH DECLARES MARTIAL LAW IN DOGPATCH!!
TAIN'T FAIR, LOCKIN' US UP BECUZ YO' THINKS WE CAIN'T RESIST "TH' WRECKER"!!
JEST GIVE US A (YUM!) CHANCE TO RESIST HER!!
AH'D LOVE TO RESIST HER FO' A HOUR OR TWO, DEAR—JEST TO SHOW YO' HOW LOYAL AH IS!!
AH KNOWS HOW LOYAL YO' IS!!—THASS WHY YO' IS LOCKED UP!!
YO' ALL BIN ASSIGNED SENTRY DUTY ON ALL ROADS LEADIN' INTO DOGPATCH! NOW, AS SOON AS YO' SEES "TH' WRECKER"—
ER-MAMMY--
WHAT DO SHE LOOK LIKE?
WHUT A SILLY QUESTION!!—WHY, SHE'S-UH-AH MEANS-SHE'S-GULP!-SAY!!-NOBODY NEVAH TOLE US WHUT SHE LOOKS LIKE!!
BUT, SHECKS, GALS!!—EV'RY WIFE KNOWS A ENEMY WHEN SHE SEES HER!! THAR'S A WIFELY INSTINK INSIDE US THAT WARNS US WHEN SHE'S NEAR!!
11-29

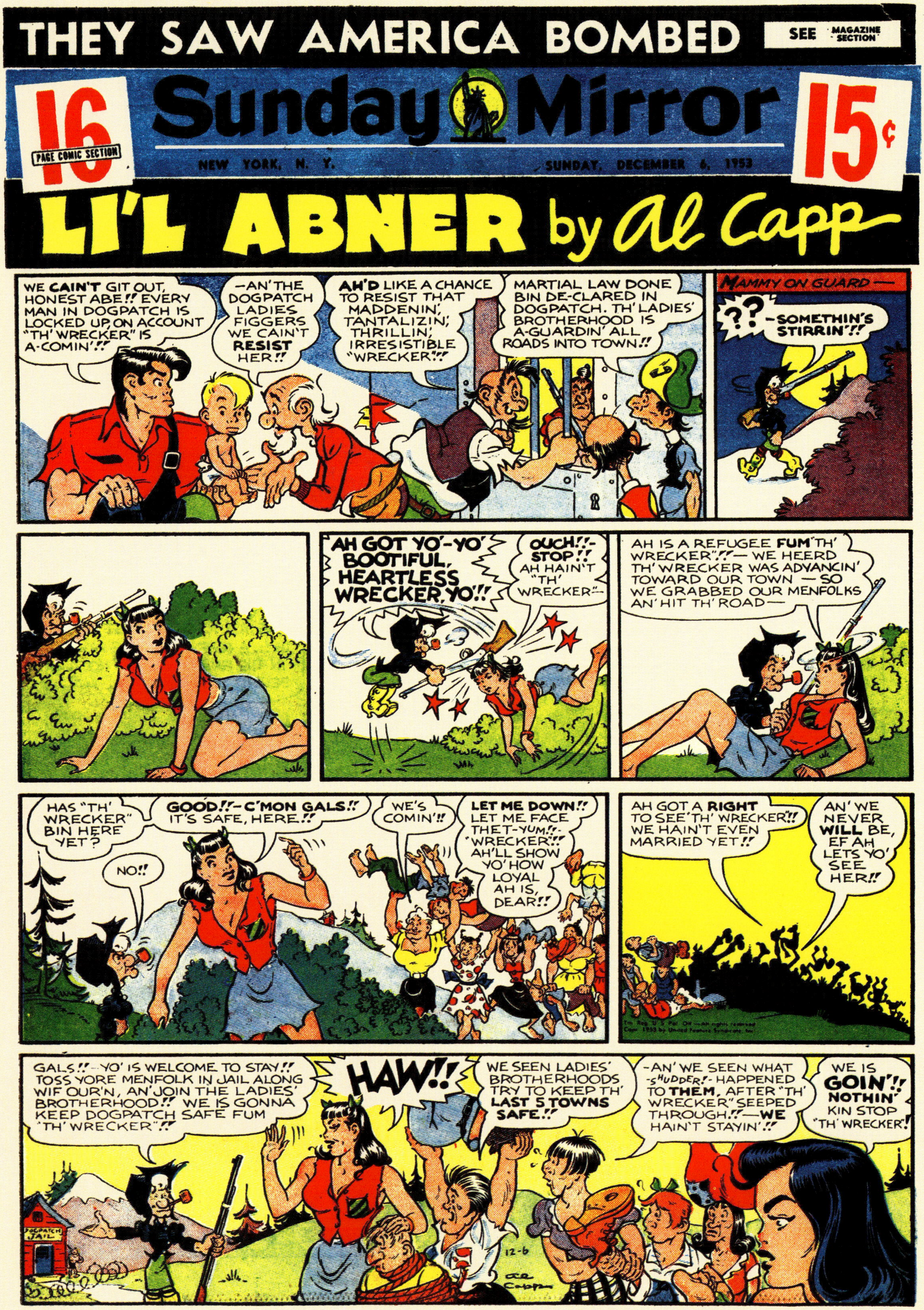
THEY SAW AMERICA BOMBED
SEE MAGAZINE SECTION
16 PAGE COMIC SECTION
Sunday Mirror
NEW YORK, N. Y.
SUNDAY, DECEMBER 6, 1953
15¢
LI'L ABNER by Al Capp
WE CAIN'T GIT OUT, HONEST ABE!! EVERY MAN IN DOGPATCH IS LOCKED UP, ON ACCOUNT "TH' WRECKER" IS A-COMIN'!!
–AN' THE DOGPATCH LADIES FIGGERS WE CAIN'T RESIST HER!!
AH'D LIKE A CHANCE TO RESIST THAT MADDENIN', TANTALIZIN', THRILLIN', IRRESISTIBLE "WRECKER"!!
MARTIAL LAW DONE BIN DE-CLARED IN DOGPATCH. TH' LADIES' BROTHERHOOD IS A-GUARDIN' ALL ROADS INTO TOWN!!
MAMMY ON GUARD –
??–SOMETHIN'S STIRRIN'!!
AH GOT YO'–YO' BOOTIFUL, HEARTLESS WRECKER, YO'!!
OUCH!!–STOP!! AH HAIN'T "TH' WRECKER"–
AH IS A REFUGEE FUM TH' WRECKER"!!– WE HEERD TH' WRECKER WAS ADVANCIN' TOWARD OUR TOWN – SO WE GRABBED OUR MENFOLKS AN' HIT TH' ROAD–
HAS "TH' WRECKER" BIN HERE YET?
NO!!
GOOD!!–C'MON GALS!! IT'S SAFE, HERE!!
WE'S COMIN'!!
LET ME DOWN!! LET ME FACE THET–YUM!!–"WRECKER"!! AH'LL SHOW YO' HOW LOYAL AH IS, DEAR!!
AH GOT A RIGHT TO SEE TH' WRECKER"!! WE HAIN'T EVEN MARRIED YET!!
AN' WE NEVER WILL BE, EF AH LETS YO' SEE HER!!
GALS!!–YO' IS WELCOME TO STAY!! TOSS YORE MENFOLK IN JAIL ALONG WIF OUR'N, AN' JOIN THE LADIES' BROTHERHOOD!! WE IS GONNA KEEP DOGPATCH SAFE FUM "TH' WRECKER"!!
HAW!!
WE SEEN LADIES' BROTHERHOODS TRY TO KEEP TH' LAST 5 TOWNS SAFE!!
–AN' WE SEEN WHAT –SHUDDER!– HAPPENED TO THEM, AFTER "TH' WRECKER" SEEPED THROUGH!!–WE HAIN'T STAYIN'!!
WE IS GOIN'!! NOTHIN' KIN STOP "TH' WRECKER"!
DOGPATCH JAIL
12-6
Al Capp

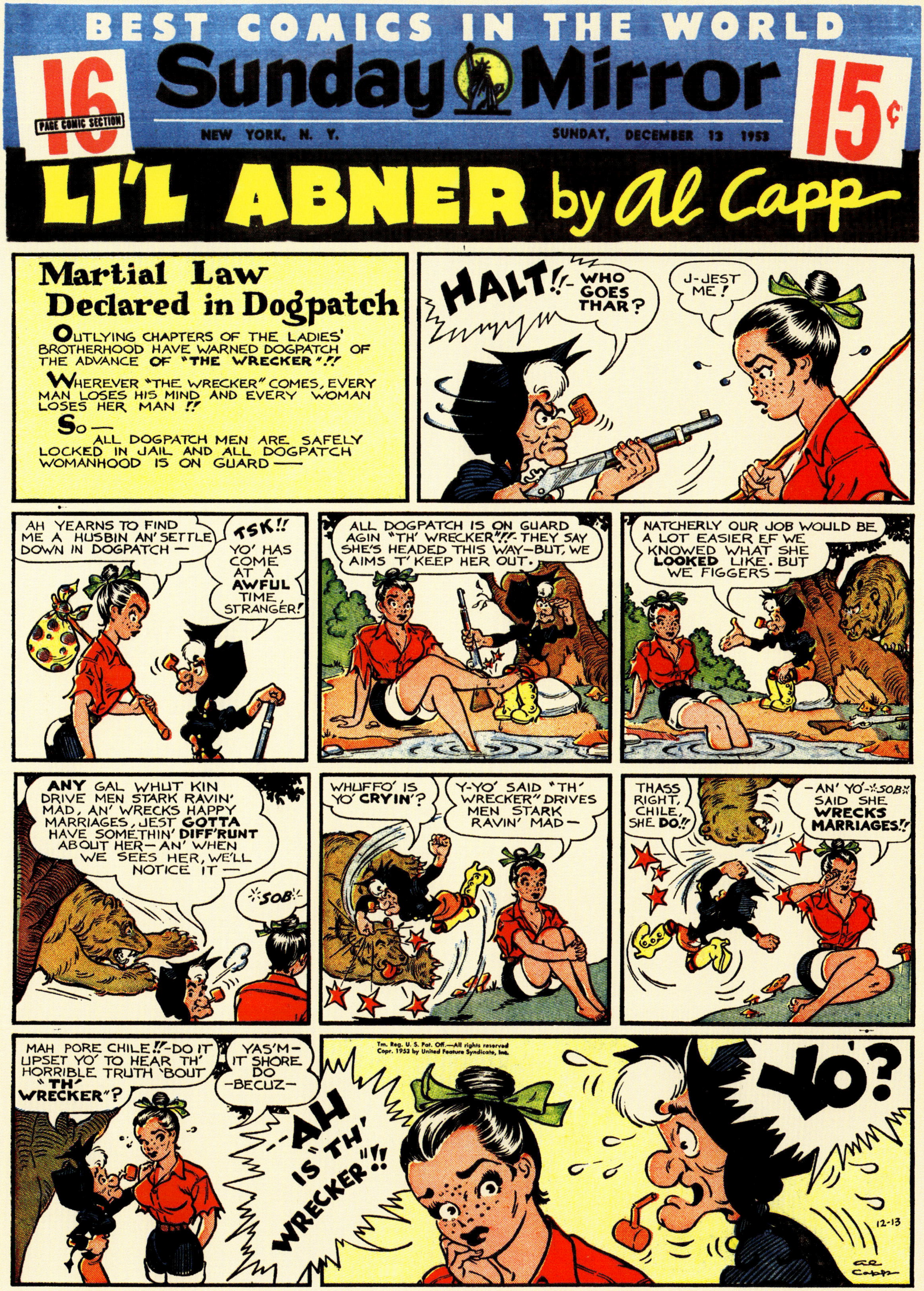
BEST COMICS IN THE WORLD
16 PAGE COMIC SECTION
Sunday Mirror
15¢
NEW YORK, N. Y.
SUNDAY, DECEMBER 13 1953
LI'L ABNER by Al Capp
Martial Law Declared in Dogpatch
OUTLYING CHAPTERS OF THE LADIES' BROTHERHOOD HAVE WARNED DOGPATCH OF THE ADVANCE OF "THE WRECKER"!!
WHEREVER "THE WRECKER" COMES, EVERY MAN LOSES HIS MIND AND EVERY WOMAN LOSES HER MAN !!
SO— ALL DOGPATCH MEN ARE SAFELY LOCKED IN JAIL AND ALL DOGPATCH WOMANHOOD IS ON GUARD—
HALT!!– WHO GOES THAR?
J-JEST ME!
AH YEARNS TO FIND ME A HUSBIN AN' SETTLE DOWN IN DOGPATCH—
TSK!! YO' HAS COME AT A AWFUL TIME, STRANGER!
ALL DOGPATCH IS ON GUARD AGIN "TH' WRECKER"!!– THEY SAY SHE'S HEADED THIS WAY–BUT, WE AIMS T' KEEP HER OUT.
NATCHERLY OUR JOB WOULD BE A LOT EASIER EF WE KNOWED WHAT SHE LOOKED LIKE. BUT WE FIGGERS—
ANY GAL WHUT KIN DRIVE MEN STARK RAVIN' MAD, AN' WRECKS HAPPY MARRIAGES, JEST GOTTA HAVE SOMETHIN' DIFF'RUNT ABOUT HER–AN' WHEN WE SEES HER, WE'LL NOTICE IT—
SOB
WHUFFO' IS YO' CRYIN'?
Y-YO' SAID "TH' WRECKER" DRIVES MEN STARK RAVIN' MAD—
THASS RIGHT, CHILE, SHE DO!!
–AN' YO'–SOB– SAID SHE WRECKS MARRIAGES!!
MAH PORE CHILE!!–DO IT UPSET YO' TO HEAR TH' HORRIBLE TRUTH 'BOUT "TH' WRECKER"?
YAS'M– IT SHORE DO –BECUZ–
Tm. Reg. U. S. Pat. Off.—All rights reserved
Copr. 1953 by United Feature Syndicate, Inc.
AH IS "TH' WRECKER"!!
YO'?
12-13
AL CAPP

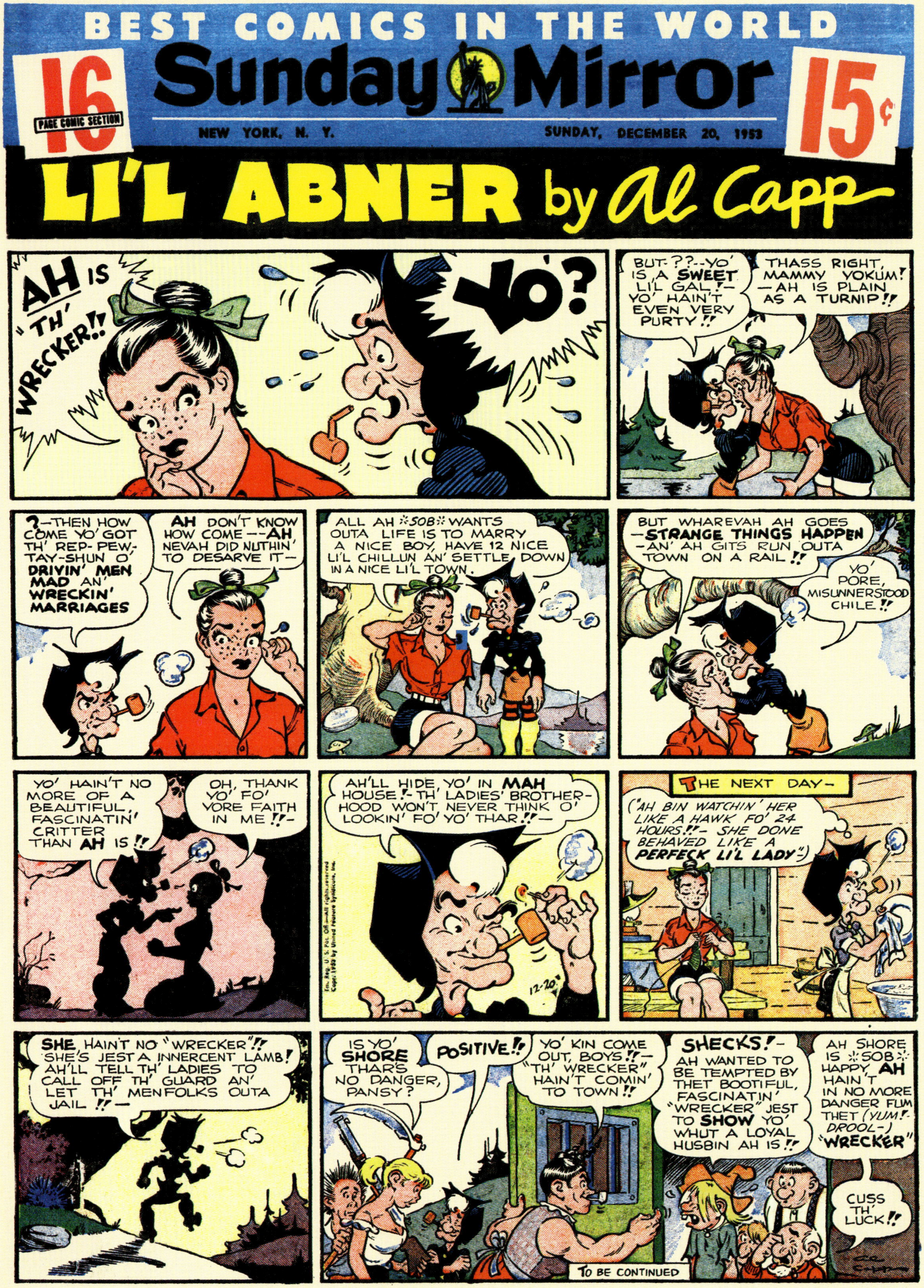

BEST COMICS IN THE WORLD
16 PAGE COMIC SECTION
Sunday Mirror
15¢
NEW YORK, N. Y.
SUNDAY, DECEMBER 20, 1953
LI'L ABNER by Al Capp
AH IS "TH' WRECKER"!!
YO'?
BUT-??--YO' IS A SWEET LI'L GAL!-YO' HAIN'T EVEN VERY PURTY!!
THASS RIGHT, MAMMY YOKUM!-AH IS PLAIN AS A TURNIP!!
?-THEN HOW COME YO' GOT TH' REP-PEW-TAY-SHUN O' DRIVIN' MEN MAD AN' WRECKIN' MARRIAGES
AH DON'T KNOW HOW COME--AH NEVAH DID NUTHIN' TO DESARVE IT-
ALL AH *SOB* WANTS OUTA LIFE IS TO MARRY A NICE BOY, HAVE 12 NICE LI'L CHILLUN AN' SETTLE DOWN IN A NICE LI'L TOWN.
BUT WHAREVAH AH GOES -STRANGE THINGS HAPPEN -AN' AH GITS RUN OUTA TOWN ON A RAIL!!
YO' PORE, MISUNNERSTOOD CHILE!!
YO' HAIN'T NO MORE OF A BEAUTIFUL, FASCINATIN' CRITTER THAN AH IS!!
OH, THANK YO' FO' YORE FAITH IN ME!!-
AH'LL HIDE YO' IN MAH HOUSE!-TH' LADIES' BROTHER-HOOD WON'T NEVER THINK O' LOOKIN' FO' YO' THAR!!-
Tm. Reg. U. S. Pat. Off.—All rights reserved Copr. 1953 by United Feature Syndicate, Inc.
12-20
THE NEXT DAY-
("AH BIN WATCHIN' HER LIKE A HAWK FO' 24 HOURS!!- SHE DONE BEHAVED LIKE A PERFECK LI'L LADY")
SHE HAIN'T NO "WRECKER"!! SHE'S JEST A INNERCENT LAMB! AH'LL TELL TH' LADIES TO CALL OFF TH' GUARD AN' LET TH' MENFOLKS OUTA JAIL!!-
IS YO' SHORE THAR'S NO DANGER, PANSY?
POSITIVE!!
YO' KIN COME OUT, BOYS!!-"TH' WRECKER" HAIN'T COMIN' TO TOWN!!
SHECKS!-AH WANTED TO BE TEMPTED BY THET BOOTIFUL, FASCINATIN' "WRECKER" JEST TO SHOW YO' WHUT A LOYAL HUSBIN AH IS!!
AH SHORE IS *SOB* HAPPY AH HAIN'T IN NO MORE DANGER FUM THET (YUM!-DROOL-) "WRECKER"
CUSS TH' LUCK!!
TO BE CONTINUED

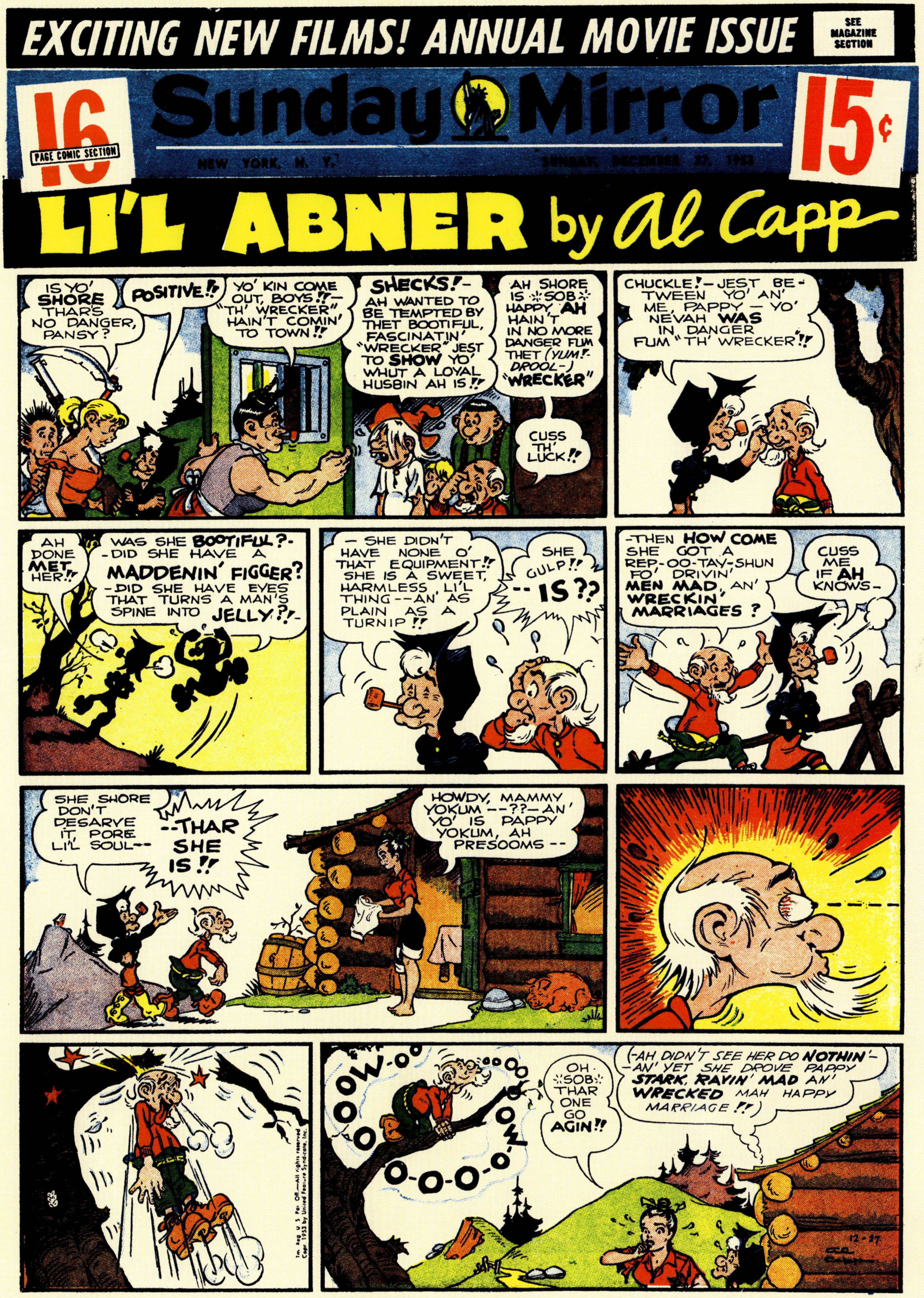
EXCITING NEW FILMS! ANNUAL MOVIE ISSUE
SEE MAGAZINE SECTION
16 PAGE COMIC SECTION
Sunday Mirror
15¢
NEW YORK, N. Y.
SUNDAY, DECEMBER 27, 1953
LI'L ABNER by Al Capp
IS YO' SHORE THAR'S NO DANGER, PANSY?
POSITIVE!!
YO' KIN COME OUT, BOYS!!— "TH' WRECKER" HAIN'T COMIN' TO TOWN!!
SHECKS!— AH WANTED TO BE TEMPTED BY THET BOOTIFUL, FASCINATIN' "WRECKER" JEST TO SHOW YO' WHUT A LOYAL HUSBIN AH IS!!
AH SHORE IS *SOB* HAPPY AH HAIN'T IN NO MORE DANGER FUM THET (YUM!- DROOL-) "WRECKER"
CUSS TH' LUCK!!
CHUCKLE!— JEST BE-TWEEN YO' AN' ME, PAPPY — YO' NEVAH WAS IN DANGER FUM "TH' WRECKER"!!
AH DONE MET HER!!
WAS SHE BOOTIFUL?- -DID SHE HAVE A MADDENIN' FIGGER? -DID SHE HAVE EYES THAT TURNS A MAN'S SPINE INTO JELLY?!-
— SHE DIDN'T HAVE NONE O' THAT EQUIPMENT!! SHE IS A SWEET, HARMLESS, LI'L THING--AN' AS PLAIN AS A TURNIP!!
SHE GULP!! --IS??
-THEN HOW COME SHE GOT A REP-OO-TAY-SHUN FO' DRIVIN' MEN MAD, AN' WRECKIN' MARRIAGES ?
CUSS ME IF AH KNOWS-
SHE SHORE DON'T DESARVE IT, PORE LI'L SOUL--
--THAR SHE IS!!
HOWDY, MAMMY YOKUM --??— AN' YO' IS PAPPY YOKUM, AH PRESOOMS --
Tm. Reg. U S Pat. Off.—All rights reserved
Copr. 1953 by United Feature Syndicate, Inc.
OOW-OOOOO-O-O-O-O-O-O
OH *SOB* THAR ONE GO AGIN!!
(-AH DIDN'T SEE HER DO NOTHIN'- -AN' YET SHE DROVE PAPPY STARK, RAVIN' MAD AN' WRECKED MAH HAPPY MARRIAGE !!)
12-27

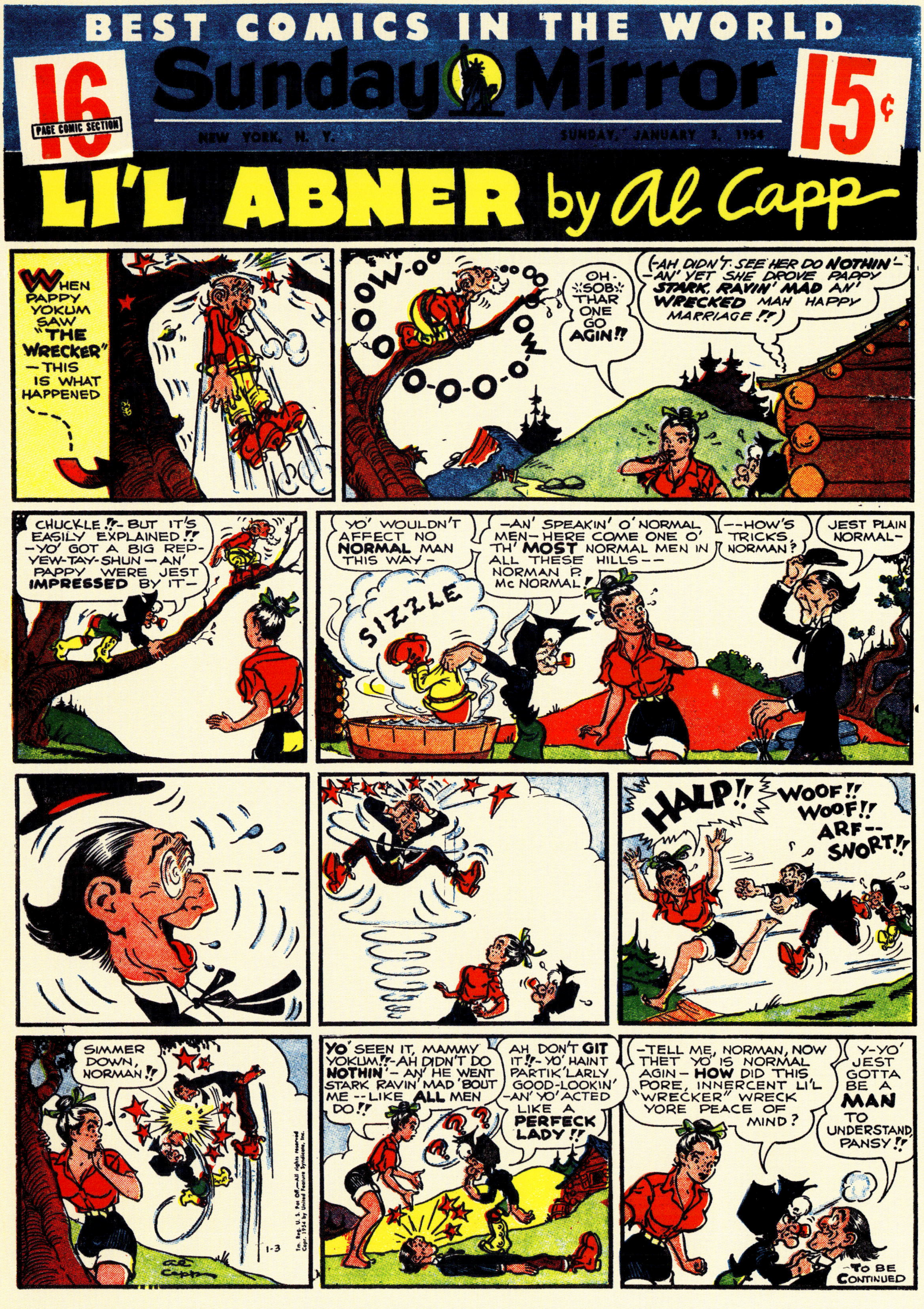

BEST COMICS IN THE WORLD
16 PAGE COMIC SECTION
Sunday Mirror
NEW YORK, N. Y.
SUNDAY, JANUARY 3, 1954
15¢
LI'L ABNER by Al Capp
WHEN PAPPY YOKUM SAW "THE WRECKER" —THIS IS WHAT HAPPENED
OOOW-OOOO
OOW-O-O-O-O
OH-SOB-THAR ONE GO AGIN!!
—AH DIDN'T SEE HER DO NOTHIN'—AN' YET SHE DROVE PAPPY STARK, RAVIN' MAD AN' WRECKED MAH HAPPY MARRIAGE!!
CHUCKLE!!—BUT IT'S EASILY EXPLAINED!!—YO' GOT A BIG REP-YEW-TAY-SHUN—AN' PAPPY WERE JEST IMPRESSED BY IT—
YO' WOULDN'T AFFECT NO NORMAL MAN THIS WAY—
—AN' SPEAKIN' O' NORMAL MEN—HERE COME ONE O' TH' MOST NORMAL MEN IN ALL THESE HILLS—NORMAN P. Mc NORMAL!
SIZZLE
—HOW'S TRICKS, NORMAN?
JEST PLAIN NORMAL—
HALP!!
WOOF!! WOOF!! ARF—SNORT!!
SIMMER DOWN, NORMAN!!
1-3
Tm. Reg. U. S. Pat Off.—All rights reserved
Copr. 1954 by United Feature Syndicate, Inc.
YO' SEEN IT, MAMMY YOKUM!!—AH DIDN'T DO NOTHIN'—AN' HE WENT STARK RAVIN' MAD 'BOUT ME—LIKE ALL MEN DO!!
AH DON'T GIT IT!!—YO' HAINT PARTIK'LARLY GOOD-LOOKIN'—AN' YO' ACTED LIKE A PERFECK LADY!!
—TELL ME, NORMAN, NOW THET YO' IS NORMAL AGIN—HOW DID THIS PORE, INNERCENT LI'L "WRECKER" WRECK YORE PEACE OF MIND?
Y-YO' JEST GOTTA BE A MAN TO UNDERSTAND PANSY!!
—TO BE CONTINUED

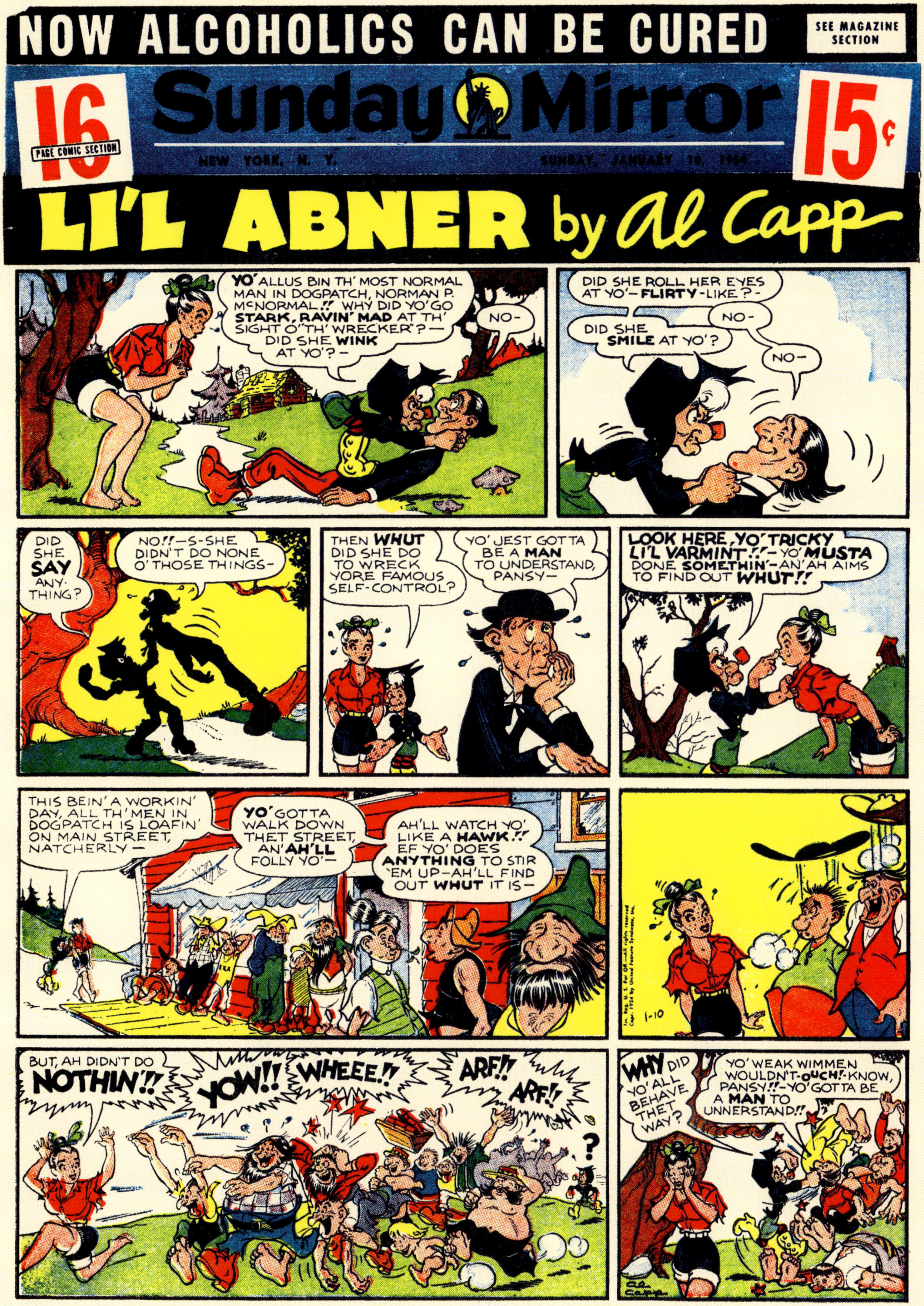

NOW ALCOHOLICS CAN BE CURED
SEE MAGAZINE SECTION
16
PAGE COMIC SECTION
Sunday Mirror
NEW YORK, N. Y.
SUNDAY, JANUARY 10, 1954
15¢
LI'L ABNER by Al Capp
YO' ALLUS BIN TH' MOST NORMAL MAN IN DOGPATCH, NORMAN P. McNORMAL.!! WHY DID YO'GO STARK, RAVIN' MAD AT TH' SIGHT O' "TH' WRECKER"? — DID SHE WINK AT YO'? —
NO-
DID SHE ROLL HER EYES AT YO'- FLIRTY-LIKE? -
NO-
DID SHE SMILE AT YO'?
NO-
DID SHE SAY ANY-THING?
NO!!-S-SHE DIDN'T DO NONE O' THOSE THINGS-
THEN WHUT DID SHE DO TO WRECK YORE FAMOUS SELF-CONTROL?
YO' JEST GOTTA BE A MAN TO UNDERSTAND, PANSY-
LOOK HERE, YO' TRICKY LI'L VARMINT!!- YO' MUSTA DONE SOMETHIN'- AN' AH AIMS TO FIND OUT WHUT!!
THIS BEIN' A WORKIN' DAY, ALL TH' MEN IN DOGPATCH IS LOAFIN' ON MAIN STREET, NATCHERLY —
YO' GOTTA WALK DOWN THET STREET, AN' AH'LL FOLLY YO'—
AH'LL WATCH YO' LIKE A HAWK.!! EF YO' DOES ANYTHING TO STIR 'EM UP-AH'LL FIND OUT WHUT IT IS—
1-10
BUT, AH DIDN'T DO NOTHIN'!!
YOW!!
WHEEE!!
ARF!!
ARF!!
?
WHY DID YO' ALL BEHAVE THET WAY?
YO' WEAK WIMMEN WOULDN'T-OUCH!-KNOW, PANSY!!-YO' GOTTA BE A MAN TO UNNERSTAND!!

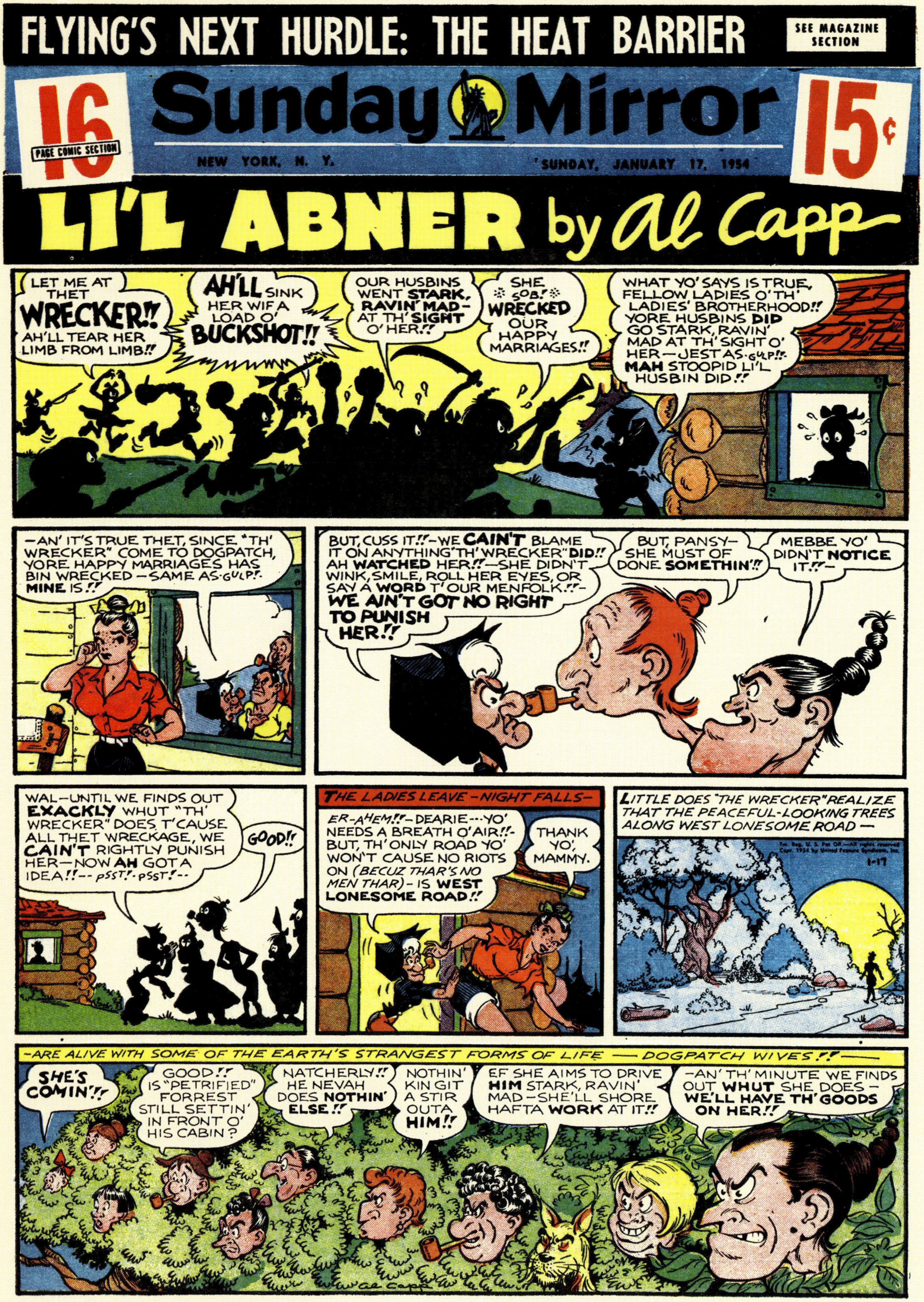

FLYING'S NEXT HURDLE: THE HEAT BARRIER
SEE MAGAZINE SECTION
16
PAGE COMIC SECTION
Sunday Mirror
15¢
NEW YORK, N. Y.
SUNDAY, JANUARY 17, 1954
LI'L ABNER by Al Capp
LET ME AT THET WRECKER!! AH'LL TEAR HER LIMB FROM LIMB!!
AH'LL SINK HER WIF A LOAD O' BUCKSHOT!!
OUR HUSBINS WENT STARK, RAVIN' MAD - AT TH' SIGHT O' HER!!
SHE - SOB! - WRECKED OUR HAPPY MARRIAGES!!
WHAT YO' SAYS IS TRUE, FELLOW LADIES O' TH' LADIES' BROTHERHOOD!! YORE HUSBINS DID GO STARK, RAVIN' MAD AT TH' SIGHT O' HER - JEST AS - GULP!! - MAH STOOPID LI'L HUSBIN DID!!
-AN' IT'S TRUE THET, SINCE "TH' WRECKER" COME TO DOGPATCH, YORE HAPPY MARRIAGES HAS BIN WRECKED - SAME AS - GULP! - MINE IS!!
BUT, CUSS IT!! - WE CAIN'T BLAME IT ON ANYTHING "TH' WRECKER" DID!! AH WATCHED HER!! - SHE DIDN'T WINK, SMILE, ROLL HER EYES, OR SAY A WORD T' OUR MENFOLK!! - WE AIN'T GOT NO RIGHT TO PUNISH HER!!
BUT, PANSY - SHE MUST OF DONE SOMETHIN'!!
MEBBE YO' DIDN'T NOTICE IT!! -
WAL - UNTIL WE FINDS OUT EXACKLY WHUT "TH' WRECKER" DOES T' CAUSE ALL THET WRECKAGE, WE CAIN'T RIGHTLY PUNISH HER - NOW AH GOT A IDEA!! -- PSST! - PSST! --
GOOD!!
THE LADIES LEAVE - NIGHT FALLS -
ER-AHEM!! - DEARIE --- YO' NEEDS A BREATH O' AIR!! - BUT, TH' ONLY ROAD YO' WON'T CAUSE NO RIOTS ON (BECUZ THAR'S NO MEN THAR) - IS WEST LONESOME ROAD!!
THANK YO', MAMMY.
LITTLE DOES "THE WRECKER" REALIZE THAT THE PEACEFUL-LOOKING TREES ALONG WEST LONESOME ROAD —
1-17
— ARE ALIVE WITH SOME OF THE EARTH'S STRANGEST FORMS OF LIFE — DOGPATCH WIVES!!
SHE'S COMIN'!!
GOOD!! IS "PETRIFIED" FORREST STILL SETTIN' IN FRONT O' HIS CABIN?
NATCHERLY!! HE NEVAH DOES NOTHIN' ELSE!!
NOTHIN' KIN GIT A STIR OUTA HIM!!
EF SHE AIMS TO DRIVE HIM STARK, RAVIN' MAD - SHE'LL SHORE HAFTA WORK AT IT!!
-AN' TH' MINUTE WE FINDS OUT WHUT SHE DOES - WE'LL HAVE TH' GOODS ON HER!!

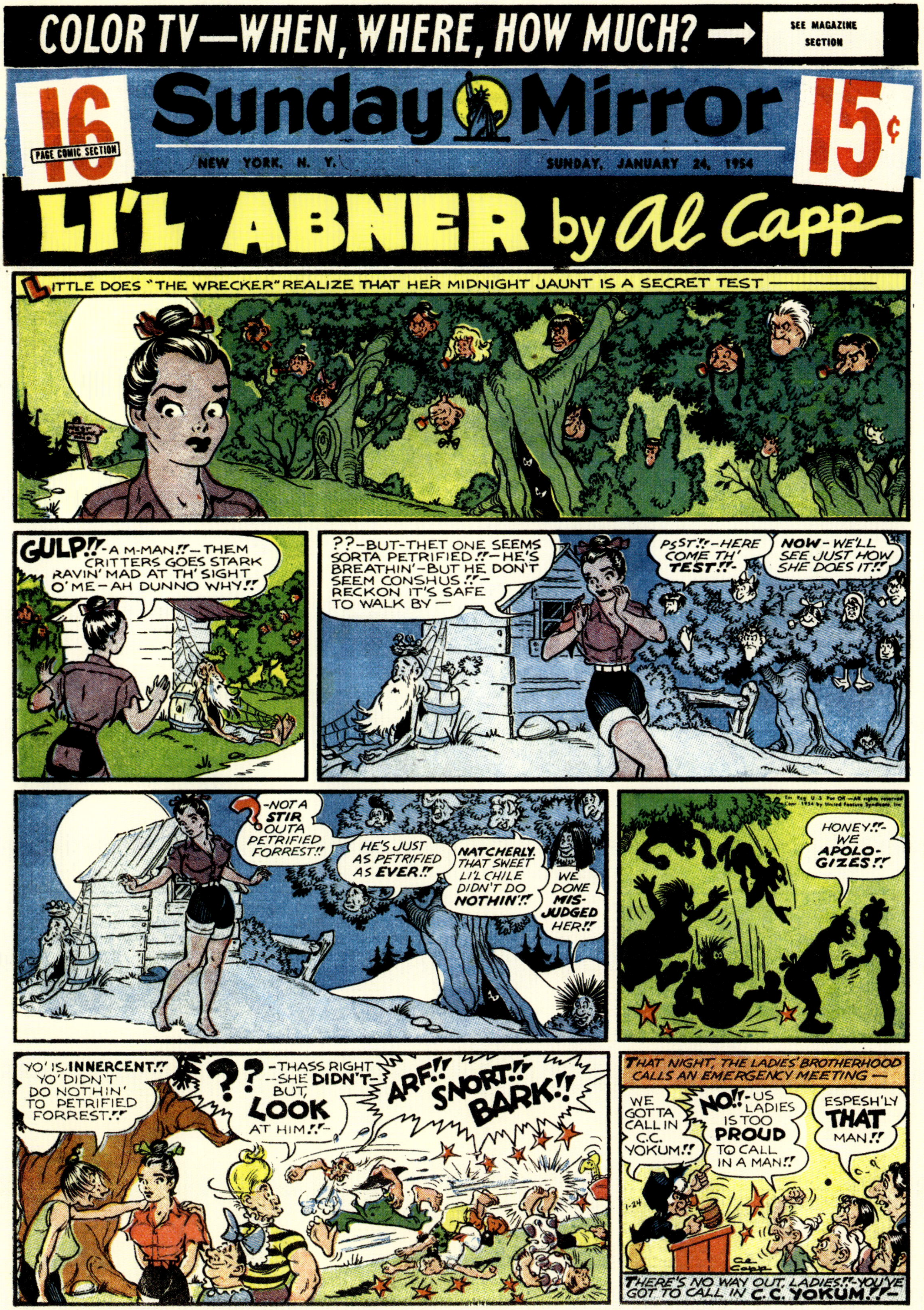
COLOR TV—WHEN, WHERE, HOW MUCH?
SEE MAGAZINE SECTION
16 PAGE COMIC SECTION
Sunday Mirror
15¢
NEW YORK, N. Y.
SUNDAY, JANUARY 24, 1954
LI'L ABNER by Al Capp
LITTLE DOES "THE WRECKER" REALIZE THAT HER MIDNIGHT JAUNT IS A SECRET TEST —
GULP!!-A M-MAN!!—THEM CRITTERS GOES STARK RAVIN' MAD AT TH' SIGHT O'ME—AH DUNNO WHY!!
??-BUT-THET ONE SEEMS SORTA PETRIFIED!!-HE'S BREATHIN'-BUT HE DON'T SEEM CONSHUS!!-RECKON IT'S SAFE TO WALK BY —
PSST!!-HERE COME TH' TEST!!-
NOW-WE'LL SEE JUST HOW SHE DOES IT!!
?-NOT A STIR OUTA PETRIFIED FORREST!!
HE'S JUST AS PETRIFIED AS EVER!!
NATCHERLY. THAT SWEET LI'L CHILE DIDN'T DO NOTHIN'!!
WE DONE MIS-JUDGED HER!!
HONEY!!-WE APOLO-GIZES!!
YO' IS INNERCENT!! YO' DIDN'T DO NOTHIN' TO PETRIFIED FORREST!!
??-THASS RIGHT --SHE DIDN'T-BUT, LOOK AT HIM!!-
ARF!! SNORT!! BARK!!
THAT NIGHT, THE LADIES' BROTHERHOOD CALLS AN EMERGENCY MEETING —
WE GOTTA CALL IN C.C. YOKUM!!
NO!!-US LADIES IS TOO PROUD TO CALL IN A MAN!!
ESPESH'LY THAT MAN!!
THERE'S NO WAY OUT, LADIES!!-YOU'VE GOT TO CALL IN C.C. YOKUM!!-

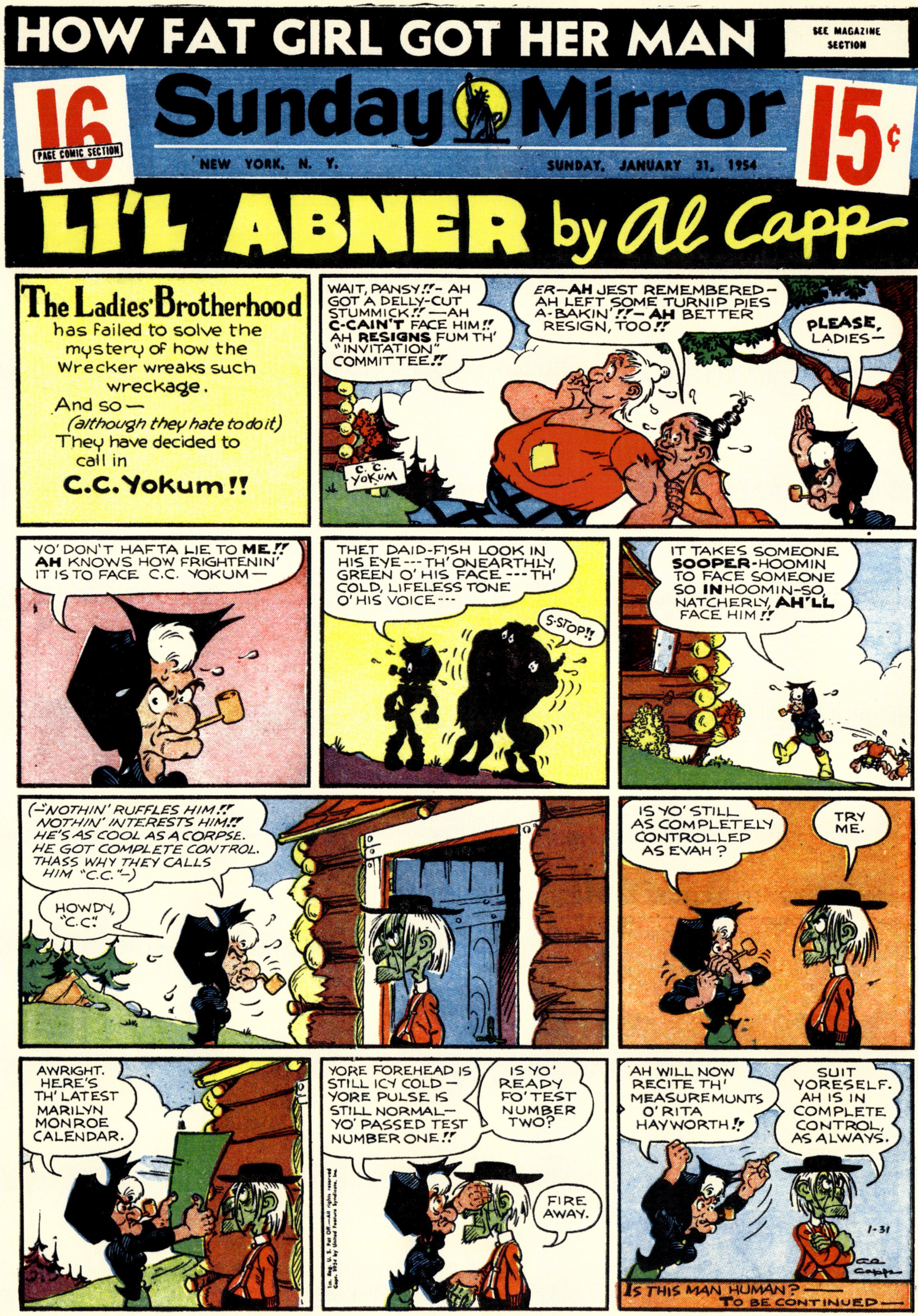

HOW FAT GIRL GOT HER MAN
SEE MAGAZINE SECTION
16 PAGE COMIC SECTION
Sunday Mirror
15¢
NEW YORK, N. Y.
SUNDAY, JANUARY 31, 1954
LI'L ABNER by Al Capp
The Ladies' Brotherhood has failed to solve the mystery of how the Wrecker wreaks such wreckage. And so — (although they hate to do it) They have decided to call in C.C. Yokum!!
WAIT, PANSY!!- AH GOT A DELLY-CUT STUMMICK!! —AH C-CAIN'T FACE HIM!! AH RESIGNS FUM TH' "INVITATION" COMMITTEE!!
ER—AH JEST REMEMBERED—AH LEFT SOME TURNIP PIES A-BAKIN'!!—AH BETTER RESIGN, TOO!!
PLEASE, LADIES—
C. C. YOKUM
YO' DON'T HAFTA LIE TO ME!! AH KNOWS HOW FRIGHTENIN' IT IS TO FACE C.C. YOKUM—
THET DAID-FISH LOOK IN HIS EYE---TH' ONEARTHLY GREEN O' HIS FACE---TH' COLD, LIFELESS TONE O' HIS VOICE---
S-STOP!!
IT TAKES SOMEONE SOOPER-HOOMIN TO FACE SOMEONE SO INHOOMIN-SO, NATCHERLY, AH'LL FACE HIM!!
(—"NOTHIN' RUFFLES HIM!! NOTHIN' INTERESTS HIM!! HE'S AS COOL AS A CORPSE. HE GOT COMPLETE CONTROL. THASS WHY THEY CALLS HIM "C.C."—)
HOWDY, "C.C."
IS YO' STILL AS COMPLETELY CONTROLLED AS EVAH?
TRY ME.
AWRIGHT. HERE'S TH' LATEST MARILYN MONROE CALENDAR.
YORE FOREHEAD IS STILL ICY COLD — YORE PULSE IS STILL NORMAL— YO' PASSED TEST NUMBER ONE!!
IS YO' READY FO' TEST NUMBER TWO?
FIRE AWAY.
AH WILL NOW RECITE TH' MEASUREMUNTS O' RITA HAYWORTH!!
SUIT YORESELF. AH IS IN COMPLETE CONTROL, AS ALWAYS.
1-31
Al Capp
IS THIS MAN HUMAN? — TO BE CONTINUED —

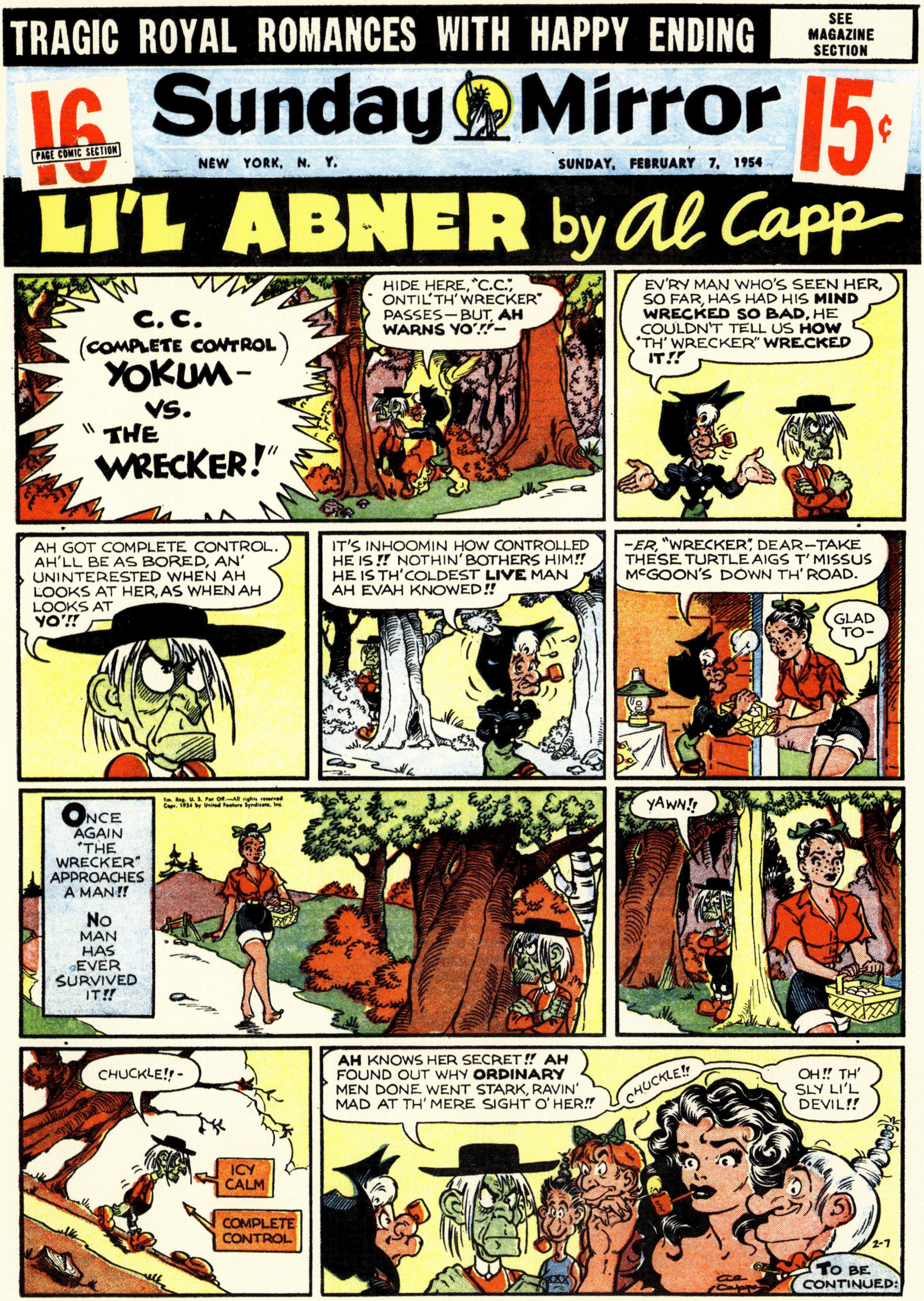
TRAGIC ROYAL ROMANCES WITH HAPPY ENDING
SEE MAGAZINE SECTION
16 PAGE COMIC SECTION
Sunday Mirror
15¢
NEW YORK, N. Y.
SUNDAY, FEBRUARY 7, 1954
LI'L ABNER by Al Capp
C. C. (COMPLETE CONTROL) YOKUM - VS. "THE WRECKER!"
HIDE HERE, "C.C.," ONTIL TH' WRECKER" PASSES—BUT, AH WARNS YO'!!—
EV'RY MAN WHO'S SEEN HER, SO FAR, HAS HAD HIS MIND WRECKED SO BAD, HE COULDN'T TELL US HOW "TH' WRECKER" WRECKED IT!!
AH GOT COMPLETE CONTROL. AH'LL BE AS BORED, AN' UNINTERESTED WHEN AH LOOKS AT HER, AS WHEN AH LOOKS AT YO'!!
IT'S INHOOMIN HOW CONTROLLED HE IS!! NOTHIN' BOTHERS HIM!! HE IS TH' COLDEST LIVE MAN AH EVAH KNOWED!!
-ER, "WRECKER," DEAR—TAKE THESE TURTLE AIGS T' MISSUS McGOON'S DOWN TH' ROAD.
GLAD TO-
Tm. Reg. U. S. Pat Off.—All rights reserved Copr. 1954 by United Feature Syndicate, Inc.
ONCE AGAIN "THE WRECKER" APPROACHES A MAN!!
NO MAN HAS EVER SURVIVED IT!!
YAWN!!
CHUCKLE!!-
ICY CALM
COMPLETE CONTROL
AH KNOWS HER SECRET!! AH FOUND OUT WHY ORDINARY MEN DONE WENT STARK, RAVIN' MAD AT TH' MERE SIGHT O' HER!!
CHUCKLE!!
OH!! TH' SLY LI'L DEVIL!!
2-7
TO BE CONTINUED:

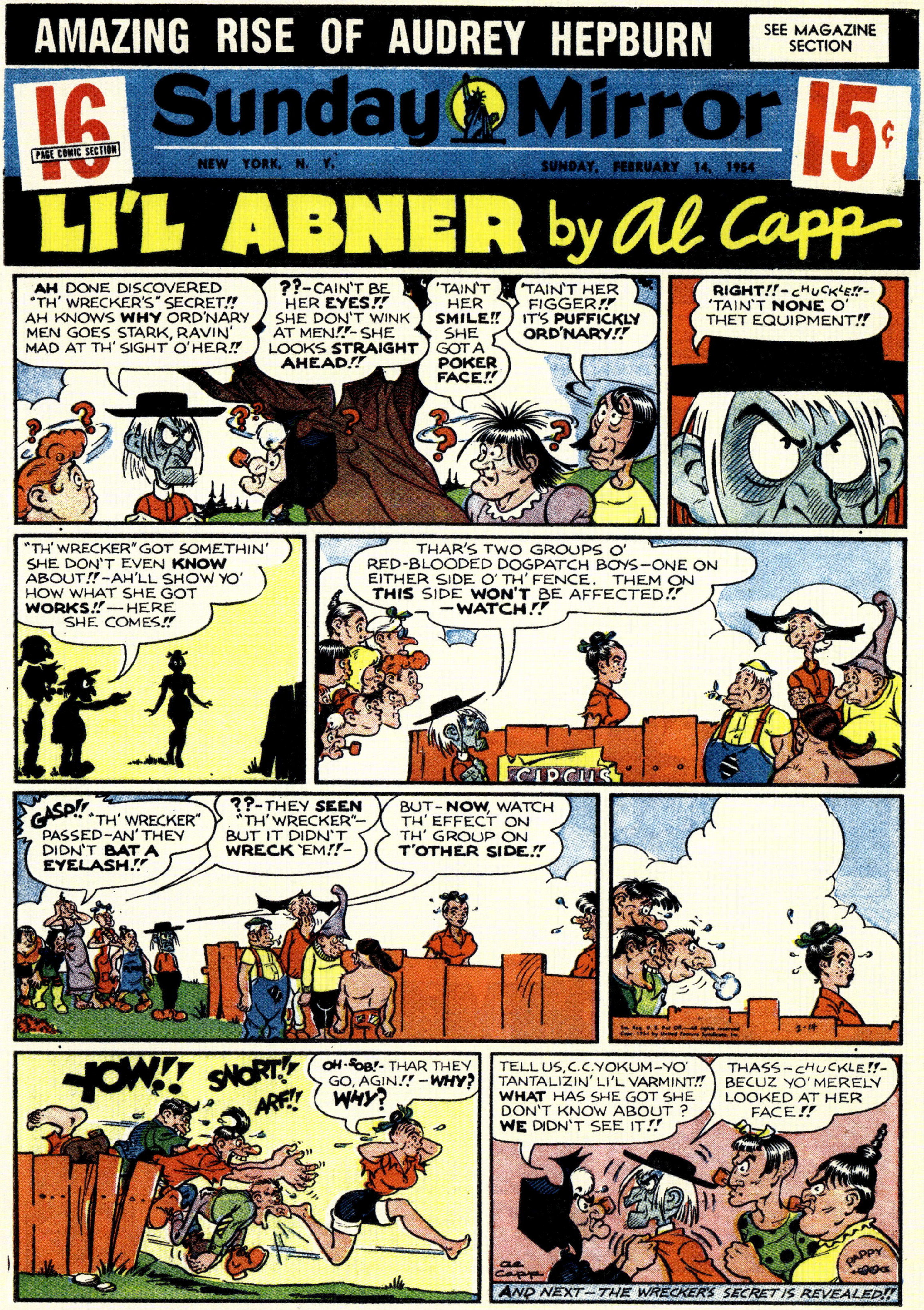

AMAZING RISE OF AUDREY HEPBURN
SEE MAGAZINE SECTION
16 PAGE COMIC SECTION
Sunday Mirror
15¢
NEW YORK, N. Y.
SUNDAY, FEBRUARY 14, 1954
LI'L ABNER by Al Capp
AH DONE DISCOVERED "TH' WRECKER'S" SECRET!! AH KNOWS WHY ORD'NARY MEN GOES STARK, RAVIN' MAD AT TH' SIGHT O'HER!!
??-CAIN'T BE HER EYES!! SHE DON'T WINK AT MEN!!-SHE LOOKS STRAIGHT AHEAD!!
'TAIN'T HER SMILE!! SHE GOT A POKER FACE!!
'TAIN'T HER FIGGER!! IT'S PUFFICKLY ORD'NARY!!
RIGHT!!-CHUCKLE!!-'TAIN'T NONE O' THET EQUIPMENT!!
"TH' WRECKER" GOT SOMETHIN' SHE DON'T EVEN KNOW ABOUT!!-AH'LL SHOW YO' HOW WHAT SHE GOT WORKS!!-HERE SHE COMES!!
THAR'S TWO GROUPS O' RED-BLOODED DOGPATCH BOYS-ONE ON EITHER SIDE O' TH' FENCE. THEM ON THIS SIDE WON'T BE AFFECTED!!-WATCH!!
CIRCUS
GASP!! "TH' WRECKER" PASSED-AN' THEY DIDN'T BAT A EYELASH!!
??-THEY SEEN "TH' WRECKER"-BUT IT DIDN'T WRECK 'EM!!-
BUT-NOW, WATCH TH' EFFECT ON TH' GROUP ON T'OTHER SIDE!!
2-14
YOW!!
SNORT!!
ARF!!
OH-SOB!-THAR THEY GO, AGIN!!-WHY? WHY?
TELL US, C.C. YOKUM-YO' TANTALIZIN' LI'L VARMINT!! WHAT HAS SHE GOT SHE DON'T KNOW ABOUT? WE DIDN'T SEE IT!!
THASS-CHUCKLE!!-BECUZ YO' MERELY LOOKED AT HER FACE!!
AL CAPP
AND NEXT-THE WRECKER'S SECRET IS REVEALED!!

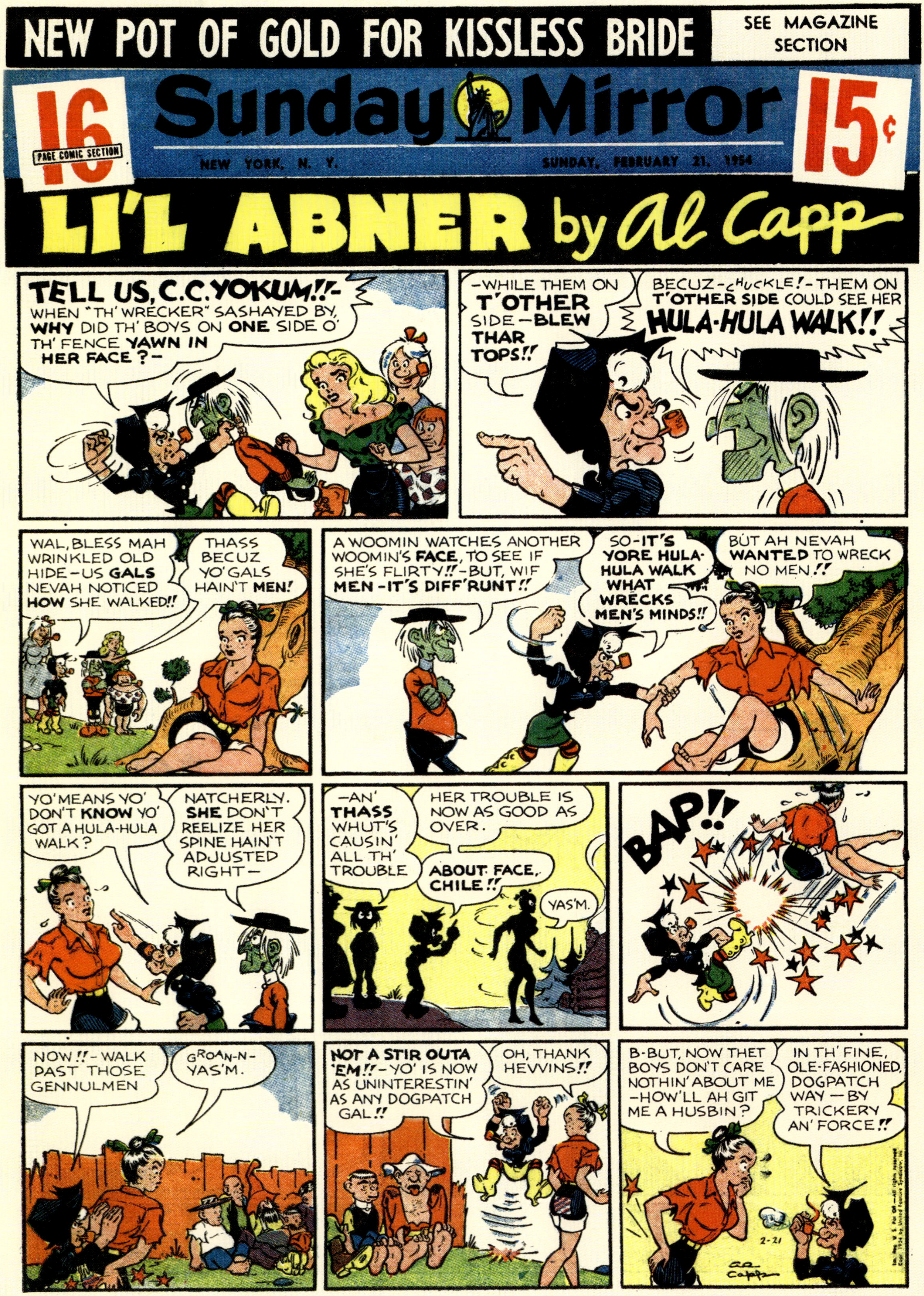

NEW POT OF GOLD FOR KISSLESS BRIDE
SEE MAGAZINE SECTION
16 PAGE COMIC SECTION
Sunday Mirror
15¢
NEW YORK, N. Y.
SUNDAY, FEBRUARY 21, 1954
LI'L ABNER by Al Capp
TELL US, C.C. YOKUM!!- WHEN "TH' WRECKER" SASHAYED BY, WHY DID TH' BOYS ON ONE SIDE O' TH' FENCE YAWN IN HER FACE?-
-WHILE THEM ON T'OTHER SIDE-BLEW THAR TOPS!!
BECUZ-CHUCKLE!-THEM ON T'OTHER SIDE COULD SEE HER HULA-HULA WALK!!
WAL, BLESS MAH WRINKLED OLD HIDE-US GALS NEVAH NOTICED HOW SHE WALKED!!
THASS BECUZ YO' GALS HAIN'T MEN!
A WOOMIN WATCHES ANOTHER WOOMIN'S FACE, TO SEE IF SHE'S FLIRTY!!-BUT, WIF MEN-IT'S DIFF'RUNT!!
SO-IT'S YORE HULA-HULA WALK WHAT WRECKS MEN'S MINDS!!
BUT AH NEVAH WANTED TO WRECK NO MEN!!
YO' MEANS YO' DON'T KNOW YO' GOT A HULA-HULA WALK?
NATCHERLY. SHE DON'T REELIZE HER SPINE HAIN'T ADJUSTED RIGHT-
-AN' THASS WHUT'S CAUSIN' ALL TH' TROUBLE
HER TROUBLE IS NOW AS GOOD AS OVER.
ABOUT FACE, CHILE!!
YAS'M.
BAP!!
NOW!!-WALK PAST THOSE GENNULMEN
GROAN-N-YAS'M.
NOT A STIR OUTA 'EM!!-YO' IS NOW AS UNINTERESTIN' AS ANY DOGPATCH GAL!!
OH, THANK HEVVINS!!
B-BUT, NOW THET BOYS DON'T CARE NOTHIN' ABOUT ME-HOW'LL AH GIT ME A HUSBIN?
IN TH' FINE, OLE-FASHIONED, DOGPATCH WAY-BY TRICKERY AN' FORCE!!
2-21
Al Capp

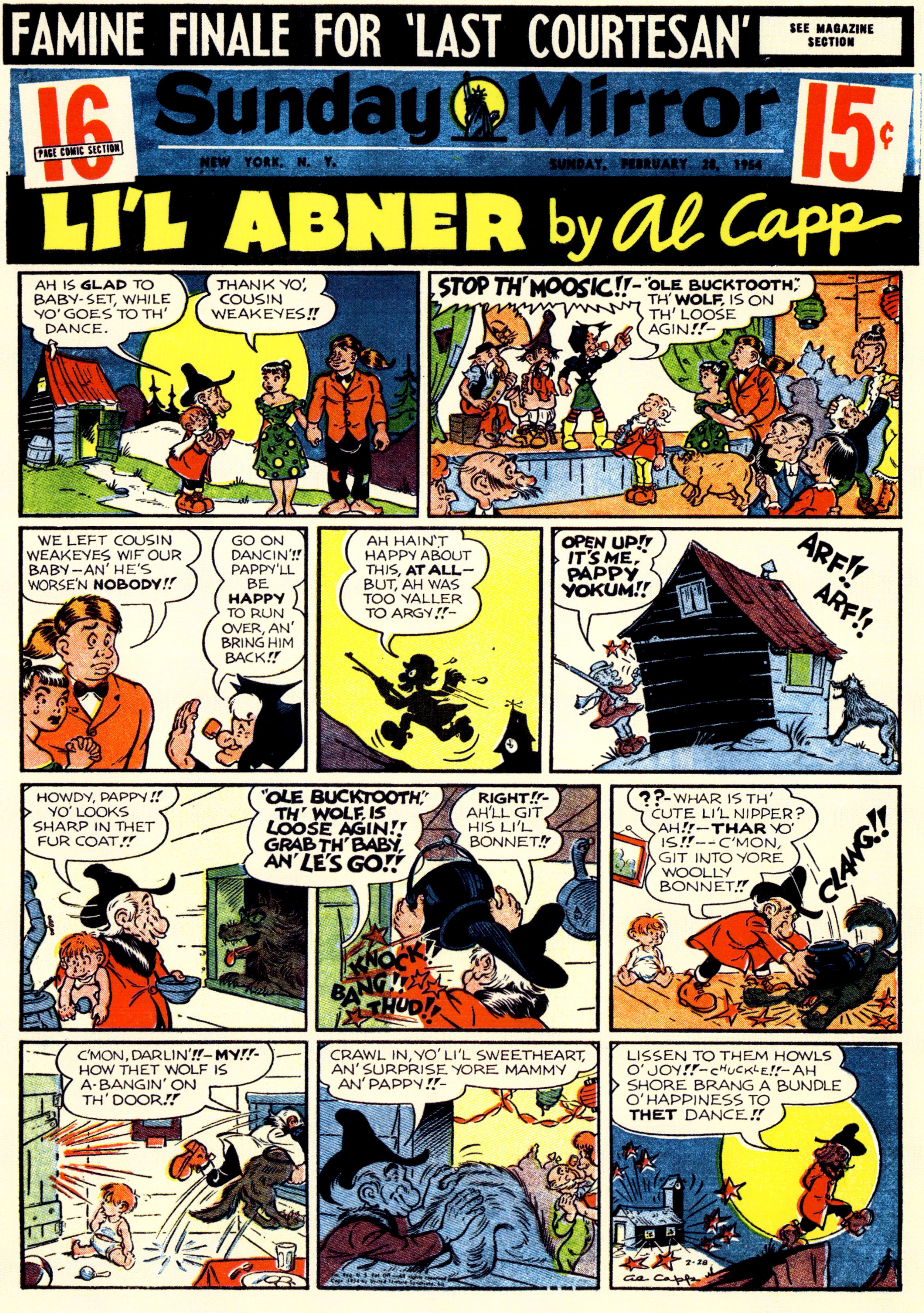
FAMINE FINALE FOR 'LAST COURTESAN'
SEE MAGAZINE SECTION
16
PAGE COMIC SECTION
Sunday Mirror
NEW YORK, N. Y.
SUNDAY, FEBRUARY 28, 1954
15¢
LI'L ABNER by Al Capp
AH IS GLAD TO BABY-SET, WHILE YO' GOES TO TH' DANCE.
THANK YO', COUSIN WEAKEYES!!
STOP TH' MOOSIC!!-'OLE BUCKTOOTH,' TH' WOLF, IS ON TH' LOOSE AGIN!!-
WE LEFT COUSIN WEAKEYES WIF OUR BABY-AN' HE'S WORSE'N NOBODY!!
GO ON DANCIN'!! PAPPY'LL BE HAPPY TO RUN OVER, AN' BRING HIM BACK!!
AH HAIN'T HAPPY ABOUT THIS, AT ALL-BUT, AH WAS TOO YALLER TO ARGY!!-
OPEN UP!! IT'S ME, PAPPY YOKUM!!
ARF!! ARF!!
HOWDY, PAPPY!! YO' LOOKS SHARP IN THET FUR COAT!!
'OLE BUCKTOOTH,' TH' WOLF, IS LOOSE AGIN!! GRAB TH' BABY, AN' LE'S GO!!
RIGHT!!-AH'LL GIT HIS LI'L BONNET!!
KNOCK!! BANG!! THUD!!
??-WHAR IS TH' CUTE LI'L NIPPER? AH!!-THAR YO' IS!!--C'MON, GIT INTO YORE WOOLLY BONNET!!
CLANG!!
C'MON, DARLIN'!!-MY!!-HOW THET WOLF IS A-BANGIN' ON TH' DOOR!!
CRAWL IN, YO' LI'L SWEETHEART, AN' SURPRISE YORE MAMMY AN' PAPPY!!-
LISSEN TO THEM HOWLS O' JOY!!-CHUCKLE!!-AH SHORE BRANG A BUNDLE O' HAPPINESS TO THET DANCE!!
2-28
Al Capp

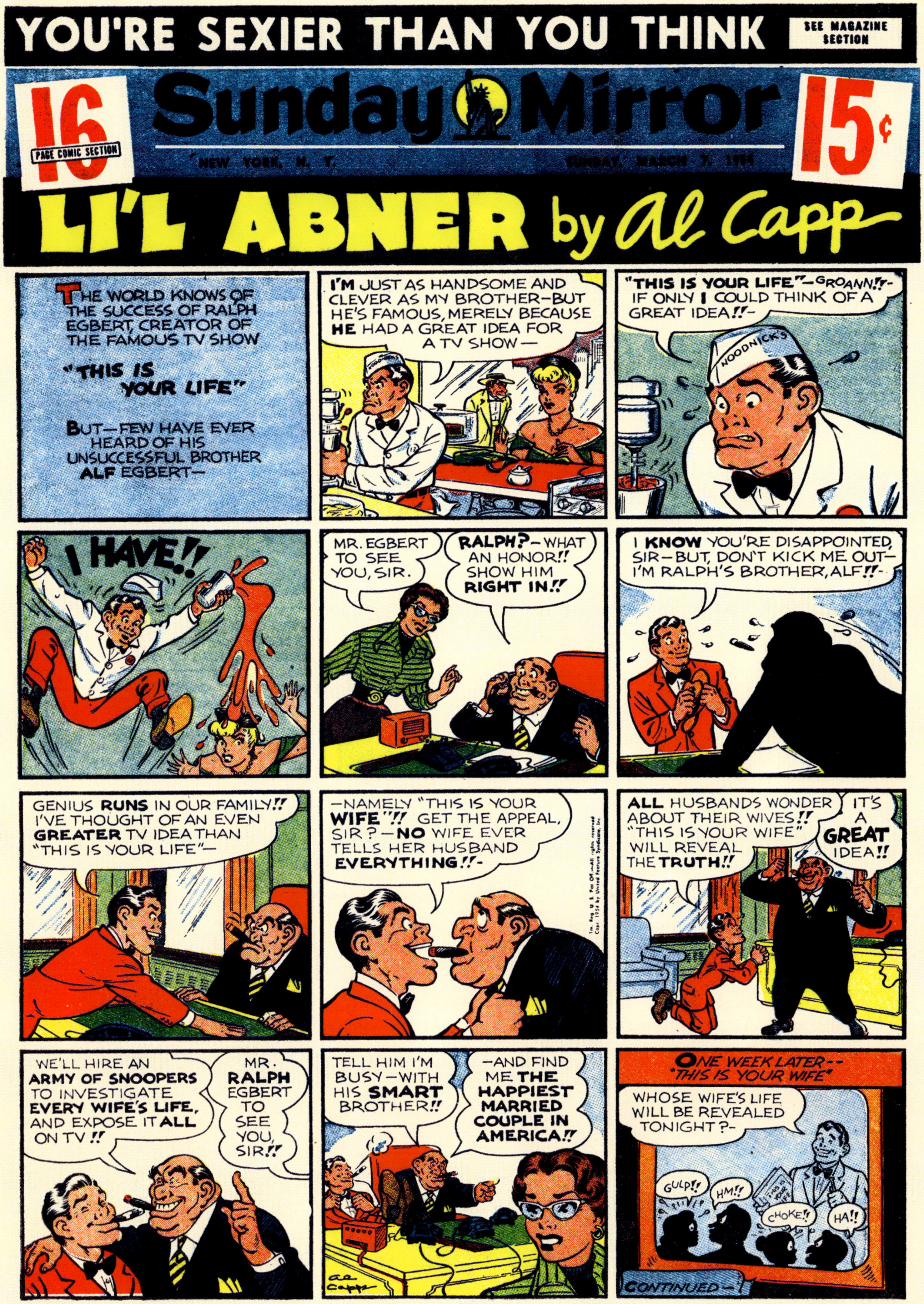
YOU'RE SEXIER THAN YOU THINK
SEE MAGAZINE SECTION
16 PAGE COMIC SECTION
Sunday Mirror
NEW YORK, N. Y.
15¢
LI'L ABNER by Al Capp
THE WORLD KNOWS OF THE SUCCESS OF RALPH EGBERT, CREATOR OF THE FAMOUS TV SHOW "THIS IS YOUR LIFE" BUT—FEW HAVE EVER HEARD OF HIS UNSUCCESSFUL BROTHER ALF EGBERT—
I'M JUST AS HANDSOME AND CLEVER AS MY BROTHER—BUT HE'S FAMOUS, MERELY BECAUSE HE HAD A GREAT IDEA FOR A TV SHOW—
"THIS IS YOUR LIFE"—GROANN!!—IF ONLY I COULD THINK OF A GREAT IDEA!!—
NOODNICK'S
I HAVE!!
MR. EGBERT TO SEE YOU, SIR.
RALPH?—WHAT AN HONOR!! SHOW HIM RIGHT IN!!
I KNOW YOU'RE DISAPPOINTED, SIR—BUT, DON'T KICK ME OUT—I'M RALPH'S BROTHER, ALF!!—
GENIUS RUNS IN OUR FAMILY!! I'VE THOUGHT OF AN EVEN GREATER TV IDEA THAN "THIS IS YOUR LIFE"—
—NAMELY "THIS IS YOUR WIFE"!! GET THE APPEAL, SIR?—NO WIFE EVER TELLS HER HUSBAND EVERYTHING!!—
ALL HUSBANDS WONDER ABOUT THEIR WIVES!! "THIS IS YOUR WIFE" WILL REVEAL THE TRUTH!!
IT'S A GREAT IDEA!!
WE'LL HIRE AN ARMY OF SNOOPERS TO INVESTIGATE EVERY WIFE'S LIFE, AND EXPOSE IT ALL ON TV!!
MR. RALPH EGBERT TO SEE YOU, SIR!!
TELL HIM I'M BUSY—WITH HIS SMART BROTHER!!
—AND FIND ME THE HAPPIEST MARRIED COUPLE IN AMERICA!!
ONE WEEK LATER-- "THIS IS YOUR WIFE"
WHOSE WIFE'S LIFE WILL BE REVEALED TONIGHT?—
GULP!!
HM!!
CHOKE!!
HA!!
CONTINUED—

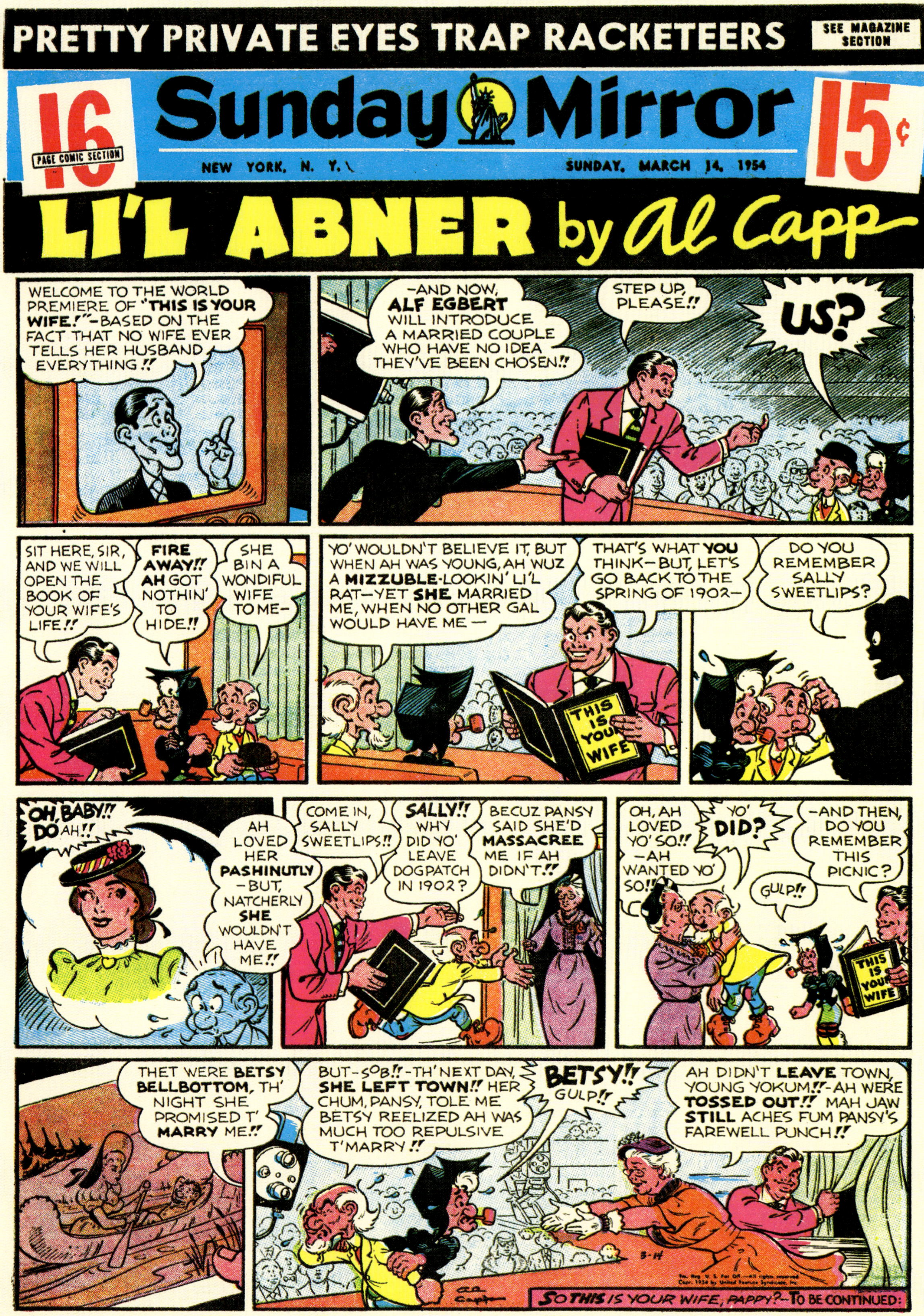

PRETTY PRIVATE EYES TRAP RACKETEERS
SEE MAGAZINE SECTION
16 PAGE COMIC SECTION
Sunday Mirror
15¢
NEW YORK, N. Y.
SUNDAY, MARCH 14, 1954
LI'L ABNER by Al Capp
WELCOME TO THE WORLD PREMIERE OF "THIS IS YOUR WIFE!"-BASED ON THE FACT THAT NO WIFE EVER TELLS HER HUSBAND EVERYTHING!!
-AND NOW, ALF EGBERT WILL INTRODUCE A MARRIED COUPLE WHO HAVE NO IDEA THEY'VE BEEN CHOSEN!!
STEP UP, PLEASE!!
US?
SIT HERE, SIR, AND WE WILL OPEN THE BOOK OF YOUR WIFE'S LIFE!!
FIRE AWAY!! AH GOT NOTHIN' TO HIDE!!
SHE BIN A WONDIFUL WIFE TO ME-
YO' WOULDN'T BELIEVE IT, BUT WHEN AH WAS YOUNG, AH WUZ A MIZZUBLE-LOOKIN' LI'L RAT-YET SHE MARRIED ME, WHEN NO OTHER GAL WOULD HAVE ME —
THIS IS YOUR WIFE
THAT'S WHAT YOU THINK-BUT, LET'S GO BACK TO THE SPRING OF 1902—
DO YOU REMEMBER SALLY SWEETLIPS?
OH, BABY!! DO AH!!
AH LOVED HER PASHINUTLY -BUT, NATCHERLY SHE WOULDN'T HAVE ME!!
COME IN, SALLY SWEETLIPS!!
SALLY!! WHY DID YO' LEAVE DOGPATCH IN 1902?
BECUZ PANSY SAID SHE'D MASSACREE ME IF AH DIDN'T!!
OH, AH LOVED YO' SO!! -AH WANTED YO' SO!!
YO' DID?
-AND THEN, DO YOU REMEMBER THIS PICNIC?
GULP!!
THIS IS YOUR WIFE
THET WERE BETSY BELLBOTTOM, TH' NIGHT SHE PROMISED T' MARRY ME!!
BUT-SOB!!-TH' NEXT DAY, SHE LEFT TOWN!! HER CHUM, PANSY, TOLE ME BETSY REELIZED AH WAS MUCH TOO REPULSIVE T'MARRY!!
BETSY!! GULP!!
AH DIDN'T LEAVE TOWN, YOUNG YOKUM!!-AH WERE TOSSED OUT!! MAH JAW STILL ACHES FUM PANSY'S FAREWELL PUNCH!!
3-14
Al Capp
SO THIS IS YOUR WIFE, PAPPY?-TO BE CONTINUED!

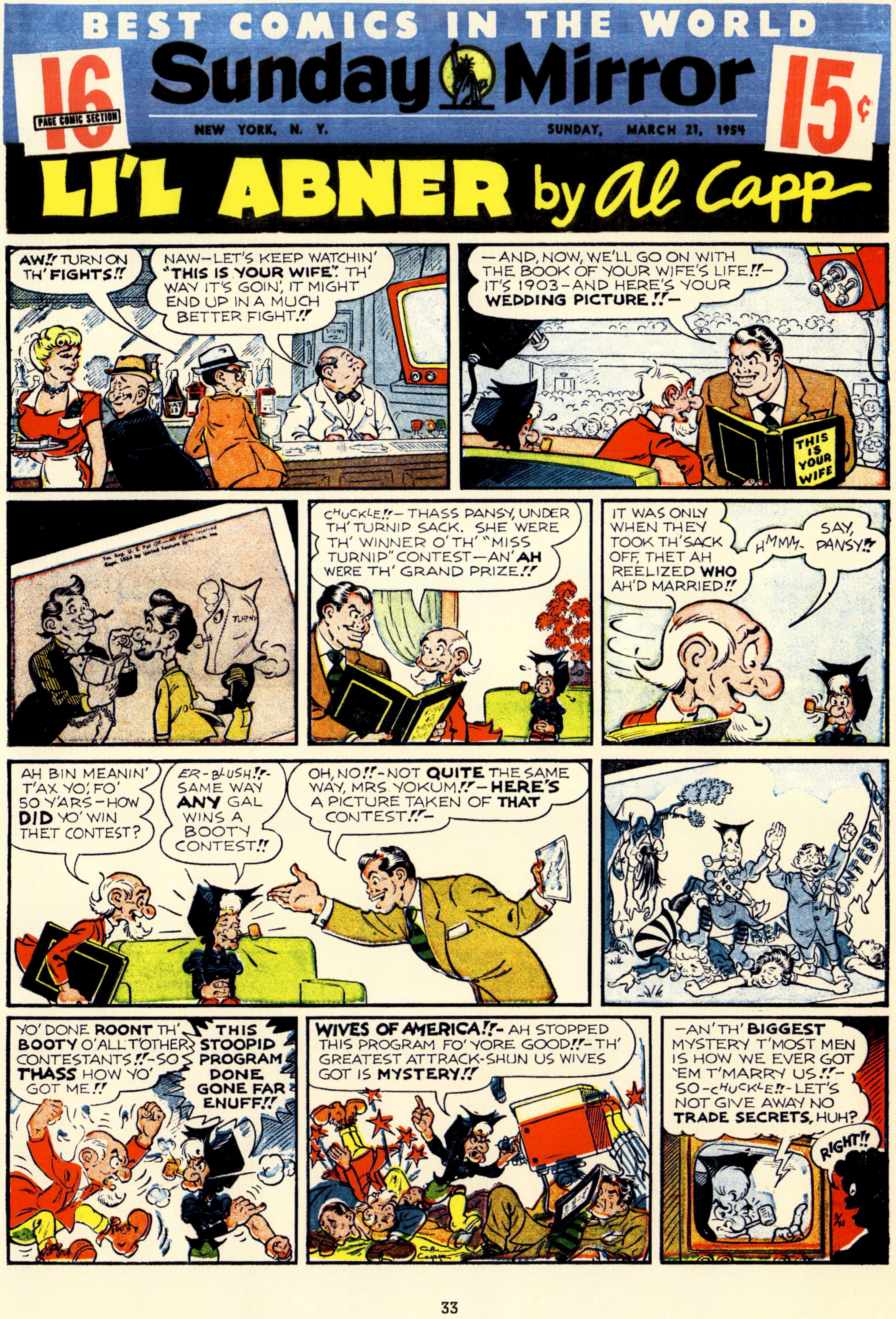
BEST COMICS IN THE WORLD
Sunday Mirror
16 PAGE COMIC SECTION
15¢
NEW YORK, N. Y.
SUNDAY, MARCH 21, 1954
LI'L ABNER by Al Capp
AW!! TURN ON TH' FIGHTS!!
NAW—LET'S KEEP WATCHIN' "THIS IS YOUR WIFE". TH' WAY IT'S GOIN', IT MIGHT END UP IN A MUCH BETTER FIGHT!!
—AND, NOW, WE'LL GO ON WITH THE BOOK OF YOUR WIFE'S LIFE!!— IT'S 1903—AND HERE'S YOUR WEDDING PICTURE!!—
THIS IS YOUR WIFE
CHUCKLE!!—THASS PANSY, UNDER TH' TURNIP SACK. SHE WERE TH' WINNER O'TH' "MISS TURNIP" CONTEST—AN' AH WERE TH' GRAND PRIZE!!
IT WAS ONLY WHEN THEY TOOK TH'SACK OFF, THET AH REELIZED WHO AH'D MARRIED!!
HMMM-
SAY, PANSY!!
AH BIN MEANIN' T'AX YO', FO' 50 Y'ARS—HOW DID YO' WIN THET CONTEST?
ER-BLUSH!!- SAME WAY ANY GAL WINS A BOOTY CONTEST!!
OH, NO!!—NOT QUITE THE SAME WAY, MRS. YOKUM!!—HERE'S A PICTURE TAKEN OF THAT CONTEST!!—
CONTEST
YO' DONE ROONT TH' BOOTY O'ALL T'OTHER CONTESTANTS!!—SO THASS HOW YO' GOT ME!!
THIS STOOPID PROGRAM DONE GONE FAR ENUFF!!
WIVES OF AMERICA!!—AH STOPPED THIS PROGRAM FO' YORE GOOD!!—TH' GREATEST ATTRACK-SHUN US WIVES GOT IS MYSTERY!!
—AN' TH' BIGGEST MYSTERY T'MOST MEN IS HOW WE EVER GOT 'EM T'MARRY US!!— SO—CHUCKLE!!—LET'S NOT GIVE AWAY NO TRADE SECRETS, HUH?
RIGHT!!

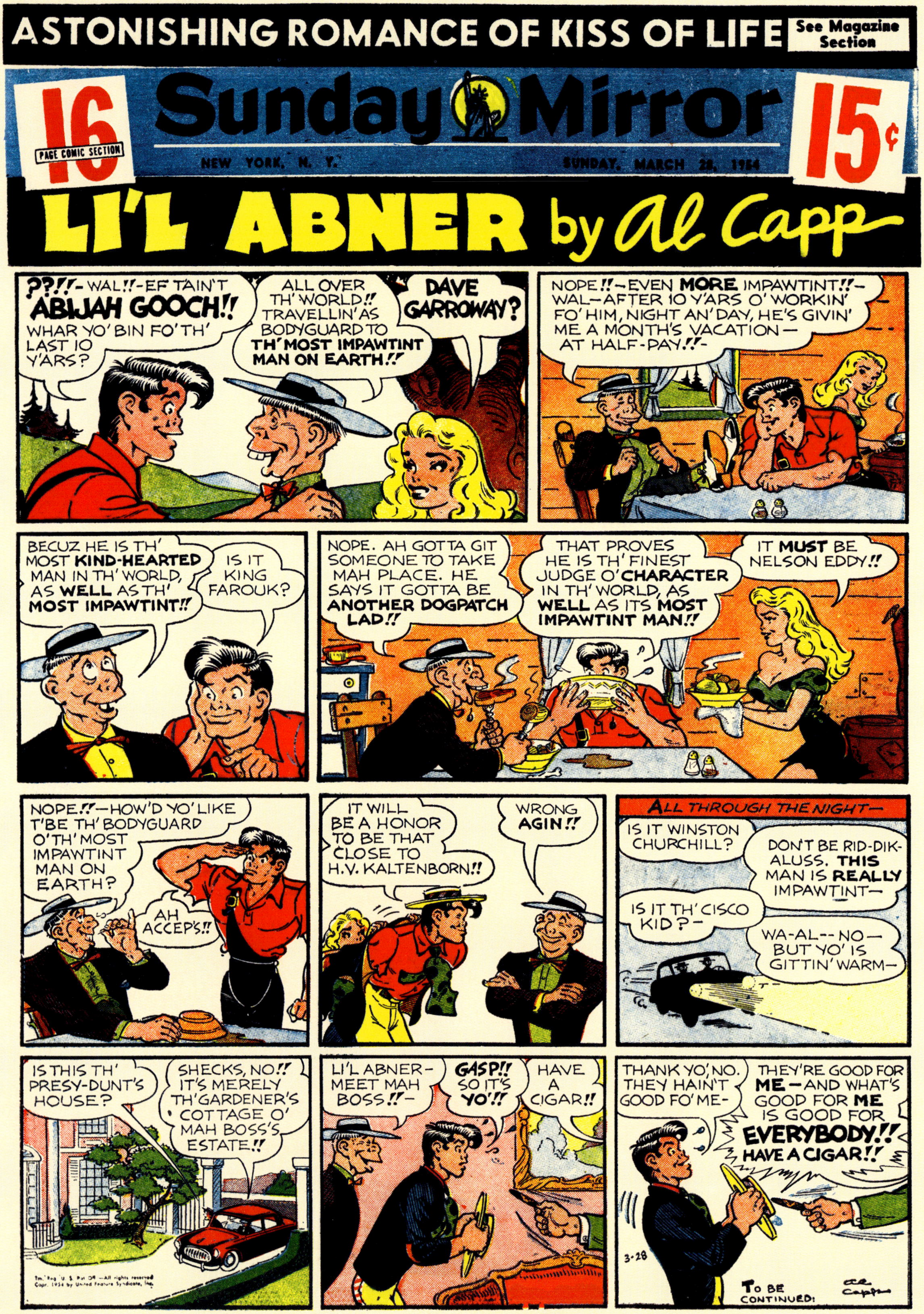
ASTONISHING ROMANCE OF KISS OF LIFE
See Magazine Section
16 PAGE COMIC SECTION
Sunday Mirror
NEW YORK, N. Y.
SUNDAY, MARCH 28, 1954
15¢
LI'L ABNER by Al Capp
??!!-WAL!!-EF TAIN'T ABIJAH GOOCH!! WHAR YO' BIN FO' TH' LAST 10 Y'ARS?
ALL OVER TH' WORLD!! TRAVELLIN' AS BODYGUARD TO TH' MOST IMPAWTINT MAN ON EARTH!!
DAVE GARROWAY?
NOPE!!-EVEN MORE IMPAWTINT!!-WAL-AFTER 10 Y'ARS O' WORKIN' FO' HIM, NIGHT AN' DAY, HE'S GIVIN' ME A MONTH'S VACATION-AT HALF-PAY!!-
BECUZ HE IS TH' MOST KIND-HEARTED MAN IN TH' WORLD, AS WELL AS TH' MOST IMPAWTINT!!
IS IT KING FAROUK?
NOPE. AH GOTTA GIT SOMEONE TO TAKE MAH PLACE. HE SAYS IT GOTTA BE ANOTHER DOGPATCH LAD!!
THAT PROVES HE IS TH' FINEST JUDGE O' CHARACTER IN TH' WORLD, AS WELL AS ITS MOST IMPAWTINT MAN!!
IT MUST BE NELSON EDDY!!
NOPE!!-HOW'D YO' LIKE T'BE TH' BODYGUARD O' TH' MOST IMPAWTINT MAN ON EARTH?
AH ACCEP'S!!
IT WILL BE A HONOR TO BE THAT CLOSE TO H.V. KALTENBORN!!
WRONG AGIN!!
ALL THROUGH THE NIGHT-
IS IT WINSTON CHURCHILL?
DON'T BE RID-DIK-ALUSS. THIS MAN IS REALLY IMPAWTINT-
IS IT TH' CISCO KID?-
WA-AL--NO-BUT YO' IS GITTIN' WARM-
IS THIS TH' PRESY-DUNT'S HOUSE?
SHECKS, NO!! IT'S MERELY TH' GARDENER'S COTTAGE O' MAH BOSS'S ESTATE!!
Tm. Reg. U. S. Pat. Off.—All rights reserved
Copr. 1954 by United Feature Syndicate, Inc.
LI'L ABNER-MEET MAH BOSS!!-
GASP!! SO IT'S YO'!!
HAVE A CIGAR!!
THANK YO', NO. THEY HAIN'T GOOD FO' ME-
THEY'RE GOOD FOR ME-AND WHAT'S GOOD FOR ME IS GOOD FOR EVERYBODY!! HAVE A CIGAR!!
3-28
TO BE CONTINUED:

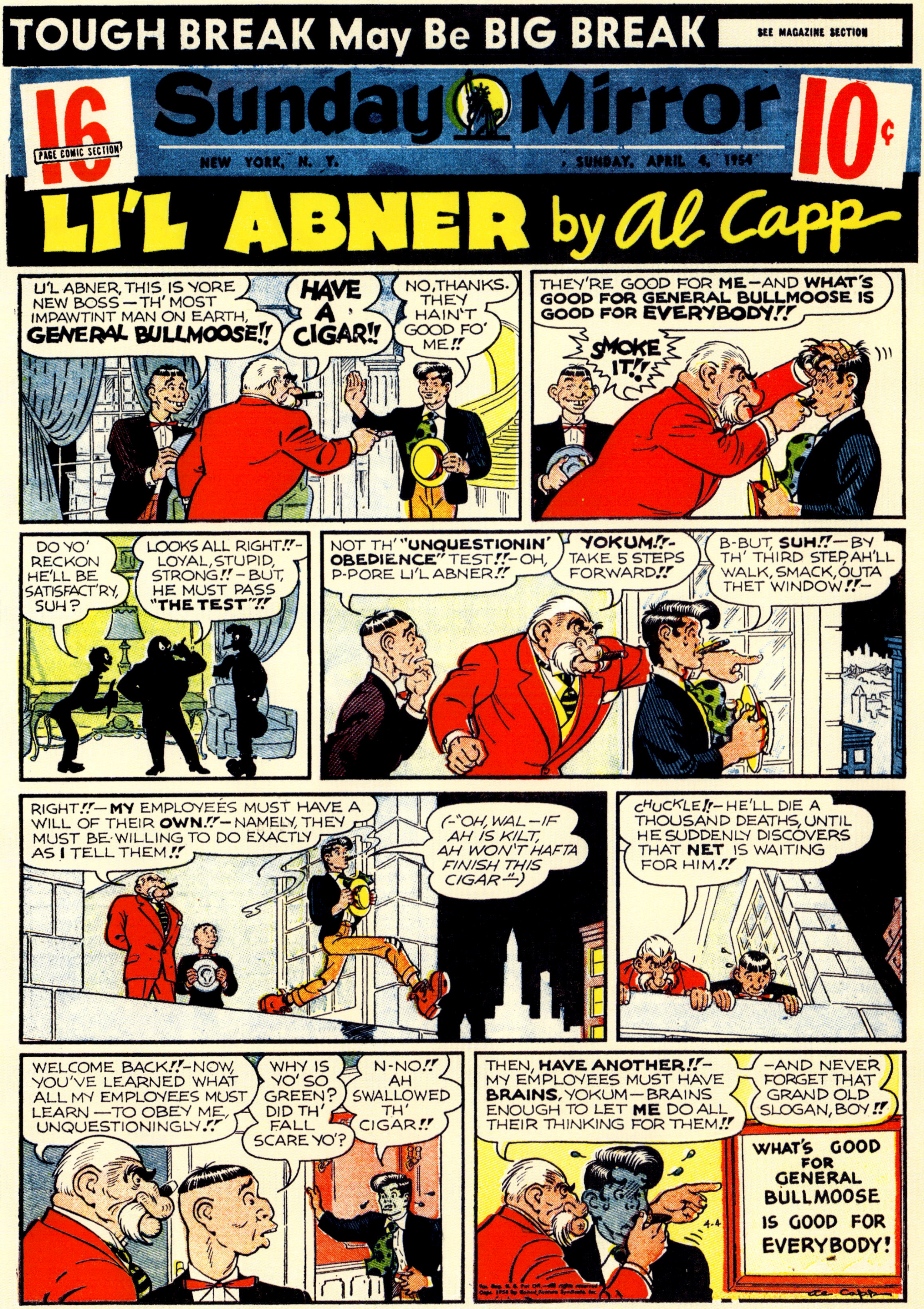
TOUGH BREAK May Be BIG BREAK
SEE MAGAZINE SECTION
16 PAGE COMIC SECTION
Sunday Mirror
NEW YORK, N. Y.
SUNDAY, APRIL 4, 1954
10¢
LI'L ABNER by Al Capp
LI'L ABNER, THIS IS YORE NEW BOSS — TH' MOST IMPAWTINT MAN ON EARTH, GENERAL BULLMOOSE!!
HAVE A CIGAR!!
NO, THANKS. THEY HAIN'T GOOD FO' ME.!!
THEY'RE GOOD FOR ME — AND WHAT'S GOOD FOR GENERAL BULLMOOSE IS GOOD FOR EVERYBODY!!
SMOKE IT!!
DO YO' RECKON HE'LL BE SATISFACT'RY, SUH?
LOOKS ALL RIGHT!!— LOYAL, STUPID, STRONG!! — BUT, HE MUST PASS "THE TEST"!!
NOT TH' "UNQUESTIONIN' OBEDIENCE" TEST!!— OH, P-PORE LI'L ABNER!!
YOKUM!!— TAKE 5 STEPS FORWARD!!
B-BUT, SUH!!— BY TH' THIRD STEP AH'LL WALK, SMACK, OUTA THET WINDOW!!—
RIGHT!!— MY EMPLOYEES MUST HAVE A WILL OF THEIR OWN!!— NAMELY, THEY MUST BE WILLING TO DO EXACTLY AS I TELL THEM!!
(—"OH, WAL — IF AH IS KILT, AH WON'T HAFTA FINISH THIS CIGAR"—)
CHUCKLE!!— HE'LL DIE A THOUSAND DEATHS, UNTIL HE SUDDENLY DISCOVERS THAT NET IS WAITING FOR HIM!!
WELCOME BACK!!— NOW, YOU'VE LEARNED WHAT ALL MY EMPLOYEES MUST LEARN — TO OBEY ME, UNQUESTIONINGLY!!
WHY IS YO' SO GREEN? DID TH' FALL SCARE YO'?
N-NO!! AH SWALLOWED TH' CIGAR!!
THEN, HAVE ANOTHER!!— MY EMPLOYEES MUST HAVE BRAINS, YOKUM — BRAINS ENOUGH TO LET ME DO ALL THEIR THINKING FOR THEM!!
—AND NEVER FORGET THAT GRAND OLD SLOGAN, BOY!!
WHAT'S GOOD FOR GENERAL BULLMOOSE IS GOOD FOR EVERYBODY!
4-4
Al Capp

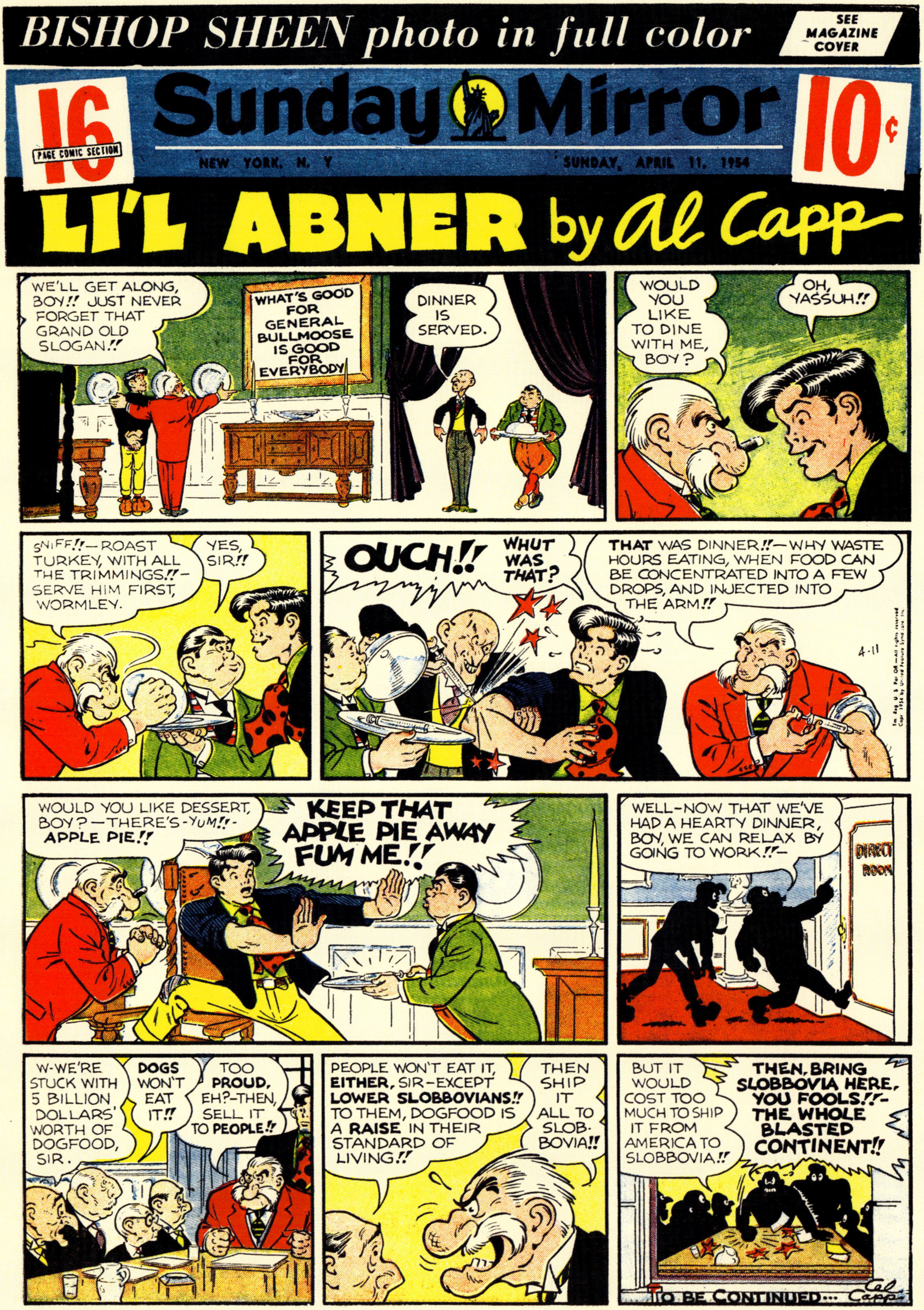
BISHOP SHEEN photo in full color
SEE MAGAZINE COVER
16 PAGE COMIC SECTION
Sunday Mirror
10¢
NEW YORK, N. Y.
SUNDAY, APRIL 11, 1954
LI'L ABNER by Al Capp
WE'LL GET ALONG, BOY!! JUST NEVER FORGET THAT GRAND OLD SLOGAN!!
WHAT'S GOOD FOR GENERAL BULLMOOSE IS GOOD FOR EVERYBODY
DINNER IS SERVED.
WOULD YOU LIKE TO DINE WITH ME, BOY?
OH, YASSUH!!
SNIFF!!—ROAST TURKEY, WITH ALL THE TRIMMINGS!!—SERVE HIM FIRST, WORMLEY.
YES, SIR!!
OUCH!!
WHUT WAS THAT?
THAT WAS DINNER!!—WHY WASTE HOURS EATING, WHEN FOOD CAN BE CONCENTRATED INTO A FEW DROPS, AND INJECTED INTO THE ARM!!
4-11
WOULD YOU LIKE DESSERT, BOY?—THERE'S-YUM!!-APPLE PIE!!
KEEP THAT APPLE PIE AWAY FUM ME!!
WELL-NOW THAT WE'VE HAD A HEARTY DINNER, BOY, WE CAN RELAX BY GOING TO WORK!!—
W-WE'RE STUCK WITH 5 BILLION DOLLARS' WORTH OF DOGFOOD, SIR.
DOGS WON'T EAT IT!!
TOO PROUD, EH?—THEN, SELL IT TO PEOPLE!!
PEOPLE WON'T EAT IT, EITHER, SIR—EXCEPT LOWER SLOBBOVIANS!! TO THEM, DOGFOOD IS A RAISE IN THEIR STANDARD OF LIVING!!
THEN SHIP IT ALL TO SLOBBOVIA!!
BUT IT WOULD COST TOO MUCH TO SHIP IT FROM AMERICA TO SLOBBOVIA!!
THEN, BRING SLOBBOVIA HERE, YOU FOOLS!!—THE WHOLE BLASTED CONTINENT!!
TO BE CONTINUED...
Al Capp

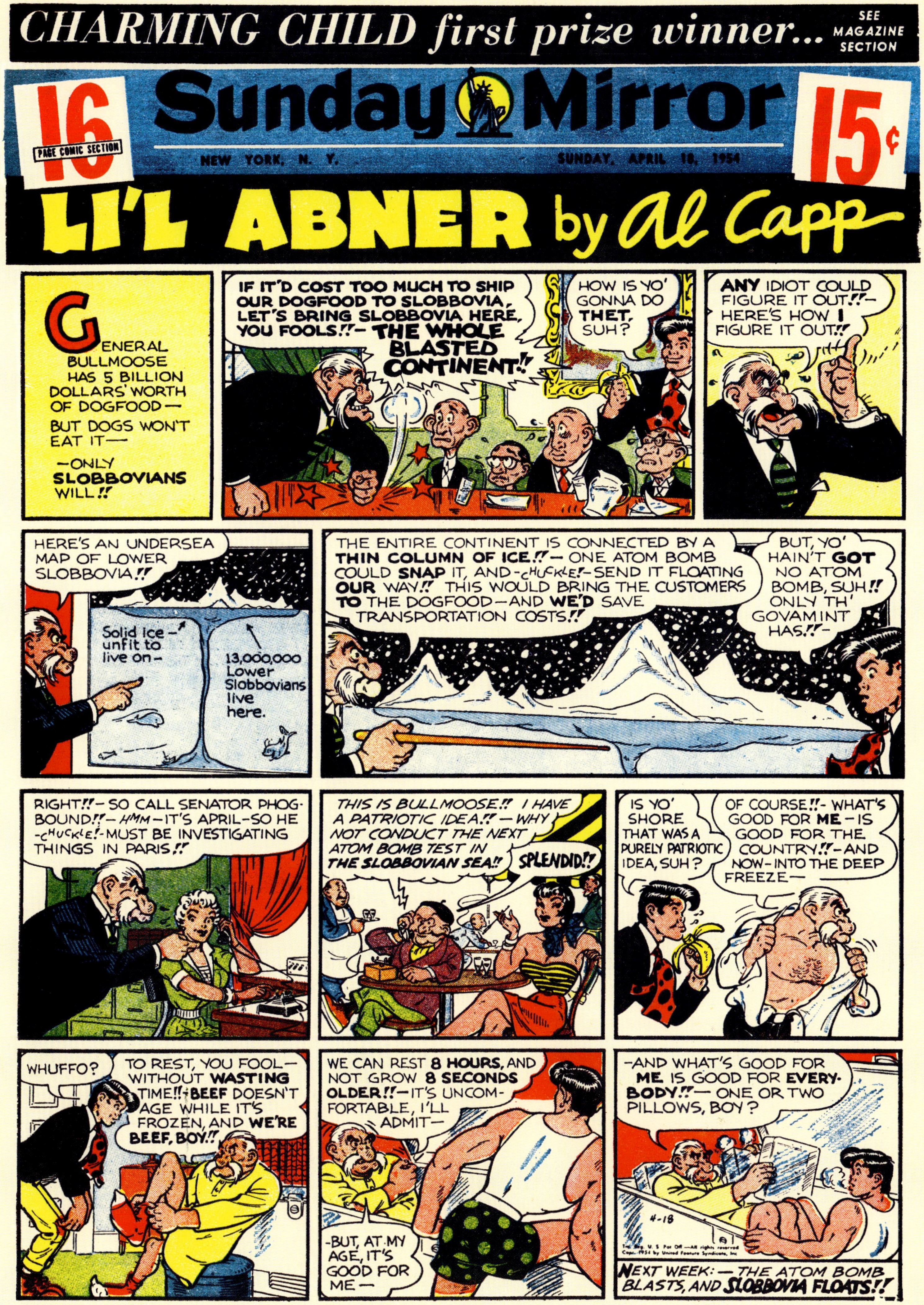

CHARMING CHILD first prize winner...
SEE MAGAZINE SECTION
16 PAGE COMIC SECTION
Sunday Mirror
NEW YORK, N. Y.
SUNDAY, APRIL 18, 1954
15¢
LI'L ABNER by Al Capp
GENERAL BULLMOOSE HAS 5 BILLION DOLLARS' WORTH OF DOGFOOD — BUT DOGS WON'T EAT IT — —ONLY SLOBBOVIANS WILL!!
IF IT'D COST TOO MUCH TO SHIP OUR DOGFOOD TO SLOBBOVIA, LET'S BRING SLOBBOVIA HERE, YOU FOOLS!!— THE WHOLE BLASTED CONTINENT!!
HOW IS YO' GONNA DO THET, SUH?
ANY IDIOT COULD FIGURE IT OUT!!— HERE'S HOW I FIGURE IT OUT!!
HERE'S AN UNDERSEA MAP OF LOWER SLOBBOVIA!!
Solid ice — unfit to live on —
13,000,000 Lower Slobbovians live here.
THE ENTIRE CONTINENT IS CONNECTED BY A THIN COLUMN OF ICE!!— ONE ATOM BOMB COULD SNAP IT, AND -chuckle!- SEND IT FLOATING OUR WAY!! THIS WOULD BRING THE CUSTOMERS TO THE DOGFOOD — AND WE'D SAVE TRANSPORTATION COSTS!!
BUT, YO' HAIN'T GOT NO ATOM BOMB, SUH!! ONLY TH' GOVAMINT HAS!!—
RIGHT!!— SO CALL SENATOR PHOGBOUND!!— HMM — IT'S APRIL — SO HE -chuckle!- MUST BE INVESTIGATING THINGS IN PARIS!!
THIS IS BULLMOOSE!! I HAVE A PATRIOTIC IDEA!! — WHY NOT CONDUCT THE NEXT ATOM BOMB TEST IN THE SLOBBOVIAN SEA!!
SPLENDID!!
IS YO' SHORE THAT WAS A PURELY PATRIOTIC IDEA, SUH?
OF COURSE!!— WHAT'S GOOD FOR ME — IS GOOD FOR THE COUNTRY!!— AND NOW — INTO THE DEEP FREEZE —
WHUFFO?
TO REST, YOU FOOL — WITHOUT WASTING TIME!!— BEEF DOESN'T AGE WHILE IT'S FROZEN, AND WE'RE BEEF, BOY!!
WE CAN REST 8 HOURS, AND NOT GROW 8 SECONDS OLDER!!— IT'S UNCOMFORTABLE, I'LL ADMIT —
-BUT, AT MY AGE, IT'S GOOD FOR ME —
—AND WHAT'S GOOD FOR ME IS GOOD FOR EVERYBODY!!— ONE OR TWO PILLOWS, BOY?
4-18
NEXT WEEK: — THE ATOM BOMB BLASTS, AND SLOBBOVIA FLOATS!!

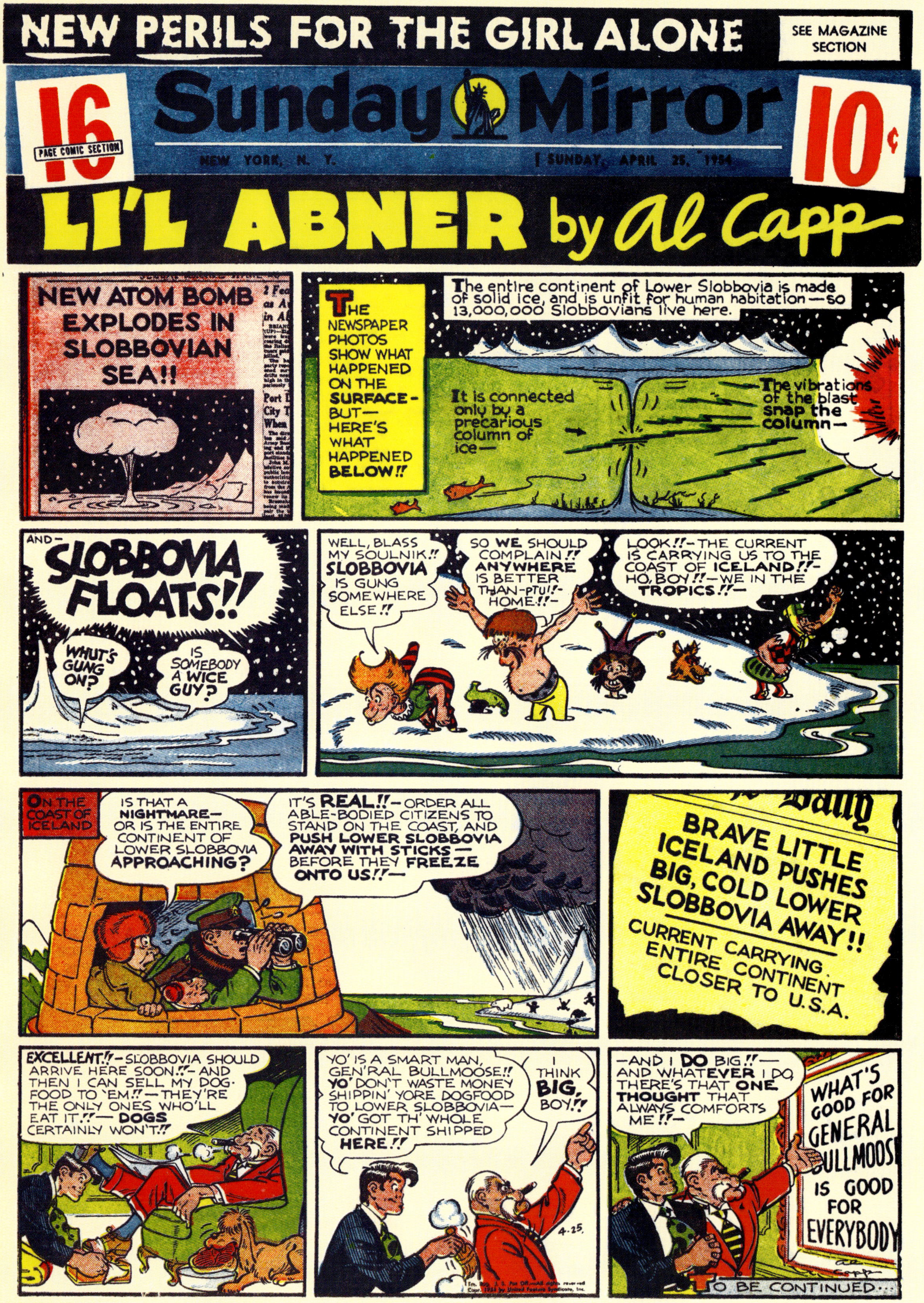
NEW PERILS FOR THE GIRL ALONE
SEE MAGAZINE SECTION
16 PAGE COMIC SECTION
Sunday Mirror
NEW YORK, N. Y.
SUNDAY, APRIL 25, 1954
10¢
LI'L ABNER by Al Capp
NEW ATOM BOMB EXPLODES IN SLOBBOVIAN SEA!!
THE NEWSPAPER PHOTOS SHOW WHAT HAPPENED ON THE SURFACE - BUT— HERE'S WHAT HAPPENED BELOW!!
The entire continent of Lower Slobbovia is made of solid ice, and is unfit for human habitation — so 13,000,000 Slobbovians live here.
It is connected only by a precarious column of ice—
The vibrations of the blast snap the column—
AND—
SLOBBOVIA FLOATS!!
WHUT'S GUNG ON?
IS SOMEBODY A WICE GUY?
WELL, BLASS MY SOULNIK!! SLOBBOVIA IS GUNG SOMEWHERE ELSE!!
SO WE SHOULD COMPLAIN!! ANYWHERE IS BETTER THAN-PTUI!- HOME!!-
LOOK!!- THE CURRENT IS CARRYING US TO THE COAST OF ICELAND!!- HO, BOY!!- WE IN THE TROPICS!!-
ON THE COAST OF ICELAND
IS THAT A NIGHTMARE— OR IS THE ENTIRE CONTINENT OF LOWER SLOBBOVIA APPROACHING?
IT'S REAL!!- ORDER ALL ABLE-BODIED CITIZENS TO STAND ON THE COAST, AND PUSH LOWER SLOBBOVIA AWAY WITH STICKS — BEFORE THEY FREEZE ONTO US!!—
BRAVE LITTLE ICELAND PUSHES BIG, COLD LOWER SLOBBOVIA AWAY!!
CURRENT CARRYING ENTIRE CONTINENT CLOSER TO U.S.A.
EXCELLENT!!- SLOBBOVIA SHOULD ARRIVE HERE SOON!!- AND THEN I CAN SELL MY DOG-FOOD TO 'EM!! — THEY'RE THE ONLY ONES WHO'LL EAT IT!!— DOGS CERTAINLY WON'T!!
YO' IS A SMART MAN, GEN'RAL BULLMOOSE!! YO' DON'T WASTE MONEY SHIPPIN' YORE DOGFOOD TO LOWER SLOBBOVIA— YO' GOT TH' WHOLE CONTINENT SHIPPED HERE!!
I THINK BIG, BOY!!
4-25
—AND I DO BIG!!— AND WHATEVER I DO, THERE'S THAT ONE THOUGHT THAT ALWAYS COMFORTS ME!!—
WHAT'S GOOD FOR GENERAL BULLMOOSE IS GOOD FOR EVERYBODY
TO BE CONTINUED...

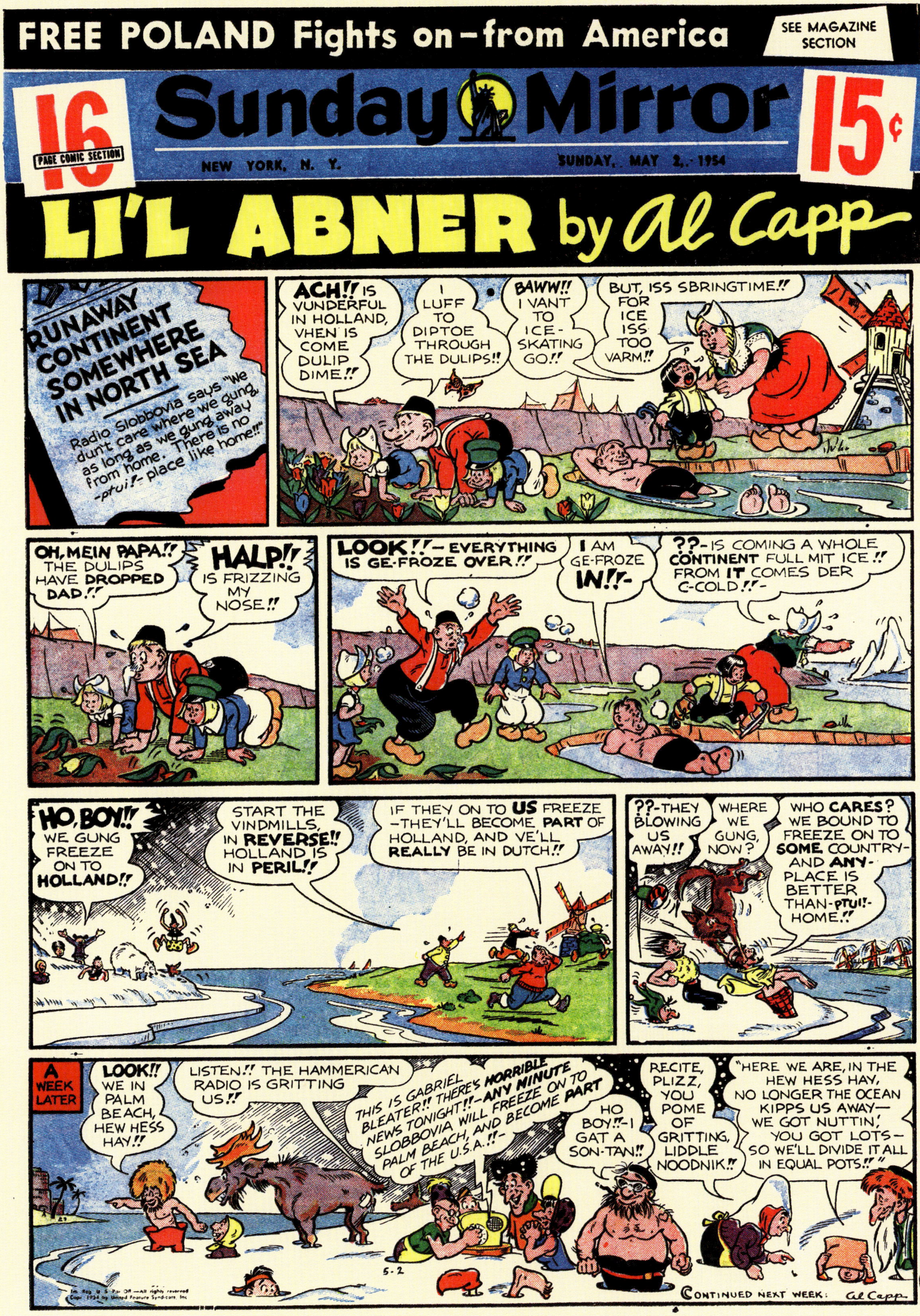

FREE POLAND Fights on—from America
SEE MAGAZINE SECTION
16
PAGE COMIC SECTION
Sunday Mirror
15¢
NEW YORK, N. Y.
SUNDAY, MAY 2, 1954
LI'L ABNER by Al Capp
RUNAWAY CONTINENT SOMEWHERE IN NORTH SEA
Radio Slobbovia says "We dun't care where we gung, as long as we gung away from home. There is no -ptui!- place like home!!"
ACH!! IS VUNDERFUL IN HOLLAND, VHEN IS COME DULIP DIME!!
I LUFF TO DIPTOE THROUGH THE DULIPS!!
BAWW!! I VANT TO ICE-SKATING GO!!
BUT, ISS SBRINGTIME!! FOR ICE ISS TOO VARM!!
OH, MEIN PAPA!! THE DULIPS HAVE DROPPED DAD!!
HALP!! IS FRIZZING MY NOSE!!
LOOK!!—EVERYTHING IS GE-FROZE OVER!!
I AM GE-FROZE IN!!-
??-IS COMING A WHOLE CONTINENT FULL MIT ICE!! FROM IT COMES DER C-COLD!!-
HO, BOY!! WE GUNG FREEZE ON TO HOLLAND!!
START THE VINDMILLS, IN REVERSE!! HOLLAND IS IN PERIL!!
IF THEY ON TO US FREEZE —THEY'LL BECOME PART OF HOLLAND, AND VE'LL REALLY BE IN DUTCH!!
??-THEY BLOWING US AWAY!!
WHERE WE GUNG, NOW?
WHO CARES? WE BOUND TO FREEZE ON TO SOME COUNTRY-AND ANY-PLACE IS BETTER THAN-PTUI!-HOME!!
A WEEK LATER
LOOK!! WE IN PALM BEACH, HEW HESS HAY!!
LISTEN!! THE HAMMERICAN RADIO IS GRITTING US!!
THIS IS GABRIEL BLEATER!! THERE'S HORRIBLE NEWS TONIGHT!!-ANY MINUTE SLOBBOVIA WILL FREEZE ON TO PALM BEACH, AND BECOME PART OF THE U.S.A.!!-
HO BOY!!-I GAT A SON-TAN!!
RECITE, PLIZZ, YOU POME OF GRITTING, LIDDLE NOODNIK!!
"HERE WE ARE, IN THE HEW HESS HAY, NO LONGER THE OCEAN KIPPS US AWAY— WE GOT NUTTIN', YOU GOT LOTS— SO WE'LL DIVIDE IT ALL IN EQUAL POTS!!"
5-2
CONTINUED NEXT WEEK: Al Capp

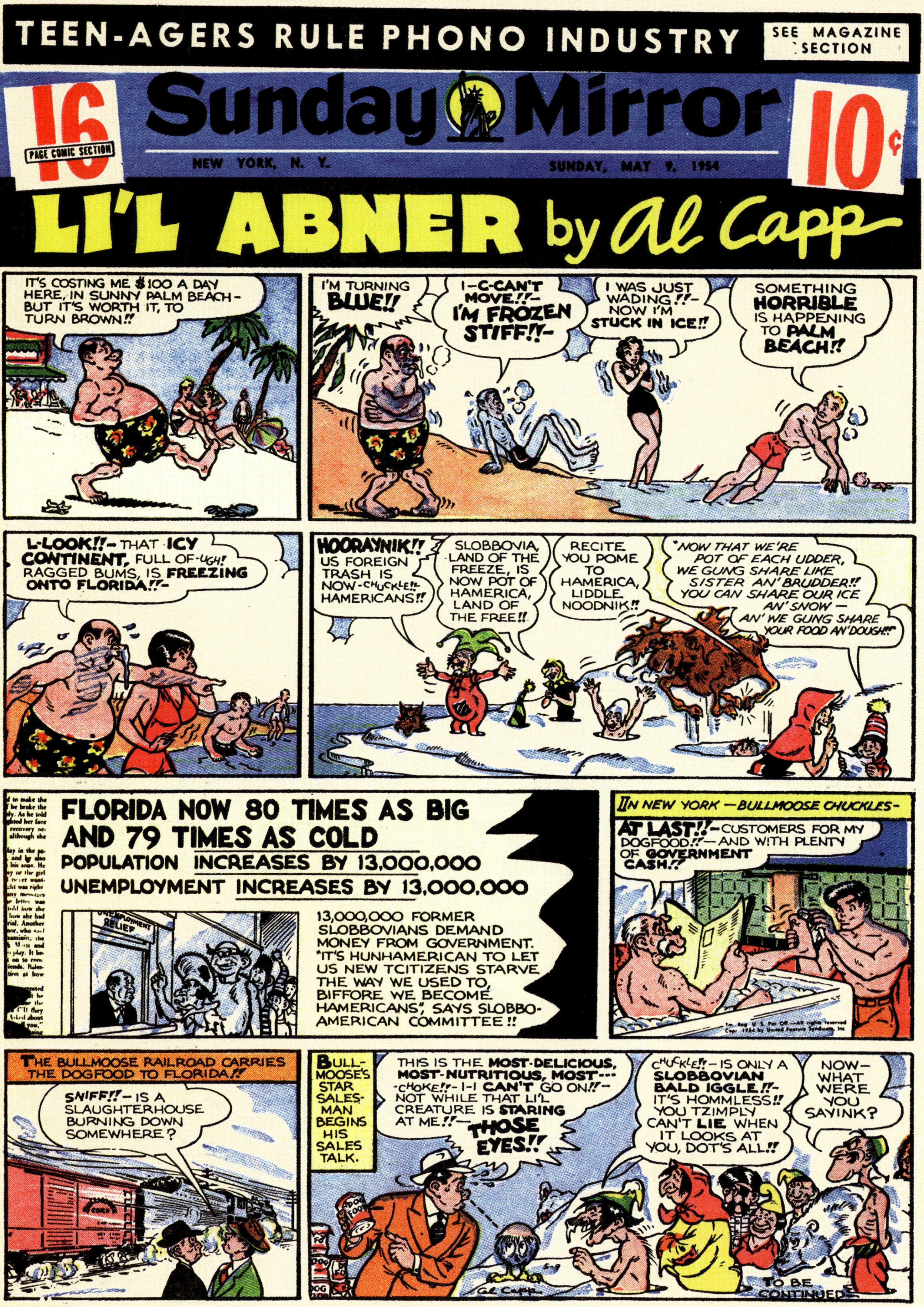
TEEN-AGERS RULE PHONO INDUSTRY
SEE MAGAZINE SECTION
16 PAGE COMIC SECTION
Sunday Mirror
10¢
NEW YORK, N. Y.
SUNDAY, MAY 9, 1954
LI'L ABNER by Al Capp
IT'S COSTING ME $100 A DAY HERE, IN SUNNY PALM BEACH - BUT IT'S WORTH IT, TO TURN BROWN!!
I'M TURNING BLUE!!
I-C-CAN'T MOVE!!- I'M FROZEN STIFF!!-
I WAS JUST WADING!!- NOW I'M STUCK IN ICE!!
SOMETHING HORRIBLE IS HAPPENING TO PALM BEACH!!
L-LOOK!!- THAT ICY CONTINENT, FULL OF-UGH! RAGGED BUMS, IS FREEZING ONTO FLORIDA!!-
HOORAYNIK!! US FOREIGN TRASH IS NOW-CHUCKLE!!- HAMERICANS!!
SLOBBOVIA, LAND OF THE FREEZE, IS NOW POT OF HAMERICA, LAND OF THE FREE!!
RECITE YOU POME TO HAMERICA, LIDDLE NOODNIK!!
"NOW THAT WE'RE POT OF EACH UDDER, WE GUNG SHARE LIKE SISTER AN' BRUDDER!! YOU CAN SHARE OUR ICE AN' SNOW - AN' WE GUNG SHARE YOUR FOOD AN' DOUGH!!"
FLORIDA NOW 80 TIMES AS BIG AND 79 TIMES AS COLD
POPULATION INCREASES BY 13,000,000
UNEMPLOYMENT INCREASES BY 13,000,000
UNEMPLOYMENT RELIEF
13,000,000 FORMER SLOBBOVIANS DEMAND MONEY FROM GOVERNMENT. "IT'S HUNHAMERICAN TO LET US NEW TCITIZENS STARVE THE WAY WE USED TO, BIFFORE WE BECOME HAMERICANS," SAYS SLOBBO-AMERICAN COMMITTEE!!
IN NEW YORK - BULLMOOSE CHUCKLES -
AT LAST!!- CUSTOMERS FOR MY DOGFOOD!!- AND WITH PLENTY OF GOVERNMENT CASH!!
THE BULLMOOSE RAILROAD CARRIES THE DOGFOOD TO FLORIDA!!
SNIFF!!- IS A SLAUGHTERHOUSE BURNING DOWN SOMEWHERE?
BULLMOOSE'S STAR SALESMAN BEGINS HIS SALES TALK.
THIS IS THE MOST-DELICIOUS, MOST-NUTRITIOUS, MOST--- -CHOKE!!- I-I CAN'T GO ON!!- NOT WHILE THAT LI'L CREATURE IS STARING AT ME!!-
THOSE EYES!!
CHUCKLE!!- IS ONLY A SLOBBOVIAN BALD IGGLE!!- IT'S HOMMLESS!! YOU TZIMPLY CAN'T LIE WHEN IT LOOKS AT YOU, DOT'S ALL!!
NOW- WHAT WERE YOU SAYINK?
Al Capp
TO BE CONTINUED

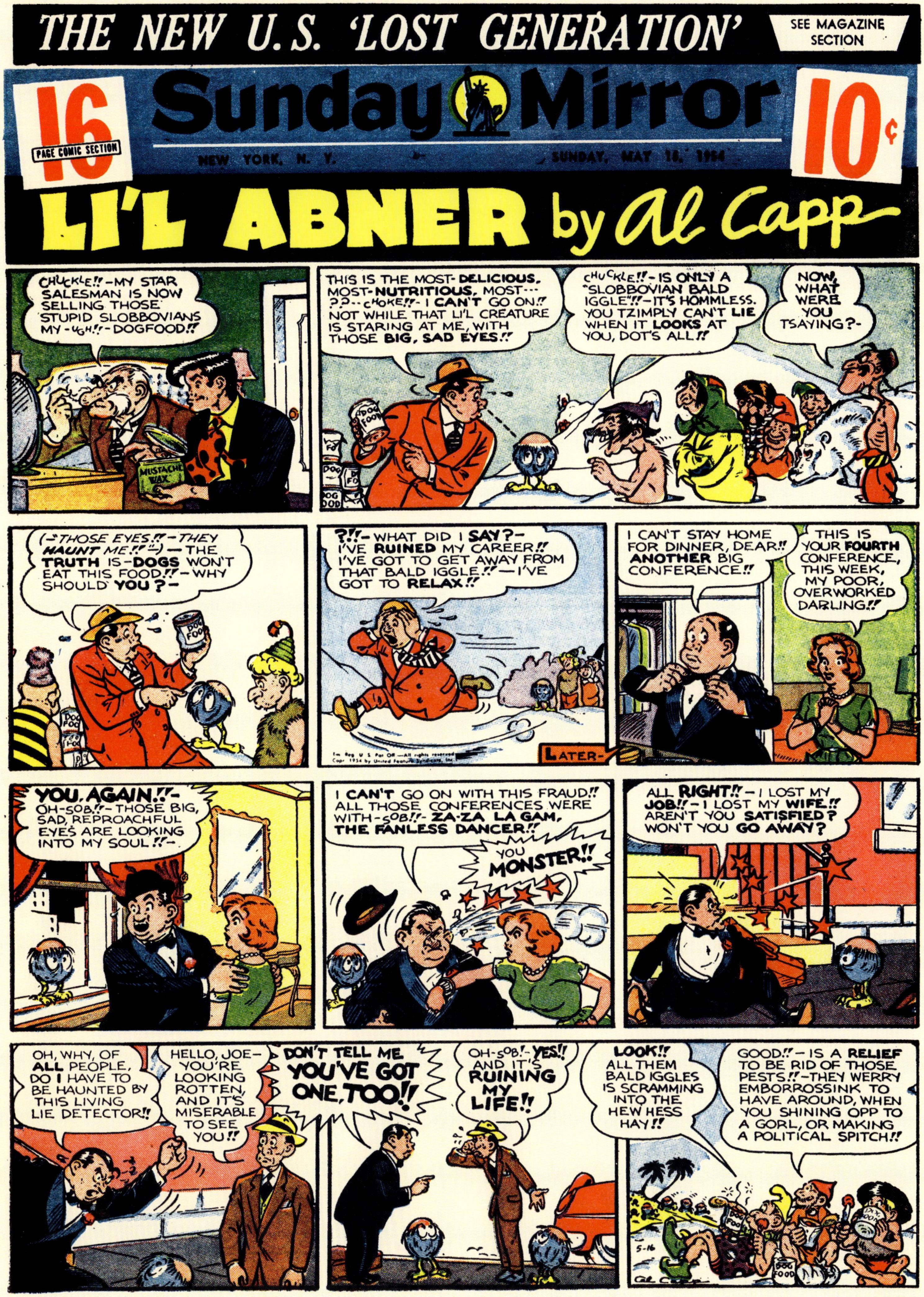
THE NEW U.S. 'LOST GENERATION'
SEE MAGAZINE SECTION
16
PAGE COMIC SECTION
Sunday Mirror
NEW YORK, N. Y.
SUNDAY, MAY 16, 1954
10¢
LI'L ABNER by Al Capp
CHUCKLE!! –MY STAR SALESMAN IS NOW SELLING THOSE STUPID SLOBBOVIANS MY –UGH!!– DOGFOOD!!
MUSTACHE WAX
THIS IS THE MOST-DELICIOUS. MOST-NUTRITIOUS. MOST-- ?? --CHOKE!!– I CAN'T GO ON.!! NOT WHILE THAT LI'L CREATURE IS STARING AT ME, WITH THOSE BIG, SAD EYES.!!
CHUCKLE!!– IS ONLY A "SLOBBOVIAN BALD IGGLE"!!– IT'S HOMMLESS. YOU TZIMPLY CAN'T LIE WHEN IT LOOKS AT YOU, DOT'S ALL!!
NOW, WHAT WERE YOU TSAYING?-
DOG FOOD
(–THOSE EYES!!– THEY HAUNT ME!!–) –THE TRUTH IS–DOGS WON'T EAT THIS FOOD!!– WHY SHOULD YOU?–
DOG FOOD
?!!– WHAT DID I SAY?– I'VE RUINED MY CAREER!! I'VE GOT TO GET AWAY FROM THAT BALD IGGLE!!– I'VE GOT TO RELAX!!
LATER–
I CAN'T STAY HOME FOR DINNER, DEAR!! ANOTHER BIG CONFERENCE!!
THIS IS YOUR FOURTH CONFERENCE, THIS WEEK, MY POOR, OVERWORKED DARLING!!
YOU, AGAIN!!– OH-SOB!!– THOSE BIG, SAD, REPROACHFUL EYES ARE LOOKING INTO MY SOUL!!–
I CAN'T GO ON WITH THIS FRAUD!! ALL THOSE CONFERENCES WERE WITH-SOB!!– ZA-ZA LA GAM, THE FANLESS DANCER!!
YOU MONSTER!!
ALL RIGHT!!– I LOST MY JOB!!– I LOST MY WIFE!! AREN'T YOU SATISFIED? WON'T YOU GO AWAY?
OH, WHY, OF ALL PEOPLE, DO I HAVE TO BE HAUNTED BY THIS LIVING LIE DETECTOR!!
HELLO, JOE– YOU'RE LOOKING ROTTEN, AND IT'S MISERABLE TO SEE YOU!!
DON'T TELL ME YOU'VE GOT ONE, TOO!!
OH-SOB!– YES!! AND IT'S RUINING MY LIFE!!
LOOK!! ALL THEM BALD IGGLES IS SCRAMMING INTO THE HEW HESS HAY!!
GOOD!!– IS A RELIEF TO BE RID OF THOSE PESTS!!– THEY WERRY EMBORROSSINK TO HAVE AROUND, WHEN YOU SHINING OPP TO A GORL, OR MAKING A POLITICAL SPITCH!!
DOG FOOD
5-16
AL CAPP

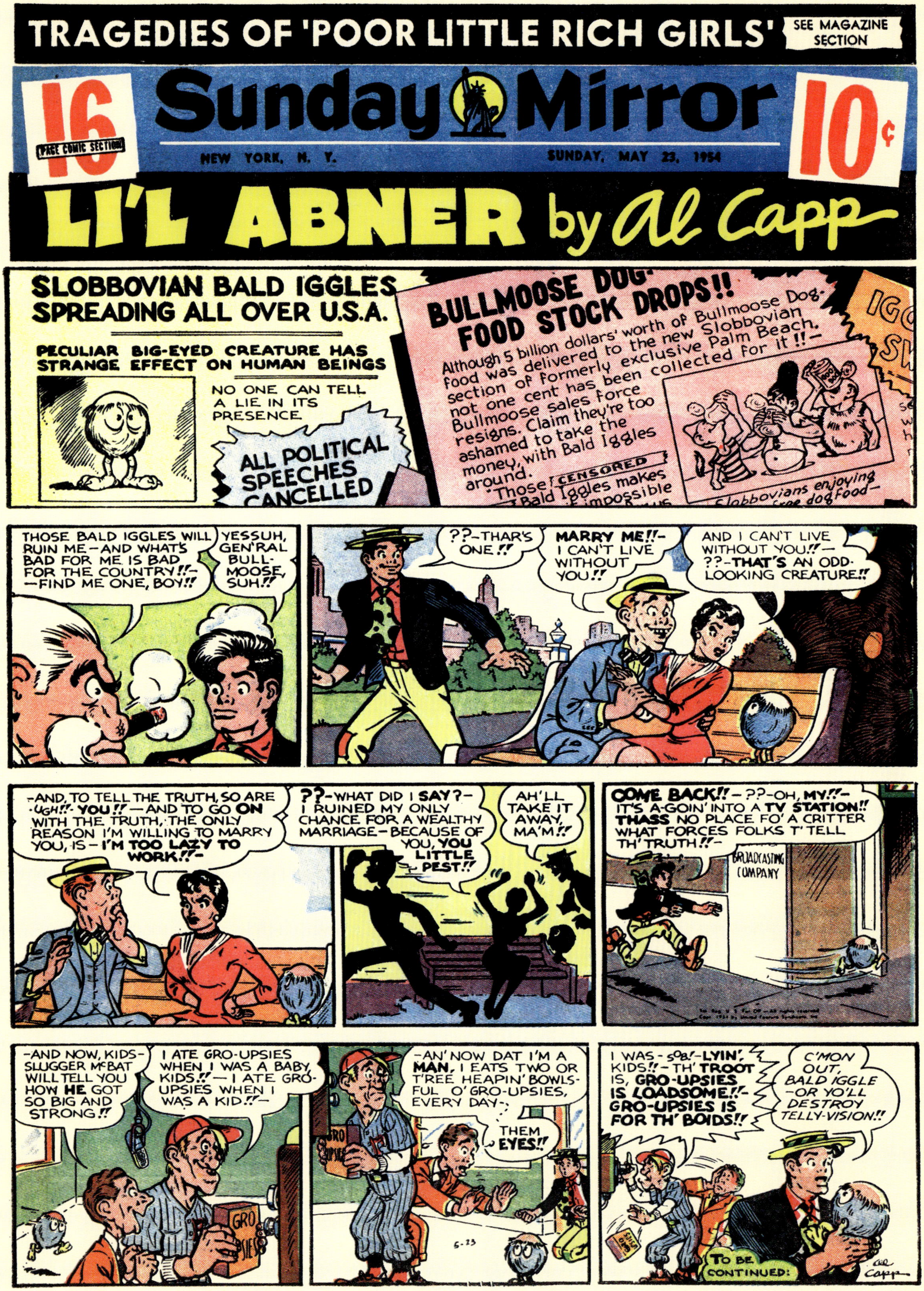

TRAGEDIES OF 'POOR LITTLE RICH GIRLS'
SEE MAGAZINE SECTION
16 PAGE COMIC SECTION
Sunday Mirror
NEW YORK, N. Y.
SUNDAY, MAY 23, 1954
10¢
LI'L ABNER by Al Capp
SLOBBOVIAN BALD IGGLES SPREADING ALL OVER U.S.A.
PECULIAR BIG-EYED CREATURE HAS STRANGE EFFECT ON HUMAN BEINGS
NO ONE CAN TELL A LIE IN ITS PRESENCE
ALL POLITICAL SPEECHES CANCELLED
BULLMOOSE DOG-FOOD STOCK DROPS!!
Although 5 billion dollars' worth of Bullmoose Dog-food was delivered to the new Slobbovian section of formerly exclusive Palm Beach, not one cent has been collected for it!!— Bullmoose sales force resigns. Claim they're too ashamed to take the money, with Bald Iggles around.
"Those CENSORED Bald Iggles makes
Slobbovians enjoying free dog food—
THOSE BALD IGGLES WILL RUIN ME—AND WHAT'S BAD FOR ME IS BAD FOR THE COUNTRY!!—FIND ME ONE, BOY!!
YESSUH, GEN'RAL BULL-MOOSE, SUH!!
??—THAR'S ONE!!
MARRY ME!!— I CAN'T LIVE WITHOUT YOU!!
AND I CAN'T LIVE WITHOUT YOU!!— ??—THAT'S AN ODD-LOOKING CREATURE!!
—AND, TO TELL THE TRUTH, SO ARE —UGH!!— YOU!!—AND TO GO ON WITH THE TRUTH, THE ONLY REASON I'M WILLING TO MARRY YOU, IS—I'M TOO LAZY TO WORK!!—
??—WHAT DID I SAY?— I RUINED MY ONLY CHANCE FOR A WEALTHY MARRIAGE—BECAUSE OF YOU, YOU LITTLE PEST!!
AH'LL TAKE IT AWAY, MA'M!!
COME BACK!!—??—OH, MY!!— IT'S A-GOIN' INTO A TV STATION!! THASS NO PLACE FO' A CRITTER WHAT FORCES FOLKS T' TELL TH' TRUTH!!—
BROADCASTING COMPANY
—AND NOW, KIDS—SLUGGER McBAT WILL TELL YOU HOW HE GOT SO BIG AND STRONG!!
I ATE GRO-UPSIES WHEN I WAS A BABY, KIDS!!—I ATE GRO-UPSIES WHEN I WAS A KID!!—
GRO-UPSIES
—AN' NOW DAT I'M A MAN, I EATS TWO OR T'REE HEAPIN' BOWLS-FUL O' GRO-UPSIES, EVERY DAY—
THEM EYES!!
5-23
I WAS—SOB!—LYIN', KIDS!!—TH' TROOT IS, GRO-UPSIES IS LOADSOME!!—GRO-UPSIES IS FOR TH' BOIDS!!
C'MON OUT, BALD IGGLE —OR YO'LL DESTROY TELLY-VISION!!
TO BE CONTINUED:
AL CAPP

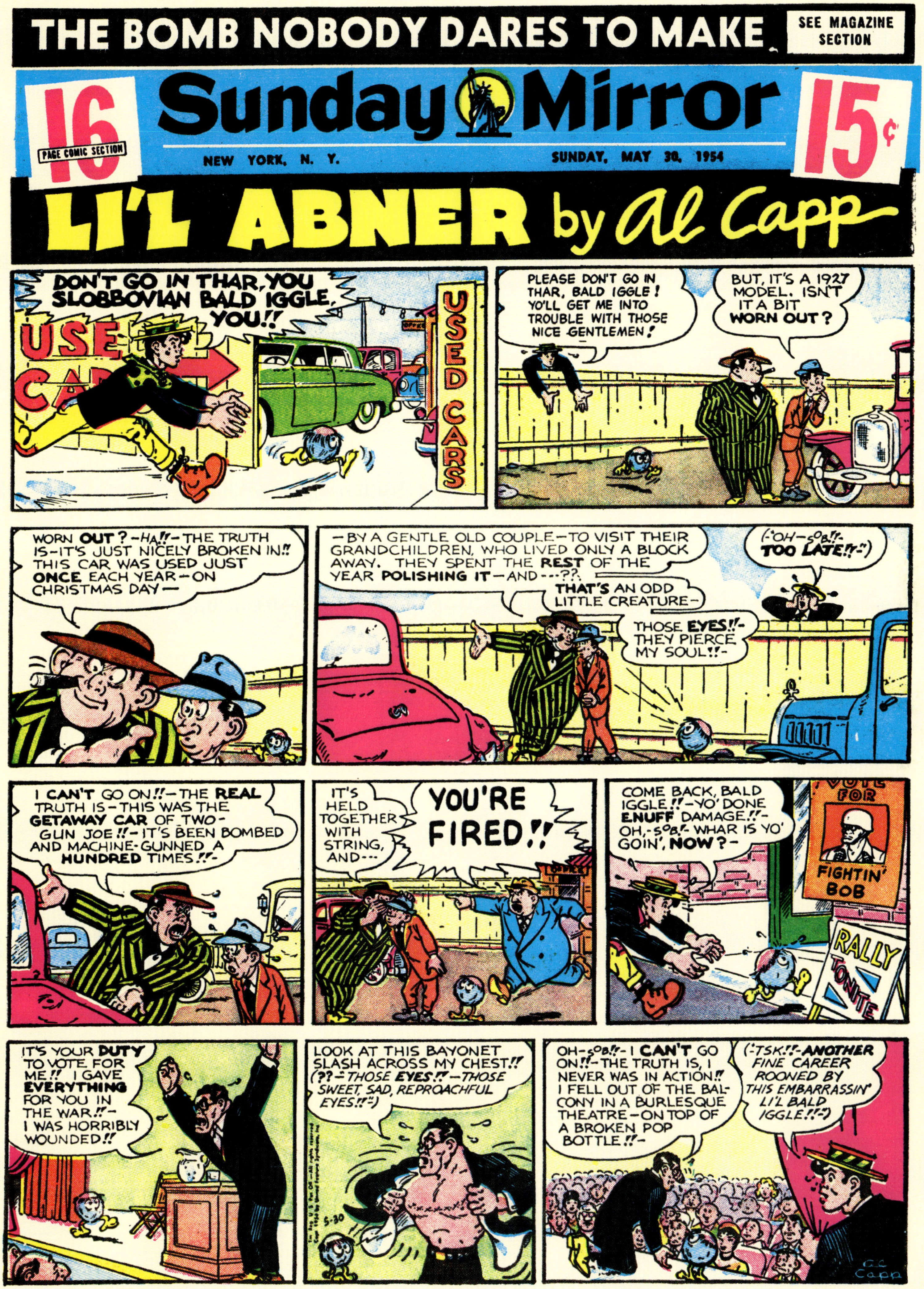
THE BOMB NOBODY DARES TO MAKE
SEE MAGAZINE SECTION
16
PAGE COMIC SECTION
Sunday Mirror
NEW YORK, N. Y.
SUNDAY, MAY 30, 1954
15¢
LI'L ABNER by Al Capp
DON'T GO IN THAR, YOU SLOBBOVIAN BALD IGGLE, YOU!!
USED CARS
PLEASE DON'T GO IN THAR, BALD IGGLE! YO'LL GET ME INTO TROUBLE WITH THOSE NICE GENTLEMEN!
BUT, IT'S A 1927 MODEL. ISN'T IT A BIT WORN OUT?
WORN OUT?-HA!!-THE TRUTH IS-IT'S JUST NICELY BROKEN IN!! THIS CAR WAS USED JUST ONCE EACH YEAR-ON CHRISTMAS DAY-
-BY A GENTLE OLD COUPLE-TO VISIT THEIR GRANDCHILDREN, WHO LIVED ONLY A BLOCK AWAY. THEY SPENT THE REST OF THE YEAR POLISHING IT-AND--??
(-OH-SOB!!-TOO LATE!!-)
THAT'S AN ODD LITTLE CREATURE-
THOSE EYES!!-THEY PIERCE MY SOUL!!-
I CAN'T GO ON!!-THE REAL TRUTH IS-THIS WAS THE GETAWAY CAR OF TWO-GUN JOE!!-IT'S BEEN BOMBED AND MACHINE-GUNNED A HUNDRED TIMES!!-
IT'S HELD TOGETHER WITH STRING, AND---
YOU'RE FIRED!!
COME BACK, BALD IGGLE!!-YO' DONE ENUFF DAMAGE!!-OH,-SOB!-WHAR IS YO' GOIN', NOW?-
VOTE FOR FIGHTIN' BOB
RALLY TONITE
IT'S YOUR DUTY TO VOTE FOR ME!! I GAVE EVERYTHING FOR YOU IN THE WAR!!-I WAS HORRIBLY WOUNDED!!
LOOK AT THIS BAYONET SLASH ACROSS MY CHEST!! (??-THOSE EYES!!-THOSE SWEET, SAD, REPROACHFUL EYES!!-)
OH-SOB!!-I CAN'T GO ON!!-THE TRUTH IS, I NEVER WAS IN ACTION!! I FELL OUT OF THE BALCONY IN A BURLESQUE THEATRE-ON TOP OF A BROKEN POP BOTTLE!!-
(-TSK!!-ANOTHER FINE CAREER ROONED BY THIS EMBARRASSIN' LI'L BALD IGGLE!!-)
AL CAPP

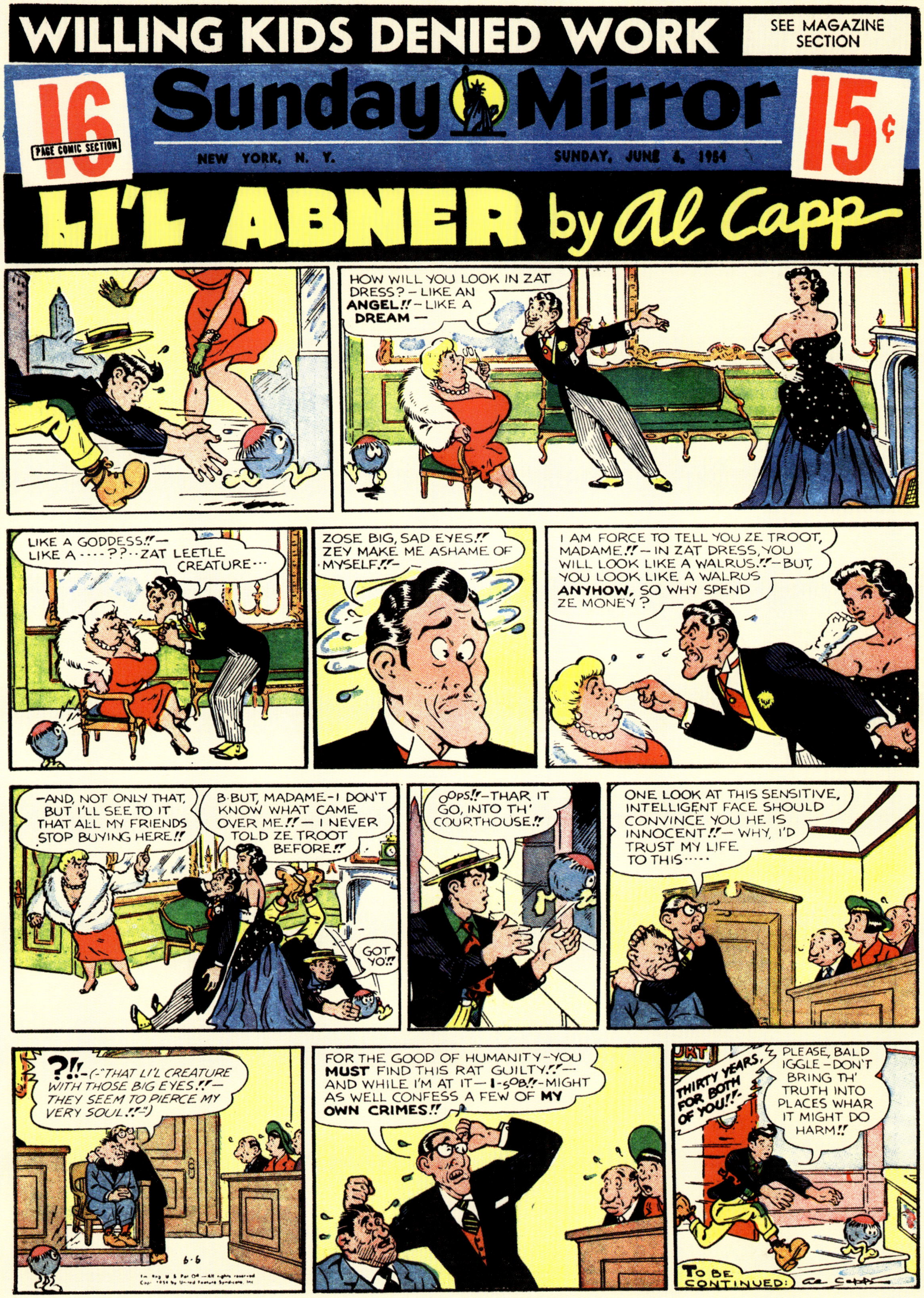
WILLING KIDS DENIED WORK
SEE MAGAZINE SECTION
16 PAGE COMIC SECTION
Sunday Mirror
15¢
NEW YORK, N. Y.
SUNDAY, JUNE 6, 1954
LI'L ABNER by Al Capp
HOW WILL YOU LOOK IN ZAT DRESS? – LIKE AN ANGEL!! – LIKE A DREAM –
LIKE A GODDESS!! – LIKE A - - - - ?? - - ZAT LEETLE CREATURE - - -
ZOSE BIG, SAD EYES!! ZEY MAKE ME ASHAME OF MYSELF!! –
I AM FORCE TO TELL YOU ZE TROOT, MADAME!! – IN ZAT DRESS, YOU WILL LOOK LIKE A WALRUS!! – BUT, YOU LOOK LIKE A WALRUS ANYHOW, SO WHY SPEND ZE MONEY?
–AND, NOT ONLY THAT, BUT I'LL SEE TO IT THAT ALL MY FRIENDS STOP BUYING HERE!!
B-BUT, MADAME – I DON'T KNOW WHAT CAME OVER ME!! – I NEVER TOLD ZE TROOT BEFORE!!
GOT YO!!
OOPS!! – THAR IT GO, INTO TH' COURTHOUSE!!
ONE LOOK AT THIS SENSITIVE, INTELLIGENT FACE SHOULD CONVINCE YOU HE IS INNOCENT!! – WHY, I'D TRUST MY LIFE TO THIS - - - - -
?!! – ("THAT LI'L CREATURE WITH THOSE BIG EYES!! – THEY SEEM TO PIERCE MY VERY SOUL!!")
6-6
FOR THE GOOD OF HUMANITY – YOU MUST FIND THIS RAT GUILTY!! – AND WHILE I'M AT IT – I – SOB!! – MIGHT AS WELL CONFESS A FEW OF MY OWN CRIMES!!
THIRTY YEARS, FOR BOTH OF YOU!!
PLEASE, BALD IGGLE – DON'T BRING TH' TRUTH INTO PLACES WHAR IT MIGHT DO HARM!!
TO BE CONTINUED:
AL CAPP

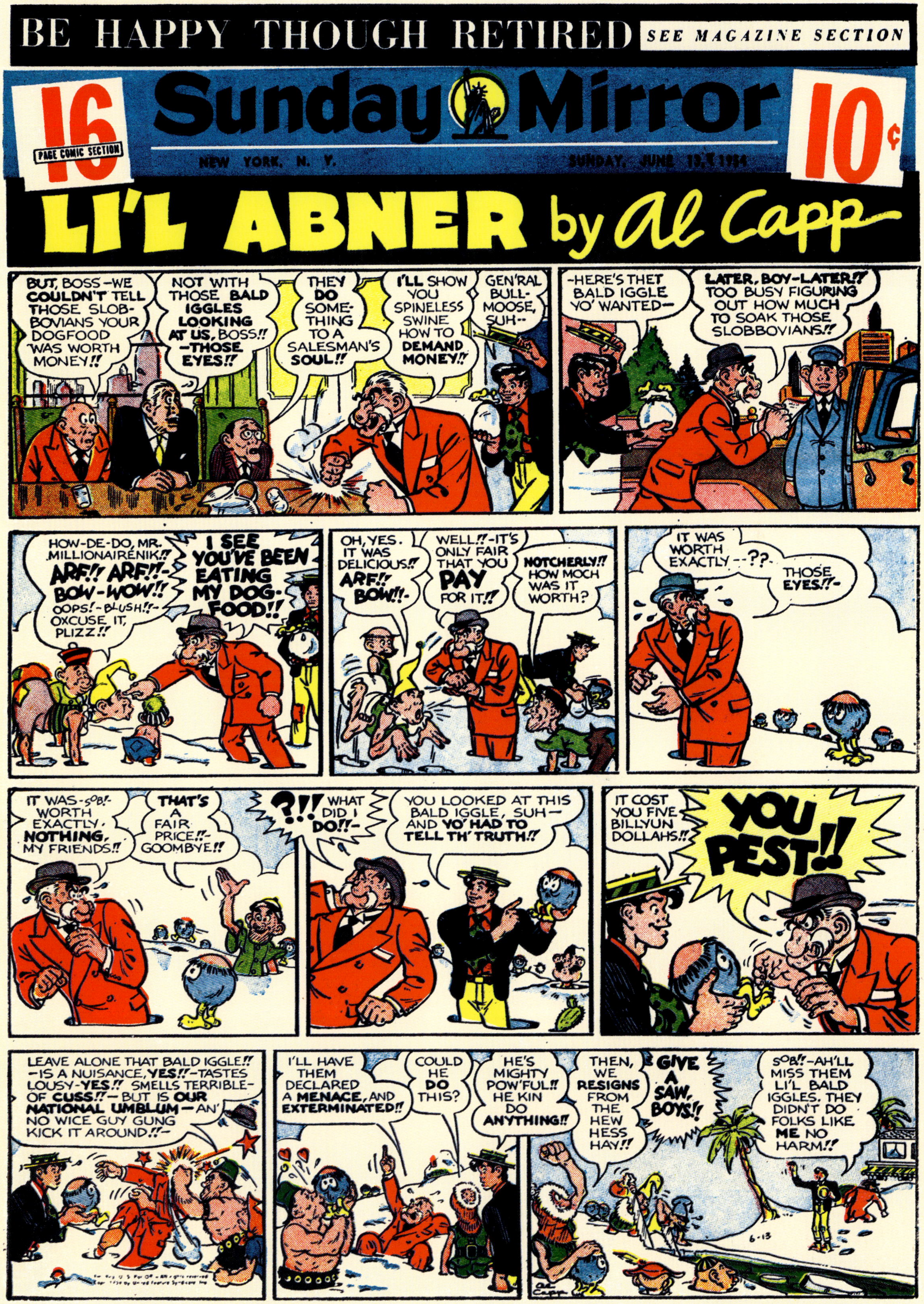

BE HAPPY THOUGH RETIRED
SEE MAGAZINE SECTION
16
PAGE COMIC SECTION
Sunday Mirror
NEW YORK, N. Y.
SUNDAY, JUNE 13, 1954
10¢
LI'L ABNER by Al Capp
BUT, BOSS–WE COULDN'T TELL THOSE SLOBBOVIANS YOUR DOGFOOD WAS WORTH MONEY!!
NOT WITH THOSE BALD IGGLES LOOKING AT US, BOSS!! –THOSE EYES!!
THEY DO SOMETHING TO A SALESMAN'S SOUL!!
I'LL SHOW YOU SPINELESS SWINE HOW TO DEMAND MONEY!!
GEN'RAL BULLMOOSE, SUH--
-HERE'S THET BALD IGGLE YO' WANTED-
LATER, BOY-LATER!! TOO BUSY FIGURING OUT HOW MUCH TO SOAK THOSE SLOBBOVIANS!!
HOW-DE-DO, MR. MILLIONAIRÉNIK!! ARF!! ARF!!– BOW-WOW!! OOPS!–BLUSH!!– OXCUSE IT, PLIZZ!!
I SEE YOU'VE BEEN EATING MY DOG-FOOD!!
OH, YES. IT WAS DELICIOUS!! ARF!! BOW!!-
WELL!!–IT'S ONLY FAIR THAT YOU PAY FOR IT!!
NOTCHERLY!! HOW MOCH WAS IT WORTH?
IT WAS WORTH EXACTLY – –??–
THOSE EYES!!–
IT WAS–SOB!!– WORTH EXACTLY NOTHING, MY FRIENDS!!
THAT'S A FAIR PRICE!!– GOOMBYE!!
?!! WHAT DID I DO!!–
YOU LOOKED AT THIS BALD IGGLE, SUH – AND YO' HAD TO TELL TH' TRUTH!!
IT COST YOU FIVE BILLYUN DOLLAHS!!
YOU PEST!!
LEAVE ALONE THAT BALD IGGLE!! –IS A NUISANCE, YES!!–TASTES LOUSY–YES!! SMELLS TERRIBLE–OF CUSS!!–BUT IS OUR NATIONAL UMBLUM–AN' NO WICE GUY GUNG KICK IT AROUND!!–
I'LL HAVE THEM DECLARED A MENACE, AND EXTERMINATED!!
COULD HE DO THIS?
HE'S MIGHTY POW'FUL!! HE KIN DO ANYTHING!!
THEN, WE RESIGNS FROM THE HEW HESS HAY!!
GIVE A SAW, BOYS!!
SOB!!–AH'LL MISS THEM LI'L BALD IGGLES. THEY DIDN'T DO FOLKS LIKE ME NO HARM!!
6-13
Al Capp

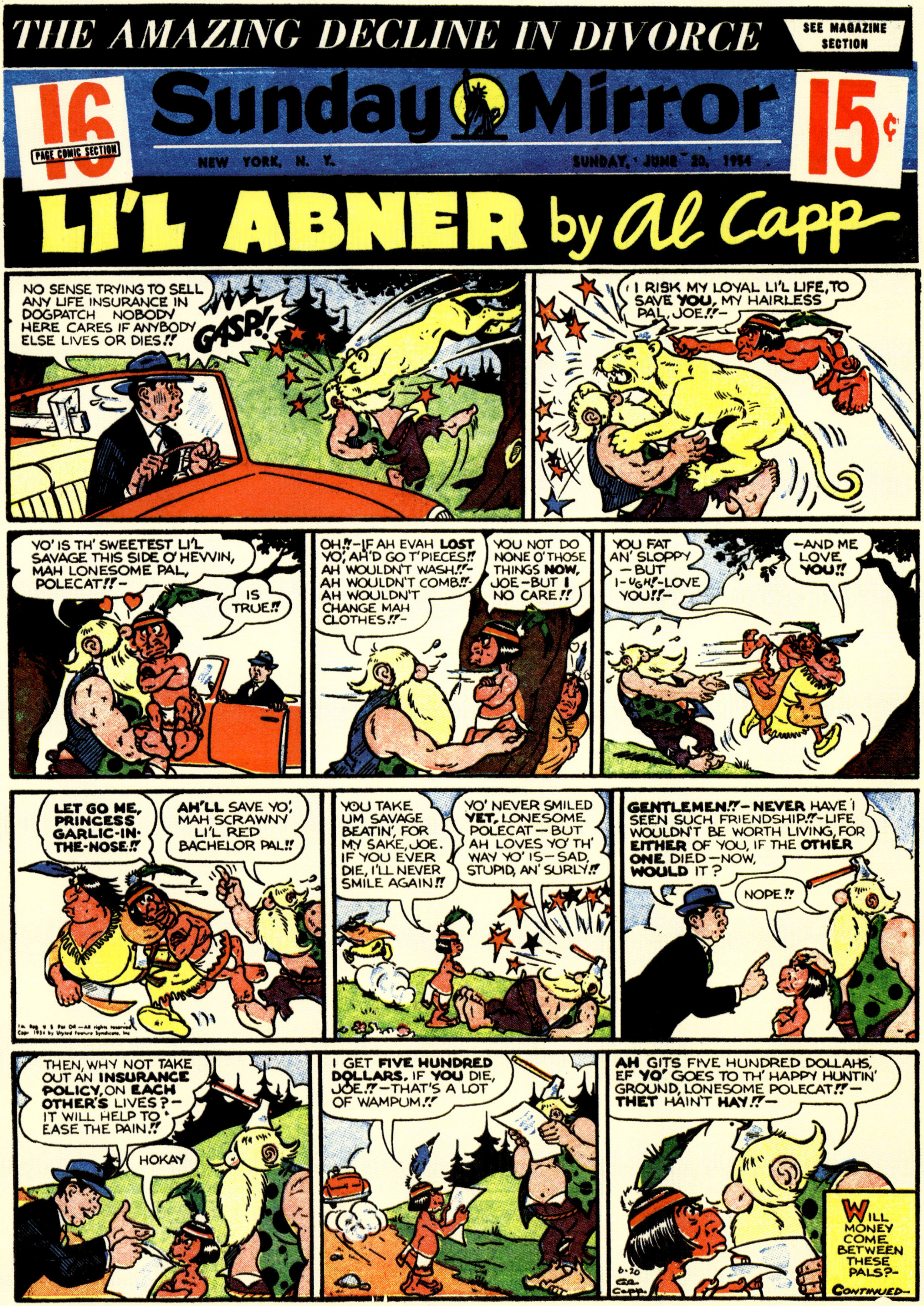

THE AMAZING DECLINE IN DIVORCE
SEE MAGAZINE SECTION
16 PAGE COMIC SECTION
Sunday Mirror
NEW YORK, N. Y.
SUNDAY, JUNE 20, 1954
15¢
LI'L ABNER by Al Capp
NO SENSE TRYING TO SELL ANY LIFE INSURANCE IN DOGPATCH. NOBODY HERE CARES IF ANYBODY ELSE LIVES OR DIES!!
GASP!
I RISK MY LOYAL LI'L LIFE, TO SAVE YOU, MY HAIRLESS PAL, JOE.!!–
YO' IS TH' SWEETEST LI'L SAVAGE THIS SIDE O' HEVVIN, MAH LONESOME PAL, POLECAT!!–
IS TRUE!!
OH!!–IF AH EVAH LOST YO', AH'D GO T'PIECES!! AH WOULDN'T WASH!!– AH WOULDN'T COMB!!– AH WOULDN'T CHANGE MAH CLOTHES!!–
YOU NOT DO NONE O' THOSE THINGS NOW, JOE–BUT I NO CARE!!
YOU FAT AN' SLOPPY –BUT I–UGH!–LOVE YOU!!–
–AND ME LOVE YOU!!
LET GO ME, PRINCESS GARLIC-IN-THE-NOSE!!
AH'LL SAVE YO', MAH SCRAWNY LI'L RED BACHELOR PAL!!
YOU TAKE UM SAVAGE BEATIN', FOR MY SAKE, JOE. IF YOU EVER DIE, I'LL NEVER SMILE AGAIN!!
YO' NEVER SMILED YET, LONESOME POLECAT–BUT AH LOVES YO' TH' WAY YO' IS–SAD, STUPID, AN' SURLY!!
GENTLEMEN!!–NEVER HAVE I SEEN SUCH FRIENDSHIP!!–LIFE WOULDN'T BE WORTH LIVING, FOR EITHER OF YOU, IF THE OTHER ONE DIED–NOW, WOULD IT?
NOPE.!!
THEN, WHY NOT TAKE OUT AN INSURANCE POLICY, ON EACH OTHER'S LIVES?– IT WILL HELP TO EASE THE PAIN.!!
HOKAY
I GET FIVE HUNDRED DOLLARS, IF YOU DIE, JOE.!!–THAT'S A LOT OF WAMPUM.!!
AH GITS FIVE HUNDRED DOLLAHS, EF YO' GOES TO TH' HAPPY HUNTIN' GROUND, LONESOME POLECAT!!– THET HAIN'T HAY.!!–
WILL MONEY COME BETWEEN THESE PALS?– CONTINUED–
6-20
Al Capp

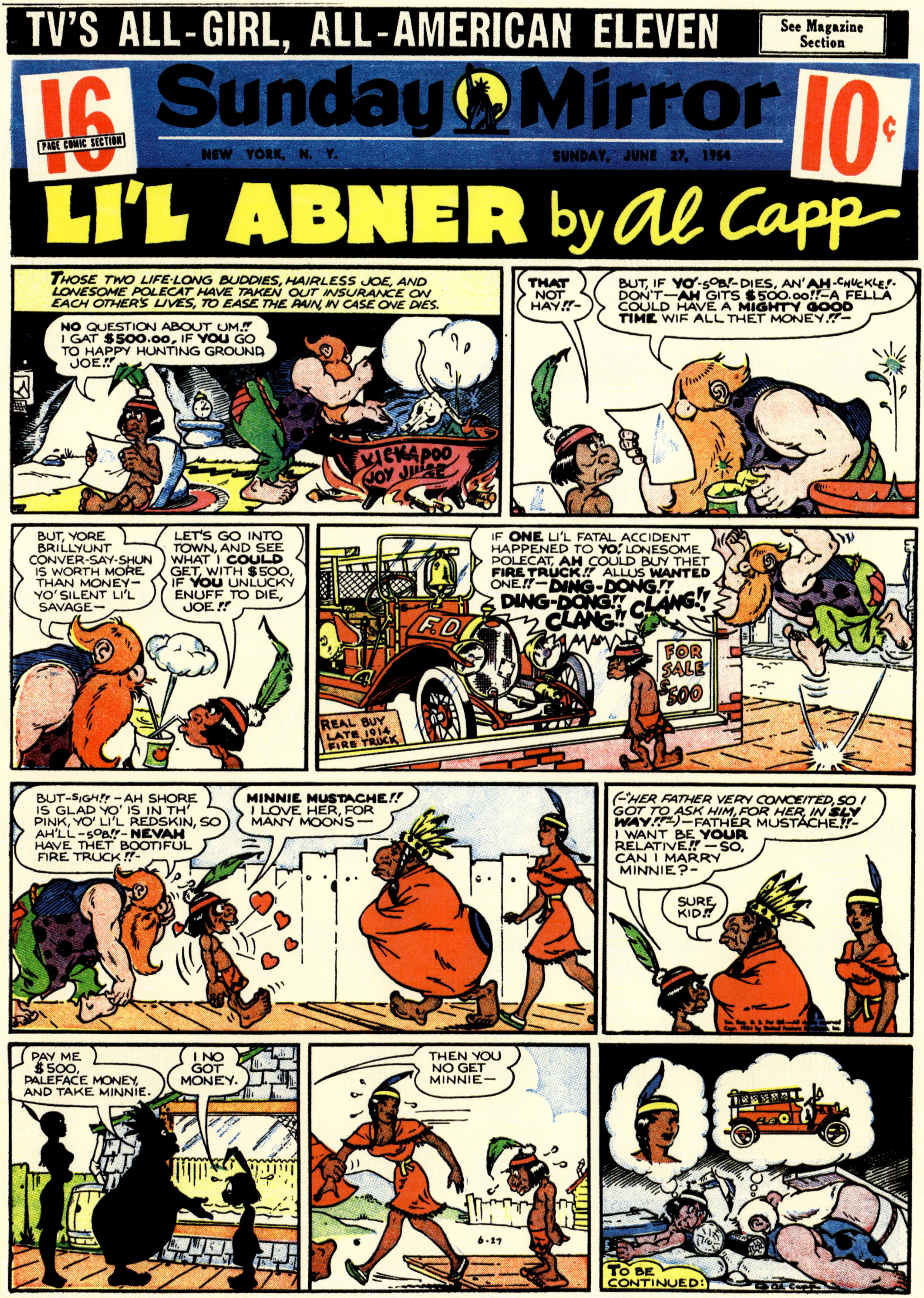
TV'S ALL-GIRL, ALL-AMERICAN ELEVEN
See Magazine Section
16
PAGE COMIC SECTION
Sunday Mirror
NEW YORK, N. Y.
SUNDAY, JUNE 27, 1954
10¢
LI'L ABNER by Al Capp
THOSE TWO LIFE-LONG BUDDIES, HAIRLESS JOE, AND LONESOME POLECAT HAVE TAKEN OUT INSURANCE ON EACH OTHER'S LIVES, TO EASE THE PAIN, IN CASE ONE DIES.
NO QUESTION ABOUT UM.!! I GAT $500.00, IF YOU GO TO HAPPY HUNTING GROUND, JOE.!!
KICKAPOO JOY JUICE
THAT NOT HAY.!!-
BUT, IF YO'-SOB!-DIES, AN' AH-CHUCKLE!-DON'T-AH GITS $500.00!!-A FELLA COULD HAVE A MIGHTY GOOD TIME WIF ALL THET MONEY.!!-
BUT, YORE BRILLYUNT CONVER-SAY-SHUN IS WORTH MORE THAN MONEY-YO' SILENT LI'L SAVAGE-
LET'S GO INTO TOWN, AND SEE WHAT I COULD GET, WITH $500, IF YOU UNLUCKY ENUFF TO DIE, JOE.!!
IF ONE LI'L FATAL ACCIDENT HAPPENED TO YO', LONESOME POLECAT, AH COULD BUY THET FIRE TRUCK.!! ALLUS WANTED ONE.!!-DING-DONG.!!
DING-DONG!! CLANG!! CLANG!!
F.D.
FOR SALE $500
REAL BUY LATE 1914 FIRE TRUCK
BUT-SIGH!!-AH SHORE IS GLAD YO' IS IN TH' PINK, YO' LI'L REDSKIN, SO AH'LL-SOB!!-NEVAH HAVE THET BOOTIFUL FIRE TRUCK.!!-
MINNIE MUSTACHE.!! I LOVE HER, FOR MANY MOONS—
(-"HER FATHER VERY CONCEITED, SO I GOT TO ASK HIM, FOR HER, IN SLY WAY.!!"-)-FATHER MUSTACHE.!!-I WANT BE YOUR RELATIVE.!!-SO, CAN I MARRY MINNIE?-
SURE, KID.!!
PAY ME $500, PALEFACE MONEY, AND TAKE MINNIE.
I NO GOT MONEY.
THEN YOU NO GET MINNIE—
6-27
TO BE CONTINUED:
Al Capp

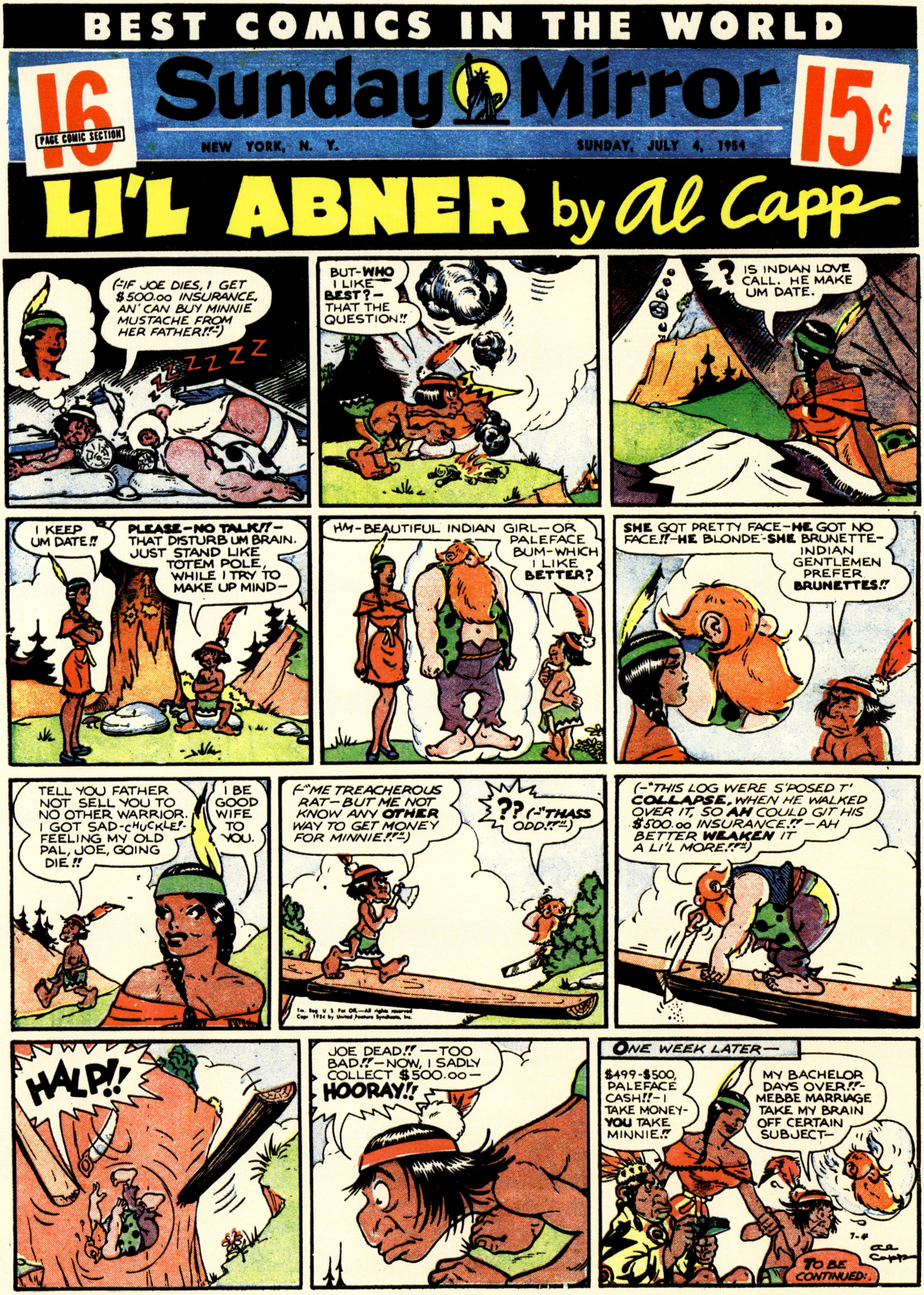
BEST COMICS IN THE WORLD
16 PAGE COMIC SECTION
Sunday Mirror
15¢
NEW YORK, N. Y.
SUNDAY, JULY 4, 1954
LI'L ABNER by Al Capp
(-IF JOE DIES, I GET $500.00 INSURANCE, AN' CAN BUY MINNIE MUSTACHE FROM HER FATHER!!-)
ZZZZZZ
BUT-WHO I LIKE BEST?-THAT THE QUESTION!!
? IS INDIAN LOVE CALL. HE MAKE UM DATE.
I KEEP UM DATE!!
PLEASE-NO TALK!!-THAT DISTURB UM BRAIN. JUST STAND LIKE TOTEM POLE, WHILE I TRY TO MAKE UP MIND-
HM-BEAUTIFUL INDIAN GIRL-OR PALEFACE BUM-WHICH I LIKE BETTER?
SHE GOT PRETTY FACE-HE GOT NO FACE.!!-HE BLONDE-SHE BRUNETTE-INDIAN GENTLEMEN PREFER BRUNETTES!!
TELL YOU FATHER NOT SELL YOU TO NO OTHER WARRIOR. I GOT SAD-chuckle!-FEELING MY OLD PAL, JOE, GOING DIE!!
I BE GOOD WIFE TO YOU.
(-"ME TREACHEROUS RAT-BUT ME NOT KNOW ANY OTHER WAY TO GET MONEY FOR MINNIE!!"-)
?? (-"THASS ODD!!"-)
(-"THIS LOG WERE S'POSED T' COLLAPSE, WHEN HE WALKED OVER IT, SO AH COULD GIT HIS $500.00 INSURANCE.!!-AH BETTER WEAKEN IT A LI'L MORE.!!"-)
HALP!!
JOE DEAD!!-TOO BAD!!-NOW, I SADLY COLLECT $500.00-HOORAY!!
ONE WEEK LATER-
$499-$500, PALEFACE CASH!!-I TAKE MONEY-YOU TAKE MINNIE!!
MY BACHELOR DAYS OVER!!-MEBBE MARRIAGE TAKE MY BRAIN OFF CERTAIN SUBJECT-
TO BE CONTINUED.

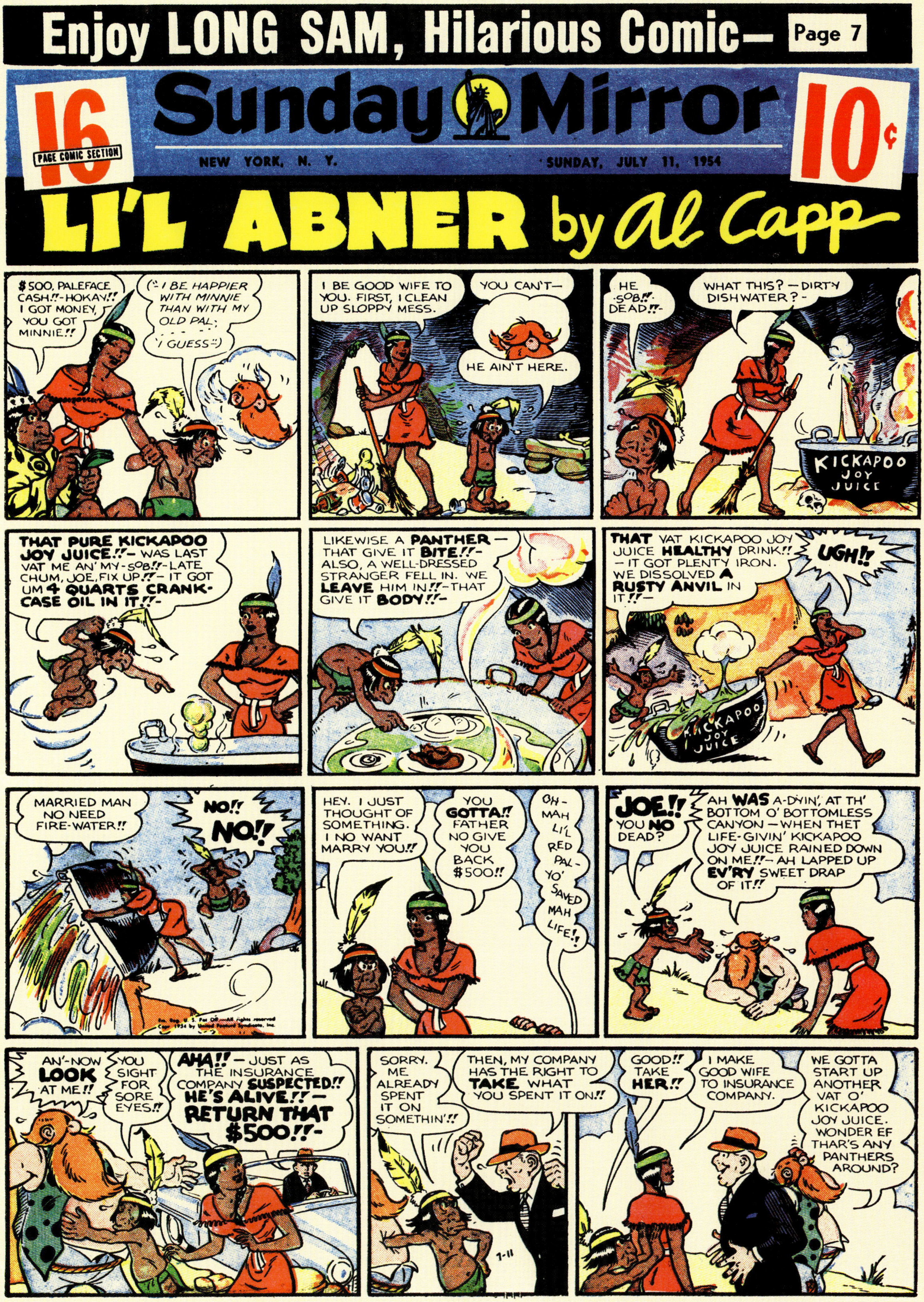

Enjoy LONG SAM, Hilarious Comic— Page 7
16 PAGE COMIC SECTION
Sunday Mirror
NEW YORK, N. Y.
SUNDAY, JULY 11, 1954
10¢
LI'L ABNER by Al Capp
$500, PALEFACE CASH!!–HOKAY!! I GOT MONEY, YOU GOT MINNIE!!
("I BE HAPPIER WITH MINNIE THAN WITH MY OLD PAL; - - - I GUESS-")
I BE GOOD WIFE TO YOU. FIRST, I CLEAN UP SLOPPY MESS.
YOU CAN'T–
HE AIN'T HERE.
HE -SOB!!- DEAD!!-
WHAT THIS? – DIRTY DISHWATER? –
KICKAPOO JOY JUICE
THAT PURE KICKAPOO JOY JUICE!!– WAS LAST VAT ME AN' MY-SOB!!-LATE CHUM, JOE, FIX UP!!– IT GOT UM 4 QUARTS CRANK-CASE OIL IN IT!!–
LIKEWISE A PANTHER – THAT GIVE IT BITE!!– ALSO, A WELL-DRESSED STRANGER FELL IN. WE LEAVE HIM IN!!–THAT GIVE IT BODY!!–
THAT VAT KICKAPOO JOY JUICE HEALTHY DRINK!! – IT GOT PLENTY IRON. WE DISSOLVED A RUSTY ANVIL IN IT!!–
UGH!!
KICKAPOO JOY JUICE
MARRIED MAN NO NEED FIRE-WATER!!
NO!! NO!!
HEY. I JUST THOUGHT OF SOMETHING. I NO WANT MARRY YOU!!
YOU GOTTA!! FATHER NO GIVE YOU BACK $500!!
OH – MAH LI'L RED PAL – YO' SAVED MAH LIFE!!
JOE!! YOU NO DEAD?
AH WAS A-DYIN', AT TH' BOTTOM O' BOTTOMLESS CANYON – WHEN THET LIFE-GIVIN' KICKAPOO JOY JUICE RAINED DOWN ON ME!!– AH LAPPED UP EV'RY SWEET DRAP OF IT!!
AN'-NOW LOOK AT ME!!
YOU SIGHT FOR SORE EYES!!
AHA!! – JUST AS THE INSURANCE COMPANY SUSPECTED!! HE'S ALIVE!!– RETURN THAT $500!!–
SORRY. ME ALREADY SPENT IT ON SOMETHIN'!!
THEN, MY COMPANY HAS THE RIGHT TO TAKE WHAT YOU SPENT IT ON!!
GOOD!! TAKE HER!!
I MAKE GOOD WIFE TO INSURANCE COMPANY.
WE GOTTA START UP ANOTHER VAT O' KICKAPOO JOY JUICE. WONDER EF THAR'S ANY PANTHERS AROUND?

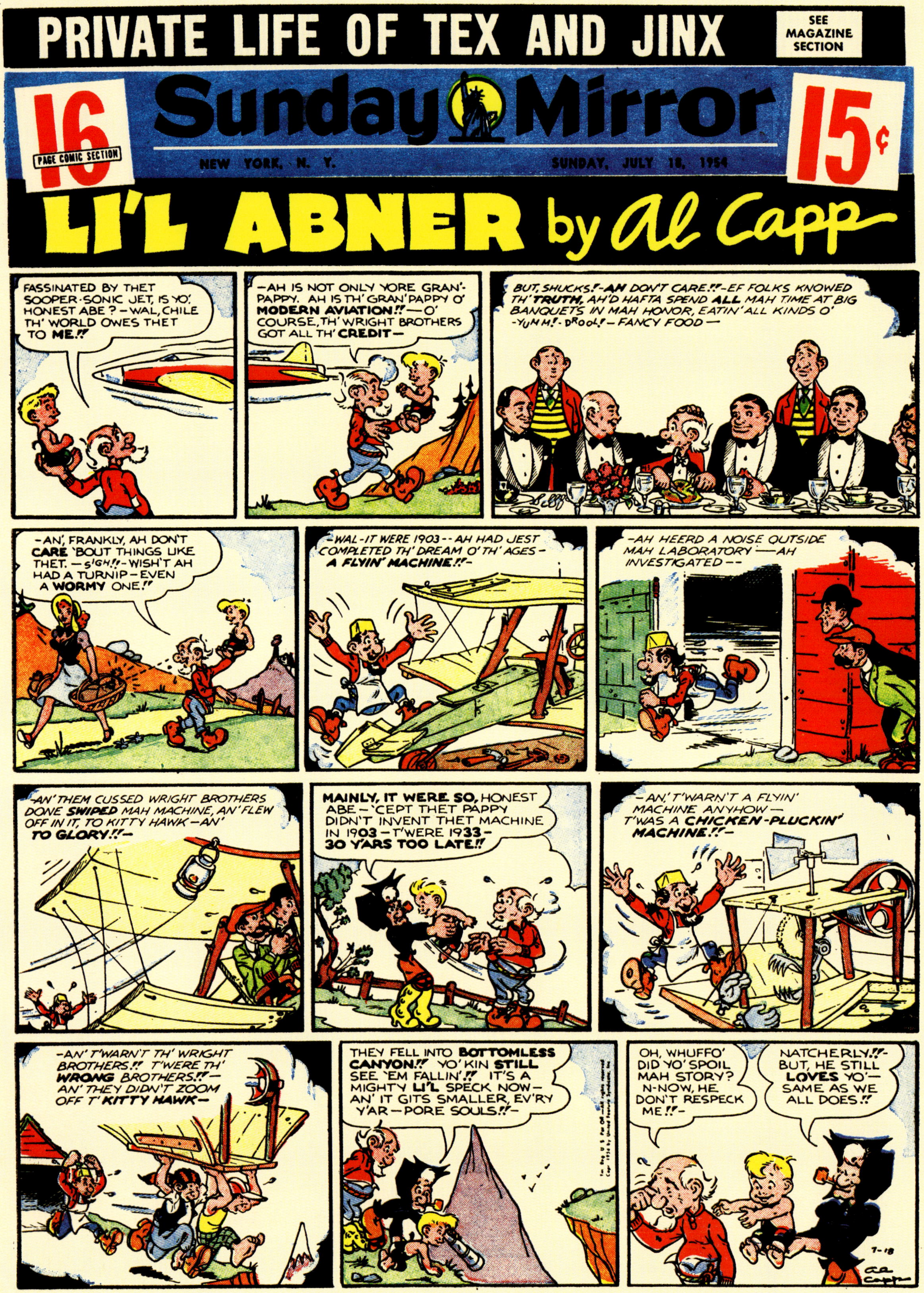
PRIVATE LIFE OF TEX AND JINX
SEE MAGAZINE SECTION
16 PAGE COMIC SECTION
Sunday Mirror
NEW YORK, N. Y.
SUNDAY, JULY 18, 1954
15¢
LI'L ABNER by Al Capp
FASSINATED BY THET SOOPER-SONIC JET, IS YO', HONEST ABE? —WAL, CHILE TH' WORLD OWES THET TO ME.!!
—AH IS NOT ONLY YORE GRAN'-PAPPY. AH IS TH' GRAN'PAPPY O' MODERN AVIATION!! —O' COURSE, TH' WRIGHT BROTHERS GOT ALL TH' CREDIT—
BUT, SHUCKS!-AH DON'T CARE!!-EF FOLKS KNOWED TH' TRUTH, AH'D HAFTA SPEND ALL MAH TIME AT BIG BANQUETS IN MAH HONOR, EATIN' ALL KINDS O' -YUMM!-DROOL!-FANCY FOOD—
—AN', FRANKLY, AH DON'T CARE 'BOUT THINGS LIKE THET. —SIGH!!-WISH'T AH HAD A TURNIP—EVEN A WORMY ONE.!!
—WAL-IT WERE 1903--AH HAD JEST COMPLETED TH' DREAM O' TH' AGES—A FLYIN' MACHINE!!—
—AH HEERD A NOISE OUTSIDE MAH LABORATORY——AH INVESTIGATED——
—AN' THEM CUSSED WRIGHT BROTHERS DONE SWIPED MAH MACHINE, AN' FLEW OFF IN IT, TO KITTY HAWK—AN' TO GLORY!!—
MAINLY, IT WERE SO, HONEST ABE—'CEPT THET PAPPY DIDN'T INVENT THET MACHINE IN 1903—T'WERE 1933—30 YARS TOO LATE!!
—AN' T'WARN'T A FLYIN' MACHINE ANYHOW—T'WAS A CHICKEN-PLUCKIN' MACHINE!!—
—AN' T'WARN'T TH' WRIGHT BROTHERS!! T'WERE TH' WRONG BROTHERS!!—AN' THEY DIDN'T ZOOM OFF T' KITTY HAWK—
THEY FELL INTO BOTTOMLESS CANYON!! YO' KIN STILL SEE 'EM FALLIN'!! IT'S A MIGHTY LI'L SPECK NOW—AN' IT GITS SMALLER EV'RY Y'AR—PORE SOULS!!—
OH, WHUFFO' DID YO' SPOIL MAH STORY? N-NOW, HE DON'T RESPECK ME!!—
NATCHERLY!!—BUT, HE STILL LOVES YO'—SAME AS WE ALL DOES!!
7-18

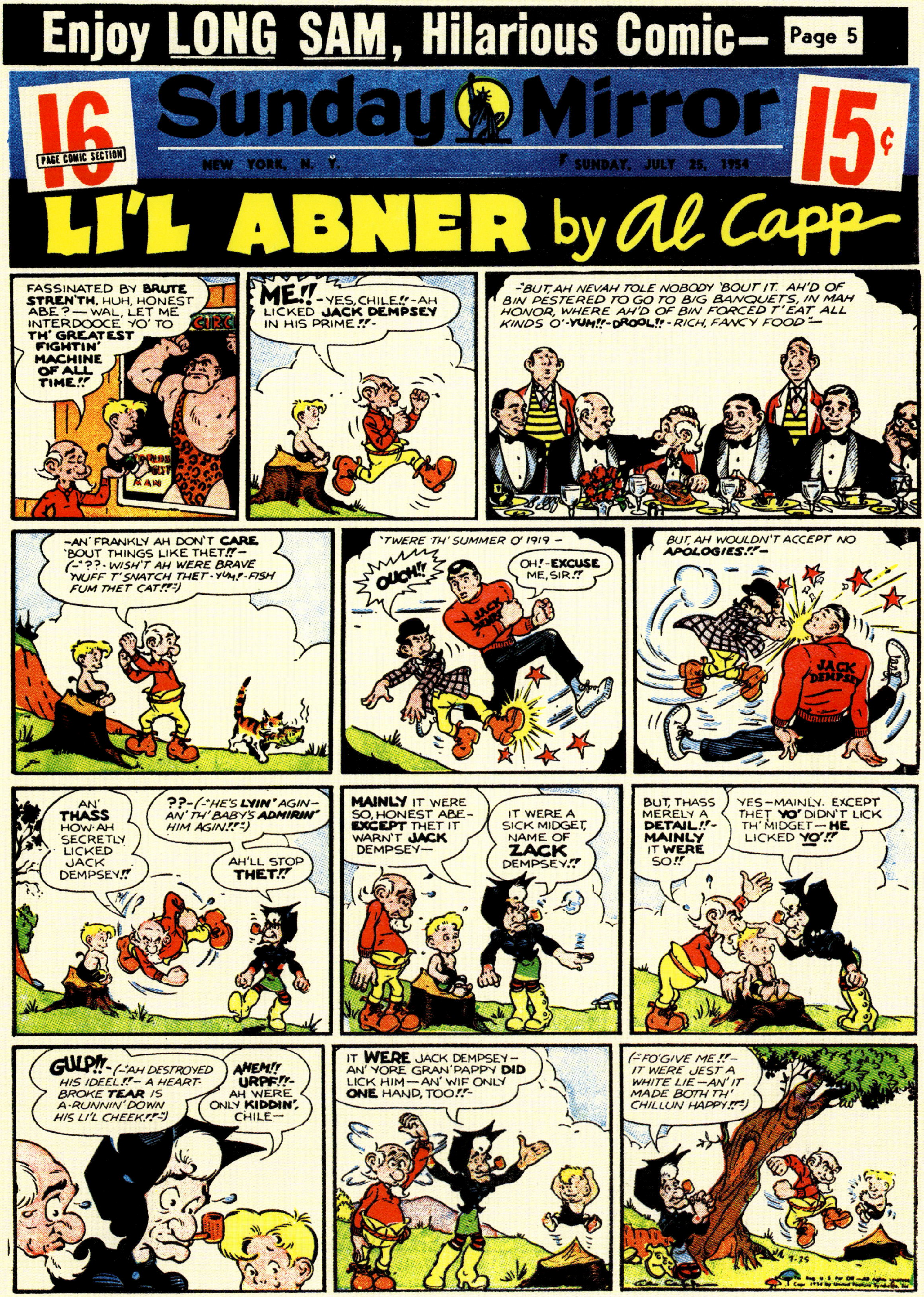
Enjoy LONG SAM, Hilarious Comic— Page 5
16 PAGE COMIC SECTION
Sunday Mirror
NEW YORK, N. Y.
SUNDAY, JULY 25, 1954
15¢
LI'L ABNER by Al Capp
FASSINATED BY BRUTE STREN'TH, HUH, HONEST ABE? — WAL, LET ME INTERDOOCE YO' TO TH' GREATEST FIGHTIN' MACHINE OF ALL TIME!!
ME!! -YES, CHILE!! -AH LICKED JACK DEMPSEY IN HIS PRIME!! -
-BUT, AH NEVAH TOLE NOBODY 'BOUT IT. AH'D OF BIN PESTERED TO GO TO BIG BANQUETS, IN MAH HONOR, WHERE AH'D OF BIN FORCED T'EAT ALL KINDS O'-YUM!!-DROOL!!-RICH, FANCY FOOD—
-AN' FRANKLY AH DON'T CARE 'BOUT THINGS LIKE THET!! — (-??-WISH'T AH WERE BRAVE 'NUFF T'SNATCH THET-YUM!-FISH FUM THET CAT!!-)
'TWERE TH' SUMMER O' 1919 —
OUCH!!
OH! -EXCUSE ME, SIR!!
JACK DEMPSEY
BUT, AH WOULDN'T ACCEPT NO APOLOGIES!! —
JACK DEMPSEY
AN' THASS HOW AH SECRETLY LICKED JACK DEMPSEY!!
??-(-HE'S LYIN' AGIN—AN' TH' BABY'S ADMIRIN' HIM AGIN!!-)
AH'LL STOP THET!!
MAINLY IT WERE SO, HONEST ABE—EXCEPT THET IT WARN'T JACK DEMPSEY—
IT WERE A SICK MIDGET, NAME OF ZACK DEMPSEY!!
BUT, THASS MERELY A DETAIL!! - MAINLY IT WERE SO!!
YES—MAINLY. EXCEPT THET YO' DIDN'T LICK TH' MIDGET—HE LICKED YO'!!
GULP!! - (-AH DESTROYED HIS IDEEL!! — A HEART-BROKE TEAR IS A-RUNNIN' DOWN HIS LI'L CHEEK!!-)
AHEM!! URPF!! - AH WERE ONLY KIDDIN', CHILE—
IT WERE JACK DEMPSEY—AN' YORE GRAN'PAPPY DID LICK HIM—AN' WIF ONLY ONE HAND, TOO!! -
(-FO'GIVE ME!! — IT WERE JEST A WHITE LIE—AN' IT MADE BOTH TH' CHILLUN HAPPY!!-)

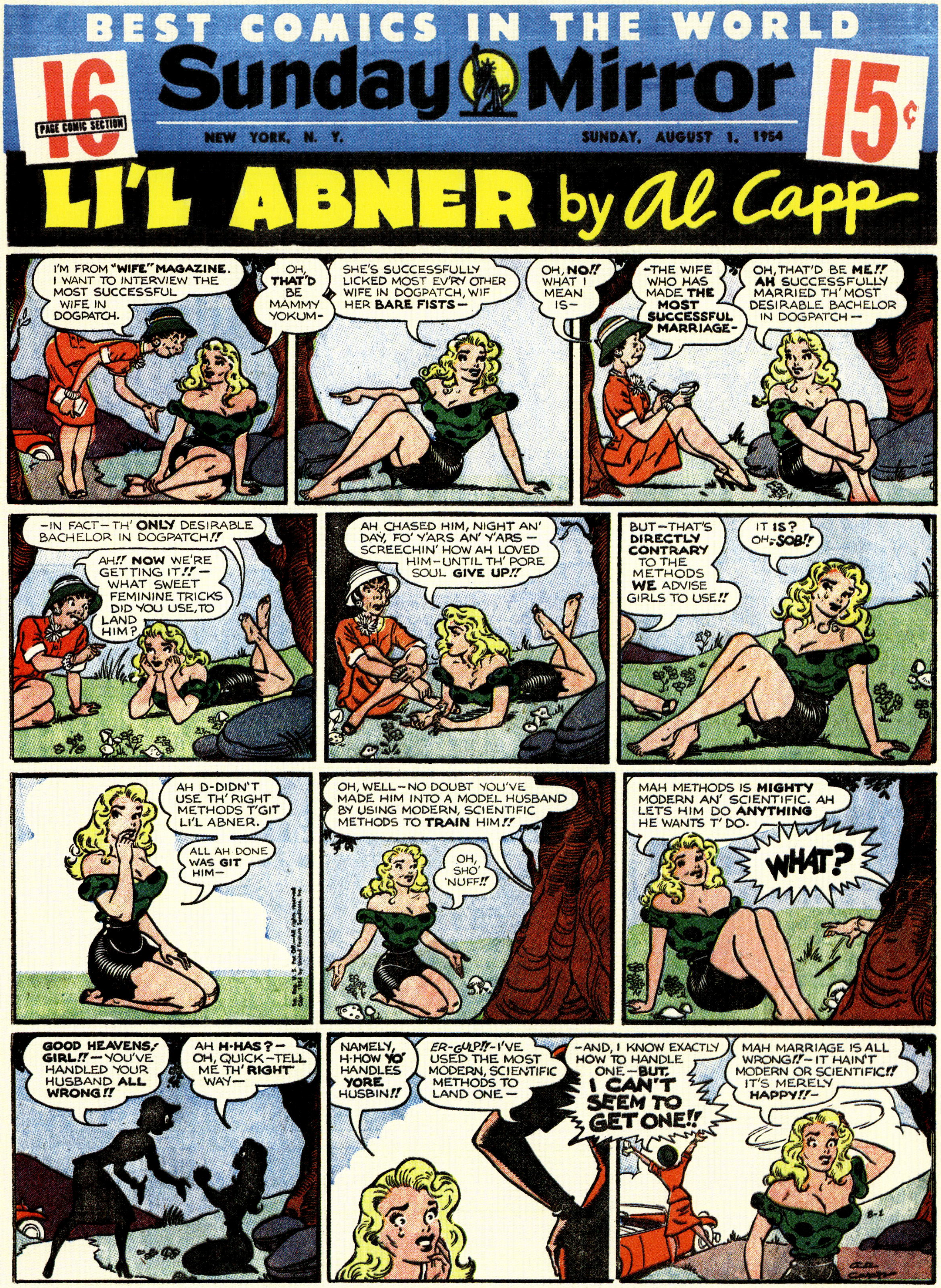

BEST COMICS IN THE WORLD
16
PAGE COMIC SECTION
Sunday Mirror
15¢
NEW YORK, N. Y.
SUNDAY, AUGUST 1, 1954
LI'L ABNER by Al Capp
I'M FROM "WIFE" MAGAZINE. I WANT TO INTERVIEW THE MOST SUCCESSFUL WIFE IN DOGPATCH.
OH, THAT'D BE MAMMY YOKUM-
SHE'S SUCCESSFULLY LICKED MOST EV'RY OTHER WIFE IN DOGPATCH, WIF HER BARE FISTS-
OH, NO!! WHAT I MEAN IS-
-THE WIFE WHO HAS MADE THE MOST SUCCESSFUL MARRIAGE-
OH, THAT'D BE ME!! AH SUCCESSFULLY MARRIED TH' MOST DESIRABLE BACHELOR IN DOGPATCH-
-IN FACT-TH' ONLY DESIRABLE BACHELOR IN DOGPATCH!!
AH!! NOW WE'RE GETTING IT!!-WHAT SWEET FEMININE TRICKS DID YOU USE, TO LAND HIM?
AH CHASED HIM, NIGHT AN' DAY, FO' Y'ARS AN' Y'ARS-SCREECHIN' HOW AH LOVED HIM-UNTIL TH' PORE SOUL GIVE UP!!
BUT-THAT'S DIRECTLY CONTRARY TO THE METHODS WE ADVISE GIRLS TO USE!!
IT IS? OH-SOB!!
AH D-DIDN'T USE TH' RIGHT METHODS T'GIT LI'L ABNER.
ALL AH DONE WAS GIT HIM-
OH, WELL-NO DOUBT YOU'VE MADE HIM INTO A MODEL HUSBAND BY USING MODERN, SCIENTIFIC METHODS TO TRAIN HIM!!
OH, SHO' 'NUFF!!
MAH METHODS IS MIGHTY MODERN AN' SCIENTIFIC. AH LETS HIM DO ANYTHING HE WANTS T' DO.
WHAT?
GOOD HEAVENS, GIRL!!-YOU'VE HANDLED YOUR HUSBAND ALL WRONG!!
AH H-HAS?-OH, QUICK-TELL ME TH' RIGHT WAY-
NAMELY, H-HOW YO' HANDLES YORE HUSBIN!!
ER-GULP!!-I'VE USED THE MOST MODERN, SCIENTIFIC METHODS TO LAND ONE-
-AND, I KNOW EXACTLY HOW TO HANDLE ONE-BUT, I CAN'T SEEM TO GET ONE!!
MAH MARRIAGE IS ALL WRONG!!-IT HAIN'T MODERN OR SCIENTIFIC!! IT'S MERELY HAPPY!!-
8-1

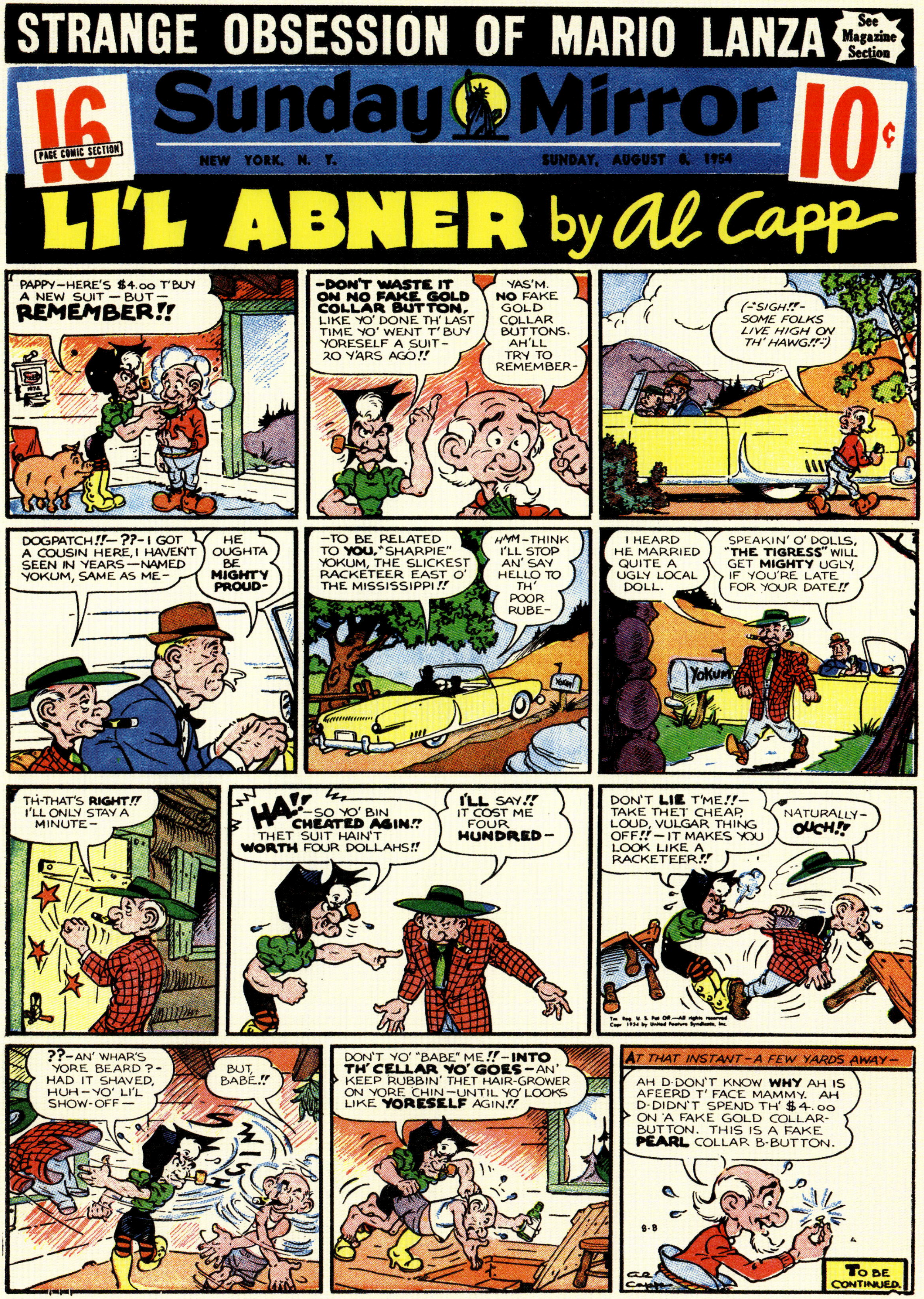

STRANGE OBSESSION OF MARIO LANZA
See Magazine Section
16
PAGE COMIC SECTION
Sunday Mirror
10¢
NEW YORK, N. Y.
SUNDAY, AUGUST 8, 1954
LI'L ABNER by Al Capp
PAPPY—HERE'S $4.00 T'BUY A NEW SUIT—BUT—REMEMBER!!
—DON'T WASTE IT ON NO FAKE GOLD COLLAR BUTTON, LIKE YO' DONE TH' LAST TIME YO' WENT T' BUY YORESELF A SUIT-20 YARS AGO!!
YAS'M. NO FAKE GOLD COLLAR BUTTONS. AH'LL TRY TO REMEMBER-
(-SIGH!!-SOME FOLKS LIVE HIGH ON TH' HAWG!!-)
DOGPATCH!!—??-I GOT A COUSIN HERE, I HAVEN'T SEEN IN YEARS—NAMED YOKUM, SAME AS ME-
HE OUGHTA BE MIGHTY PROUD-
—TO BE RELATED TO YOU, "SHARPIE" YOKUM, THE SLICKEST RACKETEER EAST O' THE MISSISSIPPI!!
HMM—THINK I'LL STOP AN' SAY HELLO TO TH' POOR RUBE-
YOKUM
I HEARD HE MARRIED QUITE A UGLY LOCAL DOLL.
SPEAKIN' O' DOLLS, "THE TIGRESS" WILL GET MIGHTY UGLY, IF YOU'RE LATE FOR YOUR DATE!!
YOKUM
TH-THAT'S RIGHT!! I'LL ONLY STAY A MINUTE-
HA!!—SO YO' BIN CHEATED AGIN!? THET SUIT HAIN'T WORTH FOUR DOLLAHS!!
I'LL SAY!! IT COST ME FOUR HUNDRED-
DON'T LIE T'ME!!—TAKE THET CHEAP, LOUD, VULGAR THING OFF!!—IT MAKES YOU LOOK LIKE A RACKETEER!!
NATURALLY-OUCH!!
??—AN' WHAR'S YORE BEARD?—HAD IT SHAVED, HUH—YO' LI'L SHOW-OFF—
BUT, BABE!!
SWISH
DON'T YO' "BABE" ME!!—INTO TH' CELLAR YO' GOES—AN' KEEP RUBBIN' THET HAIR-GROWER ON YORE CHIN—UNTIL YO' LOOKS LIKE YORESELF AGIN!!
AT THAT INSTANT—A FEW YARDS AWAY—
AH D-DON'T KNOW WHY AH IS AFEERD T' FACE MAMMY. AH D-DIDN'T SPEND TH' $4.00 ON A FAKE GOLD COLLAR-BUTTON. THIS IS A FAKE PEARL COLLAR B-BUTTON.
8-8
Al Capp
TO BE CONTINUED.

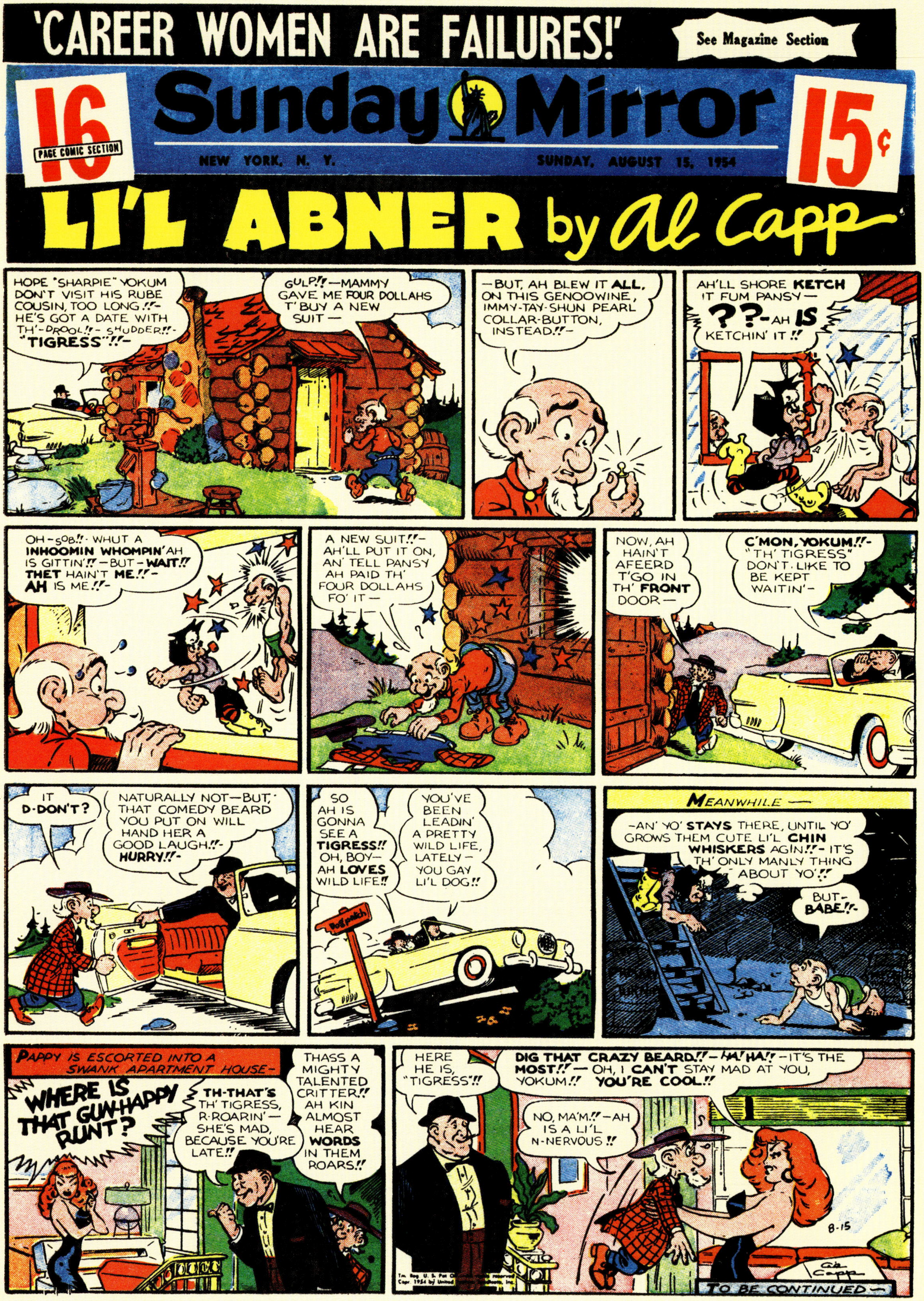

'CAREER WOMEN ARE FAILURES!'
See Magazine Section
16 PAGE COMIC SECTION
Sunday Mirror
15¢
NEW YORK, N. Y.
SUNDAY, AUGUST 15, 1954
LI'L ABNER by Al Capp
HOPE "SHARPIE" YOKUM DON'T VISIT HIS RUBE COUSIN, TOO LONG!! - HE'S GOT A DATE WITH TH'-DROOL!!-SHUDDER!!- "TIGRESS"!!-
GULP!!-MAMMY GAVE ME FOUR DOLLAHS T' BUY A NEW SUIT-
-BUT, AH BLEW IT ALL, ON THIS GENOOWINE, IMMY-TAY-SHUN PEARL COLLAR-BUTTON, INSTEAD!!-
AH'LL SHORE KETCH IT FUM PANSY-
??-AH IS KETCHIN' IT!!
OH-SOB!!-WHUT A INHOOMIN WHOMPIN' AH IS GITTIN'!!-BUT-WAIT!! THET HAIN'T ME!!- AH IS ME!!-
A NEW SUIT!!- AH'LL PUT IT ON, AN' TELL PANSY AH PAID TH' FOUR DOLLAHS FO' IT-
NOW, AH HAIN'T AFEERD T'GO IN TH' FRONT DOOR-
C'MON, YOKUM!!- "TH' TIGRESS" DON'T LIKE TO BE KEPT WAITIN'-
IT D-DON'T?
NATURALLY NOT-BUT, THAT COMEDY BEARD YOU PUT ON WILL HAND HER A GOOD LAUGH!!- HURRY!!-
SO AH IS GONNA SEE A TIGRESS!! OH, BOY- AH LOVES WILD LIFE!!
YOU'VE BEEN LEADIN' A PRETTY WILD LIFE, LATELY- YOU GAY LI'L DOG!!
MEANWHILE-
-AN' YO' STAYS THERE, UNTIL YO' GROWS THEM CUTE LI'L CHIN WHISKERS AGIN!!-IT'S TH' ONLY MANLY THING ABOUT YO'!!
BUT- BABE!!-
PAPPY IS ESCORTED INTO A SWANK APARTMENT HOUSE-
WHERE IS THAT GUN-HAPPY RUNT?
TH-THAT'S TH' TIGRESS, R-ROARIN'- SHE'S MAD, BECAUSE YOU'RE LATE!!
THASS A MIGHTY TALENTED CRITTER!! AH KIN ALMOST HEAR WORDS IN THEM ROARS!!
HERE HE IS, "TIGRESS"!!
DIG THAT CRAZY BEARD!!-HA! HA!!-IT'S THE MOST!!-OH, I CAN'T STAY MAD AT YOU, YOKUM!! YOU'RE COOL!!
NO, MA'M!!-AH IS A LI'L N-NERVOUS!!
8-15
Al Capp
TO BE CONTINUED-

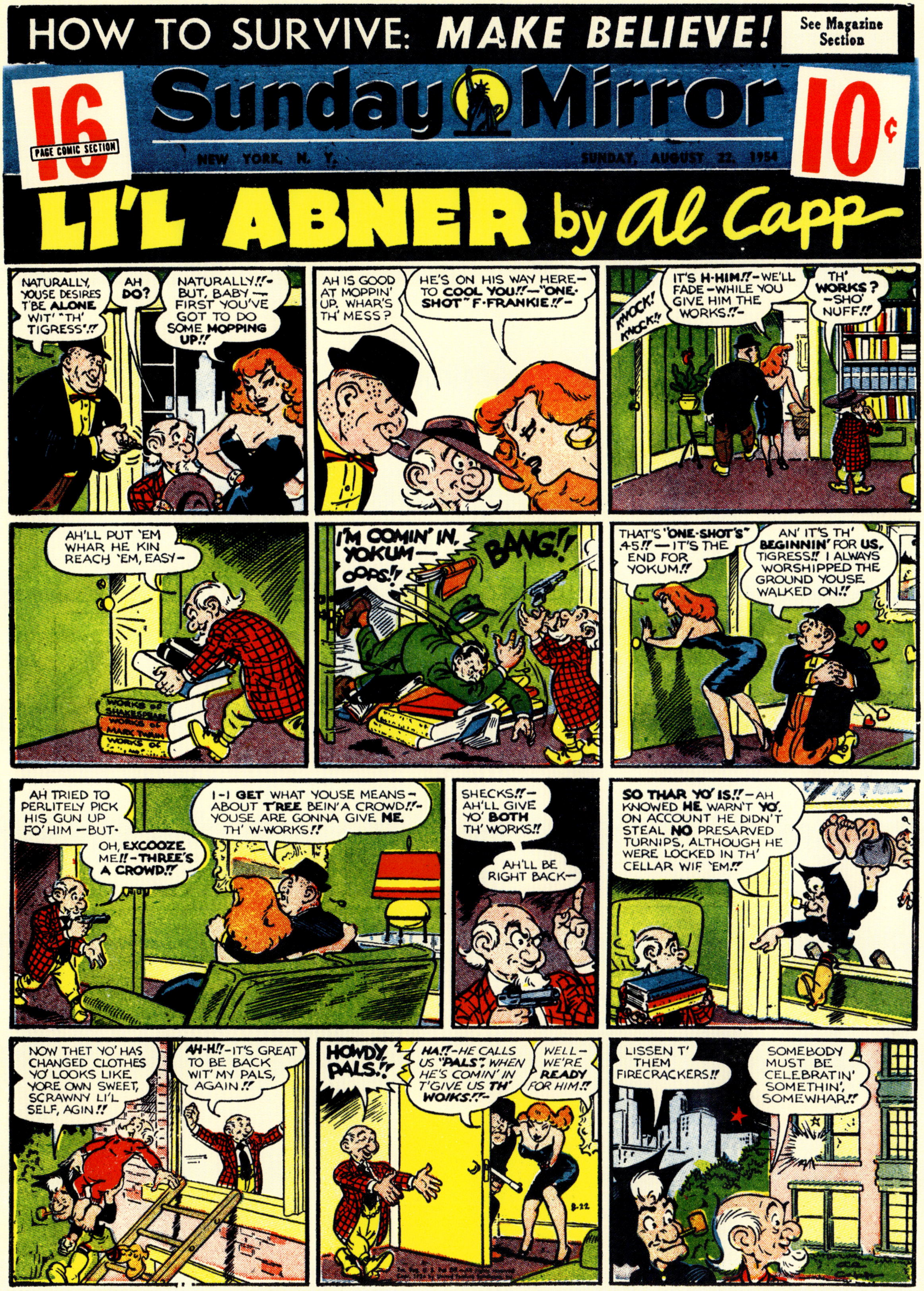

HOW TO SURVIVE: MAKE BELIEVE!
See Magazine Section
16 PAGE COMIC SECTION
Sunday Mirror
NEW YORK, N. Y.
SUNDAY, AUGUST 22, 1954
10¢
LI'L ABNER by Al Capp
NATURALLY, YOUSE DESIRES T'BE ALONE WIT' "TH' TIGRESS"!?
AH DO?
NATURALLY!!- BUT, BABY — FIRST YOU'VE GOT TO DO SOME MOPPING UP!!
AH IS GOOD AT MOPPIN' UP. WHAR'S TH' MESS?
HE'S ON HIS WAY HERE— TO COOL YOU!!—"ONE-SHOT" F-FRANKIE!!—
KNOCK! KNOCK!!
IT'S H-HIM!!—WE'LL FADE—WHILE YOU GIVE HIM THE WORKS!!—
TH' WORKS? —SHO' NUFF!!
AH'LL PUT 'EM WHAR HE KIN REACH 'EM, EASY—
I'M COMIN' IN, YOKUM—
OOPS!!
BANG!!
THAT'S "ONE-SHOT'S" .45!!—IT'S THE END FOR YOKUM!!
AN' IT'S TH' BEGINNIN' FOR US, TIGRESS!! I ALWAYS WORSHIPPED THE GROUND YOUSE WALKED ON!!
AH TRIED TO PERLITELY PICK HIS GUN UP FO' HIM — BUT-
OH, EXCOOZE ME!!—THREE'S A CROWD!!
I-I GET WHAT YOUSE MEANS— ABOUT T'REE BEIN' A CROWD!!— YOUSE ARE GONNA GIVE ME TH' W-WORKS!!
SHECKS!!— AH'LL GIVE YO' BOTH TH' WORKS!!
AH'LL BE RIGHT BACK—
SO THAR YO' IS!!—AH KNOWED HE WARN'T YO', ON ACCOUNT HE DIDN'T STEAL NO PRESARVED TURNIPS, ALTHOUGH HE WERE LOCKED IN TH' CELLAR WIF 'EM!!
NOW THET YO' HAS CHANGED CLOTHES YO' LOOKS LIKE YORE OWN SWEET, SCRAWNY LI'L SELF, AGIN!!
AH-H!!—IT'S GREAT TO BE BACK WIT' MY PALS, AGAIN!!
HOWDY, PALS!!
HA!!—HE CALLS US "PALS," WHEN HE'S COMIN' IN T'GIVE US TH' WOIKS!!—
WELL— WE'RE READY FOR HIM!!
LISSEN T' THEM FIRECRACKERS!!
SOMEBODY MUST BE CELEBRATIN' SOMETHIN', SOMEWHAR!!

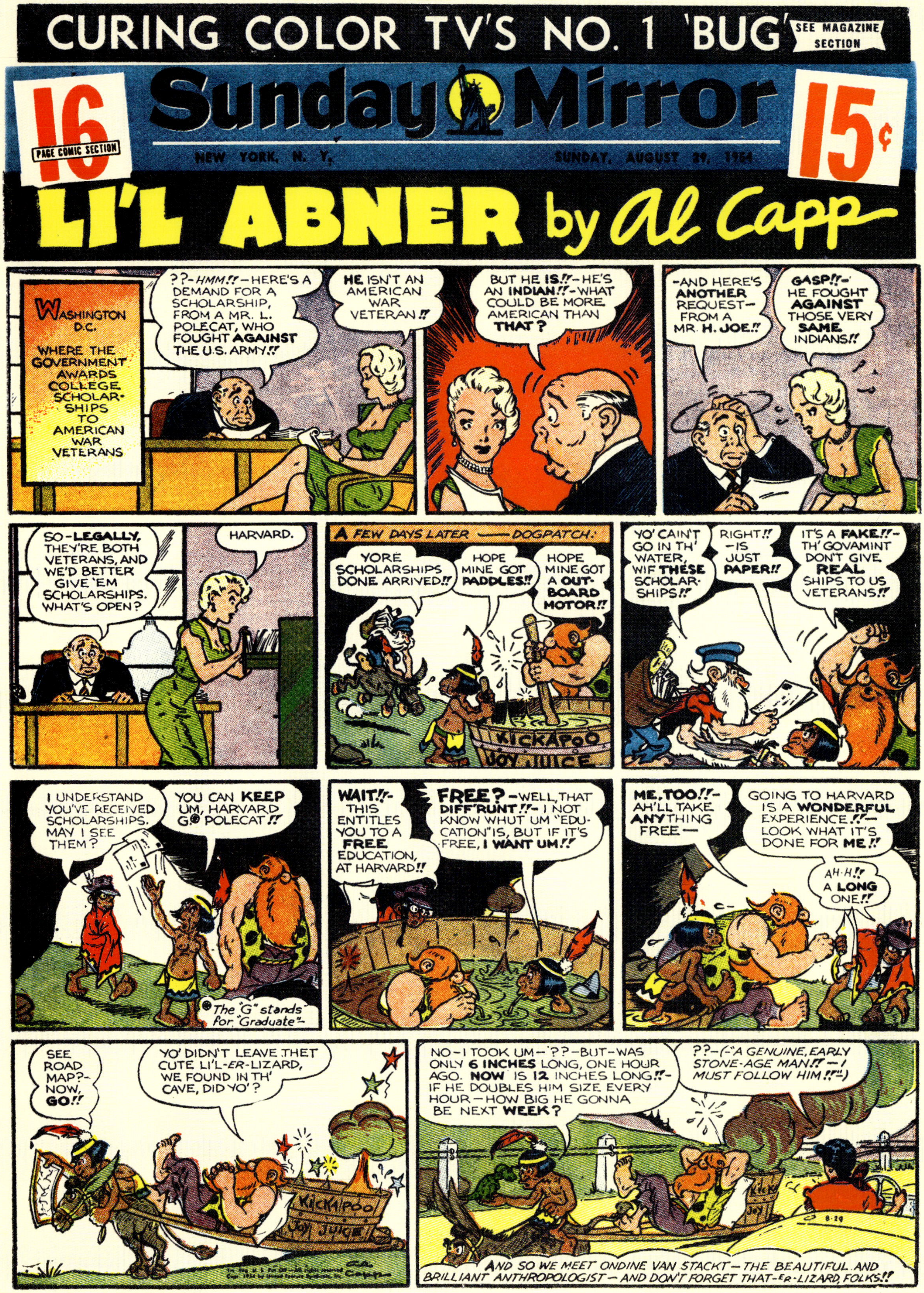

CURING COLOR TV'S NO. 1 'BUG'
SEE MAGAZINE SECTION
16 PAGE COMIC SECTION
Sunday Mirror
15¢
NEW YORK, N. Y.
SUNDAY, AUGUST 29, 1954
LI'L ABNER by Al Capp
WASHINGTON D.C. WHERE THE GOVERNMENT AWARDS COLLEGE SCHOLARSHIPS TO AMERICAN WAR VETERANS
??-HMM!!-HERE'S A DEMAND FOR A SCHOLARSHIP, FROM A MR. L. POLECAT, WHO FOUGHT AGAINST THE U.S. ARMY!!
HE ISN'T AN AMERICAN WAR VETERAN!!
BUT HE IS!!-HE'S AN INDIAN!!-WHAT COULD BE MORE AMERICAN THAN THAT?
-AND HERE'S ANOTHER REQUEST-FROM A MR. H. JOE.!!
GASP!!-HE FOUGHT AGAINST THOSE VERY SAME INDIANS!!
SO-LEGALLY, THEY'RE BOTH VETERANS, AND WE'D BETTER GIVE 'EM SCHOLARSHIPS. WHAT'S OPEN?
HARVARD.
A FEW DAYS LATER —— DOGPATCH:
YORE SCHOLARSHIPS DONE ARRIVED!!
HOPE MINE GOT PADDLES!!
HOPE MINE GOT A OUT-BOARD MOTOR!!
KICKAPOO JOY JUICE
YO' CAIN'T GO IN TH' WATER, WIF THESE SCHOLARSHIPS!!
RIGHT!!-IS JUST PAPER!!
IT'S A FAKE!!-TH' GOVAMINT DON'T GIVE REAL SHIPS TO US VETERANS!!
I UNDERSTAND YOU'VE RECEIVED SCHOLARSHIPS. MAY I SEE THEM?
YOU CAN KEEP UM, HARVARD G.* POLECAT!!
*The "G" stands for "Graduate"-
WAIT!!-THIS ENTITLES YOU TO A FREE EDUCATION, AT HARVARD!!
FREE?-WELL, THAT DIFF'RUNT!!-I NOT KNOW WHUT UM "EDUCATION" IS, BUT IF IT'S FREE, I WANT UM!!
ME, TOO!!-AH'LL TAKE ANYTHING FREE—
GOING TO HARVARD IS A WONDERFUL EXPERIENCE!!-LOOK WHAT IT'S DONE FOR ME!!
AH-H!! A LONG ONE!!
SEE ROAD MAP?-NOW, GO!!
YO' DIDN'T LEAVE THET CUTE LI'L-ER-LIZARD, WE FOUND IN TH' CAVE, DID YO'?
KICKAPOO JOY JUICE
NO-I TOOK UM-??-BUT-WAS ONLY 6 INCHES LONG, ONE HOUR AGO. NOW IS 12 INCHES LONG!!-IF HE DOUBLES HIM SIZE EVERY HOUR-HOW BIG HE GONNA BE NEXT WEEK?
??-("A GENUINE, EARLY STONE-AGE MAN!!-I MUST FOLLOW HIM!!")
AND SO WE MEET ONDINE VAN STACKT-THE BEAUTIFUL AND BRILLIANT ANTHROPOLOGIST-AND DON'T FORGET THAT-ER-LIZARD, FOLKS!!

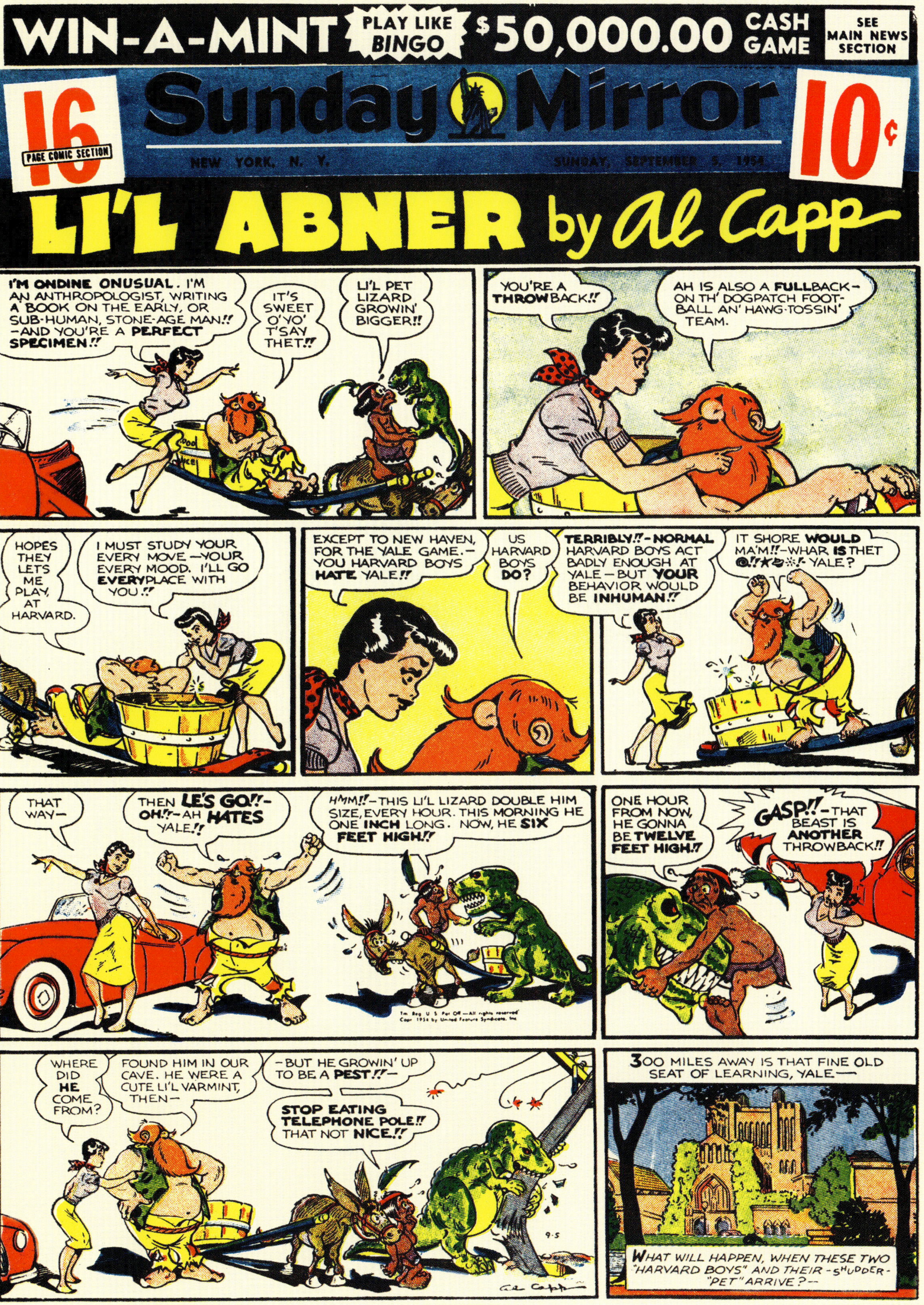
WIN-A-MINT
PLAY LIKE BINGO
$50,000.00 CASH GAME
SEE MAIN NEWS SECTION
16 PAGE COMIC SECTION
Sunday Mirror
NEW YORK, N. Y.
SUNDAY, SEPTEMBER 5, 1954
10¢
LI'L ABNER by Al Capp
I'M ONDINE ONUSUAL. I'M AN ANTHROPOLOGIST, WRITING A BOOK ON THE EARLY, OR SUB-HUMAN, STONE-AGE MAN!! -AND YOU'RE A PERFECT SPECIMEN!!
IT'S SWEET O'YO' T'SAY THET!!
LI'L PET LIZARD GROWIN' BIGGER!!
YOU'RE A THROWBACK!!
AH IS ALSO A FULLBACK— ON TH' DOGPATCH FOOT-BALL AN' HAWG-TOSSIN' TEAM.
HOPES THEY LETS ME PLAY, AT HARVARD.
I MUST STUDY YOUR EVERY MOVE—YOUR EVERY MOOD. I'LL GO EVERYPLACE WITH YOU.!!
EXCEPT TO NEW HAVEN, FOR THE YALE GAME.— YOU HARVARD BOYS HATE YALE!!
US HARVARD BOYS DO?
TERRIBLY!!—NORMAL HARVARD BOYS ACT BADLY ENOUGH AT YALE—BUT YOUR BEHAVIOR WOULD BE INHUMAN!!
IT SHORE WOULD MA'M!!—WHAR IS THET @!!★☆☆!- YALE?
THAT WAY—
THEN LE'S GO!!- OH!!—AH HATES YALE!!
HMM!!—THIS LI'L LIZARD DOUBLE HIM SIZE, EVERY HOUR. THIS MORNING HE ONE INCH LONG. NOW, HE SIX FEET HIGH!!
ONE HOUR FROM NOW, HE GONNA BE TWELVE FEET HIGH!!
GASP!!—THAT BEAST IS ANOTHER THROWBACK!!
WHERE DID HE COME FROM?
FOUND HIM IN OUR CAVE. HE WERE A CUTE LI'L VARMINT, THEN—
—BUT HE GROWIN' UP TO BE A PEST!!—
STOP EATING TELEPHONE POLE!! THAT NOT NICE!!
300 MILES AWAY IS THAT FINE OLD SEAT OF LEARNING, YALE—
WHAT WILL HAPPEN, WHEN THESE TWO "HARVARD BOYS" AND THEIR -SHUDDER- "PET" ARRIVE?—
9-5
Al Capp

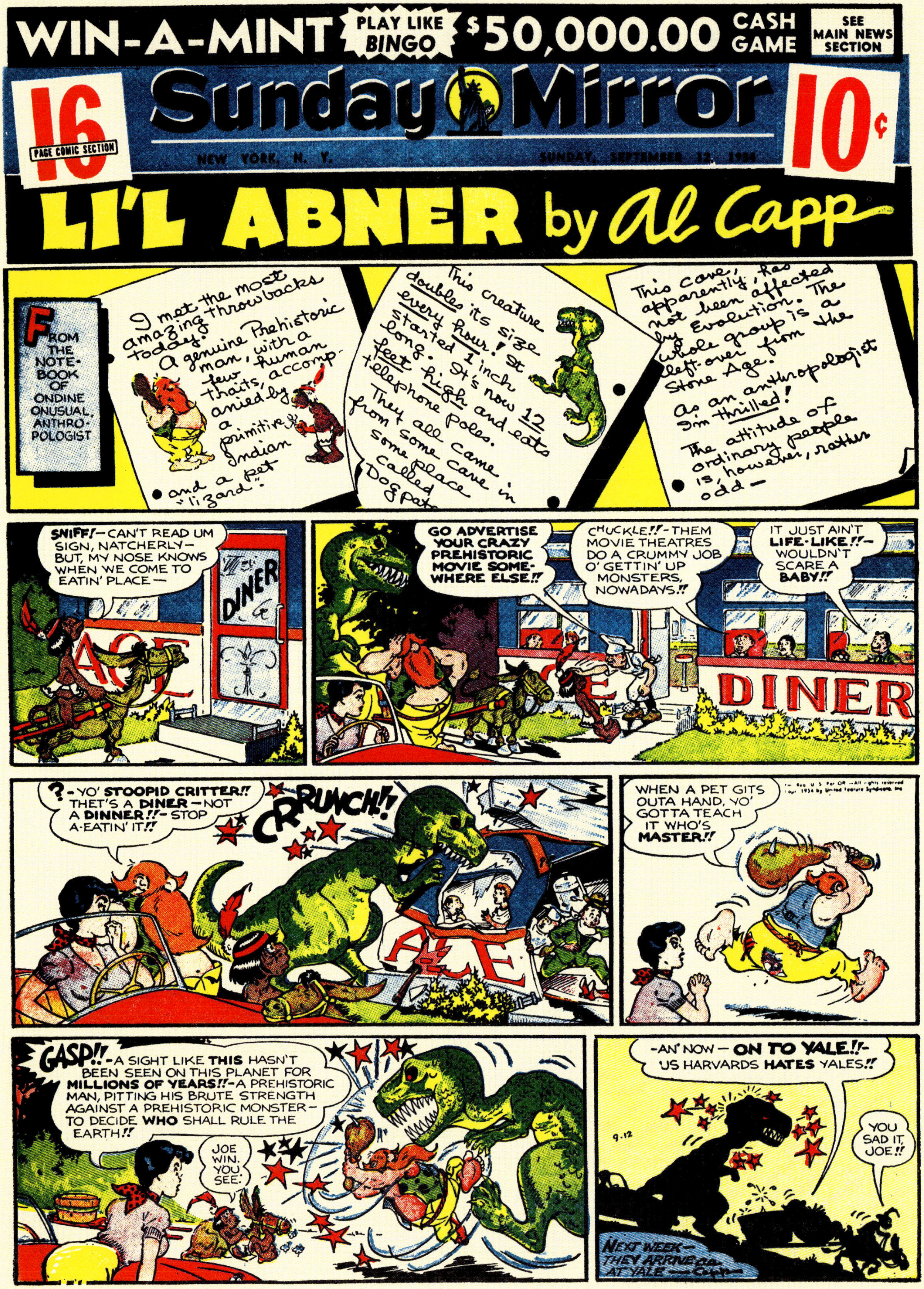

WIN-A-MINT
PLAY LIKE BINGO
$50,000.00 CASH GAME
SEE MAIN NEWS SECTION
16 PAGE COMIC SECTION
Sunday Mirror
10¢
NEW YORK, N. Y.
SUNDAY, SEPTEMBER 12, 1954
LI'L ABNER by Al Capp
FROM THE NOTE-BOOK OF ONDINE ONUSUAL, ANTHRO-POLOGIST
I met the most amazing throwbacks today. A genuine Prehistoric man, with a few human traits, accompanied by a primitive Indian and a pet "lizard".
This creature doubles its size every hour! It started 1 inch long. It's now 12 feet high and eats telephone poles. They all came from some cave in some place called Dogpatch
This cave, apparently, has not been affected by Evolution. The whole group is a left-over from the Stone Age. As an anthropologist I'm thrilled! The attitude of ordinary people is, however, rather odd –
SNIFF! – CAN'T READ UM SIGN, NATCHERLY – BUT, MY NOSE KNOWS WHEN WE COME TO EATIN' PLACE –
DINER
GO ADVERTISE YOUR CRAZY PREHISTORIC MOVIE SOMEWHERE ELSE!!
CHUCKLE!! – THEM MOVIE THEATRES DO A CRUMMY JOB O' GETTIN' UP MONSTERS, NOWADAYS!!
IT JUST AIN'T LIFE-LIKE!! – WOULDN'T SCARE A BABY!!
DINER
?– YO' STOOPID CRITTER!! THET'S A DINER – NOT A DINNER!! – STOP A-EATIN' IT!!
CRRUNCH!!
WHEN A PET GITS OUTA HAND, YO' GOTTA TEACH IT WHO'S MASTER!!
GASP!! – A SIGHT LIKE THIS HASN'T BEEN SEEN ON THIS PLANET FOR MILLIONS OF YEARS!! – A PREHISTORIC MAN, PITTING HIS BRUTE STRENGTH AGAINST A PREHISTORIC MONSTER – TO DECIDE WHO SHALL RULE THE EARTH!!
JOE WIN. YOU SEE.
– AN' NOW – ON TO YALE!! – US HARVARDS HATES YALES!!
YOU SAID IT, JOE!!
9-12
NEXT WEEK – THEY ARRIVE AT YALE – Capp

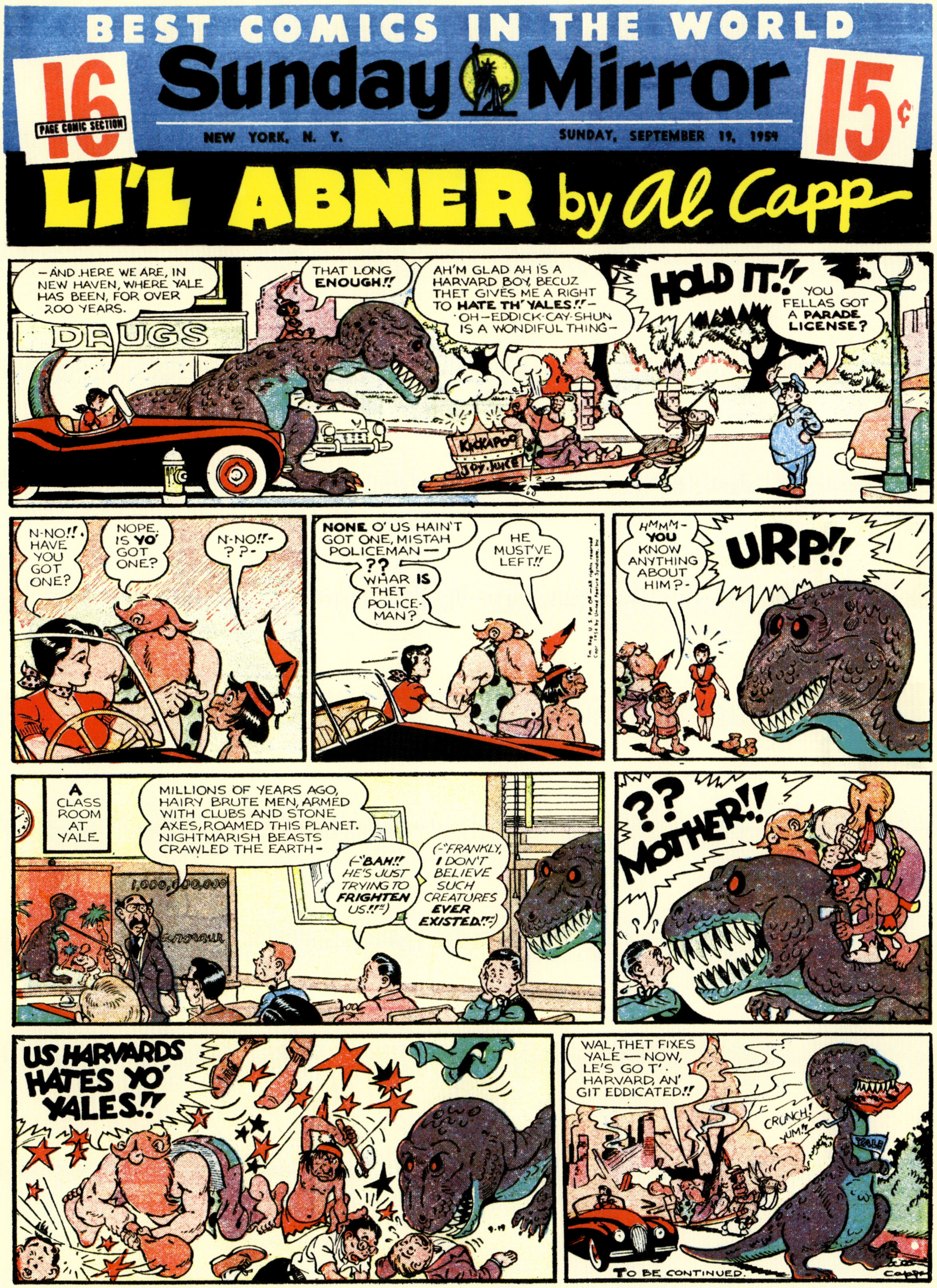

BEST COMICS IN THE WORLD
16
PAGE COMIC SECTION
Sunday Mirror
15¢
NEW YORK, N. Y.
SUNDAY, SEPTEMBER 19, 1954
LI'L ABNER by Al Capp
—AND HERE WE ARE, IN NEW HAVEN, WHERE YALE HAS BEEN, FOR OVER 200 YEARS.
DRUGS
THAT LONG ENOUGH!!
AH'M GLAD AH IS A HARVARD BOY, BECUZ THET GIVES ME A RIGHT TO HATE TH' YALES!!—OH—EDDICK-CAY-SHUN IS A WONDIFUL THING—
KICKAPOO JOY JUICE
HOLD IT!!
YOU FELLAS GOT A PARADE LICENSE?
N-NO!! HAVE YOU GOT ONE?
NOPE. IS YO' GOT ONE?
N-NO!!-??-
NONE O' US HAIN'T GOT ONE, MISTAH POLICEMAN—
??
WHAR IS THET POLICE-MAN?
HE MUST'VE LEFT!!
HMMM-YOU KNOW ANYTHING ABOUT HIM?-
URP!!
A CLASS ROOM AT YALE
MILLIONS OF YEARS AGO, HAIRY BRUTE MEN, ARMED WITH CLUBS AND STONE AXES, ROAMED THIS PLANET. NIGHTMARISH BEASTS CRAWLED THE EARTH—
(—"BAH!! HE'S JUST TRYING TO FRIGHTEN US!!"—)
(—"FRANKLY, I DON'T BELIEVE SUCH CREATURES EVER EXISTED!!"—)
??
MOTHER!!
US HARVARDS HATES YO' YALES!!
WAL, THET FIXES YALE—NOW, LE'S GO T' HARVARD AN' GIT EDDICATED!!
CRUNCH! YUM!
YALE
TO BE CONTINUED.
CAPP

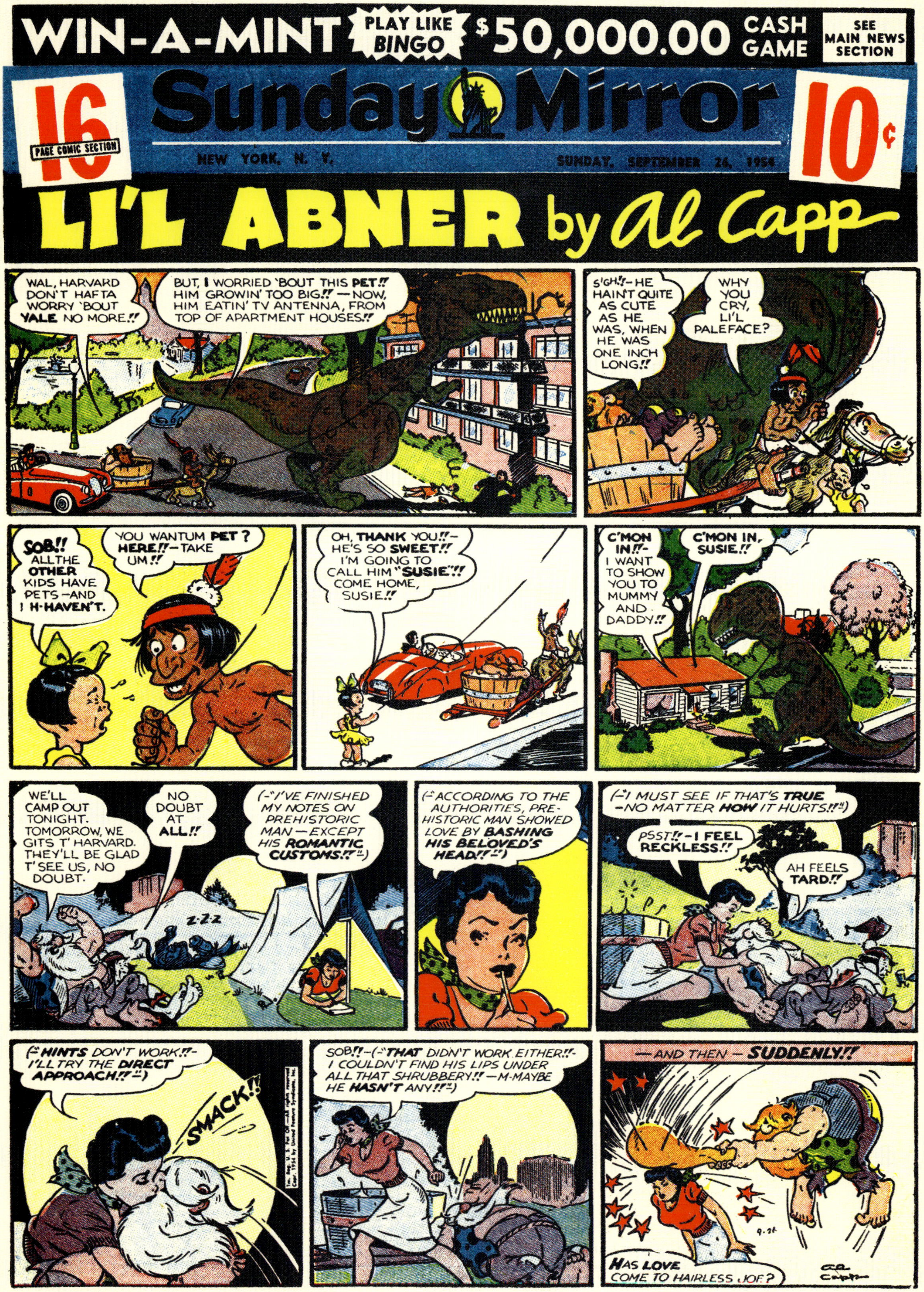
WIN-A-MINT
PLAY LIKE BINGO
$50,000.00 CASH GAME
SEE MAIN NEWS SECTION
16 PAGE COMIC SECTION
Sunday Mirror
NEW YORK, N. Y.
SUNDAY, SEPTEMBER 26, 1954
10¢
LI'L ABNER by Al Capp
WAL, HARVARD DON'T HAFTA WORRY 'BOUT YALE NO MORE.!!
BUT, I WORRIED 'BOUT THIS PET!! HIM GROWIN' TOO BIG!! — NOW, HIM EATIN' TV ANTENNA, FROM TOP OF APARTMENT HOUSES!!
S'IGH!!— HE HAIN'T QUITE AS CUTE AS HE WAS, WHEN HE WAS ONE INCH LONG!!
WHY YOU CRY, LI'L PALEFACE?
SOB!! ALL THE OTHER KIDS HAVE PETS—AND I H-HAVEN'T.
YOU WANTUM PET? HERE!!—TAKE UM!!
OH, THANK YOU!!— HE'S SO SWEET!! I'M GOING TO CALL HIM "SUSIE"!! COME HOME, SUSIE.!!
C'MON IN!!— I WANT TO SHOW YOU TO MUMMY AND DADDY!!
C'MON IN, SUSIE.!!
WE'LL CAMP OUT TONIGHT. TOMORROW, WE GITS T' HARVARD. THEY'LL BE GLAD T' SEE US, NO DOUBT.
NO DOUBT AT ALL!!
Z-Z-Z
(—"I'VE FINISHED MY NOTES ON PREHISTORIC MAN—EXCEPT HIS ROMANTIC CUSTOMS!!"—)
(—"ACCORDING TO THE AUTHORITIES, PREHISTORIC MAN SHOWED LOVE BY BASHING HIS BELOVED'S HEAD!!"—)
(—"I MUST SEE IF THAT'S TRUE —NO MATTER HOW IT HURTS!!"—)
PSST!!—I FEEL RECKLESS.!!
AH FEELS TARD.!!
(—"HINTS DON'T WORK!!— I'LL TRY THE DIRECT APPROACH!!"—)
SMACK!!
SOB!!—(—"THAT DIDN'T WORK EITHER!!— I COULDN'T FIND HIS LIPS UNDER ALL THAT SHRUBBERY!!—M-MAYBE HE HASN'T ANY!!"—)
—AND THEN — SUDDENLY!!
HAS LOVE COME TO HAIRLESS JOE?
9-26
AL CAPP

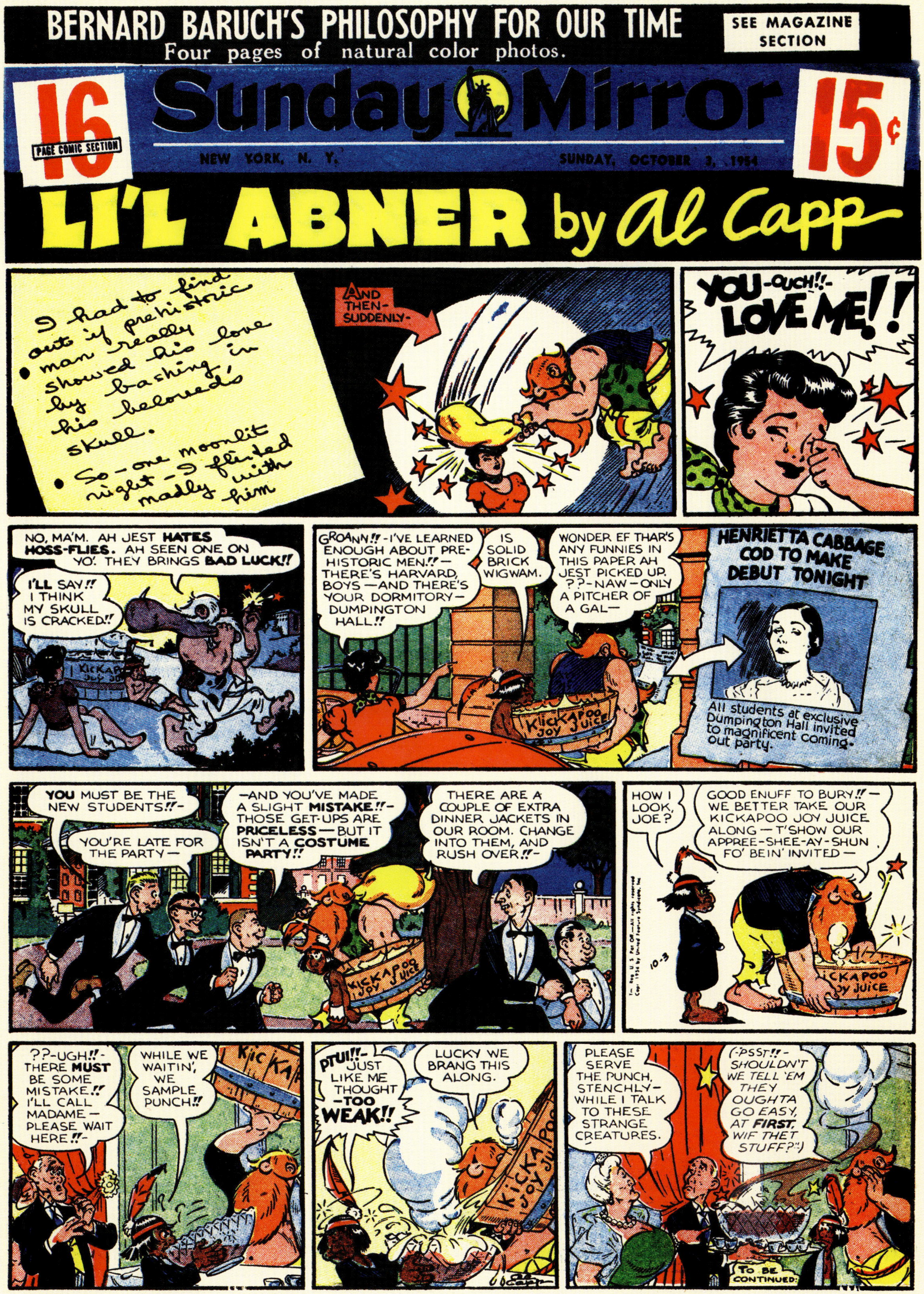
BERNARD BARUCH'S PHILOSOPHY FOR OUR TIME
Four pages of natural color photos.
SEE MAGAZINE SECTION
16
PAGE COMIC SECTION
Sunday Mirror
NEW YORK, N. Y.
SUNDAY, OCTOBER 3, 1954
15¢
LI'L ABNER by Al Capp
I had to find out if prehistoric man really showed his love by bashing in his beloved's skull.
• So - one moonlit night - I flirted madly with him
AND THEN-SUDDENLY-
YOU-OUCH!!-LOVE ME!!
NO, MA'M. AH JEST HATES HOSS-FLIES. AH SEEN ONE ON YO'. THEY BRINGS BAD LUCK!!
I'LL SAY!! I THINK MY SKULL IS CRACKED!!
GROANN!! - I'VE LEARNED ENOUGH ABOUT PREHISTORIC MEN!! - THERE'S HARVARD, BOYS - AND THERE'S YOUR DORMITORY - DUMPINGTON HALL!!
IS SOLID BRICK WIGWAM.
WONDER EF THAR'S ANY FUNNIES IN THIS PAPER AH JEST PICKED UP. ??-NAW-ONLY A PITCHER OF A GAL-
HENRIETTA CABBAGE COD TO MAKE DEBUT TONIGHT
All students at exclusive Dumpington Hall invited to magnificent coming-out party.
KICKAPOO JOY JUICE
YOU MUST BE THE NEW STUDENTS!!-
YOU'RE LATE FOR THE PARTY-
-AND YOU'VE MADE A SLIGHT MISTAKE!!- THOSE GET-UPS ARE PRICELESS - BUT IT ISN'T A COSTUME PARTY!!
THERE ARE A COUPLE OF EXTRA DINNER JACKETS IN OUR ROOM. CHANGE INTO THEM, AND RUSH OVER!!-
KICKAPOO JOY JUICE
HOW I LOOK, JOE?
GOOD ENUFF TO BURY!! - WE BETTER TAKE OUR KICKAPOO JOY JUICE ALONG - T'SHOW OUR APPREE-SHEE-AY-SHUN FO' BEIN' INVITED -
10-3
KICKAPOO JOY JUICE
??-UGH!!- THERE MUST BE SOME MISTAKE!! I'LL CALL MADAME - PLEASE WAIT HERE!!-
WHILE WE WAITIN', WE SAMPLE PUNCH!!
KICKA
PTUI!!- JUST LIKE ME THOUGHT -TOO WEAK!!
LUCKY WE BRANG THIS ALONG.
KICKAPOO JOY JUICE
PLEASE SERVE THE PUNCH, STENCHLY - WHILE I TALK TO THESE STRANGE CREATURES.
(-PSST!!- SHOULDN'T WE TELL 'EM THEY OUGHTA GO EASY, AT FIRST, WIF THET STUFF?")
TO BE CONTINUED

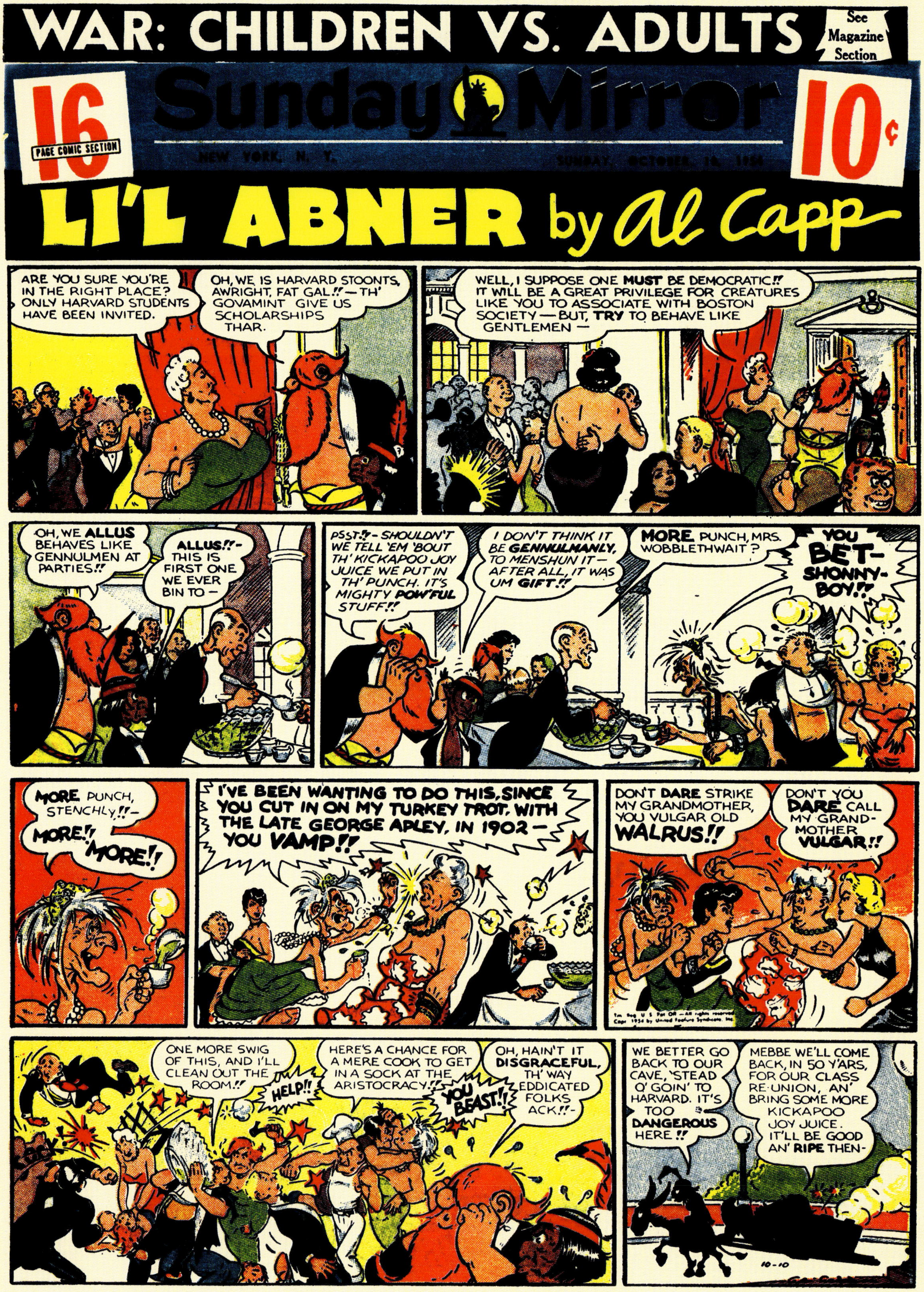
WAR: CHILDREN VS. ADULTS
See Magazine Section
16
PAGE COMIC SECTION
Sunday Mirror
NEW YORK, N. Y.
10¢
LI'L ABNER by Al Capp
ARE YOU SURE YOU'RE IN THE RIGHT PLACE? ONLY HARVARD STUDENTS HAVE BEEN INVITED.
OH, WE IS HARVARD STOONTS, AWRIGHT, FAT GAL!!—TH' GOVAMINT GIVE US SCHOLARSHIPS THAR.
WELL, I SUPPOSE ONE MUST BE DEMOCRATIC!! IT WILL BE A GREAT PRIVILEGE FOR CREATURES LIKE YOU TO ASSOCIATE WITH BOSTON SOCIETY—BUT, TRY TO BEHAVE LIKE GENTLEMEN—
OH, WE ALLUS BEHAVES LIKE GENNULMEN AT PARTIES!!
ALLUS!!—THIS IS FIRST ONE WE EVER BIN TO—
PSST!!—SHOULDN'T WE TELL 'EM 'BOUT TH' KICKAPOO JOY JUICE WE PUT IN TH' PUNCH. IT'S MIGHTY POW'FUL STUFF!!
I DON'T THINK IT BE GENNULMANLY, TO MENSHUN IT—AFTER ALL, IT WAS UM GIFT!!
MORE PUNCH, MRS. WOBBLETHWAIT?
YOU BET—SHONNY-BOY!!
MORE PUNCH, STENCHLY!!—
MORE!! MORE!!
I'VE BEEN WANTING TO DO THIS, SINCE YOU CUT IN ON MY TURKEY TROT, WITH THE LATE GEORGE APLEY, IN 1902—YOU VAMP!!
DON'T DARE STRIKE MY GRANDMOTHER, YOU VULGAR OLD WALRUS!!
DON'T YOU DARE CALL MY GRANDMOTHER VULGAR!!
ONE MORE SWIG OF THIS, AND I'LL CLEAN OUT THE ROOM!!
HELP!!
HERE'S A CHANCE FOR A MERE COOK TO GET IN A SOCK AT THE ARISTOCRACY!!
YOU BEAST!!
OH, HAIN'T IT DISGRACEFUL, TH' WAY EDDICATED FOLKS ACK!!—
WE BETTER GO BACK TO OUR CAVE, 'STEAD O' GOIN' TO HARVARD. IT'S TOO DANGEROUS HERE!!
MEBBE WE'LL COME BACK, IN 50 Y'ARS, FOR OUR CLASS RE-UNION, AN' BRING SOME MORE KICKAPOO JOY JUICE. IT'LL BE GOOD AN' RIPE THEN—
10-10

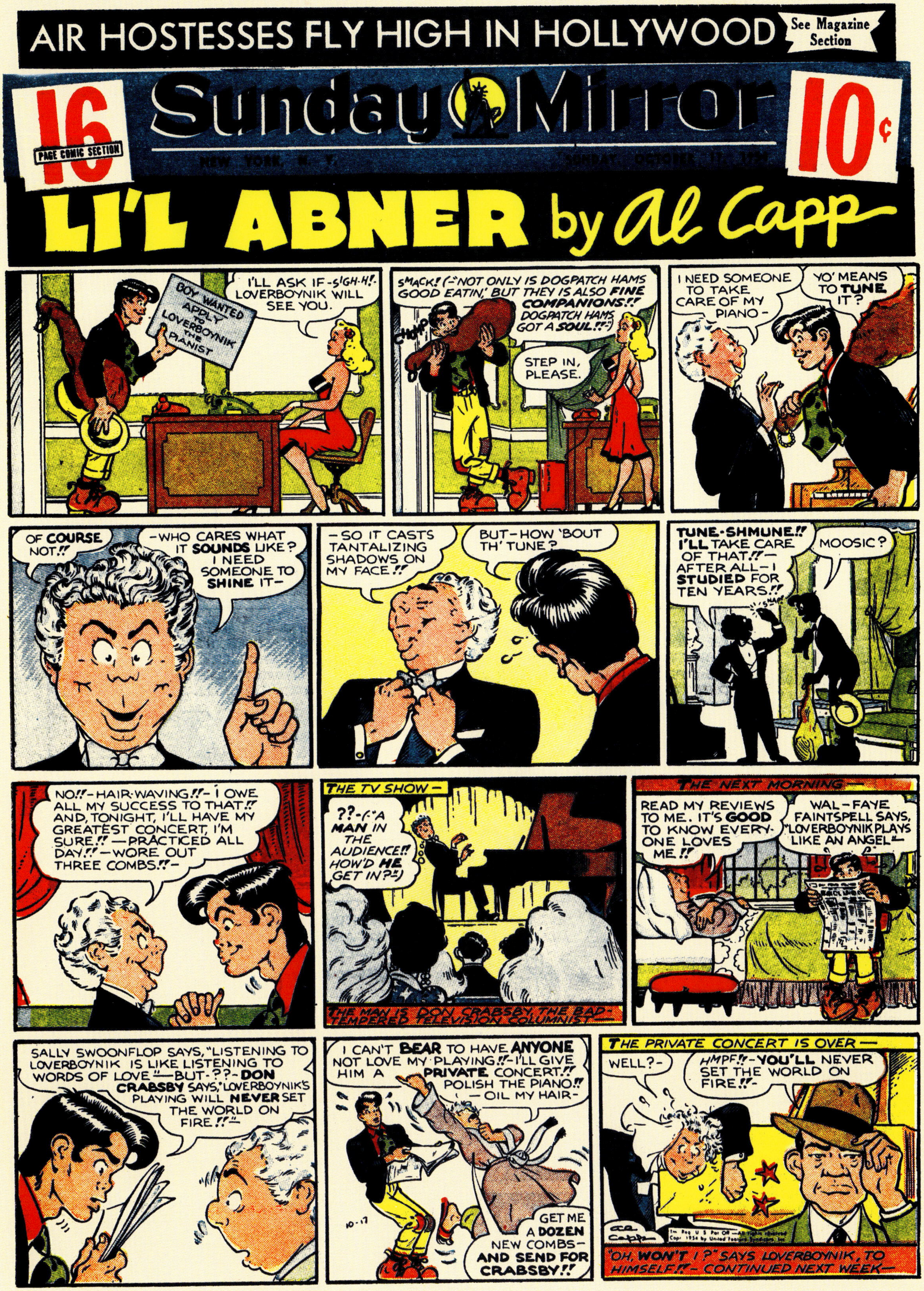

AIR HOSTESSES FLY HIGH IN HOLLYWOOD
See Magazine Section
16 PAGE COMIC SECTION
Sunday Mirror
NEW YORK, N. Y.
10¢
LI'L ABNER by Al Capp
BOY WANTED APPLY TO LOVERBOYNIK THE PIANIST
I'LL ASK IF -SIGH-H!- LOVERBOYNIK WILL SEE YOU.
SMACK!! (-"NOT ONLY IS DOGPATCH HAMS GOOD EATIN,' BUT THEY IS ALSO FINE COMPANIONS!!" DOGPATCH HAMS GOT A SOUL!!"-)
STEP IN, PLEASE.
I NEED SOMEONE TO TAKE CARE OF MY PIANO-
YO' MEANS TO TUNE IT?
OF COURSE NOT!!
-WHO CARES WHAT IT SOUNDS LIKE? I NEED SOMEONE TO SHINE IT-
-SO IT CASTS TANTALIZING SHADOWS ON MY FACE!!
BUT-HOW 'BOUT TH' TUNE?
TUNE-SHMUNE!! I'LL TAKE CARE OF THAT!!- AFTER ALL-I STUDIED FOR TEN YEARS!!
MOOSIC?
NO!!-HAIR-WAVING!!-I OWE ALL MY SUCCESS TO THAT!! AND, TONIGHT, I'LL HAVE MY GREATEST CONCERT, I'M SURE!! -PRACTICED ALL DAY!!-WORE OUT THREE COMBS!!-
THE TV SHOW-
??-(-"A MAN IN THE AUDIENCE!! HOW'D HE GET IN?"-)
THE MAN IS DON CRABSBY, THE BAD-TEMPERED TELEVISION COLUMNIST-
THE NEXT MORNING-
READ MY REVIEWS TO ME. IT'S GOOD TO KNOW EVERY-ONE LOVES ME.!!
WAL-FAYE FAINTSPELL SAYS, "LOVERBOYNIK PLAYS LIKE AN ANGEL"-
SALLY SWOONFLOP SAYS, "LISTENING TO LOVERBOYNIK IS LIKE LISTENING TO WORDS OF LOVE"-BUT-??-DON CRABSBY SAYS, "LOVERBOYNIK'S PLAYING WILL NEVER SET THE WORLD ON FIRE!!"-
I CAN'T BEAR TO HAVE ANYONE NOT LOVE MY PLAYING!!-I'LL GIVE HIM A PRIVATE CONCERT!! POLISH THE PIANO!! -OIL MY HAIR-
GET ME A DOZEN NEW COMBS- AND SEND FOR CRABSBY!!
THE PRIVATE CONCERT IS OVER-
WELL?-
HMPF!!-YOU'LL NEVER SET THE WORLD ON FIRE!!-
Al Capp
"OH, WON'T I?" SAYS LOVERBOYNIK, TO HIMSELF!!-CONTINUED NEXT WEEK-

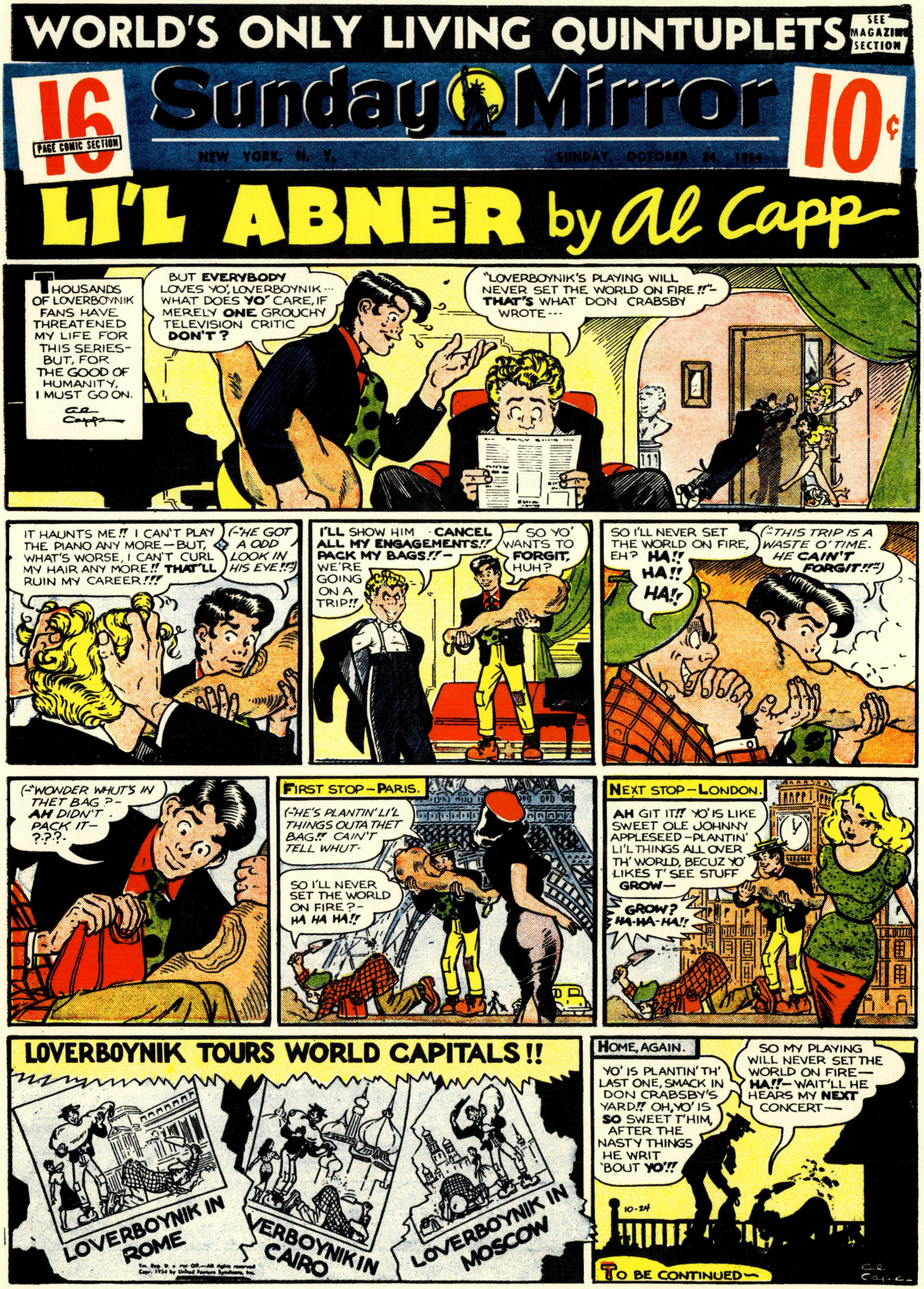

WORLD'S ONLY LIVING QUINTUPLETS
SEE MAGAZINE SECTION
16 PAGE COMIC SECTION
Sunday Mirror
10¢
NEW YORK, N. Y.
SUNDAY, OCTOBER 24, 1954
LI'L ABNER by Al Capp
THOUSANDS OF LOVERBOYNIK FANS HAVE THREATENED MY LIFE FOR THIS SERIES- BUT, FOR THE GOOD OF HUMANITY, I MUST GO ON. Al Capp
BUT EVERYBODY LOVES YO', LOVERBOYNIK··· WHAT DOES YO' CARE, IF MERELY ONE GROUCHY TELEVISION CRITIC DON'T?
"LOVERBOYNIK'S PLAYING WILL NEVER SET THE WORLD ON FIRE!!"- THAT'S WHAT DON CRABSBY WROTE---
IT HAUNTS ME!! I CAN'T PLAY THE PIANO ANY MORE—BUT, WHAT'S WORSE, I CAN'T CURL MY HAIR ANY MORE!! THAT'LL RUIN MY CAREER!!!
(-"HE GOT A ODD LOOK IN HIS EYE!!"-)
I'LL SHOW HIM - CANCEL ALL MY ENGAGEMENTS!! PACK MY BAGS!!- WE'RE GOING ON A TRIP!!
SO YO' WANTS TO FORGIT, HUH?
SO I'LL NEVER SET THE WORLD ON FIRE, EH? HA!! HA!! HA!!
(-"THIS TRIP IS A WASTE O' TIME. HE CAIN'T FORGIT!!"-)
(-"WONDER WHUT'S IN THET BAG?- AH DIDN'T PACK IT- ???.
FIRST STOP—PARIS.
(-"HE'S PLANTIN' LI'L THINGS OUTA THET BAG!! CAIN'T TELL WHUT-
SO I'LL NEVER SET THE WORLD ON FIRE?- HA HA HA!!
NEXT STOP—LONDON.
AH GIT IT!! YO' IS LIKE SWEET OLE JOHNNY APPLESEED—PLANTIN' LI'L THINGS ALL OVER TH' WORLD, BECUZ YO' LIKES T' SEE STUFF GROW—
GROW? HA-HA-HA!!
LOVERBOYNIK TOURS WORLD CAPITALS!!
LOVERBOYNIK IN ROME
VERBOYNIK IN CAIRO
LOVERBOYNIK IN MOSCOW
HOME, AGAIN.
YO' IS PLANTIN' TH' LAST ONE, SMACK IN DON CRABSBY'S YARD!! OH, YO' IS SO SWEET T'HIM, AFTER THE NASTY THINGS HE WRIT 'BOUT YO'!!
SO MY PLAYING WILL NEVER SET THE WORLD ON FIRE— HA!!— WAIT'LL HE HEARS MY NEXT CONCERT—
10-24
TO BE CONTINUED—
Al Capp

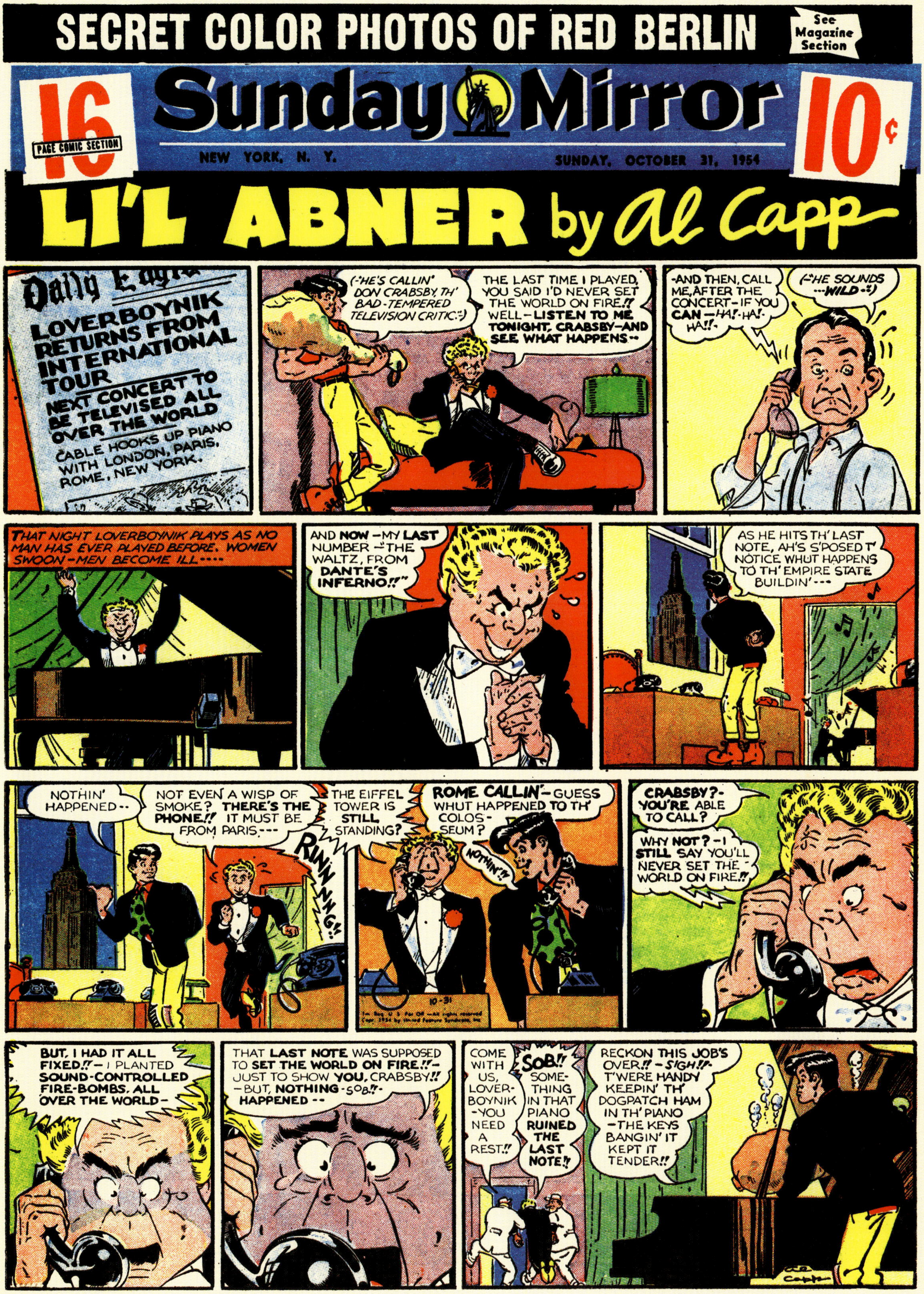

SECRET COLOR PHOTOS OF RED BERLIN
See Magazine Section
16 PAGE COMIC SECTION
Sunday Mirror
10¢
NEW YORK, N. Y.
SUNDAY, OCTOBER 31, 1954
LI'L ABNER by Al Capp
Daily Eagle
LOVERBOYNIK RETURNS FROM INTERNATIONAL TOUR
NEXT CONCERT TO BE TELEVISED ALL OVER THE WORLD
CABLE HOOKS UP PIANO WITH LONDON, PARIS, ROME, NEW YORK.
("HE'S CALLIN' DON CRABSBY, TH' BAD-TEMPERED TELEVISION CRITIC.")
THE LAST TIME I PLAYED, YOU SAID I'D NEVER SET THE WORLD ON FIRE.!! WELL— LISTEN TO ME TONIGHT, CRABSBY—AND SEE WHAT HAPPENS—
-AND THEN, CALL ME, AFTER THE CONCERT- IF YOU CAN—HA!-HA!-HA!!-
("HE SOUNDS --WILD--")
THAT NIGHT LOVERBOYNIK PLAYS AS NO MAN HAS EVER PLAYED BEFORE. WOMEN SWOON—MEN BECOME ILL----
AND NOW—MY LAST NUMBER—"THE WALTZ, FROM DANTE'S INFERNO.!!"
AS HE HITS TH' LAST NOTE, AH'S S'POSED T' NOTICE WHUT HAPPENS TO TH' EMPIRE STATE BUILDIN'---
NOTHIN' HAPPENED--
NOT EVEN A WISP OF SMOKE? THERE'S THE PHONE!! IT MUST BE FROM PARIS---
RINNNNG!!
THE EIFFEL TOWER IS STILL STANDING?
ROME CALLIN'—GUESS WHUT HAPPENED TO TH' COLOSSEUM?
NOTHIN'!!
CRABSBY?-YOU'RE ABLE TO CALL?
WHY NOT?-I STILL SAY YOU'LL NEVER SET THE WORLD ON FIRE.!!
BUT, I HAD IT ALL FIXED.!!—I PLANTED SOUND-CONTROLLED FIRE-BOMBS. ALL OVER THE WORLD—
THAT LAST NOTE WAS SUPPOSED TO SET THE WORLD ON FIRE.!!—JUST TO SHOW YOU, CRABSBY!!—BUT, NOTHING-SOB!!-HAPPENED--
COME WITH US, LOVERBOYNIK—YOU NEED A REST.!!
SOB!! SOMETHING IN THAT PIANO RUINED THE LAST NOTE!!
RECKON THIS JOB'S OVER.!!—SIGH!!—T'WERE HANDY KEEPIN' TH' DOGPATCH HAM IN TH' PIANO—THE KEYS BANGIN' IT KEPT IT TENDER!!

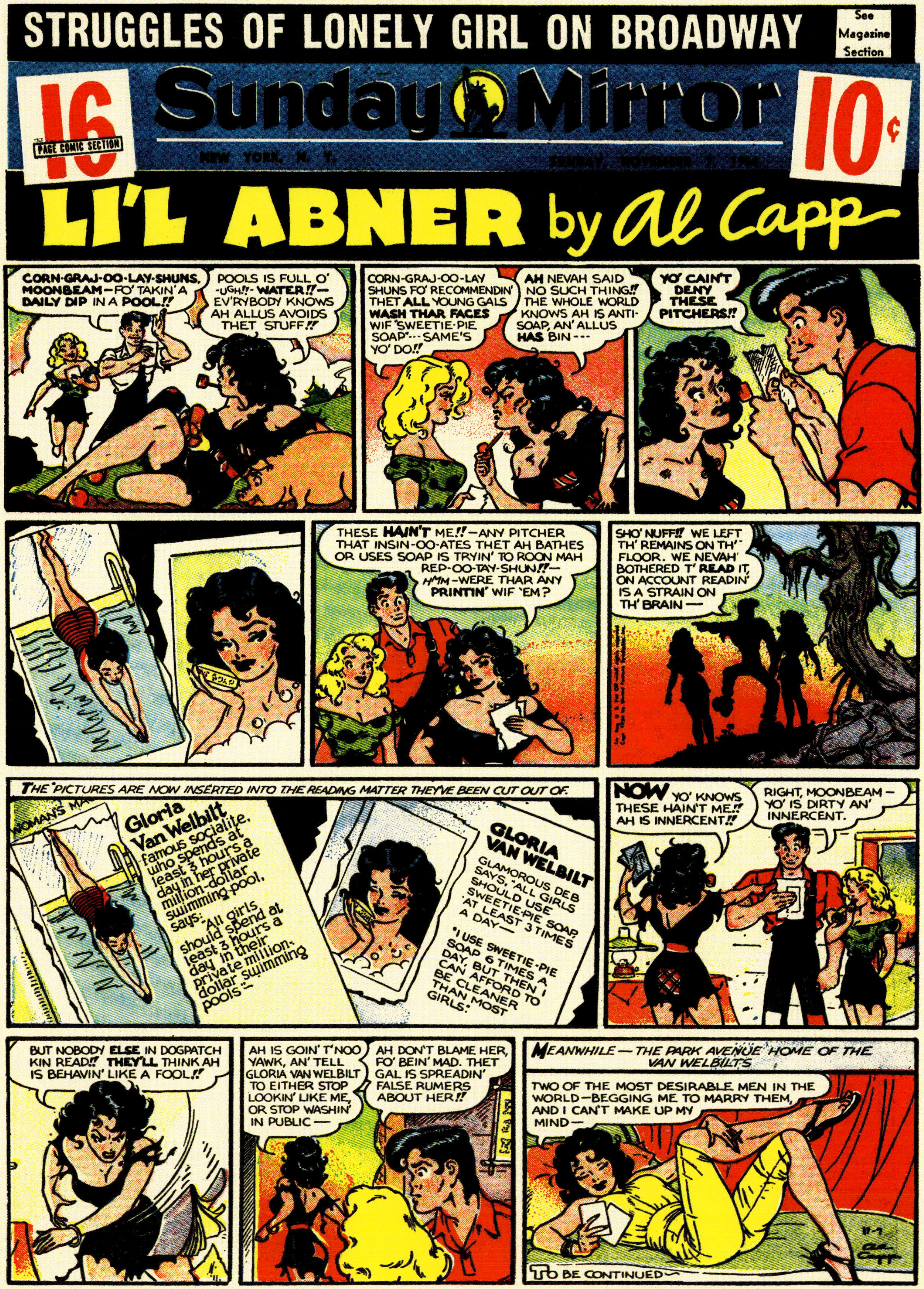
STRUGGLES OF LONELY GIRL ON BROADWAY
See Magazine Section
16 PAGE COMIC SECTION
Sunday Mirror
NEW YORK, N. Y.
10¢
LI'L ABNER by Al Capp
CORN-GRAJ-OO-LAY-SHUNS, MOONBEAM—FO' TAKIN' A DAILY DIP IN A POOL!!
POOLS IS FULL O' -UGH!!- WATER!!—EV'RYBODY KNOWS AH ALLUS AVOIDS THET STUFF!!
CORN-GRAJ-OO-LAY SHUNS FO' RECOMMENDIN' THET ALL YOUNG GALS WASH THAR FACES WIF "SWEETIE-PIE SOAP"--- SAME'S YO' DO!!
AH NEVAH SAID NO SUCH THING!! THE WHOLE WORLD KNOWS AH IS ANTI-SOAP, AN' ALLUS HAS BIN---
YO' CAIN'T DENY THESE PITCHERS!!
THESE HAIN'T ME!!—ANY PITCHER THAT INSIN-OO-ATES THET AH BATHES OR USES SOAP IS TRYIN' TO ROON MAH REP-OO-TAY-SHUN!!—HMM—WERE THAR ANY PRINTIN' WIF 'EM?
SHO' NUFF!! WE LEFT TH' REMAINS ON TH' FLOOR. WE NEVAH' BOTHERED T' READ IT, ON ACCOUNT READIN' IS A STRAIN ON TH' BRAIN—
THE PICTURES ARE NOW INSERTED INTO THE READING MATTER THEY'VE BEEN CUT OUT OF.
Gloria Van Welbilt, famous socialite, who spends at least 3 hours a day in her private million-dollar swimming-pool, says: "All girls should spend at least 3 hours a day in their private million-dollar swimming pools"—
GLORIA VAN WELBILT GLAMOROUS DEB SAYS, "ALL GIRLS SHOULD USE SWEETIE-PIE SOAP AT LEAST 3 TIMES A DAY"—
"I USE SWEETIE-PIE SOAP 6 TIMES A DAY, BUT THEN I CAN AFFORD TO BE CLEANER THAN MOST GIRLS."
NOW YO' KNOWS THESE HAIN'T ME!! AH IS INNERCENT!!
RIGHT, MOONBEAM—YO' IS DIRTY AN' INNERCENT.
BUT NOBODY ELSE IN DOGPATCH KIN READ!! THEY'LL THINK AH IS BEHAVIN' LIKE A FOOL!!
AH IS GOIN' T'NOO YAWK, AN' TELL GLORIA VAN WELBILT TO EITHER STOP LOOKIN' LIKE ME, OR STOP WASHIN' IN PUBLIC—
AH DON'T BLAME HER, FO' BEIN' MAD. THET GAL IS SPREADIN' FALSE RUMERS ABOUT HER!!
MEANWHILE—THE PARK AVENUE HOME OF THE VAN WELBILTS
TWO OF THE MOST DESIRABLE MEN IN THE WORLD—BEGGING ME TO MARRY THEM, AND I CAN'T MAKE UP MY MIND—
11-7
Al Capp
TO BE CONTINUED

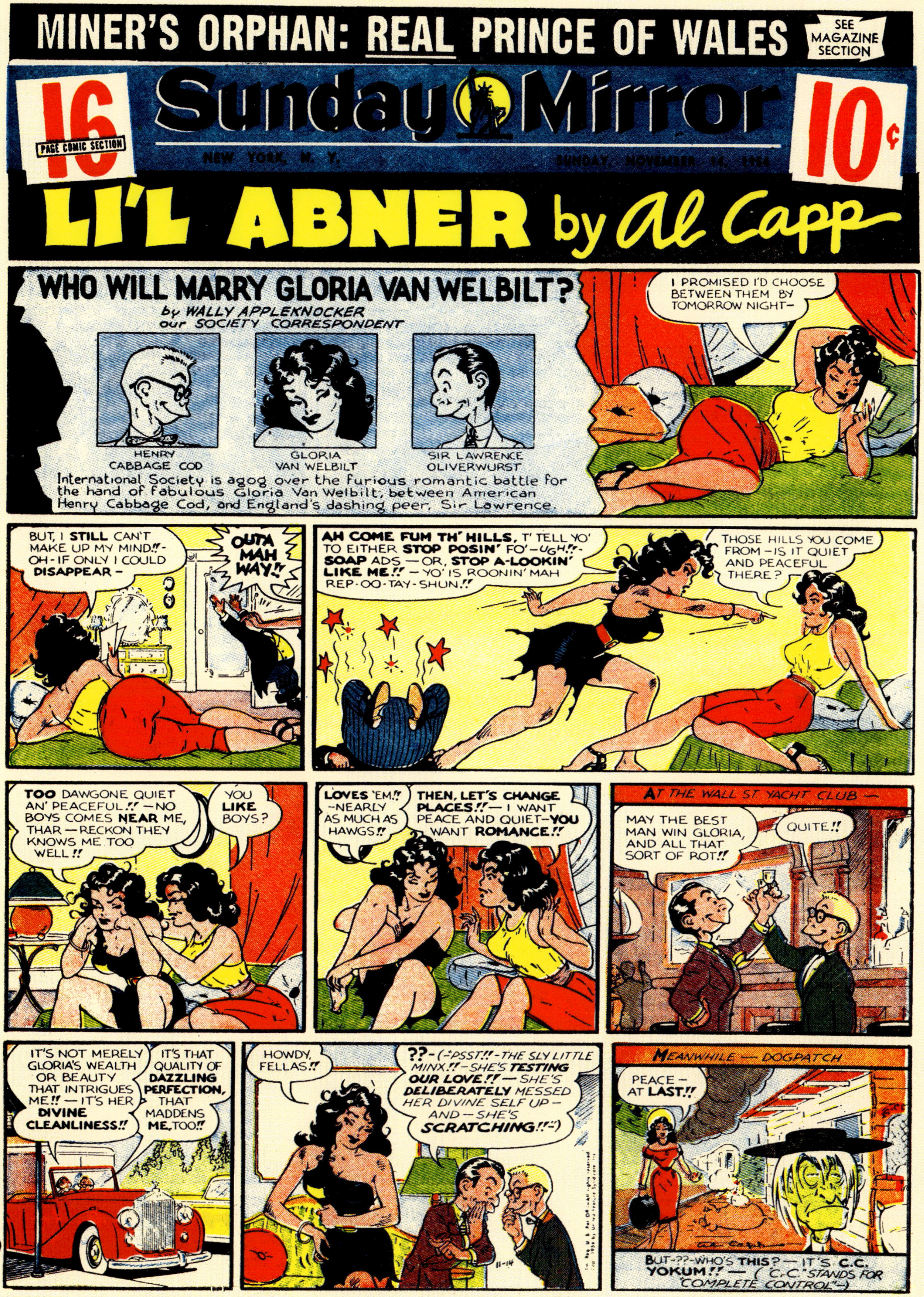
MINER'S ORPHAN: REAL PRINCE OF WALES
SEE MAGAZINE SECTION
16
PAGE COMIC SECTION
Sunday Mirror
NEW YORK, N. Y.
SUNDAY, NOVEMBER 14, 1954
10¢
LI'L ABNER by Al Capp
WHO WILL MARRY GLORIA VAN WELBILT?
by WALLY APPLEKNOCKER our SOCIETY CORRESPONDENT
HENRY CABBAGE COD
GLORIA VAN WELBILT
SIR LAWRENCE OLIVERWURST
International Society is agog over the furious romantic battle for the hand of fabulous Gloria Van Welbilt, between American Henry Cabbage Cod, and England's dashing peer, Sir Lawrence.
I PROMISED I'D CHOOSE BETWEEN THEM BY TOMORROW NIGHT–
BUT, I STILL CAN'T MAKE UP MY MIND!!– OH–IF ONLY I COULD DISAPPEAR–
OUTA MAH WAY!!
AH COME FUM TH' HILLS, T' TELL YO' TO EITHER STOP POSIN' FO'–UGH!!– SOAP ADS – OR, STOP A-LOOKIN' LIKE ME!! – YO' IS ROONIN' MAH REP-OO-TAY-SHUN!!
THOSE HILLS YOU COME FROM – IS IT QUIET AND PEACEFUL THERE?
TOO DAWGONE QUIET AN' PEACEFUL!! – NO BOYS COMES NEAR ME, THAR – RECKON THEY KNOWS ME TOO WELL!!
YOU LIKE BOYS?
LOVES 'EM!! –NEARLY AS MUCH AS HAWGS!!
THEN, LET'S CHANGE PLACES!! – I WANT PEACE AND QUIET– YOU WANT ROMANCE!!
AT THE WALL ST. YACHT CLUB –
MAY THE BEST MAN WIN GLORIA, AND ALL THAT SORT OF ROT!!
QUITE!!
IT'S NOT MERELY GLORIA'S WEALTH OR BEAUTY THAT INTRIGUES ME!! – IT'S HER DIVINE CLEANLINESS!!
IT'S THAT QUALITY OF DAZZLING PERFECTION, THAT MADDENS ME, TOO!!
HOWDY, FELLAS!!
??–(–"PSST!!–THE SLY LITTLE MINX!!–SHE'S TESTING OUR LOVE!! – SHE'S DELIBERATELY MESSED HER DIVINE SELF UP – AND – SHE'S SCRATCHING!!–")
11-14
MEANWHILE — DOGPATCH
PEACE – AT LAST!!
BUT–??–WHO'S THIS? – IT'S C.C. YOKUM!! – (C.C. "STANDS FOR "COMPLETE CONTROL"–)

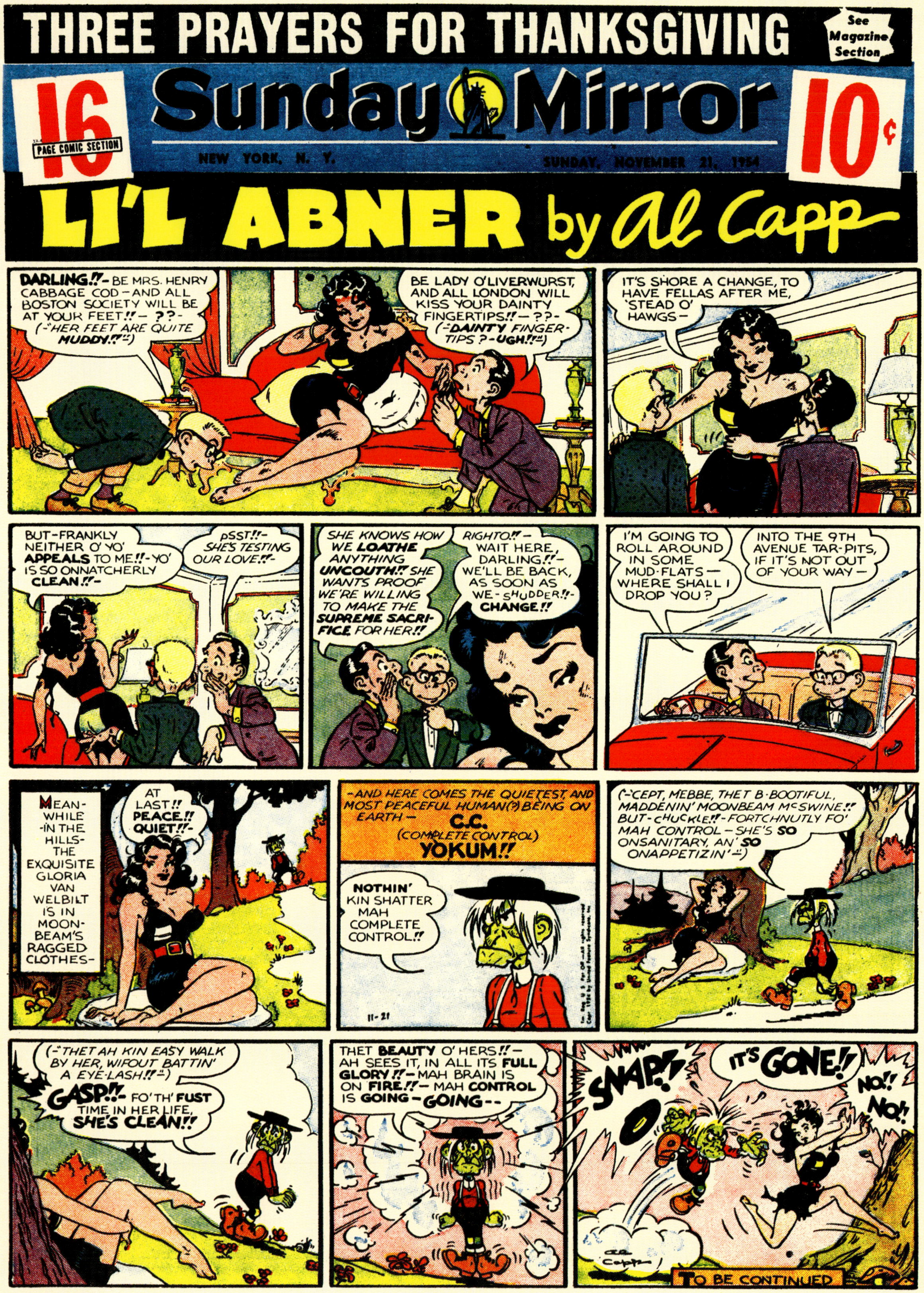
THREE PRAYERS FOR THANKSGIVING
See Magazine Section
16
PAGE COMIC SECTION
Sunday Mirror
NEW YORK, N. Y.
SUNDAY, NOVEMBER 21, 1954
10¢
LI'L ABNER by Al Capp
DARLING!!- BE MRS. HENRY CABBAGE COD-AND ALL BOSTON SOCIETY WILL BE AT YOUR FEET!!- ??- (-"HER FEET ARE QUITE MUDDY!!"-)
BE LADY O'LIVERWURST, AND ALL LONDON WILL KISS YOUR DAINTY FINGERTIPS!!- ??- (-"DAINTY FINGER-TIPS ?-UGH!!"-)
IT'S SHORE A CHANGE, TO HAVE FELLAS AFTER ME, 'STEAD O' HAWGS-
BUT-FRANKLY NEITHER O' YO' APPEALS TO ME!!-YO' IS SO ONNATCHERLY CLEAN!!-
PSST!!- SHE'S TESTING OUR LOVE!!-
SHE KNOWS HOW WE LOATHE ANYTHING UNCOUTH!! SHE WANTS PROOF WE'RE WILLING TO MAKE THE SUPREME SACRIFICE FOR HER!!
RIGHTO!!- WAIT HERE, DARLING!!- WE'LL BE BACK, AS SOON AS WE-SHUDDER!!- CHANGE!!
I'M GOING TO ROLL AROUND IN SOME MUD-FLATS- WHERE SHALL I DROP YOU?
INTO THE 9TH AVENUE TAR-PITS, IF IT'S NOT OUT OF YOUR WAY-
MEAN-WHILE -IN THE HILLS- THE EXQUISITE GLORIA VAN WELBILT IS IN MOON-BEAM'S RAGGED CLOTHES-
AT LAST!! PEACE!! QUIET!!-
-AND HERE COMES THE QUIETEST AND MOST PEACEFUL HUMAN(?) BEING ON EARTH- C.C. (COMPLETE CONTROL) YOKUM!!
NOTHIN' KIN SHATTER MAH COMPLETE CONTROL!!
11-21
(-'CEPT, MEBBE, THET B-BOOTIFUL, MADDENIN' MOONBEAM McSWINE!! BUT-CHUCKLE!!-FORTCHNUTLY FO' MAH CONTROL-SHE'S SO ONSANITARY, AN' SO ONAPPETIZIN'-)
(-THET AH KIN EASY WALK BY HER, WIFOUT BATTIN' A EYE-LASH!!-)
GASP!!- FO'TH' FUST TIME IN HER LIFE, SHE'S CLEAN!!
THET BEAUTY O' HERS!!- AH SEES IT, IN ALL ITS FULL GLORY!!-MAH BRAIN IS ON FIRE!!-MAH CONTROL IS GOING-GOING--
SNAP!!
IT'S GONE!!
NO!! NO!!
Al Capp
TO BE CONTINUED

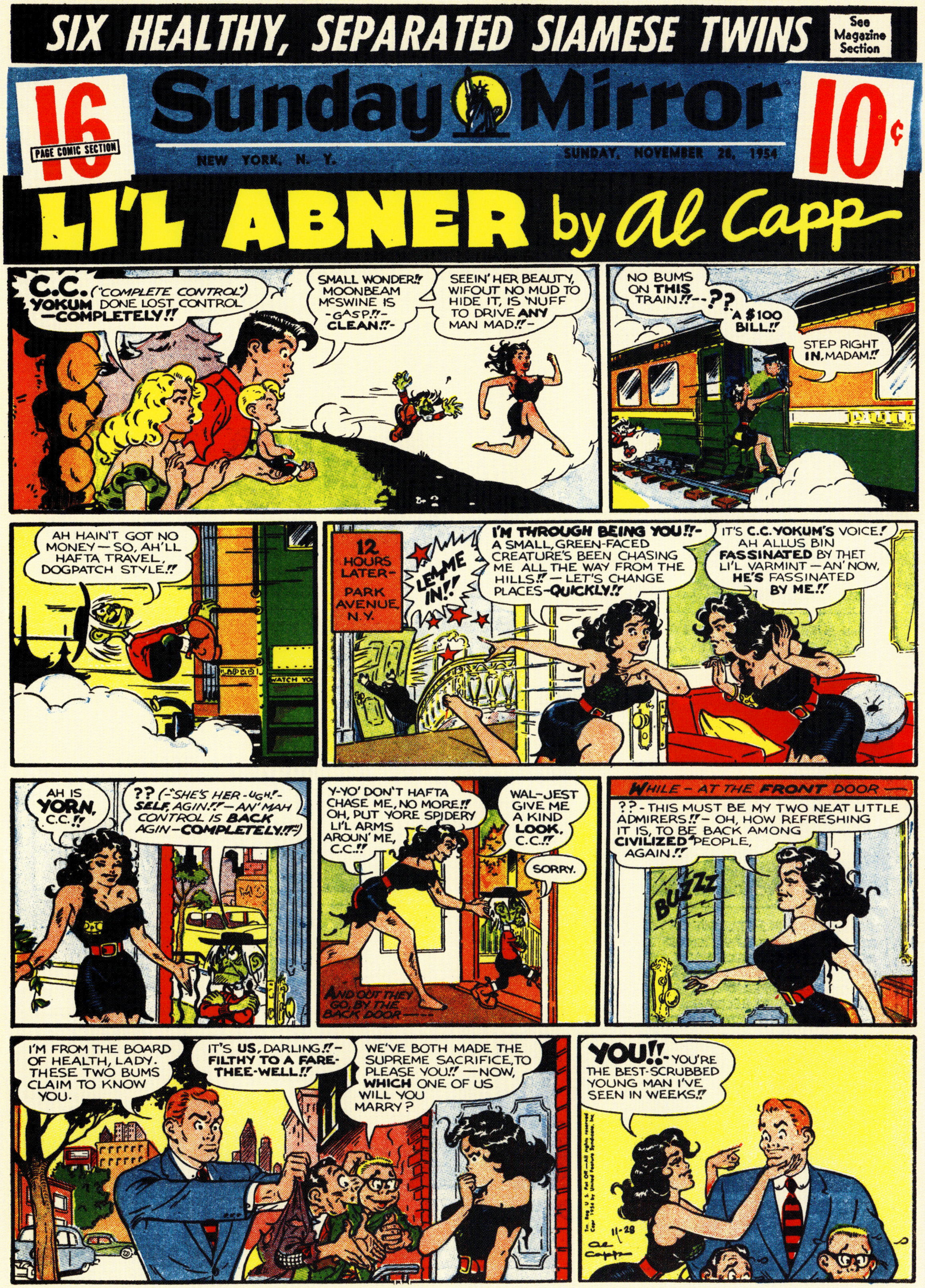

SIX HEALTHY, SEPARATED SIAMESE TWINS
See Magazine Section
16 PAGE COMIC SECTION
Sunday Mirror
NEW YORK, N. Y.
SUNDAY, NOVEMBER 28, 1954
10¢
LI'L ABNER by Al Capp
C.C. ("COMPLETE CONTROL") YOKUM DONE LOST CONTROL —COMPLETELY!!
SMALL WONDER!! MOONBEAM McSWINE IS -GASP!!- CLEAN!!-
SEEIN' HER BEAUTY, WIFOUT NO MUD TO HIDE IT, IS 'NUFF TO DRIVE ANY MAN MAD!!-
NO BUMS ON THIS TRAIN!!-- ?? A $100 BILL!!
STEP RIGHT IN, MADAM!!
AH HAIN'T GOT NO MONEY — SO, AH'LL HAFTA TRAVEL DOGPATCH STYLE!!
12 HOURS LATER- PARK AVENUE N.Y.
LEMME IN!!
I'M THROUGH BEING YOU!!- A SMALL, GREEN-FACED CREATURE'S BEEN CHASING ME ALL THE WAY FROM THE HILLS!! — LET'S CHANGE PLACES-QUICKLY!!
IT'S C.C. YOKUM'S VOICE! AH ALLUS BIN FASSINATED BY THET LI'L VARMINT — AN' NOW, HE'S FASSINATED BY ME!!
AH IS YORN, C.C.!!
?? (-"SHE'S HER -UGH!- SELF, AGIN!!" — AN' MAH CONTROL IS BACK AGIN — COMPLETELY!!")
Y-YO' DON'T HAFTA CHASE ME, NO MORE!! OH, PUT YORE SPIDERY LI'L ARMS AROUN' ME, C.C.!!
WAL-JEST GIVE ME A KIND LOOK, C.C.!!
SORRY.
AND OUT THEY GO, BY THE BACK DOOR —
WHILE - AT THE FRONT DOOR —
??-THIS MUST BE MY TWO NEAT LITTLE ADMIRERS!!- OH, HOW REFRESHING IT IS, TO BE BACK AMONG CIVILIZED PEOPLE, AGAIN!!
BUZZZ
I'M FROM THE BOARD OF HEALTH, LADY. THESE TWO BUMS CLAIM TO KNOW YOU.
IT'S US, DARLING!!- FILTHY TO A FARE-THEE-WELL!!
WE'VE BOTH MADE THE SUPREME SACRIFICE, TO PLEASE YOU!! —NOW, WHICH ONE OF US WILL YOU MARRY?
YOU!!- YOU'RE THE BEST-SCRUBBED YOUNG MAN I'VE SEEN IN WEEKS!!
11-28
Al Capp

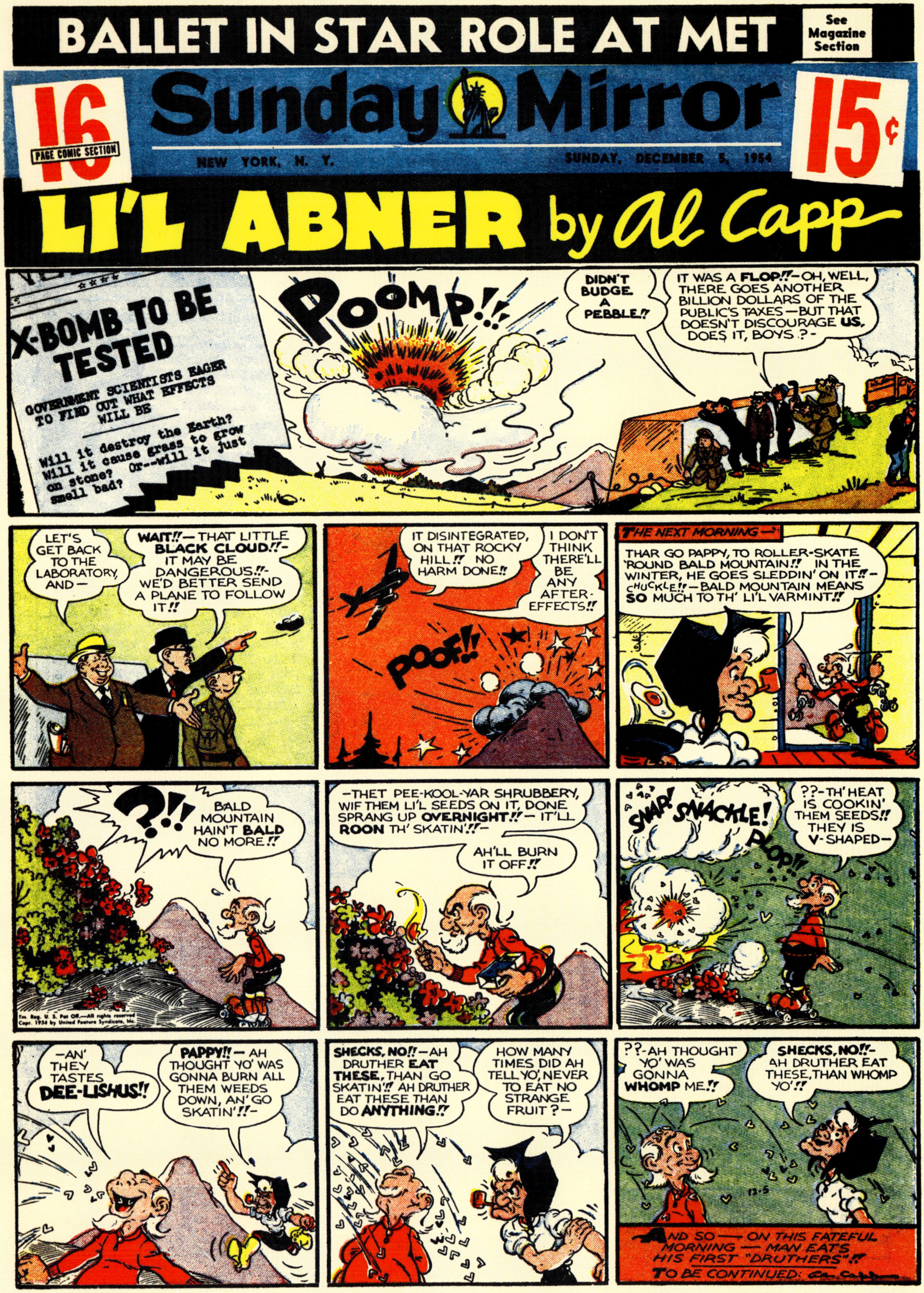

BALLET IN STAR ROLE AT MET
See Magazine Section
16 PAGE COMIC SECTION
Sunday Mirror
15¢
NEW YORK, N. Y.
SUNDAY, DECEMBER 5, 1954
LI'L ABNER by Al Capp
X-BOMB TO BE TESTED
GOVERNMENT SCIENTISTS EAGER TO FIND OUT WHAT EFFECTS WILL BE
Will it destroy the Earth? Will it cause grass to grow on stone? Or--will it just smell bad?
POOMP!!
DIDN'T BUDGE A PEBBLE.!?
IT WAS A FLOP!!–OH, WELL, THERE GOES ANOTHER BILLION DOLLARS OF THE PUBLIC'S TAXES–BUT THAT DOESN'T DISCOURAGE US. DOES IT, BOYS ?–
LET'S GET BACK TO THE LABORATORY, AND–
WAIT!!–THAT LITTLE BLACK CLOUD!!–IT MAY BE DANGEROUS!!–WE'D BETTER SEND A PLANE TO FOLLOW IT!!
IT DISINTEGRATED, ON THAT ROCKY HILL!! NO HARM DONE!!
I DON'T THINK THERE'LL BE ANY AFTER-EFFECTS!!
POOF!!
THE NEXT MORNING–
THAR GO PAPPY, TO ROLLER-SKATE 'ROUND BALD MOUNTAIN!! IN THE WINTER, HE GOES SLEDDIN' ON IT!!–CHUCKLE!!–BALD MOUNTAIN MEANS SO MUCH TO TH' LI'L VARMINT!!
?!!
BALD MOUNTAIN HAIN'T BALD NO MORE.!!
–THET PEE-KOOL-YAR SHRUBBERY, WIF THEM LI'L SEEDS ON IT, DONE SPRANG UP OVERNIGHT!!–IT'LL ROON TH' SKATIN'!!–
AH'LL BURN IT OFF!!
SNAP! SNACKLE! PLOP!!
??–TH' HEAT IS COOKIN' THEM SEEDS!! THEY IS V-SHAPED–
–AN' THEY TASTES DEE-LISHUS!!
PAPPY!!–AH THOUGHT YO' WAS GONNA BURN ALL THEM WEEDS DOWN, AN' GO SKATIN'!!–
SHECKS, NO!!–AH DRUTHER EAT THESE, THAN GO SKATIN'!! AH DRUTHER EAT THESE THAN DO ANYTHING.!!
HOW MANY TIMES DID AH TELL YO', NEVER TO EAT NO STRANGE FRUIT ?–
??–AH THOUGHT YO' WAS GONNA WHOMP ME.!!
SHECKS, NO!!–AH DRUTHER EAT THESE, THAN WHOMP YO'.!!
AND SO — ON THIS FATEFUL MORNING — MAN EATS HIS FIRST "DRUTHERS"!!
TO BE CONTINUED:

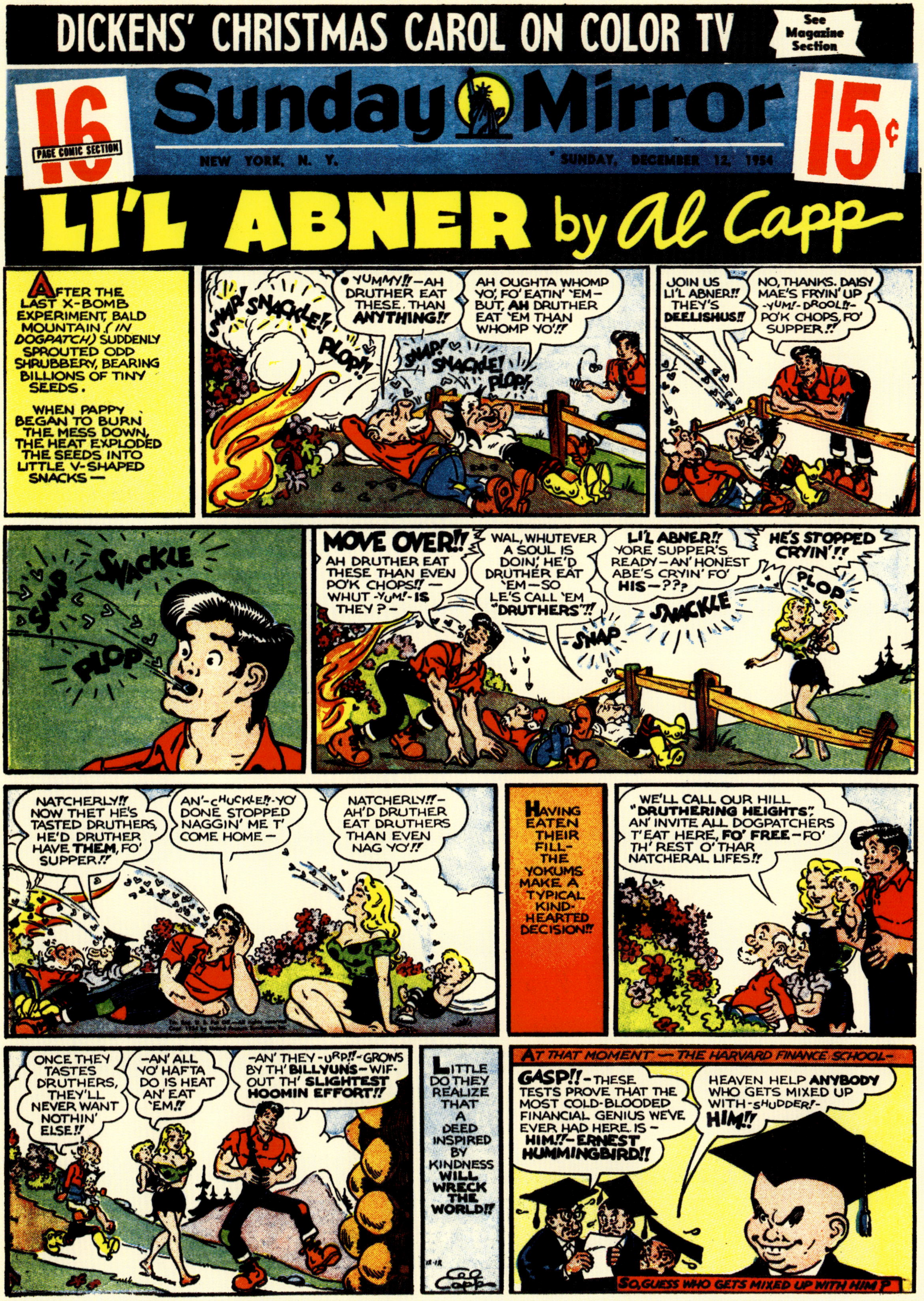
DICKENS' CHRISTMAS CAROL ON COLOR TV
See Magazine Section
16 PAGE COMIC SECTION
Sunday Mirror
15¢
NEW YORK, N. Y.
SUNDAY, DECEMBER 12, 1954
LI'L ABNER by Al Capp
AFTER THE LAST X-BOMB EXPERIMENT, BALD MOUNTAIN (IN DOGPATCH) SUDDENLY SPROUTED ODD SHRUBBERY, BEARING BILLIONS OF TINY SEEDS.
WHEN PAPPY BEGAN TO BURN THE MESS DOWN, THE HEAT EXPLODED THE SEEDS INTO LITTLE V-SHAPED SNACKS —
SNAP! SNACKLE!! PLOP!!
YUMMY!! — AH DRUTHER EAT THESE, THAN ANYTHING!!
AH OUGHTA WHOMP YO', FO' EATIN' 'EM — BUT, AH DRUTHER EAT 'EM THAN WHOMP YO'!!
SNAP! SNACKLE! PLOP!
JOIN US LI'L ABNER!! THEY'S DEELISHUS!!
NO, THANKS. DAISY MAE'S FRYIN' UP -YUM!- DROOL!!- PO'K CHOPS, FO' SUPPER!!
SNAP SNACKLE PLOP
MOVE OVER!!
AH DRUTHER EAT THESE THAN EVEN PO'K CHOPS!! — WHUT -YUM!- IS THEY? —
WAL, WHUTEVER A SOUL IS DOIN', HE'D DRUTHER EAT 'EM — SO LE'S CALL 'EM "DRUTHERS"!!
LI'L ABNER!! YORE SUPPER'S READY — AN' HONEST ABE'S CRYIN' FO' HIS — ??
HE'S STOPPED CRYIN'!!
PLOP
SNACKLE
SNAP
NATCHERLY!! NOW THET HE'S TASTED DRUTHERS, HE'D DRUTHER HAVE THEM, FO' SUPPER!!
AN'-CHUCKLE!!-YO' DONE STOPPED NAGGIN' ME T' COME HOME —
NATCHERLY!! — AH'D DRUTHER EAT DRUTHERS THAN EVEN NAG YO'!!
HAVING EATEN THEIR FILL — THE YOKUMS MAKE A TYPICAL KIND-HEARTED DECISION!!
WE'LL CALL OUR HILL "DRUTHERING HEIGHTS", AN' INVITE ALL DOGPATCHERS T'EAT HERE, FO' FREE — FO' TH' REST O' THAR NATCHERAL LIFES!!
ONCE THEY TASTES DRUTHERS, THEY'LL NEVER WANT NOTHIN' ELSE!!
-AN' ALL YO' HAFTA DO IS HEAT AN' EAT 'EM!!
-AN' THEY -URP!!- GROWS BY TH' BILLYUNS — WIF-OUT TH' SLIGHTEST HOOMIN EFFORT!!
LITTLE DO THEY REALIZE THAT A DEED INSPIRED BY KINDNESS WILL WRECK THE WORLD!!
AT THAT MOMENT — THE HARVARD FINANCE SCHOOL —
GASP!! — THESE TESTS PROVE THAT THE MOST COLD-BLOODED FINANCIAL GENIUS WE'VE EVER HAD HERE, IS — HIM!! — ERNEST HUMMINGBIRD!!
HEAVEN HELP ANYBODY WHO GETS MIXED UP WITH -SHUDDER!- HIM!!
SO, GUESS WHO GETS MIXED UP WITH HIM?
Al Capp

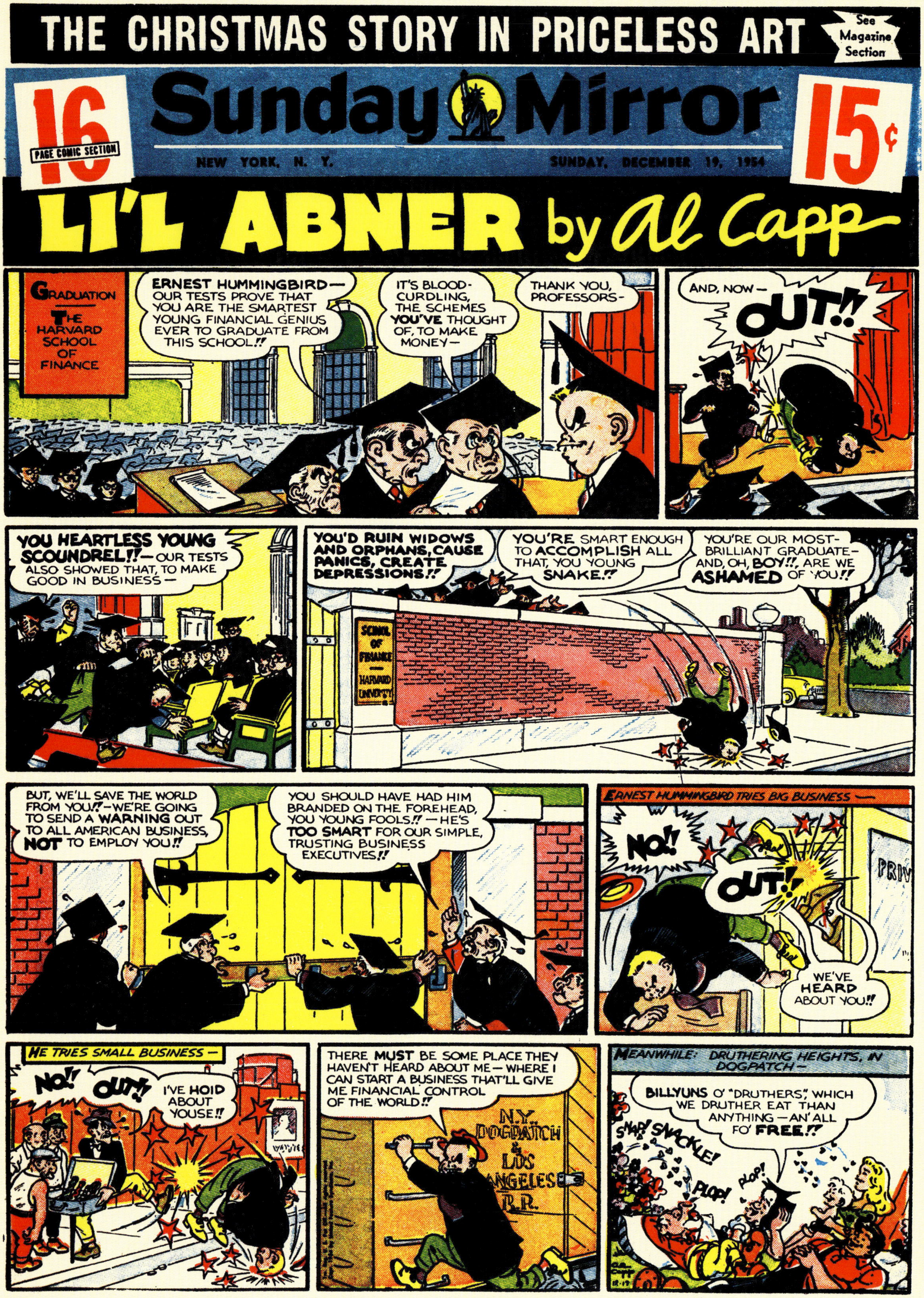
THE CHRISTMAS STORY IN PRICELESS ART
See Magazine Section
16 PAGE COMIC SECTION
Sunday Mirror
NEW YORK, N. Y.
SUNDAY, DECEMBER 19, 1954
15¢
LI'L ABNER by Al Capp
GRADUATION — THE HARVARD SCHOOL OF FINANCE
ERNEST HUMMINGBIRD — OUR TESTS PROVE THAT YOU ARE THE SMARTEST YOUNG FINANCIAL GENIUS EVER TO GRADUATE FROM THIS SCHOOL!!
IT'S BLOOD-CURDLING, THE SCHEMES YOU'VE THOUGHT OF, TO MAKE MONEY —
THANK YOU, PROFESSORS —
AND, NOW — OUT!!
YOU HEARTLESS YOUNG SCOUNDREL!! — OUR TESTS ALSO SHOWED THAT, TO MAKE GOOD IN BUSINESS —
YOU'D RUIN WIDOWS AND ORPHANS, CAUSE PANICS, CREATE DEPRESSIONS!!
YOU'RE SMART ENOUGH TO ACCOMPLISH ALL THAT, YOU YOUNG SNAKE!!
YOU'RE OUR MOST-BRILLIANT GRADUATE — AND, OH, BOY!!, ARE WE ASHAMED OF YOU!!
SCHOOL OF FINANCE — HARVARD UNIVERSITY
BUT, WE'LL SAVE THE WORLD FROM YOU!! — WE'RE GOING TO SEND A WARNING OUT TO ALL AMERICAN BUSINESS, NOT TO EMPLOY YOU!!
YOU SHOULD HAVE HAD HIM BRANDED ON THE FOREHEAD, YOU YOUNG FOOLS!! — HE'S TOO SMART FOR OUR SIMPLE, TRUSTING BUSINESS EXECUTIVES!!
ERNEST HUMMINGBIRD TRIES BIG BUSINESS —
NO!!
OUT!!
PRIV
WE'VE HEARD ABOUT YOU!!
HE TRIES SMALL BUSINESS —
NO!!
OUT!!
I'VE HOID ABOUT YOUSE!!
THERE MUST BE SOME PLACE THEY HAVEN'T HEARD ABOUT ME — WHERE I CAN START A BUSINESS THAT'LL GIVE ME FINANCIAL CONTROL OF THE WORLD!!
N.Y. DOGPATCH & LOS ANGELES R.R.
MEANWHILE: DRUTHERING HEIGHTS, IN DOGPATCH —
BILLYUNS O' "DRUTHERS," WHICH WE DRUTHER EAT THAN ANYTHING — AN' ALL FO' FREE!!
SNAP! SNACKLE!
PLOP!
PLOP!

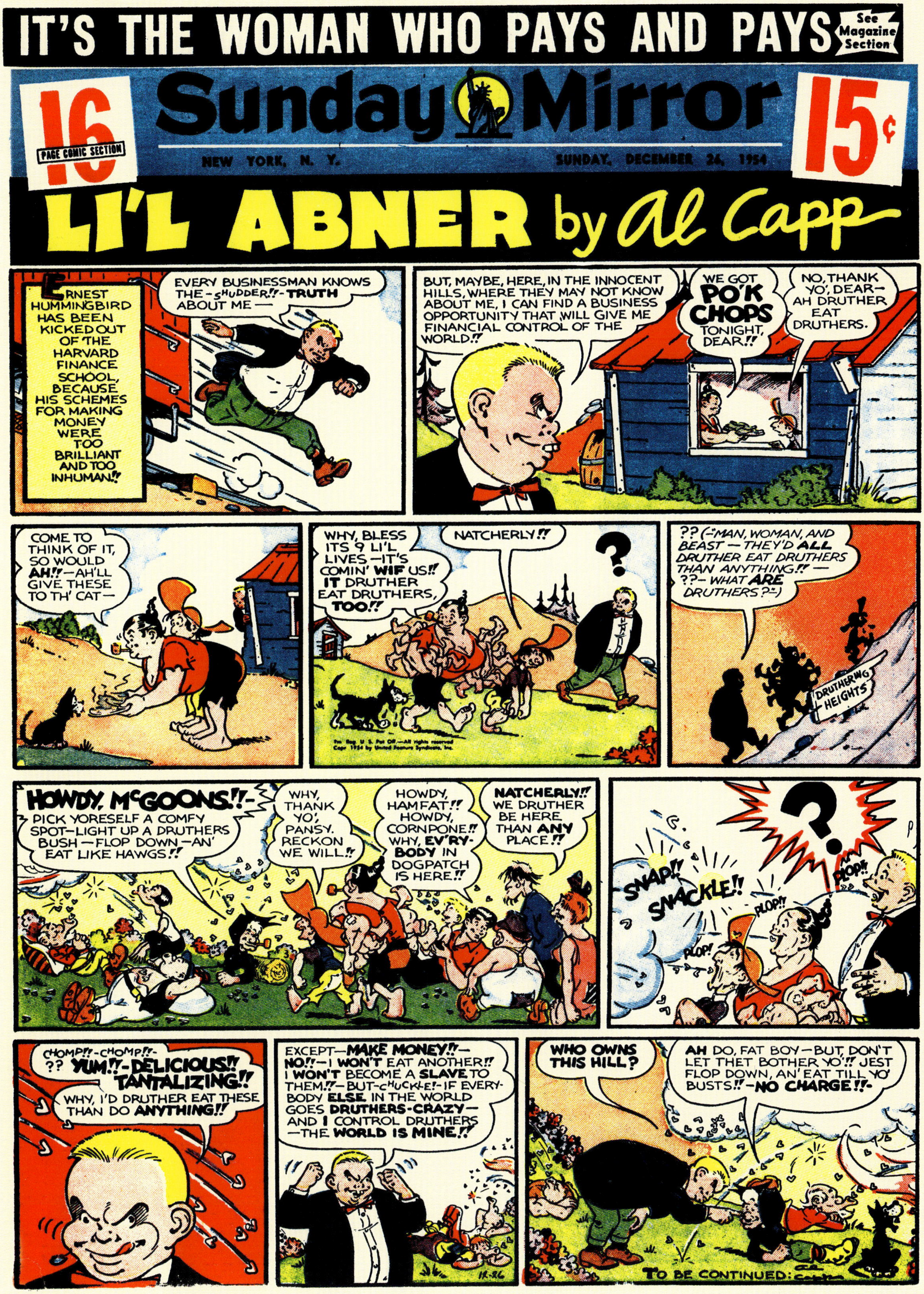
IT'S THE WOMAN WHO PAYS AND PAYS
See Magazine Section
16 PAGE COMIC SECTION
Sunday Mirror
15¢
NEW YORK, N. Y.
SUNDAY, DECEMBER 26, 1954
LI'L ABNER by Al Capp
ERNEST HUMMINGBIRD HAS BEEN KICKED OUT OF THE HARVARD FINANCE SCHOOL, BECAUSE HIS SCHEMES FOR MAKING MONEY WERE TOO BRILLIANT AND TOO INHUMAN!!
EVERY BUSINESSMAN KNOWS THE -SHUDDER!!- TRUTH ABOUT ME —
BUT, MAYBE, HERE, IN THE INNOCENT HILLS, WHERE THEY MAY NOT KNOW ABOUT ME, I CAN FIND A BUSINESS OPPORTUNITY THAT WILL GIVE ME FINANCIAL CONTROL OF THE WORLD!!
WE GOT PO'K CHOPS TONIGHT, DEAR!!
NO, THANK YO', DEAR— AH DRUTHER EAT DRUTHERS.
COME TO THINK OF IT, SO WOULD AH!!—AH'LL GIVE THESE TO TH' CAT—
WHY, BLESS ITS 9 LI'L LIVES—IT'S COMIN' WIF US!! IT DRUTHER EAT DRUTHERS, TOO!!
NATCHERLY!!
?
??(—MAN, WOMAN, AND BEAST—THEY'D ALL DRUTHER EAT DRUTHERS THAN ANYTHING!!— ??— WHAT ARE DRUTHERS?—)
DRUTHERING HEIGHTS
HOWDY, McGOONS!!— PICK YORESELF A COMFY SPOT—LIGHT UP A DRUTHERS BUSH—FLOP DOWN—AN' EAT LIKE HAWGS!!
WHY, THANK YO', PANSY. RECKON WE WILL!!
HOWDY, HAMFAT!! HOWDY, CORNPONE!! WHY, EV'RY-BODY IN DOGPATCH IS HERE!!
NATCHERLY!! WE DRUTHER BE HERE THAN ANY PLACE!!
?
SNAP!! SNACKLE!! PLOP!! PLOP!! PLOP!! PLOP!!
CHOMP!!-CHOMP!!- ?? YUM!!-DELICIOUS!! TANTALIZING!!
WHY, I'D DRUTHER EAT THESE THAN DO ANYTHING!!
EXCEPT—MAKE MONEY!!— NO!!—I WON'T EAT ANOTHER!! I WON'T BECOME A SLAVE TO THEM!!—BUT-CHUCKLE!-IF EVERY-BODY ELSE IN THE WORLD GOES DRUTHERS-CRAZY— AND I CONTROL DRUTHERS —THE WORLD IS MINE!!
WHO OWNS THIS HILL?
AH DO, FAT BOY—BUT, DON'T LET THET BOTHER YO'!! JEST FLOP DOWN, AN' EAT TILL YO' BUSTS!!—NO CHARGE!!—
TO BE CONTINUED:

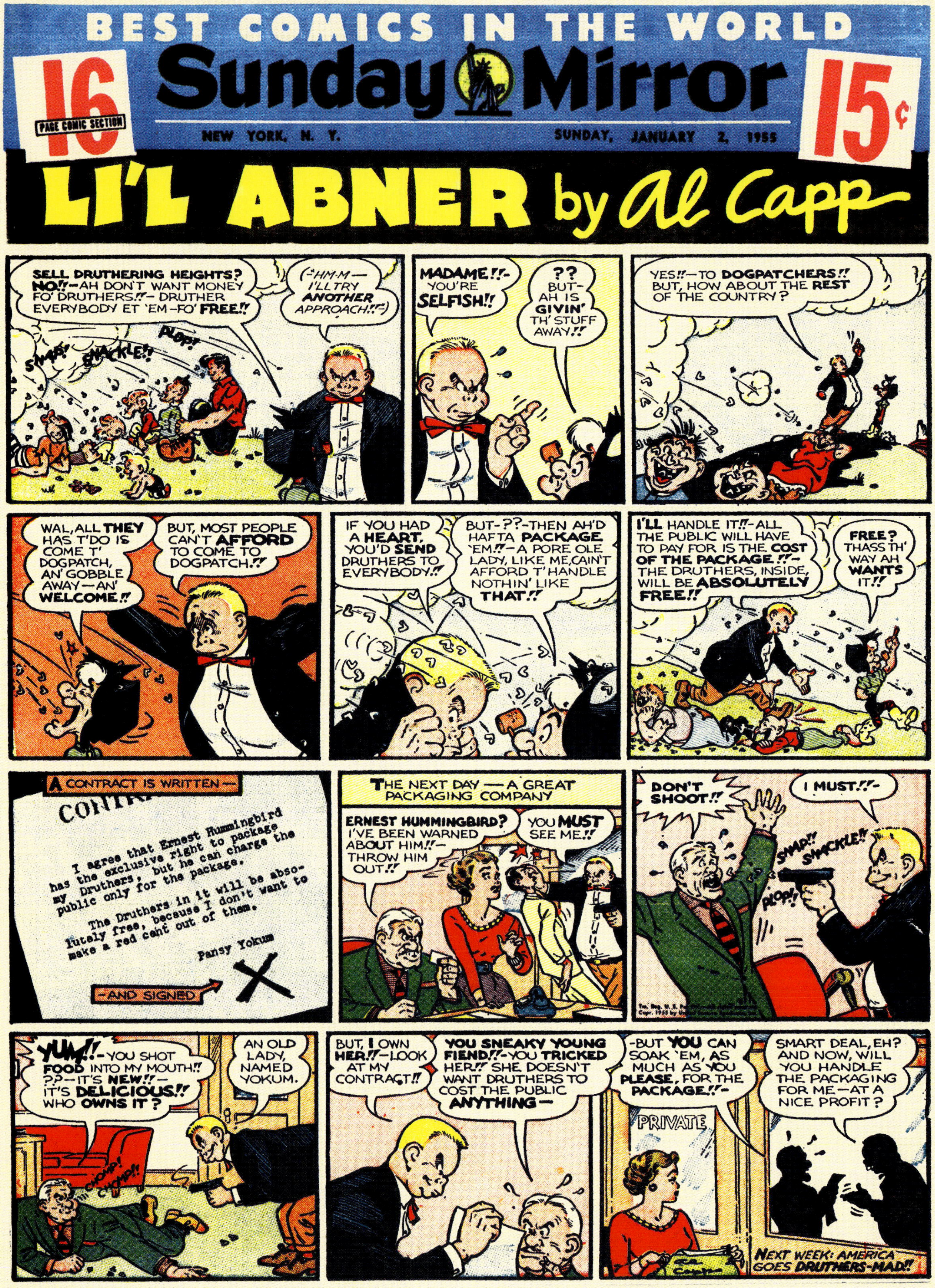

BEST COMICS IN THE WORLD
Sunday Mirror
16 PAGE COMIC SECTION
15¢
NEW YORK, N. Y.
SUNDAY, JANUARY 2, 1955
LI'L ABNER by Al Capp
SELL DRUTHERING HEIGHTS? NO!!—AH DON'T WANT MONEY FO' DRUTHERS!!—DRUTHER EVERYBODY ET 'EM—FO' FREE!!
(—HM-M— I'LL TRY ANOTHER APPROACH!!—)
SMASH!
SNACKLE!!
PLOP!
MADAME!!— YOU'RE SELFISH!!
?? BUT— AH IS GIVIN' TH' STUFF AWAY!!
YES!!—TO DOGPATCHERS!! BUT, HOW ABOUT THE REST OF THE COUNTRY?
WAL, ALL THEY HAS T'DO IS COME T' DOGPATCH, AN' GOBBLE AWAY—AN' WELCOME!!
BUT, MOST PEOPLE CAN'T AFFORD TO COME TO DOGPATCH.!!
IF YOU HAD A HEART, YOU'D SEND DRUTHERS TO EVERYBODY.!!
BUT-??-THEN AH'D HAFTA PACKAGE 'EM!!—A PORE OLE LADY, LIKE ME, CAIN'T AFFORD T' HANDLE NOTHIN' LIKE THAT!!
I'LL HANDLE IT!!—ALL THE PUBLIC WILL HAVE TO PAY FOR IS THE COST OF THE PACKAGE!!—THE DRUTHERS, INSIDE, WILL BE ABSOLUTELY FREE!!
FREE? THASS TH' WAY AH WANTS IT!!
A CONTRACT IS WRITTEN—
CONTR
I agree that Ernest Hummingbird has the exclusive right to package my Druthers, but he can charge the public only for the package.
The Druthers in it will be absolutely free, because I don't want to make a red cent out of them.
Pansy Yokum
X
—AND SIGNED
THE NEXT DAY—A GREAT PACKAGING COMPANY
ERNEST HUMMINGBIRD? I'VE BEEN WARNED ABOUT HIM!!—THROW HIM OUT!!
YOU MUST SEE ME.!!
DON'T SHOOT!!
I MUST!!—
SMASH!!
SNACKLE!!
PLOP!!
YUM!!—YOU SHOT FOOD INTO MY MOUTH!! ??—IT'S NEW!!—IT'S DELICIOUS!! WHO OWNS IT?
AN OLD LADY, NAMED YOKUM.
CHOMP! CHOMP!!
BUT, I OWN HER!!—LOOK AT MY CONTRACT!!
YOU SNEAKY YOUNG FIEND!!—YOU TRICKED HER!! SHE DOESN'T WANT DRUTHERS TO COST THE PUBLIC ANYTHING—
—BUT YOU CAN SOAK 'EM, AS MUCH AS YOU PLEASE, FOR THE PACKAGE!!—
PRIVATE
SMART DEAL, EH? AND NOW, WILL YOU HANDLE THE PACKAGING FOR ME—AT A NICE PROFIT?
NEXT WEEK: AMERICA GOES DRUTHERS-MAD!!

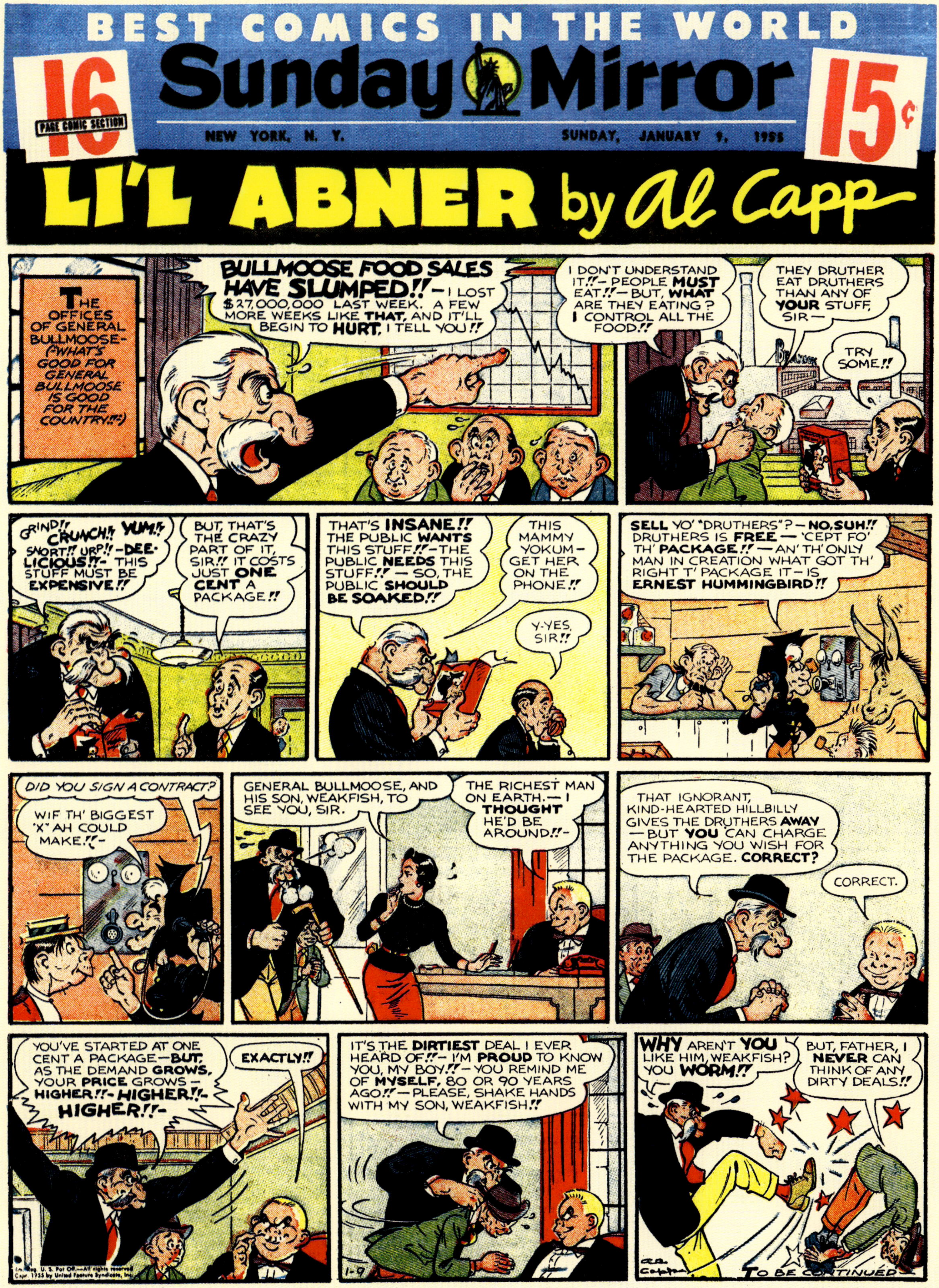
BEST COMICS IN THE WORLD
16
PAGE COMIC SECTION
Sunday Mirror
15¢
NEW YORK, N. Y.
SUNDAY, JANUARY 9, 1955
LI'L ABNER by Al Capp
THE OFFICES OF GENERAL BULLMOOSE- (WHAT'S GOOD FOR GENERAL BULLMOOSE IS GOOD FOR THE COUNTRY!!")
BULLMOOSE FOOD SALES HAVE SLUMPED!! - I LOST $27,000,000 LAST WEEK. A FEW MORE WEEKS LIKE THAT, AND IT'LL BEGIN TO HURT, I TELL YOU!!
I DON'T UNDERSTAND IT!! - PEOPLE MUST EAT!! - BUT, WHAT ARE THEY EATING? I CONTROL ALL THE FOOD!!
THEY DRUTHER EAT DRUTHERS THAN ANY OF YOUR STUFF, SIR -
TRY SOME.!!
GRIND!! CRUNCH!! YUM!! SNORT!! URP!! - DEE-LICIOUS!! - THIS STUFF MUST BE EXPENSIVE!!
BUT, THAT'S THE CRAZY PART OF IT, SIR!! IT COSTS JUST ONE CENT A PACKAGE!!
THAT'S INSANE!! THE PUBLIC WANTS THIS STUFF!! - THE PUBLIC NEEDS THIS STUFF!! - SO, THE PUBLIC SHOULD BE SOAKED!!
THIS MAMMY YOKUM - GET HER ON THE PHONE!!
Y-YES, SIR!!
SELL YO' "DRUTHERS"? - NO, SUH!! DRUTHERS IS FREE - 'CEPT FO' TH' PACKAGE!! - AN' TH' ONLY MAN IN CREATION WHAT GOT TH' RIGHT T' PACKAGE IT - IS ERNEST HUMMINGBIRD!!
DID YOU SIGN A CONTRACT?
WIF TH' BIGGEST "X" AH COULD MAKE!! -
GENERAL BULLMOOSE, AND HIS SON, WEAKFISH, TO SEE YOU, SIR.
THE RICHEST MAN ON EARTH. - I THOUGHT HE'D BE AROUND!! -
THAT IGNORANT, KIND-HEARTED HILLBILLY GIVES THE DRUTHERS AWAY - BUT YOU CAN CHARGE ANYTHING YOU WISH FOR THE PACKAGE. CORRECT?
CORRECT.
YOU'VE STARTED AT ONE CENT A PACKAGE - BUT, AS THE DEMAND GROWS, YOUR PRICE GROWS - HIGHER!! - HIGHER!! - HIGHER!! -
EXACTLY!!
IT'S THE DIRTIEST DEAL I EVER HEARD OF!! - I'M PROUD TO KNOW YOU, MY BOY!! - YOU REMIND ME OF MYSELF, 80 OR 90 YEARS AGO!! - PLEASE, SHAKE HANDS WITH MY SON, WEAKFISH!!
WHY AREN'T YOU LIKE HIM, WEAKFISH? YOU WORM!!
BUT, FATHER, I NEVER CAN THINK OF ANY DIRTY DEALS!!
1-9
AL CAPP
TO BE CONTINUED

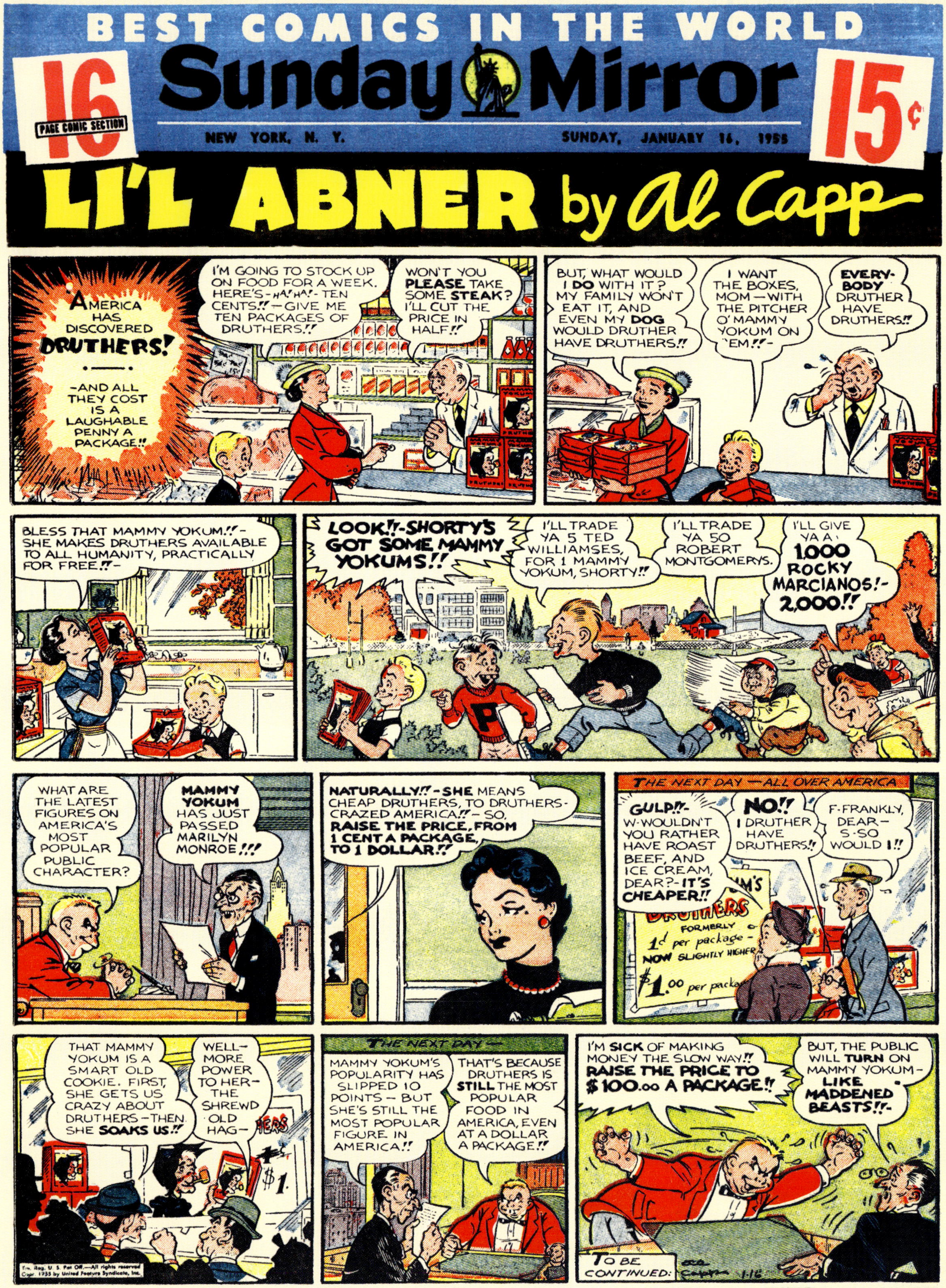
BEST COMICS IN THE WORLD
16
PAGE COMIC SECTION
Sunday Mirror
NEW YORK, N. Y.
SUNDAY, JANUARY 16, 1955
15¢
LI'L ABNER by Al Capp
"AMERICA HAS DISCOVERED DRUTHERS! -AND ALL THEY COST IS A LAUGHABLE PENNY A PACKAGE!!"
I'M GOING TO STOCK UP ON FOOD FOR A WEEK. HERE'S-HA! HA!- TEN CENTS!! -GIVE ME TEN PACKAGES OF DRUTHERS!!
WON'T YOU PLEASE TAKE SOME STEAK? I'LL CUT THE PRICE IN HALF!!
BUT, WHAT WOULD I DO WITH IT? MY FAMILY WON'T EAT IT, AND EVEN MY DOG WOULD DRUTHER HAVE DRUTHERS!!
I WANT THE BOXES, MOM -WITH THE PITCHER O' MAMMY YOKUM ON 'EM!!-
EVERY-BODY DRUTHER HAVE DRUTHERS!!
BLESS THAT MAMMY YOKUM!!- SHE MAKES DRUTHERS AVAILABLE TO ALL HUMANITY, PRACTICALLY FOR FREE!!-
LOOK!!-SHORTY'S GOT SOME MAMMY YOKUMS!!
I'LL TRADE YA 5 TED WILLIAMSES, FOR 1 MAMMY YOKUM, SHORTY!!
I'LL TRADE YA 50 ROBERT MONTGOMERYS.
I'LL GIVE YA A 1,000 ROCKY MARCIANOS!- 2,000!!
WHAT ARE THE LATEST FIGURES ON AMERICA'S MOST POPULAR PUBLIC CHARACTER?
MAMMY YOKUM HAS JUST PASSED MARILYN MONROE!!!
NATURALLY!!-SHE MEANS CHEAP DRUTHERS, TO DRUTHERS-CRAZED AMERICA!!-SO, RAISE THE PRICE, FROM 1 CENT A PACKAGE, TO 1 DOLLAR!!
THE NEXT DAY—ALL OVER AMERICA
GULP!!- W-WOULDN'T YOU RATHER HAVE ROAST BEEF, AND ICE CREAM, DEAR?-IT'S CHEAPER!!
NO!! I DRUTHER HAVE DRUTHERS!!
F-FRANKLY, DEAR- S-SO WOULD I!!
DRUTHERS
FORMERLY 1¢ per package - NOW SLIGHTLY HIGHER
$1.00 per pack
THAT MAMMY YOKUM IS A SMART OLD COOKIE. FIRST, SHE GETS US CRAZY ABOUT DRUTHERS -THEN SHE SOAKS US!!
WELL-MORE POWER TO HER-THE SHREWD OLD HAG-
$1.
THE NEXT DAY—
MAMMY YOKUM'S POPULARITY HAS SLIPPED 10 POINTS -BUT SHE'S STILL THE MOST POPULAR FIGURE IN AMERICA!!
THAT'S BECAUSE DRUTHERS IS STILL THE MOST POPULAR FOOD IN AMERICA, EVEN AT A DOLLAR A PACKAGE!!
I'M SICK OF MAKING MONEY THE SLOW WAY!! RAISE THE PRICE TO $100.00 A PACKAGE!!
BUT, THE PUBLIC WILL TURN ON MAMMY YOKUM-LIKE MADDENED BEASTS!!-
TO BE CONTINUED:
Al Capp 1-16

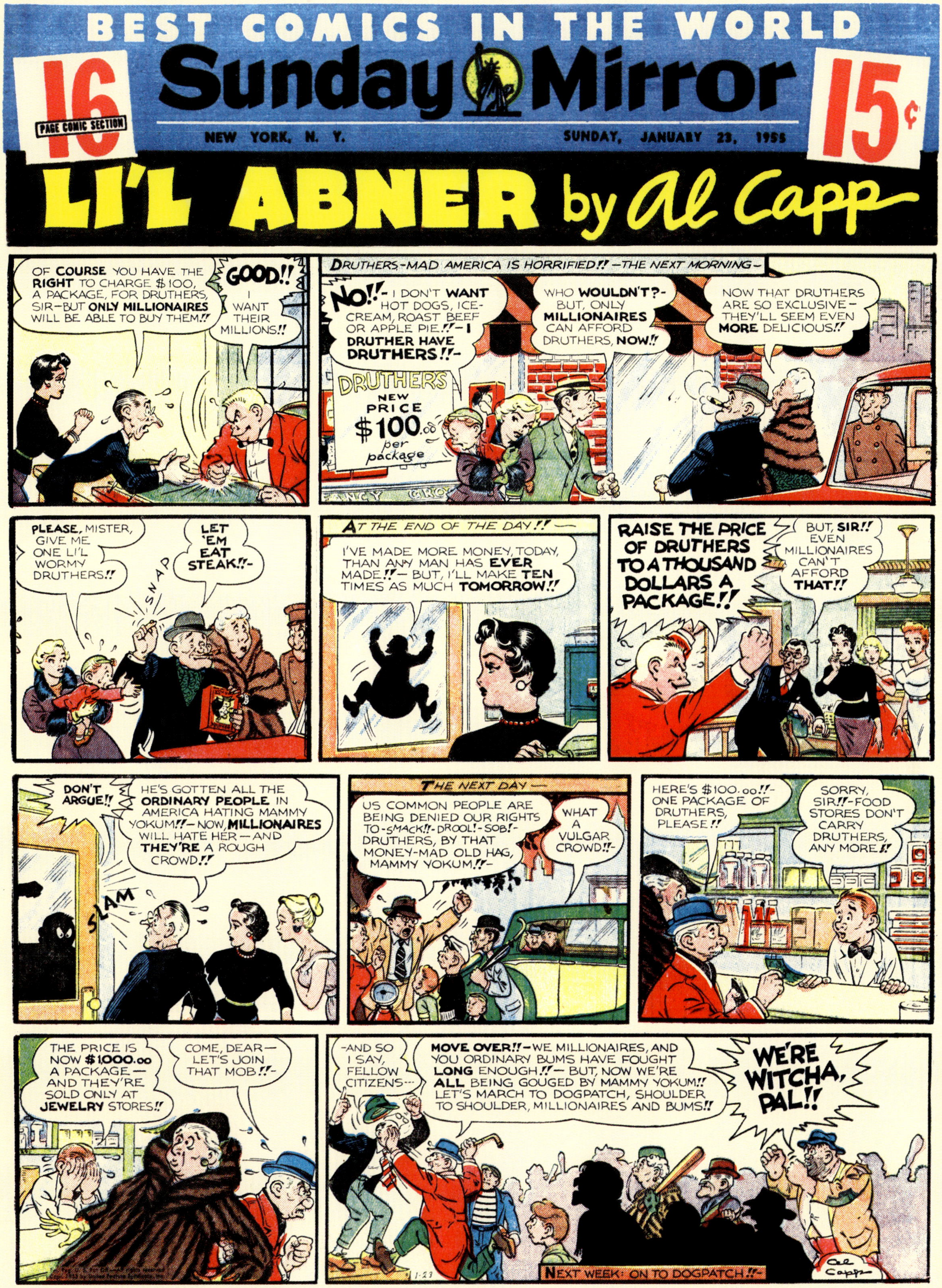
BEST COMICS IN THE WORLD
16 PAGE COMIC SECTION
Sunday Mirror
15¢
NEW YORK, N. Y.
SUNDAY, JANUARY 23, 1955
LI'L ABNER by Al Capp
OF COURSE YOU HAVE THE RIGHT TO CHARGE $100. A PACKAGE, FOR DRUTHERS, SIR—BUT ONLY MILLIONAIRES WILL BE ABLE TO BUY THEM!!
GOOD!! I WANT THEIR MILLIONS!!
DRUTHERS-MAD AMERICA IS HORRIFIED!! —THE NEXT MORNING—
NO!!—I DON'T WANT HOT DOGS, ICE-CREAM, ROAST BEEF OR APPLE PIE!!—I DRUTHER HAVE DRUTHERS!!—
WHO WOULDN'T?—BUT, ONLY MILLIONAIRES CAN AFFORD DRUTHERS, NOW!!
NOW THAT DRUTHERS ARE SO EXCLUSIVE—THEY'LL SEEM EVEN MORE DELICIOUS!!
DRUTHERS NEW PRICE $100.00 per package
PLEASE, MISTER, GIVE ME ONE LI'L WORMY DRUTHERS!!
LET 'EM EAT STEAK!!—
SNAP
AT THE END OF THE DAY!! —
I'VE MADE MORE MONEY, TODAY, THAN ANY MAN HAS EVER MADE!!—BUT, I'LL MAKE TEN TIMES AS MUCH TOMORROW!!
RAISE THE PRICE OF DRUTHERS TO A THOUSAND DOLLARS A PACKAGE!!
BUT, SIR!! EVEN MILLIONAIRES CAN'T AFFORD THAT!!
DON'T ARGUE!!
HE'S GOTTEN ALL THE ORDINARY PEOPLE IN AMERICA HATING MAMMY YOKUM!!—NOW, MILLIONAIRES WILL HATE HER—AND THEY'RE A ROUGH CROWD!!
SLAM
THE NEXT DAY —
US COMMON PEOPLE ARE BEING DENIED OUR RIGHTS TO -SMACK!!-DROOL!-SOB!- DRUTHERS, BY THAT MONEY-MAD OLD HAG, MAMMY YOKUM!!—
WHAT A VULGAR CROWD!!—
HERE'S $100.00!!—ONE PACKAGE OF DRUTHERS, PLEASE!!
SORRY, SIR!!—FOOD STORES DON'T CARRY DRUTHERS, ANY MORE!!
THE PRICE IS NOW $1,000.00 A PACKAGE—AND THEY'RE SOLD ONLY AT JEWELRY STORES!!
COME, DEAR—LET'S JOIN THAT MOB!!—
—AND SO I SAY, FELLOW CITIZENS—
MOVE OVER!!—WE MILLIONAIRES, AND YOU ORDINARY BUMS HAVE FOUGHT LONG ENOUGH!!—BUT, NOW WE'RE ALL BEING GOUGED BY MAMMY YOKUM!! LET'S MARCH TO DOGPATCH, SHOULDER TO SHOULDER, MILLIONAIRES AND BUMS!!
WE'RE WITCHA, PAL!!
NEXT WEEK: ON TO DOGPATCH!!—
Al Capp

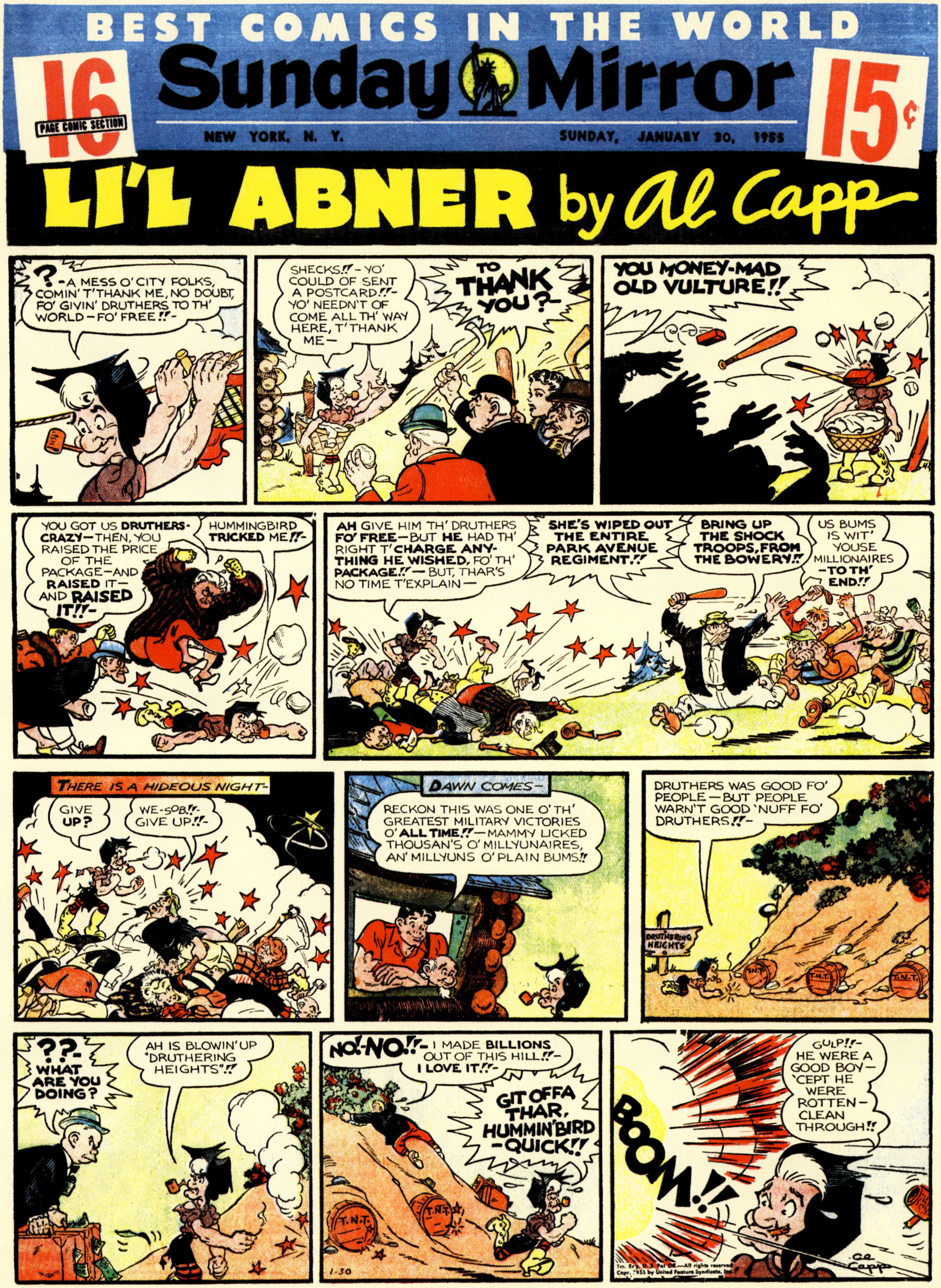
BEST COMICS IN THE WORLD
16 PAGE COMIC SECTION
Sunday Mirror
15¢
NEW YORK, N. Y.
SUNDAY, JANUARY 30, 1955
LI'L ABNER by Al Capp
?-A MESS O' CITY FOLKS, COMIN' T'THANK ME, NO DOUBT, FO' GIVIN' DRUTHERS TO TH' WORLD—FO' FREE!!-
SHECKS!!-YO' COULD OF SENT A POSTCARD!!-YO' NEEDN'T OF COME ALL TH' WAY HERE, T'THANK ME—
TO THANK YOU?-
YOU MONEY-MAD OLD VULTURE!!
YOU GOT US DRUTHERS-CRAZY—THEN, YOU RAISED THE PRICE OF THE PACKAGE—AND RAISED IT—AND RAISED IT!!-
HUMMINGBIRD TRICKED ME!!-
AH GIVE HIM TH' DRUTHERS FO' FREE—BUT HE HAD TH' RIGHT T' CHARGE ANY-THING HE WISHED, FO' TH' PACKAGE!!—BUT, THAR'S NO TIME T'EXPLAIN—
SHE'S WIPED OUT THE ENTIRE PARK AVENUE REGIMENT!!
BRING UP THE SHOCK TROOPS, FROM THE BOWERY!!
US BUMS IS WIT' YOUSE MILLIONAIRES —TO TH' END!!-
THERE IS A HIDEOUS NIGHT-
GIVE UP?
WE-SOB!!-GIVE UP!!-
DAWN COMES-
RECKON THIS WAS ONE O' TH' GREATEST MILITARY VICTORIES O' ALL TIME!!—MAMMY LICKED THOUSAN'S O' MILLYUNAIRES, AN' MILLYUNS O' PLAIN BUMS!!
DRUTHERS WAS GOOD FO' PEOPLE—BUT PEOPLE WARN'T GOOD 'NUFF FO' DRUTHERS!!-
DRUTHERING HEIGHTS
T.N.T.
??-WHAT ARE YOU DOING?
AH IS BLOWIN' UP "DRUTHERING HEIGHTS"!!
NO-NO!!-I MADE BILLIONS OUT OF THIS HILL!!-I LOVE IT!!-
GIT OFFA THAR, HUMMIN'BIRD -QUICK!!
T.N.T.
1-30
BOOM!!
GULP!!-HE WERE A GOOD BOY-'CEPT HE WERE ROTTEN-CLEAN THROUGH!!
AL CAPP

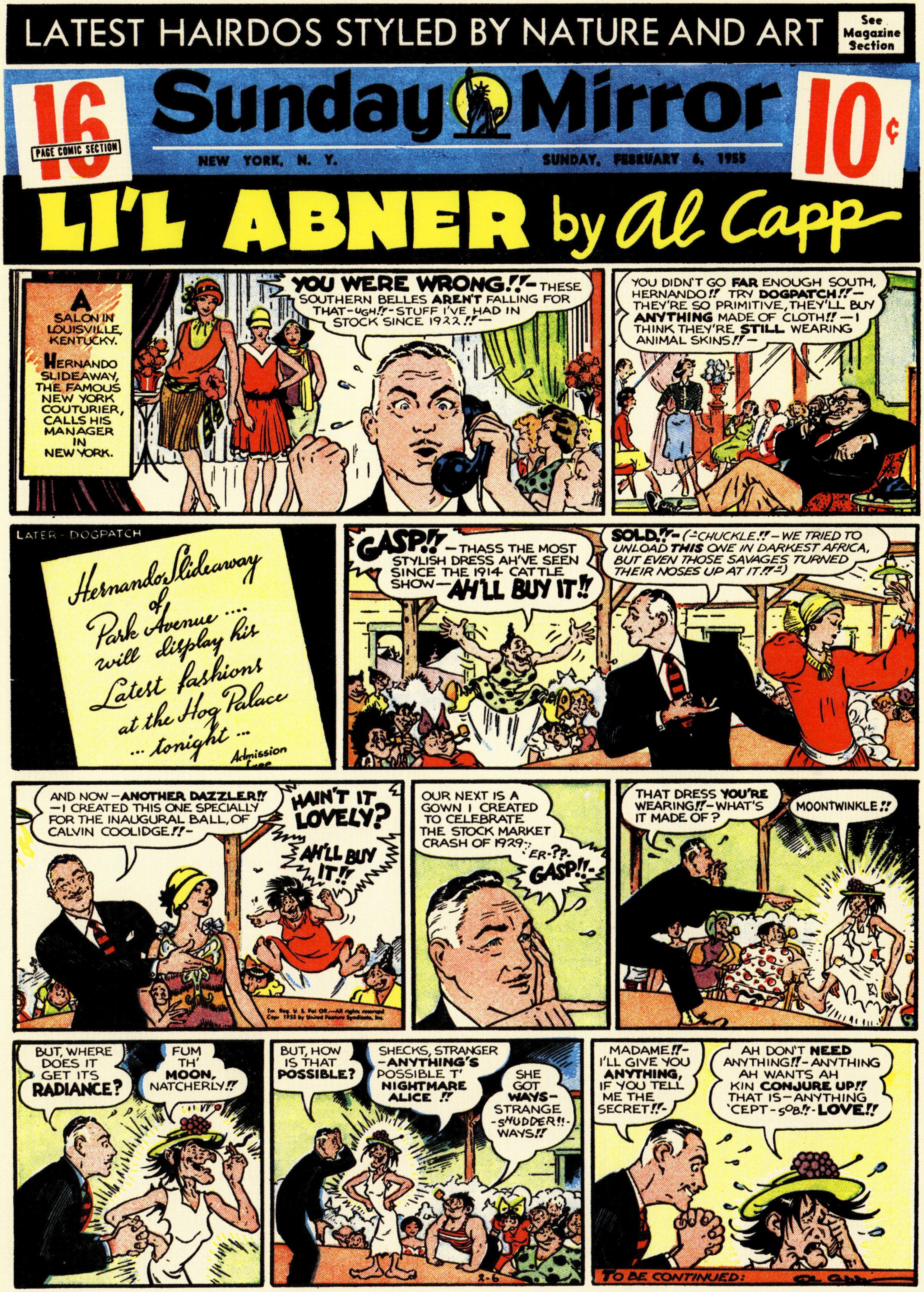
LATEST HAIRDOS STYLED BY NATURE AND ART
See Magazine Section
16 PAGE COMIC SECTION
Sunday Mirror
10¢
NEW YORK, N. Y.
SUNDAY, FEBRUARY 6, 1955
LI'L ABNER by Al Capp
A SALON IN LOUISVILLE, KENTUCKY. HERNANDO SLIDEAWAY, THE FAMOUS NEW YORK COUTURIER, CALLS HIS MANAGER IN NEW YORK.
YOU WERE WRONG!!- THESE SOUTHERN BELLES AREN'T FALLING FOR THAT-UGH!!- STUFF I'VE HAD IN STOCK SINCE 1922!!-
YOU DIDN'T GO FAR ENOUGH SOUTH, HERNANDO!! TRY DOGPATCH!!- THEY'RE SO PRIMITIVE, THEY'LL BUY ANYTHING MADE OF CLOTH!! - I THINK THEY'RE STILL WEARING ANIMAL SKINS!!-
LATER - DOGPATCH
Hernando Slideaway of Park Avenue .... will display his Latest fashions at the Hog Palace ... tonight ...
Admission free
GASP!! - THASS THE MOST STYLISH DRESS AH'VE SEEN SINCE TH' 1914 CATTLE SHOW- AH'LL BUY IT!!
SOLD!!- (-CHUCKLE!!- WE TRIED TO UNLOAD THIS ONE IN DARKEST AFRICA, BUT EVEN THOSE SAVAGES TURNED THEIR NOSES UP AT IT!!-)
AND NOW - ANOTHER DAZZLER!! - I CREATED THIS ONE SPECIALLY FOR THE INAUGURAL BALL, OF CALVIN COOLIDGE!!-
HAIN'T IT LOVELY?
AH'LL BUY IT!!
OUR NEXT IS A GOWN I CREATED TO CELEBRATE THE STOCK MARKET CRASH OF 1929-
ER-??-
GASP!!-
THAT DRESS YOU'RE WEARING!!- WHAT'S IT MADE OF?
MOONTWINKLE!!
BUT, WHERE DOES IT GET ITS RADIANCE?
FUM TH' MOON, NATCHERLY!!
BUT, HOW IS THAT POSSIBLE?
SHECKS, STRANGER - ANYTHING'S POSSIBLE T' NIGHTMARE ALICE!!
SHE GOT WAYS- STRANGE -SHUDDER!!- WAYS!!
MADAME!!- I'LL GIVE YOU ANYTHING, IF YOU TELL ME THE SECRET!!-
AH DON'T NEED ANYTHING!!- ANYTHING AH WANTS AH KIN CONJURE UP!! THAT IS- ANYTHING 'CEPT -SOB!!- LOVE!!
2-6
TO BE CONTINUED:

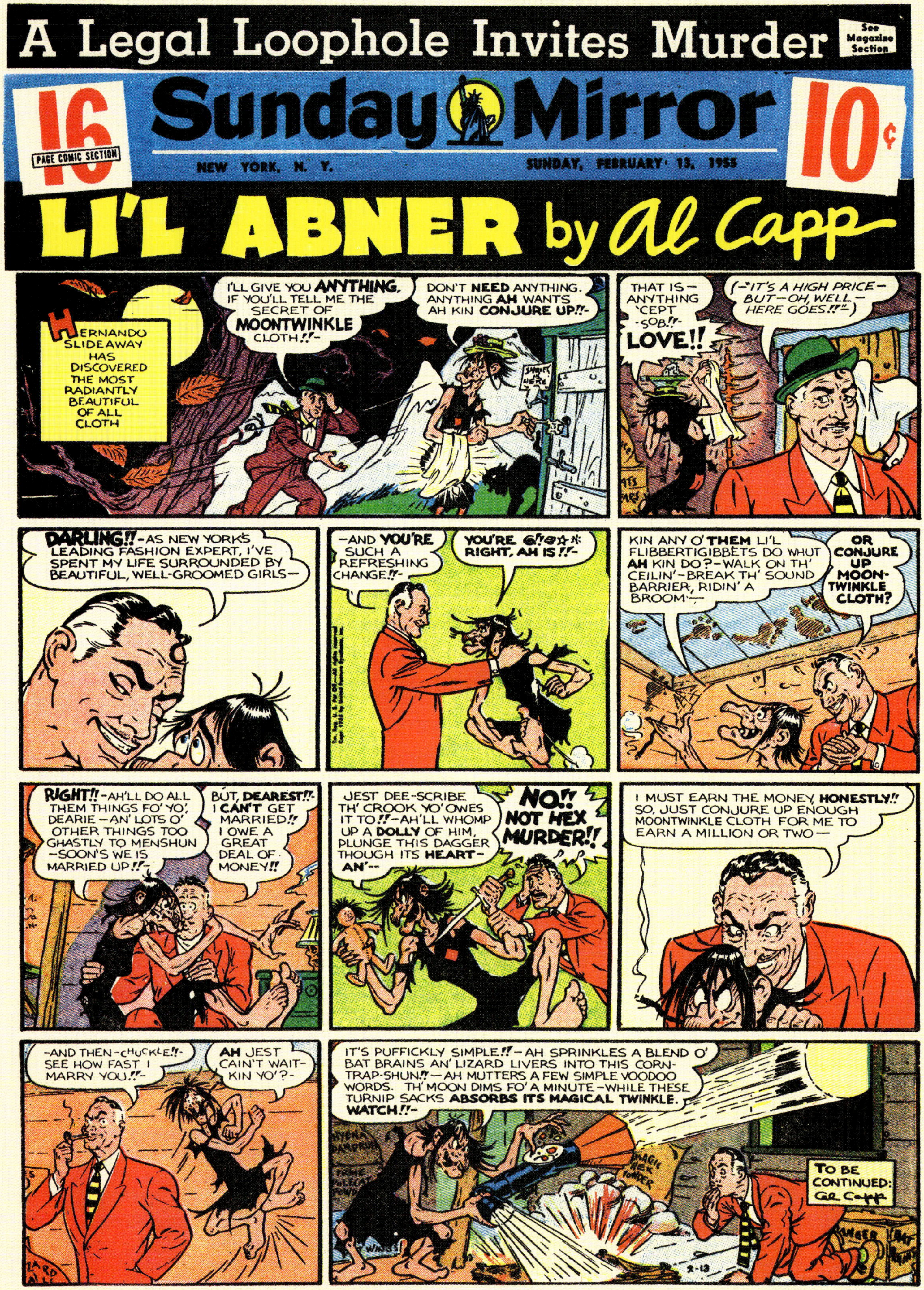
A Legal Loophole Invites Murder
See Magazine Section
16 PAGE COMIC SECTION
Sunday Mirror
10¢
NEW YORK, N. Y.
SUNDAY, FEBRUARY 13, 1955
LI'L ABNER by Al Capp
HERNANDO SLIDEAWAY HAS DISCOVERED THE MOST RADIANTLY BEAUTIFUL OF ALL CLOTH
I'LL GIVE YOU ANYTHING, IF YOU'LL TELL ME THE SECRET OF MOONTWINKLE CLOTH!!-
DON'T NEED ANYTHING. ANYTHING AH WANTS AH KIN CONJURE UP!!-
THAT IS—ANYTHING 'CEPT -SOB!!- LOVE!!
(-"IT'S A HIGH PRICE—BUT—OH, WELL—HERE GOES!!"-)
DARLING!!-AS NEW YORK'S LEADING FASHION EXPERT, I'VE SPENT MY LIFE SURROUNDED BY BEAUTIFUL, WELL-GROOMED GIRLS—
—AND YOU'RE SUCH A REFRESHING CHANGE!!-
YOU'RE ©!☺☆✳ RIGHT, AH IS!!-
KIN ANY O' THEM LI'L FLIBBERTIGIBBETS DO WHUT AH KIN DO?-WALK ON TH' CEILIN'-BREAK TH' SOUND BARRIER, RIDIN' A BROOM—
OR CONJURE UP MOON-TWINKLE CLOTH?
RIGHT!!-AH'LL DO ALL THEM THINGS FO' YO', DEARIE—AN' LOTS O' OTHER THINGS TOO GHASTLY TO MENSHUN -SOON'S WE IS MARRIED UP!!-
BUT, DEAREST!!- I CAN'T GET MARRIED!! I OWE A GREAT DEAL OF MONEY!!
JEST DEE-SCRIBE TH' CROOK YO' OWES IT TO!!-AH'LL WHOMP UP A DOLLY OF HIM, PLUNGE THIS DAGGER THOUGH ITS HEART—AN'--
NO!! NOT HEX MURDER!!
I MUST EARN THE MONEY HONESTLY!! SO, JUST CONJURE UP ENOUGH MOONTWINKLE CLOTH FOR ME TO EARN A MILLION OR TWO—
-AND THEN-CHUCKLE!!- SEE HOW FAST I MARRY YOU!!-
AH JEST CAIN'T WAIT-KIN YO'?-
IT'S PUFFICKLY SIMPLE!!—AH SPRINKLES A BLEND O' BAT BRAINS AN' LIZARD LIVERS INTO THIS CORN-TRAP-SHUN!!—AH MUTTERS A FEW SIMPLE VOODOO WORDS. TH' MOON DIMS FO' A MINUTE—WHILE THESE TURNIP SACKS ABSORBS ITS MAGICAL TWINKLE. WATCH!!-
MAGIC HEX POWDER
TO BE CONTINUED: Al Capp
2-13

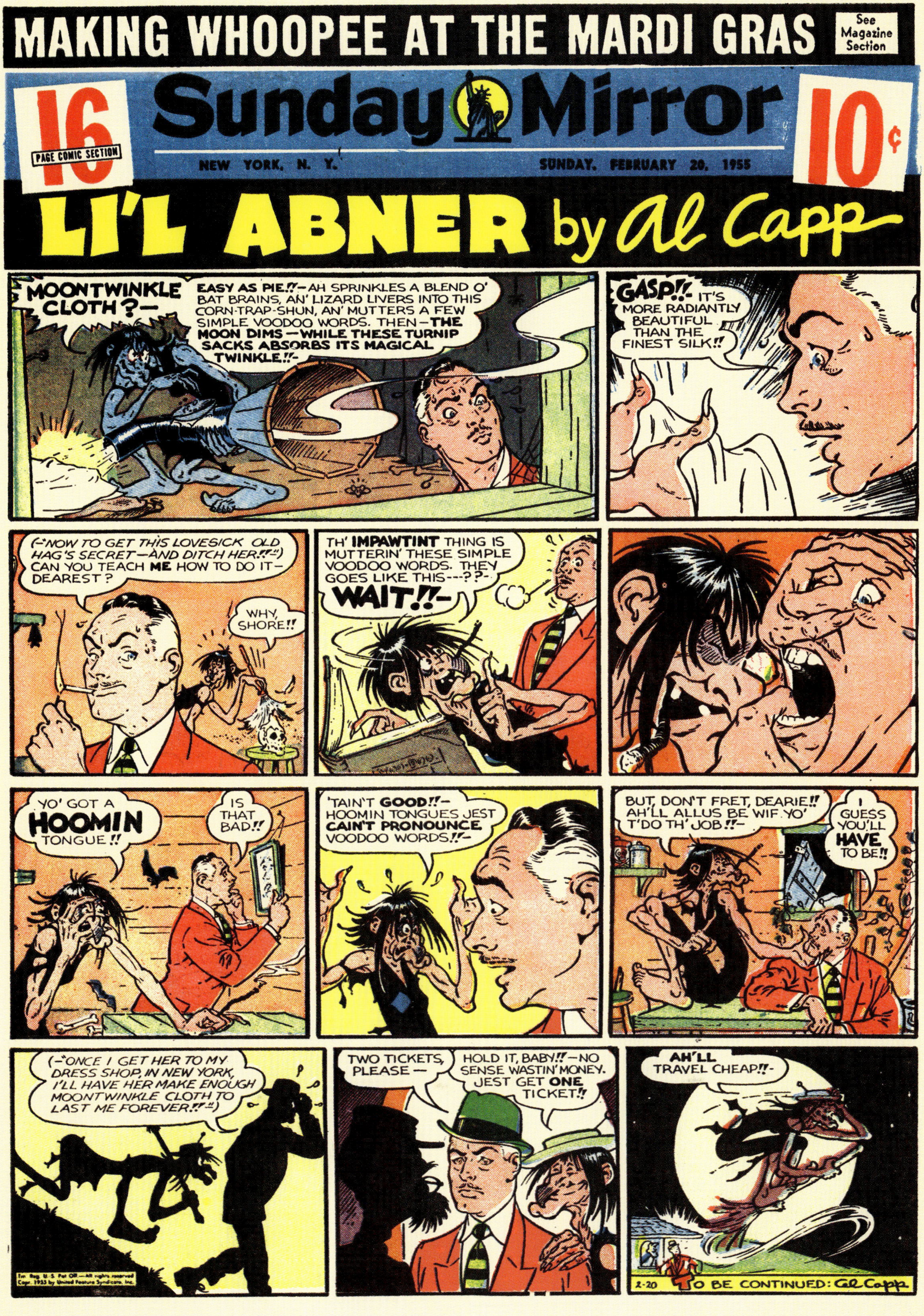

MAKING WHOOPEE AT THE MARDI GRAS
See Magazine Section
16 PAGE COMIC SECTION
Sunday Mirror
10¢
NEW YORK, N. Y.
SUNDAY, FEBRUARY 20, 1955
LI'L ABNER by Al Capp
MOONTWINKLE CLOTH?—
EASY AS PIE!!—AH SPRINKLES A BLEND O' BAT BRAINS, AN' LIZARD LIVERS INTO THIS CORN-TRAP-SHUN, AN' MUTTERS A FEW SIMPLE VOODOO WORDS. THEN—THE MOON DIMS—WHILE THESE TURNIP SACKS ABSORBS ITS MAGICAL TWINKLE!!—
GASP!! IT'S MORE RADIANTLY BEAUTIFUL THAN THE FINEST SILK!!
(—"NOW TO GET THIS LOVESICK OLD HAG'S SECRET—AND DITCH HER!!"—) CAN YOU TEACH ME HOW TO DO IT—DEAREST?
WHY, SHORE!!
TH' IMPAWTINT THING IS MUTTERIN' THESE SIMPLE VOODOO WORDS. THEY GOES LIKE THIS---??-
WAIT!!—
YO' GOT A HOOMIN TONGUE!!
IS THAT BAD!!
'TAIN'T GOOD!!—HOOMIN TONGUES JEST CAIN'T PRONOUNCE VOODOO WORDS!!—
BUT, DON'T FRET, DEARIE!! AH'LL ALLUS BE WIF YO' T'DO TH' JOB!!—
I GUESS YOU'LL HAVE TO BE!!
(—"ONCE I GET HER TO MY DRESS SHOP, IN NEW YORK, I'LL HAVE HER MAKE ENOUGH MOONTWINKLE CLOTH TO LAST ME FOREVER!!"—)
TWO TICKETS, PLEASE—
HOLD IT, BABY!!—NO SENSE WASTIN' MONEY. JEST GET ONE TICKET!!
AH'LL TRAVEL CHEAP!!—
2-20
TO BE CONTINUED: Al Capp

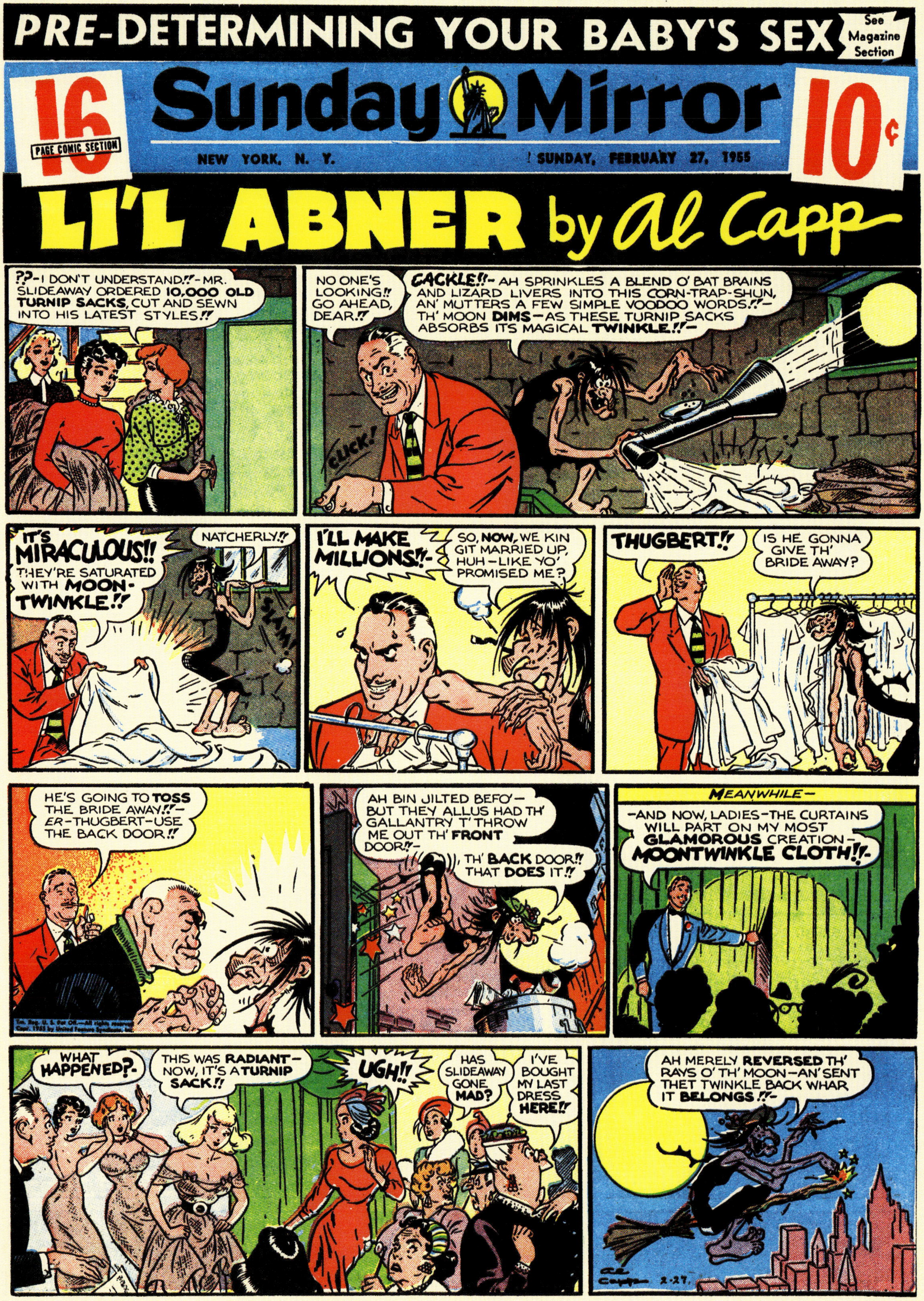

PRE-DETERMINING YOUR BABY'S SEX
See Magazine Section
16
PAGE COMIC SECTION
Sunday Mirror
10¢
NEW YORK, N. Y.
SUNDAY, FEBRUARY 27, 1955
LI'L ABNER by Al Capp
??-I DON'T UNDERSTAND!!-MR. SLIDEAWAY ORDERED 10,000 OLD TURNIP SACKS, CUT AND SEWN INTO HIS LATEST STYLES!!
NO ONE'S LOOKING!! GO AHEAD, DEAR.!!
CLICK!
CACKLE!!-AH SPRINKLES A BLEND O' BAT BRAINS AND LIZARD LIVERS INTO THIS CORN-TRAP-SHUN, AN' MUTTERS A FEW SIMPLE VOODOO WORDS!!-TH' MOON DIMS-AS THESE TURNIP SACKS ABSORBS ITS MAGICAL TWINKLE!!-
IT'S MIRACULOUS!! THEY'RE SATURATED WITH MOON-TWINKLE!!
NATCHERLY!!
SLAM!
I'LL MAKE MILLIONS!!-
SO, NOW, WE KIN GIT MARRIED UP, HUH-LIKE YO' PROMISED ME?
THUGBERT!!
IS HE GONNA GIVE TH' BRIDE AWAY?
HE'S GOING TO TOSS THE BRIDE AWAY!!-ER-THUGBERT-USE THE BACK DOOR!!
AH BIN JILTED BEFO'-BUT THEY ALLUS HAD TH' GALLANTRY T' THROW ME OUT TH' FRONT DOOR!!-
TH' BACK DOOR!! THAT DOES IT!!
MEANWHILE-
-AND NOW, LADIES-THE CURTAINS WILL PART ON MY MOST GLAMOROUS CREATION-MOONTWINKLE CLOTH!!-
WHAT HAPPENED?.
THIS WAS RADIANT-NOW, IT'S A TURNIP SACK!!
UGH!!
HAS SLIDEAWAY GONE MAD?
I'VE BOUGHT MY LAST DRESS HERE!!
AH MERELY REVERSED TH' RAYS O' TH' MOON-AN' SENT THET TWINKLE BACK WHAR IT BELONGS!!-
Al Capp 2-27

BEST COMICS IN THE WORLD
16
PAGE COMIC SECTION
Sunday Mirror
15¢
NEW YORK, N. Y.
SUNDAY, MARCH 6, 1955
LI'L ABNER by Al Capp
HOG PALACE TONIGHT PROFESSOR FLEASONG will give a LANTURN-SLIDE LECK-CHOOR ON "HOW TO JEDGE CHARACTER"
YO' CAIN'T JEDGE FOLKS' CHARACTERS BY THAR FACES!!-
FACES HAS LARNED HOW T' FOOL OTHER FACES, AN' WE MIGHT AS WELL FACE IT!!
TOES ARE TH' TRUE MIRROR O' TH' SOUL!!- TOES DON'T PUT ON AIRS!!- TOES ARE NOT TWO-FACED!!-
ONE O' TH' MOST DANGEROUS TYPES O' TOES IS- SNEAKY TOES!!-
NEVER TURN YORE BACK ON ANY-ONE WIF SNEAKY TOES. SNEAKY TOES MOVES FORWARD, WHILE TH' FOOT STANDS STILL—
—ONE O' TH' MOST APPEALIN' TYPES O' TOES – IS SHY TOES!!-
EVER MEET SOMEONE WHOSE FACE IS PROUD AN' HAUGHTY? – RIP OFF THAR SHOES!!- LOOK AT THAR TOES!!-SEE HOW SHYLY THEY PEEPS AT YO', HOPIN' YO'LL BE FOOLED BY TH' FACE!!
NEXT COMES WORRIED TOES!!- THESE HAS A TENSE, UNDEPENDABLE AIR ABOUT 'EM.
IT'S BETTER T' TURN THESE TOES IN, BECUZ IN TH' END THEY'LL TURN OUT T' BE HEELS!!-
NOW, HERE'S A TYPE O' TOE AH IS ALLUS GLAD T' SEE — GENEROUS TOES!!
PEOPLE WIF THIS TYPE O' TOES HAS A LI'L EXTRA SOMETHIN'. THEY'LL GIVE YO' TH' SHOES OFF THAR FEET —MAINLY BECUZ THEY HURT SO MUCH—
ONE O' TH' MOST UNPLEASANT TYPES O' TOES — IS GRASPING TOES!!-
ONCE THEY GETS A GRIP ON YO', THEY NEVER LETS YO' GO!!- THIS TYPE O' TOE IS FOUND ON APES, MOST RELATIVES, AN' MEMBERS O' YORE LOCAL DRAFT BOARD—
NEXT COMES HEROIC TOES.
THESE TOES IS RUGGED, BRAVE, AN' SELF-RELIANT, AN' KIN BE FOUND ON SECH PEOPLE AS JOHN WAYNE, CLARK GABLE, AN' OVETA CULP HOBBY!!
—AN' NOW COMES TH' NICEST TYPE O' TOES!! — THEY'S GOOD ENUFF T' EAT — TOE-MAY-TOES!!
GIT IT?— HA!!-HA!!- ??-MAH WALLET- IT'S GONE!!
HAW!!- FLEASONG DIDN'T NOTICE AH GOT CROOKED TOES!!

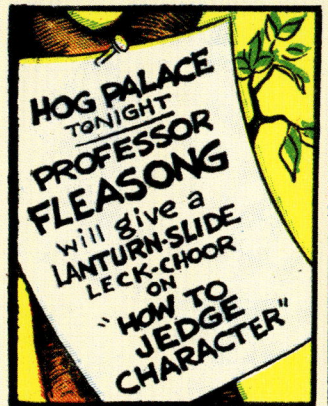

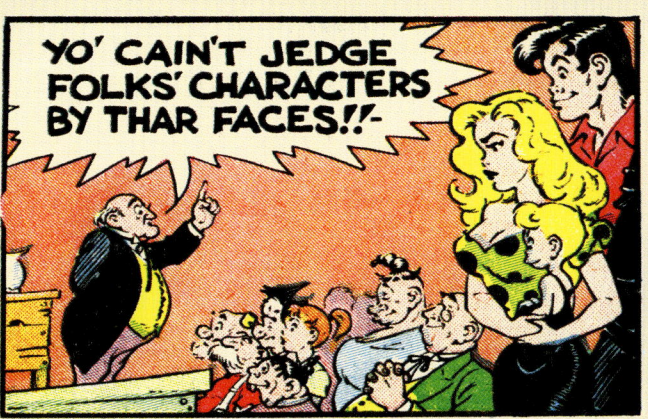

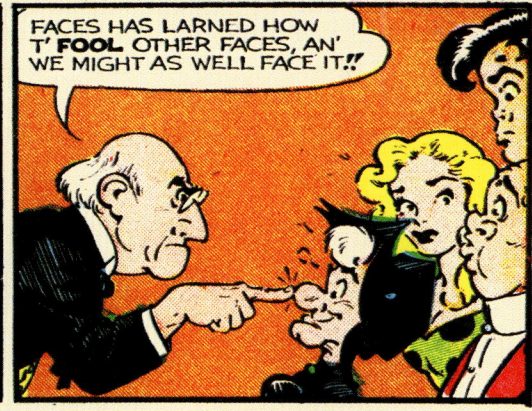

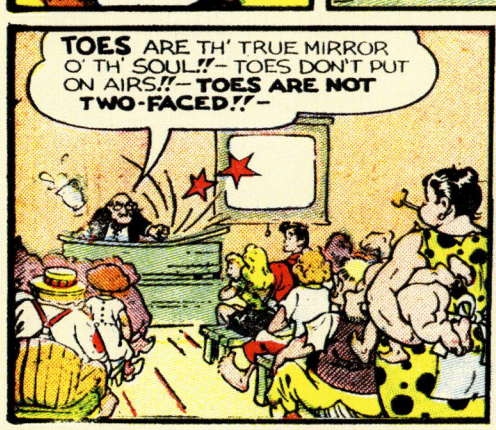

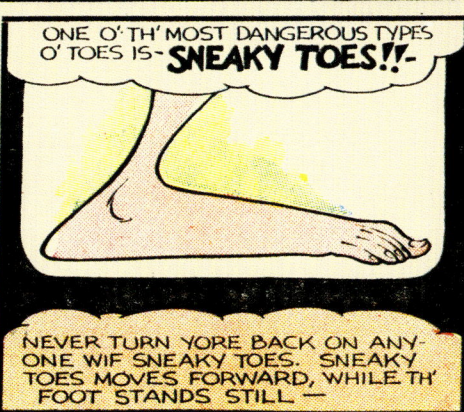

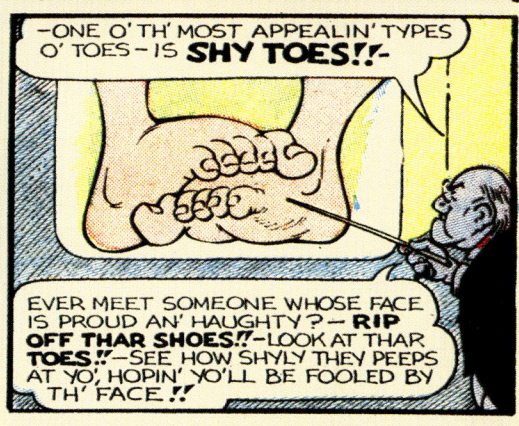

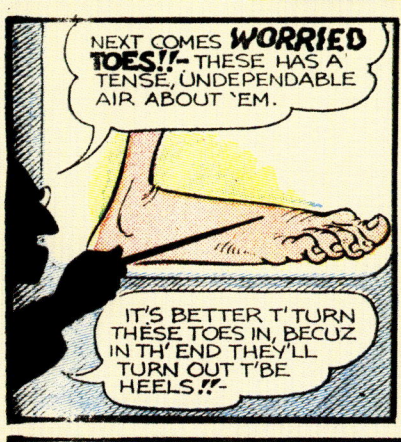

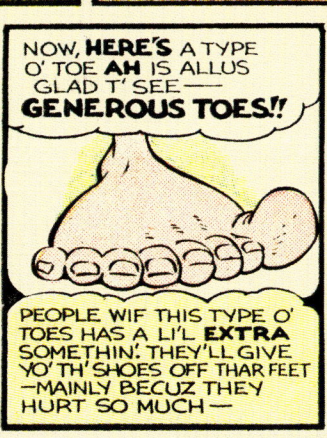

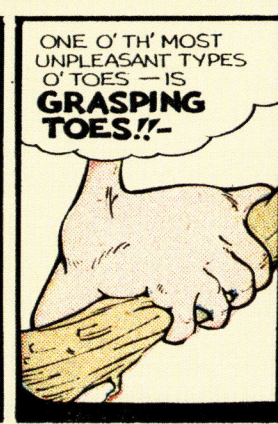

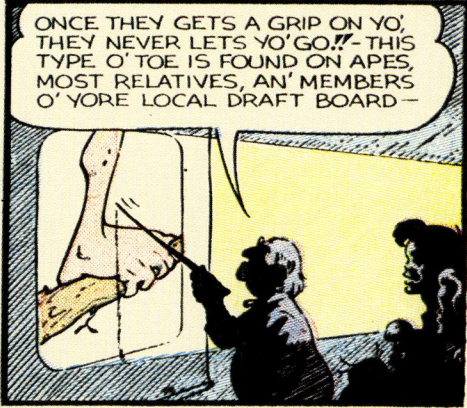

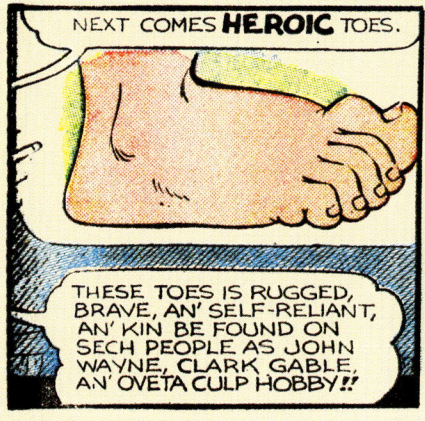

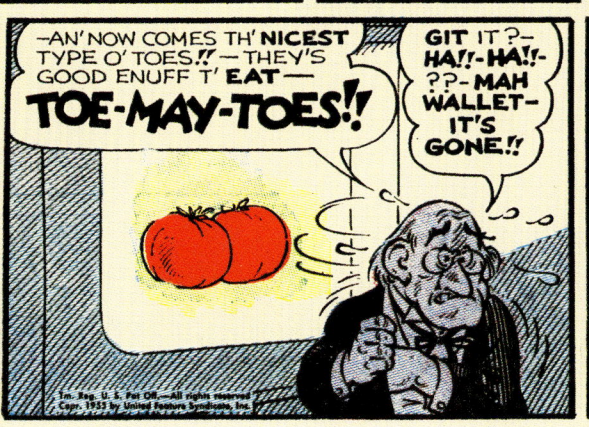

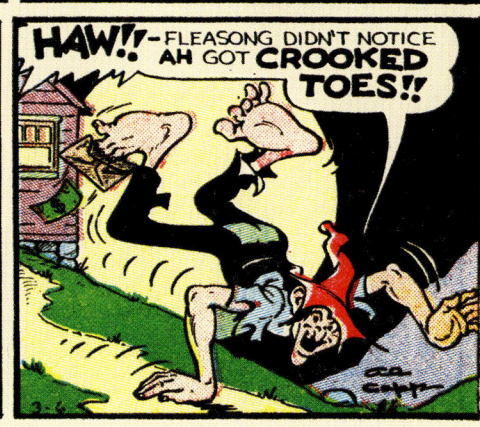

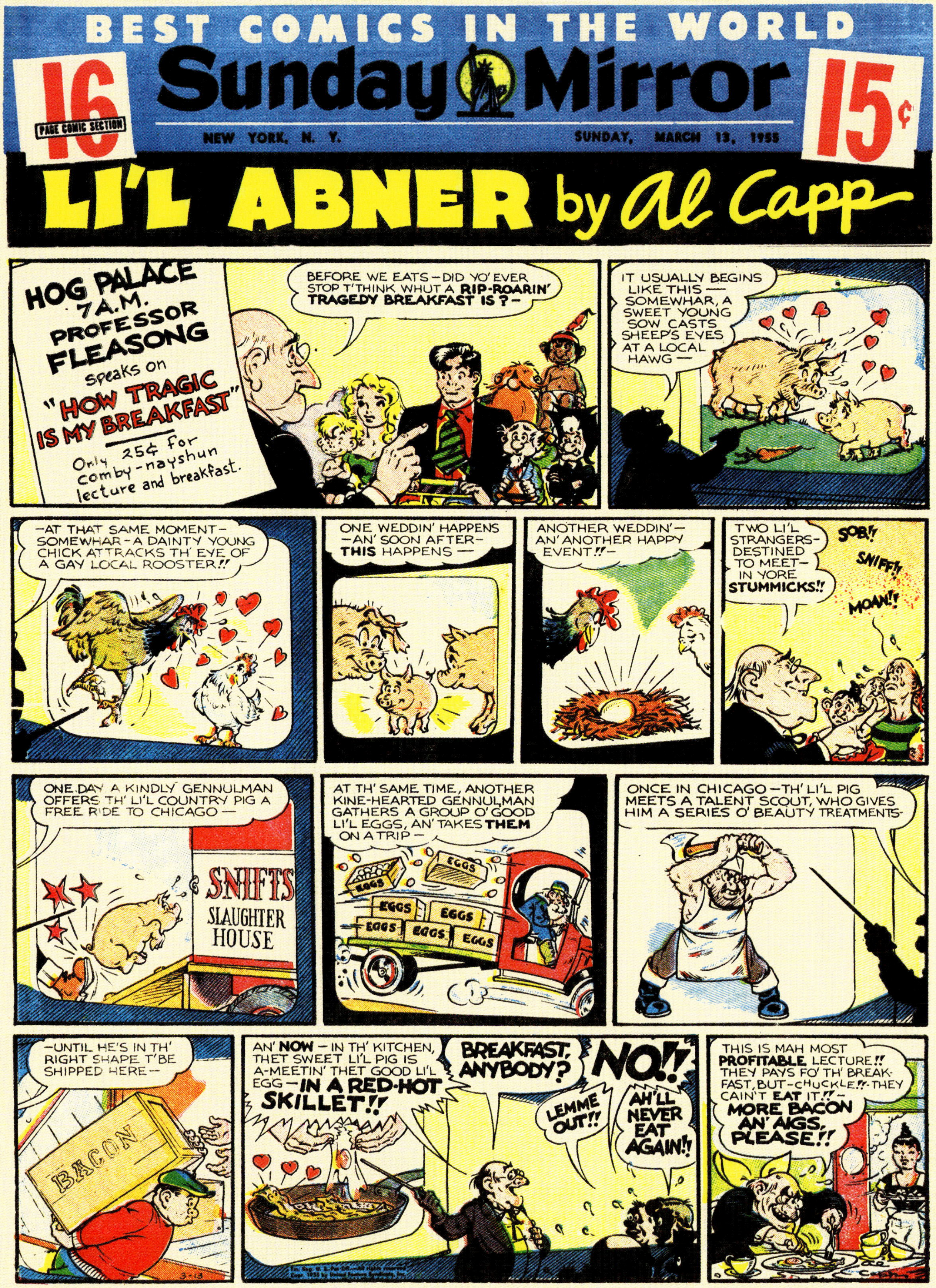

BEST COMICS IN THE WORLD
16
PAGE COMIC SECTION
Sunday Mirror
15¢
NEW YORK, N. Y.
SUNDAY, MARCH 13, 1955
LI'L ABNER by Al Capp
HOG PALACE 7 A.M. PROFESSOR FLEASONG Speaks on "HOW TRAGIC IS MY BREAKFAST" Only 25¢ for comby-nayshun lecture and breakfast.
BEFORE WE EATS—DID YO' EVER STOP T'THINK WHUT A RIP-ROARIN' TRAGEDY BREAKFAST IS?—
IT USUALLY BEGINS LIKE THIS—SOMEWHAR, A SWEET YOUNG SOW CASTS SHEEP'S EYES AT A LOCAL HAWG—
—AT THAT SAME MOMENT—SOMEWHAR—A DAINTY YOUNG CHICK ATTRACKS TH' EYE OF A GAY LOCAL ROOSTER!!
ONE WEDDIN' HAPPENS—AN' SOON AFTER—THIS HAPPENS—
ANOTHER WEDDIN'—AN' ANOTHER HAPPY EVENT!!—
TWO LI'L STRANGERS—DESTINED TO MEET—IN YORE STUMMICKS!!
SOB!!
SNIFF!!
MOAN!!
ONE DAY A KINDLY GENNULMAN OFFERS TH' LI'L COUNTRY PIG A FREE RIDE TO CHICAGO—
SNIFTS SLAUGHTER HOUSE
AT TH' SAME TIME, ANOTHER KINE-HEARTED GENNULMAN GATHERS A GROUP O' GOOD LI'L EGGS, AN' TAKES THEM ON A TRIP—
EGGS
ONCE IN CHICAGO—TH' LI'L PIG MEETS A TALENT SCOUT, WHO GIVES HIM A SERIES O' BEAUTY TREATMENTS—
—UNTIL HE'S IN TH' RIGHT SHAPE T'BE SHIPPED HERE—
BACON
AN' NOW—IN TH' KITCHEN, THET SWEET LI'L PIG IS A-MEETIN' THET GOOD LI'L EGG—IN A RED-HOT SKILLET!!
BREAKFAST, ANYBODY?
NO!!
LEMME OUT!!
AH'LL NEVER EAT AGAIN!!
THIS IS MAH MOST PROFITABLE LECTURE!! THEY PAYS FO' TH' BREAKFAST, BUT—CHUCKLE!!—THEY CAIN'T EAT IT!!—
MORE BACON AN' AIGS, PLEASE!!

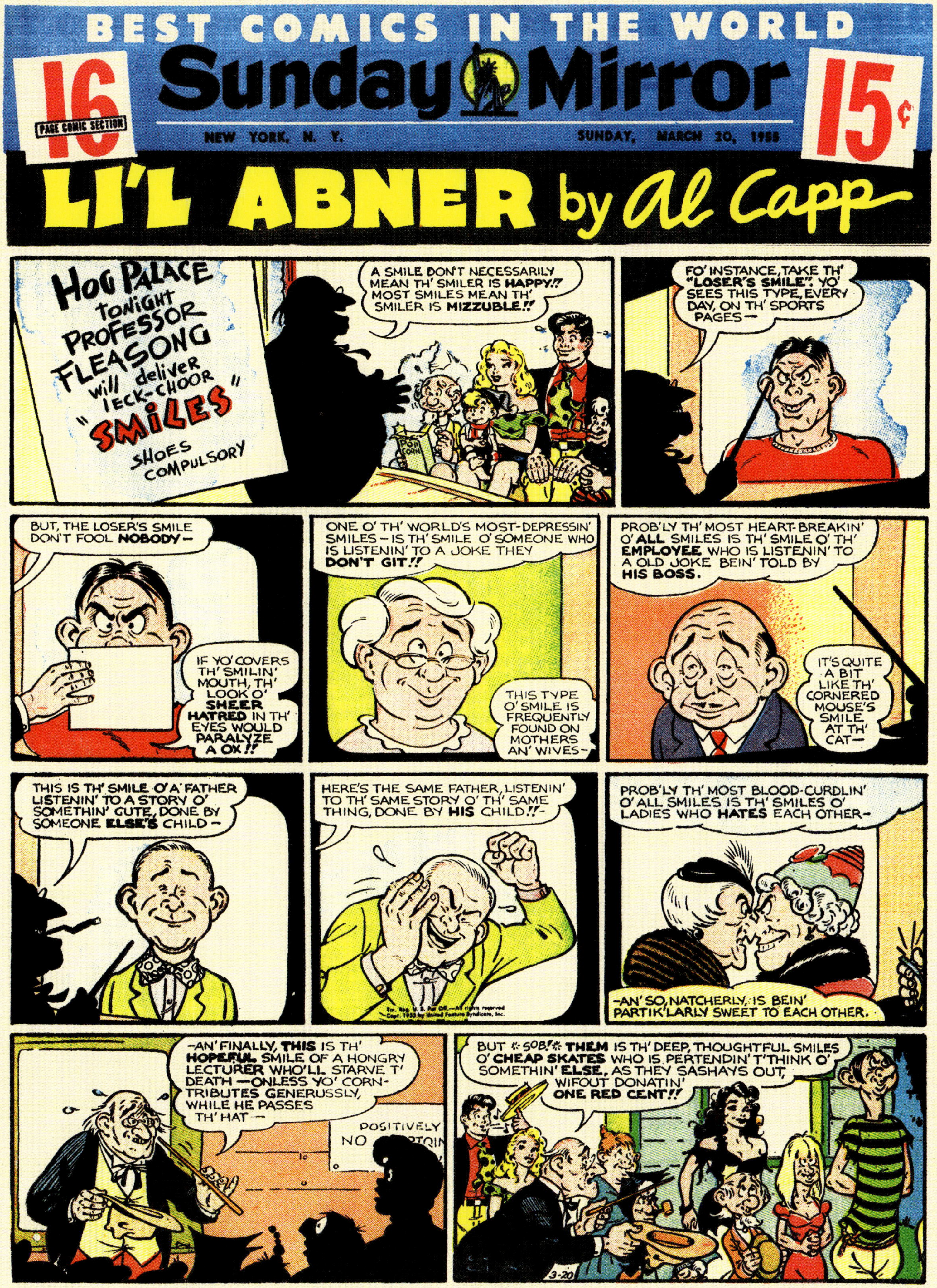

BEST COMICS IN THE WORLD
16
PAGE COMIC SECTION
Sunday Mirror
15¢
NEW YORK, N. Y.
SUNDAY, MARCH 20, 1955
LI'L ABNER by Al Capp
HOG PALACE TONIGHT PROFESSOR FLEASONG will deliver LECK-CHOOR "SMILES" SHOES COMPULSORY
A SMILE DON'T NECESSARILY MEAN TH' SMILER IS HAPPY!! MOST SMILES MEAN TH' SMILER IS MIZZUBLE!!
POP CORN
FO' INSTANCE, TAKE TH' "LOSER'S SMILE". YO' SEES THIS TYPE, EVERY DAY, ON TH' SPORTS PAGES—
BUT, THE LOSER'S SMILE DON'T FOOL NOBODY—
IF YO' COVERS TH' SMILIN' MOUTH, TH' LOOK O' SHEER HATRED IN TH' EYES WOULD PARALYZE A OX!!
ONE O' TH' WORLD'S MOST-DEPRESSIN' SMILES—IS TH' SMILE O' SOMEONE WHO IS LISTENIN' TO A JOKE THEY DON'T GIT!!
THIS TYPE O' SMILE IS FREQUENTLY FOUND ON MOTHERS AN' WIVES—
PROB'LY TH' MOST HEART-BREAKIN' O' ALL SMILES IS TH' SMILE O' TH' EMPLOYEE WHO IS LISTENIN' TO A OLD JOKE BEIN' TOLD BY HIS BOSS.
IT'S QUITE A BIT LIKE TH' CORNERED MOUSE'S SMILE, AT TH' CAT—
THIS IS TH' SMILE O' A FATHER LISTENIN' TO A STORY O' SOMETHIN' CUTE, DONE BY SOMEONE ELSE'S CHILD—
HERE'S THE SAME FATHER, LISTENIN' TO TH' SAME STORY O' TH' SAME THING, DONE BY HIS CHILD!!—
Tm. Reg. U. S. Pat. Off.—All rights reserved
Copr. 1955 by United Feature Syndicate, Inc.
PROB'LY TH' MOST BLOOD-CURDLIN' O' ALL SMILES IS TH' SMILES O' LADIES WHO HATES EACH OTHER—
—AN' SO, NATCHERLY, IS BEIN' PARTIK'LARLY SWEET TO EACH OTHER.
—AN' FINALLY, THIS IS TH' HOPEFUL SMILE OF A HONGRY LECTURER WHO'LL STARVE T' DEATH —ONLESS YO' CORN-TRIBUTES GENERUSSLY, WHILE HE PASSES TH' HAT—
POSITIVELY NO
BUT *SOB!* THEM IS TH' DEEP, THOUGHTFUL SMILES O' CHEAP SKATES WHO IS PERTENDIN' T' THINK O' SOMETHIN' ELSE, AS THEY SASHAYS OUT, WIFOUT DONATIN' ONE RED CENT!!
3-20

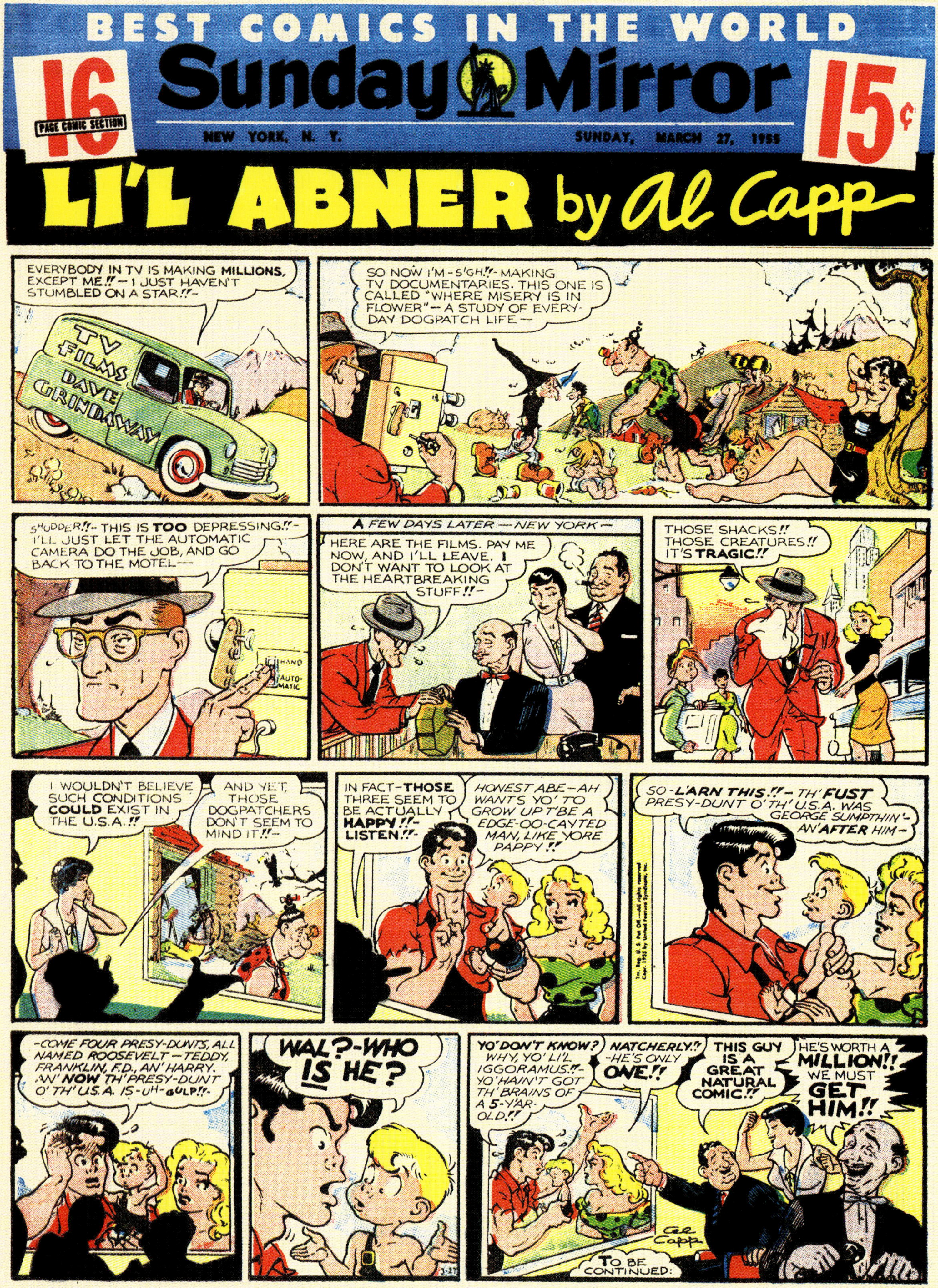

BEST COMICS IN THE WORLD
Sunday Mirror
16 PAGE COMIC SECTION
NEW YORK, N. Y.
SUNDAY, MARCH 27, 1955
15¢
LI'L ABNER by Al Capp
EVERYBODY IN TV IS MAKING MILLIONS, EXCEPT ME.!! – I JUST HAVEN'T STUMBLED ON A STAR!! –
TV FILMS DAVE GRINDAWAY
SO NOW I'M – S'GH!! – MAKING TV DOCUMENTARIES. THIS ONE IS CALLED "WHERE MISERY IS IN FLOWER" – A STUDY OF EVERY-DAY DOGPATCH LIFE –
SHUDDER!! – THIS IS TOO DEPRESSING!! – I'LL JUST LET THE AUTOMATIC CAMERA DO THE JOB, AND GO BACK TO THE MOTEL –
HAND
AUTO-MATIC
A FEW DAYS LATER – NEW YORK –
HERE ARE THE FILMS. PAY ME NOW, AND I'LL LEAVE. I DON'T WANT TO LOOK AT THE HEARTBREAKING STUFF!! –
THOSE SHACKS!! THOSE CREATURES!! IT'S TRAGIC!!
I WOULDN'T BELIEVE SUCH CONDITIONS COULD EXIST IN THE U.S.A.!!
AND YET, THOSE DOGPATCHERS DON'T SEEM TO MIND IT!! –
IN FACT – THOSE THREE SEEM TO BE ACTUALLY HAPPY!! – LISTEN!! –
HONEST ABE – AH WANTS YO' TO GROW UP T'BE A EDGE-OO-CAYTED MAN, LIKE YORE PAPPY!!
SO – L'ARN THIS!! – TH' FUST PRESY-DUNT O'TH' U.S.A. WAS GEORGE SUMPTHIN' – AN' AFTER HIM –
– COME FOUR PRESY-DUNTS, ALL NAMED ROOSEVELT – TEDDY, FRANKLIN, F.D., AN' HARRY. AN' NOW TH' PRESY-DUNT O'TH' U.S.A. IS – UH – GULP!! –
WAL? – WHO IS HE?
YO' DON'T KNOW? WHY, YO' LI'L IGGORAMUS!! – YO' HAIN'T GOT TH' BRAINS OF A 5-YAR-OLD!!
NATCHERLY!! – HE'S ONLY ONE!!
THIS GUY IS A GREAT NATURAL COMIC!!
HE'S WORTH A MILLION!! WE MUST GET HIM!!
Al Capp
TO BE CONTINUED:

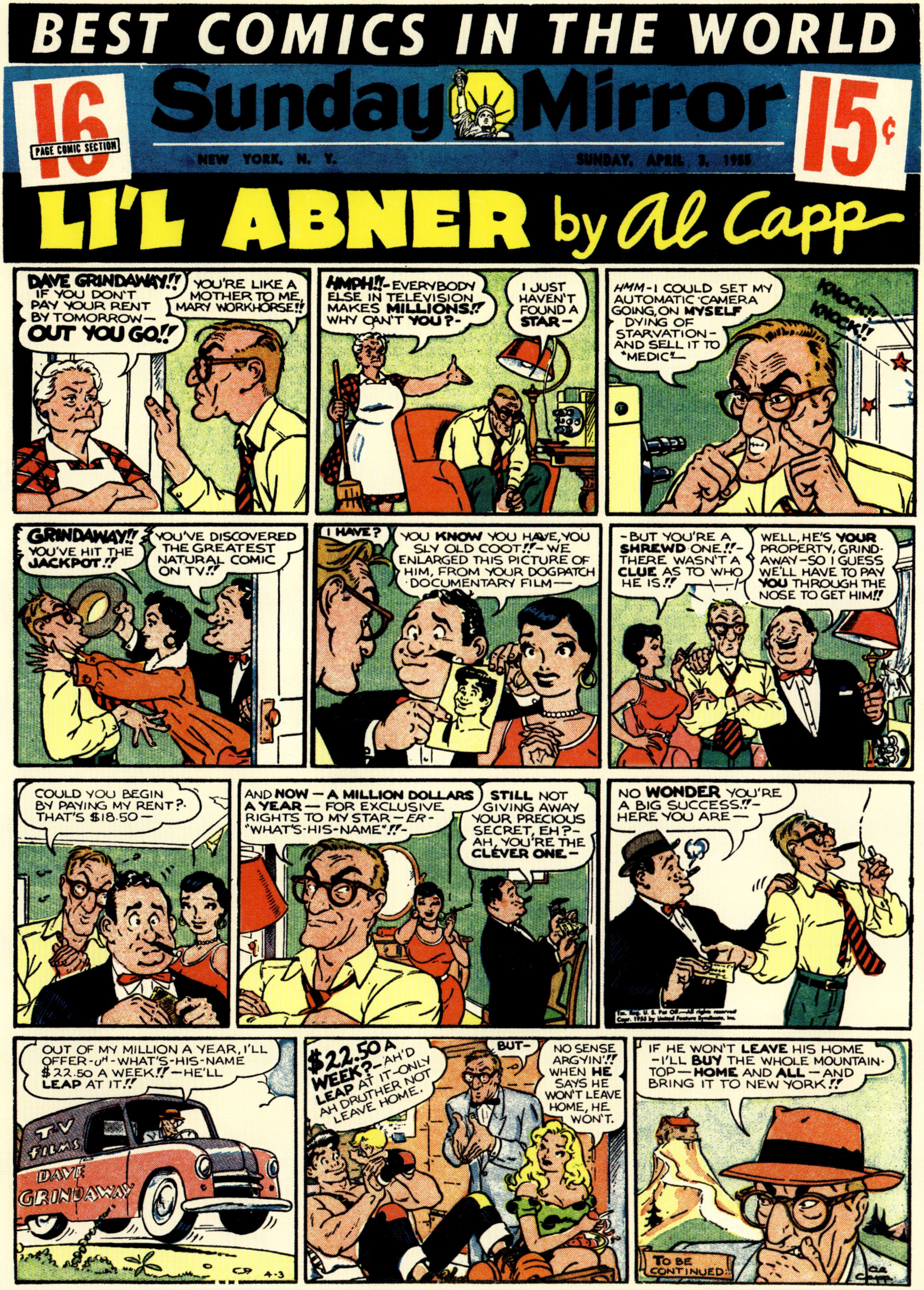
BEST COMICS IN THE WORLD
16 PAGE COMIC SECTION
Sunday Mirror
NEW YORK, N. Y.
SUNDAY, APRIL 3, 1955
15¢
LI'L ABNER by Al Capp
DAVE GRINDAWAY!! IF YOU DON'T PAY YOUR RENT BY TOMORROW— OUT YOU GO!!
YOU'RE LIKE A MOTHER TO ME, MARY WORKHORSE!!
HMPH!!— EVERYBODY ELSE IN TELEVISION MAKES MILLIONS!! WHY CAN'T YOU?—
I JUST HAVEN'T FOUND A STAR—
HMM— I COULD SET MY AUTOMATIC CAMERA GOING, ON MYSELF DYING OF STARVATION— AND SELL IT TO "MEDIC"!—
KNOCK!! KNOCK!!
GRINDAWAY!! YOU'VE HIT THE JACKPOT!!
YOU'VE DISCOVERED THE GREATEST NATURAL COMIC ON TV!!
I HAVE?
YOU KNOW YOU HAVE, YOU SLY OLD COOT!!— WE ENLARGED THIS PICTURE OF HIM, FROM YOUR DOGPATCH DOCUMENTARY FILM—
—BUT YOU'RE A SHREWD ONE!!— THERE WASN'T A CLUE AS TO WHO HE IS!!
WELL, HE'S YOUR PROPERTY, GRINDAWAY— SO I GUESS WE'LL HAVE TO PAY YOU THROUGH THE NOSE TO GET HIM!!
COULD YOU BEGIN BY PAYING MY RENT?. THAT'S $18.50—
AND NOW— A MILLION DOLLARS A YEAR— FOR EXCLUSIVE RIGHTS TO MY STAR— ER— "WHAT'S-HIS-NAME"!!—
STILL NOT GIVING AWAY YOUR PRECIOUS SECRET, EH?— AH, YOU'RE THE CLEVER ONE—
NO WONDER YOU'RE A BIG SUCCESS!!— HERE YOU ARE—
OUT OF MY MILLION A YEAR, I'LL OFFER— UH— WHAT'S-HIS-NAME $22.50 A WEEK!!— HE'LL LEAP AT IT!!
T-V FILMS DAVE GRINDAWAY
$22.50 A WEEK?— AH'D LEAP AT IT— ONLY AH DRUTHER NOT LEAVE HOME.
BUT—
NO SENSE ARGYIN'!! WHEN HE SAYS HE WON'T LEAVE HOME, HE WON'T.
IF HE WON'T LEAVE HIS HOME —I'LL BUY THE WHOLE MOUNTAIN-TOP— HOME AND ALL— AND BRING IT TO NEW YORK!!
TO BE CONTINUED

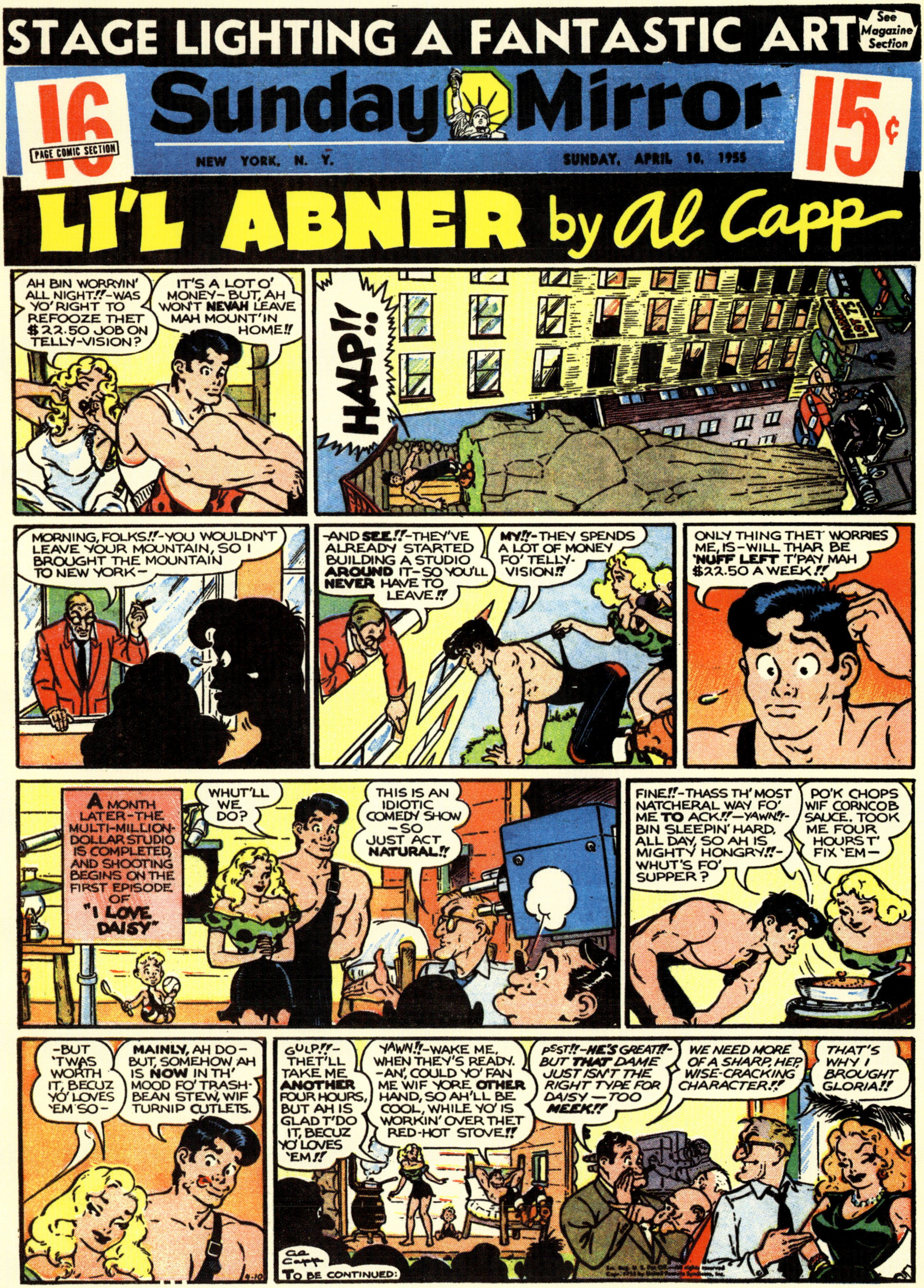

STAGE LIGHTING A FANTASTIC ART
See Magazine Section
16
PAGE COMIC SECTION
Sunday Mirror
15¢
NEW YORK, N. Y.
SUNDAY, APRIL 10, 1955
LI'L ABNER by Al Capp
AH BIN WORRYIN' ALL NIGHT!!-WAS YO' RIGHT TO REFOOZE THET $22.50 JOB ON TELLY-VISION?
IT'S A LOT O' MONEY- BUT, AH WON'T NEVAH LEAVE MAH MOUNT'IN HOME!!
HALP!!
MORNING, FOLKS!!-YOU WOULDN'T LEAVE YOUR MOUNTAIN, SO I BROUGHT THE MOUNTAIN TO NEW YORK-
-AND SEE!!-THEY'VE ALREADY STARTED BUILDING A STUDIO AROUND IT-SO YOU'LL NEVER HAVE TO LEAVE!!
MY!!-THEY SPENDS A LOT OF MONEY FO' TELLY-VISION!!
ONLY THING THET WORRIES ME, IS-WILL THAR BE 'NUFF LEFT T'PAY MAH $22.50 A WEEK!!
A MONTH LATER-THE MULTI-MILLION-DOLLAR STUDIO IS COMPLETED, AND SHOOTING BEGINS ON THE FIRST EPISODE OF "I LOVE DAISY"
WHUT'LL WE DO?
THIS IS AN IDIOTIC COMEDY SHOW -SO JUST ACT NATURAL!!
FINE!!-THASS TH' MOST NATCHERAL WAY FO' ME TO ACK!!-YAWN!!-BIN SLEEPIN' HARD ALL DAY, SO AH IS MIGHTY HONGRY!!-WHUT'S FO' SUPPER?
PO'K CHOPS WIF CORNCOB SAUCE. TOOK ME FOUR HOURS T' FIX 'EM-
-BUT 'TWAS WORTH IT, BECUZ YO' LOVES 'EM SO-
MAINLY, AH DO-BUT, SOMEHOW AH IS NOW IN TH' MOOD FO' TRASH-BEAN STEW, WIF TURNIP CUTLETS.
GULP!!-THET'LL TAKE ME ANOTHER FOUR HOURS, BUT AH IS GLAD T'DO IT, BECUZ YO' LOVES 'EM!!
YAWN!!-WAKE ME, WHEN THEY'S READY. -AN', COULD YO' FAN ME WIF YORE OTHER HAND, SO AH'LL BE COOL, WHILE YO' IS WORKIN' OVER THET RED-HOT STOVE!!
PSST!!-HE'S GREAT!!-BUT THAT DAME JUST ISN'T THE RIGHT TYPE FOR DAISY—TOO MEEK!!
WE NEED MORE OF A SHARP, HEP, WISE-CRACKING CHARACTER!!
THAT'S WHY I BROUGHT GLORIA!!
Al Capp
TO BE CONTINUED:

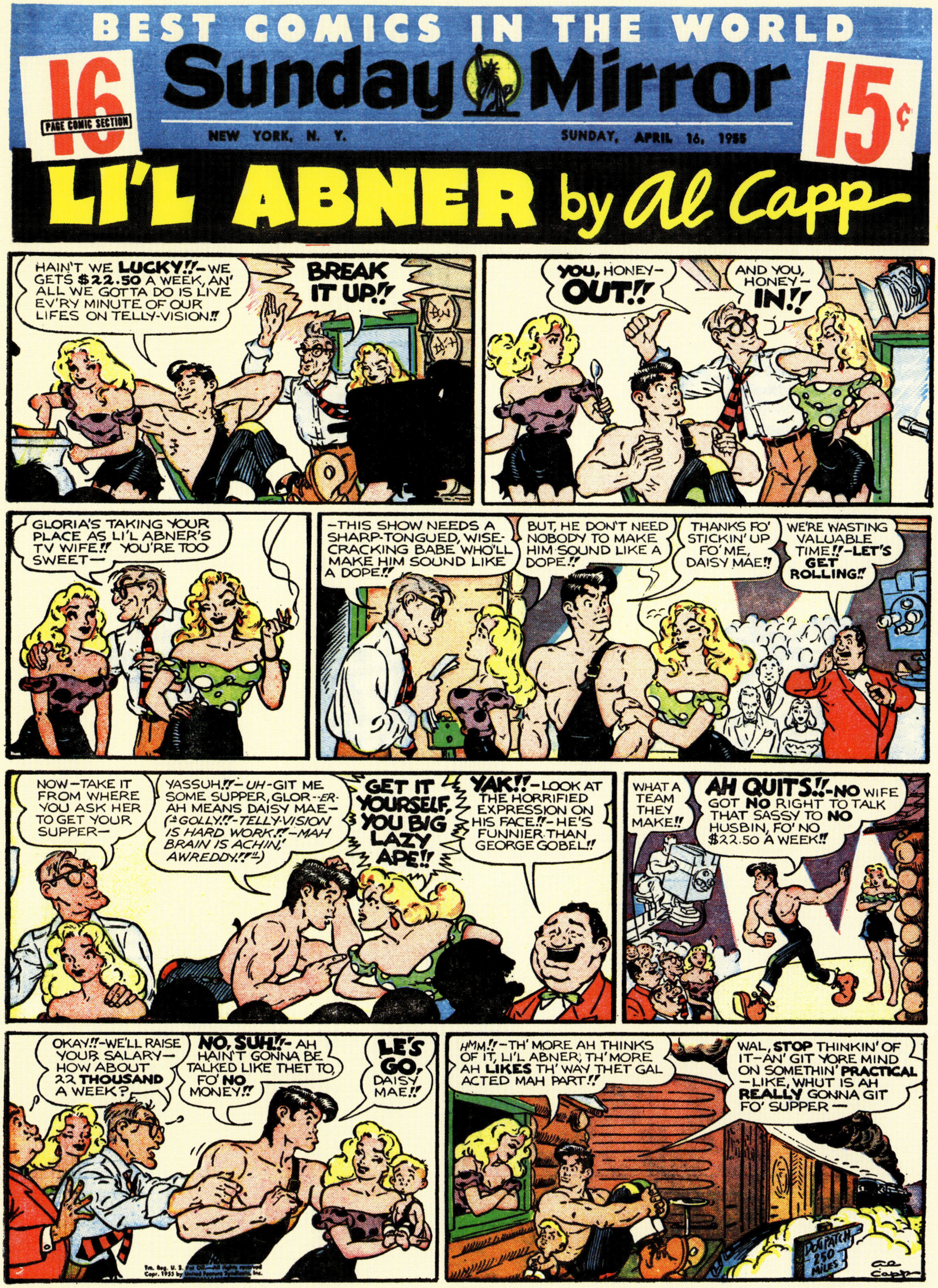

BEST COMICS IN THE WORLD
16
PAGE COMIC SECTION
Sunday Mirror
15¢
NEW YORK, N. Y.
SUNDAY, APRIL 16, 1955
LI'L ABNER by Al Capp
HAIN'T WE LUCKY!!–WE GETS $22.50 A WEEK, AN' ALL WE GOTTA DO IS LIVE EV'RY MINUTE OF OUR LIFES ON TELLY-VISION!!
BREAK IT UP!!
YOU, HONEY– OUT!!
AND YOU, HONEY– IN!!
GLORIA'S TAKING YOUR PLACE AS LI'L ABNER'S TV WIFE!! YOU'RE TOO SWEET–
–THIS SHOW NEEDS A SHARP-TONGUED, WISE-CRACKING BABE WHO'LL MAKE HIM SOUND LIKE A DOPE!!
BUT, HE DON'T NEED NOBODY TO MAKE HIM SOUND LIKE A DOPE.!!
THANKS FO' STICKIN' UP FO' ME, DAISY MAE!!
WE'RE WASTING VALUABLE TIME!!–LET'S GET ROLLING!!
NOW–TAKE IT FROM WHERE YOU ASK HER TO GET YOUR SUPPER–
YASSUH!!–UH–GIT ME SOME SUPPER, GLOR–ER–AH MEANS DAISY MAE–(–GOLLY!!–TELLY-VISION IS HARD WORK!!–MAH BRAIN IS ACHIN' AWREDDY!!–)
GET IT YOURSELF, YOU BIG LAZY APE!!
YAK!!–LOOK AT THE HORRIFIED EXPRESSION ON HIS FACE!!–HE'S FUNNIER THAN GEORGE GOBEL!!
WHAT A TEAM THEY MAKE!!
AH QUITS!!–NO WIFE GOT NO RIGHT TO TALK THAT SASSY TO NO HUSBIN, FO' NO $22.50 A WEEK!!
OKAY!!–WE'LL RAISE YOUR SALARY– HOW ABOUT 22 THOUSAND A WEEK?
NO, SUH!!–AH HAIN'T GONNA BE TALKED LIKE THET TO, FO' NO MONEY!!
LE'S GO, DAISY MAE!!
HMM!!–TH' MORE AH THINKS OF IT, LI'L ABNER, TH' MORE AH LIKES TH' WAY THET GAL ACTED MAH PART!!
WAL, STOP THINKIN' OF IT–AN' GIT YORE MIND ON SOMETHIN' PRACTICAL –LIKE, WHUT IS AH REALLY GONNA GIT FO' SUPPER–
DOGPATCH 250 MILES
Al Capp

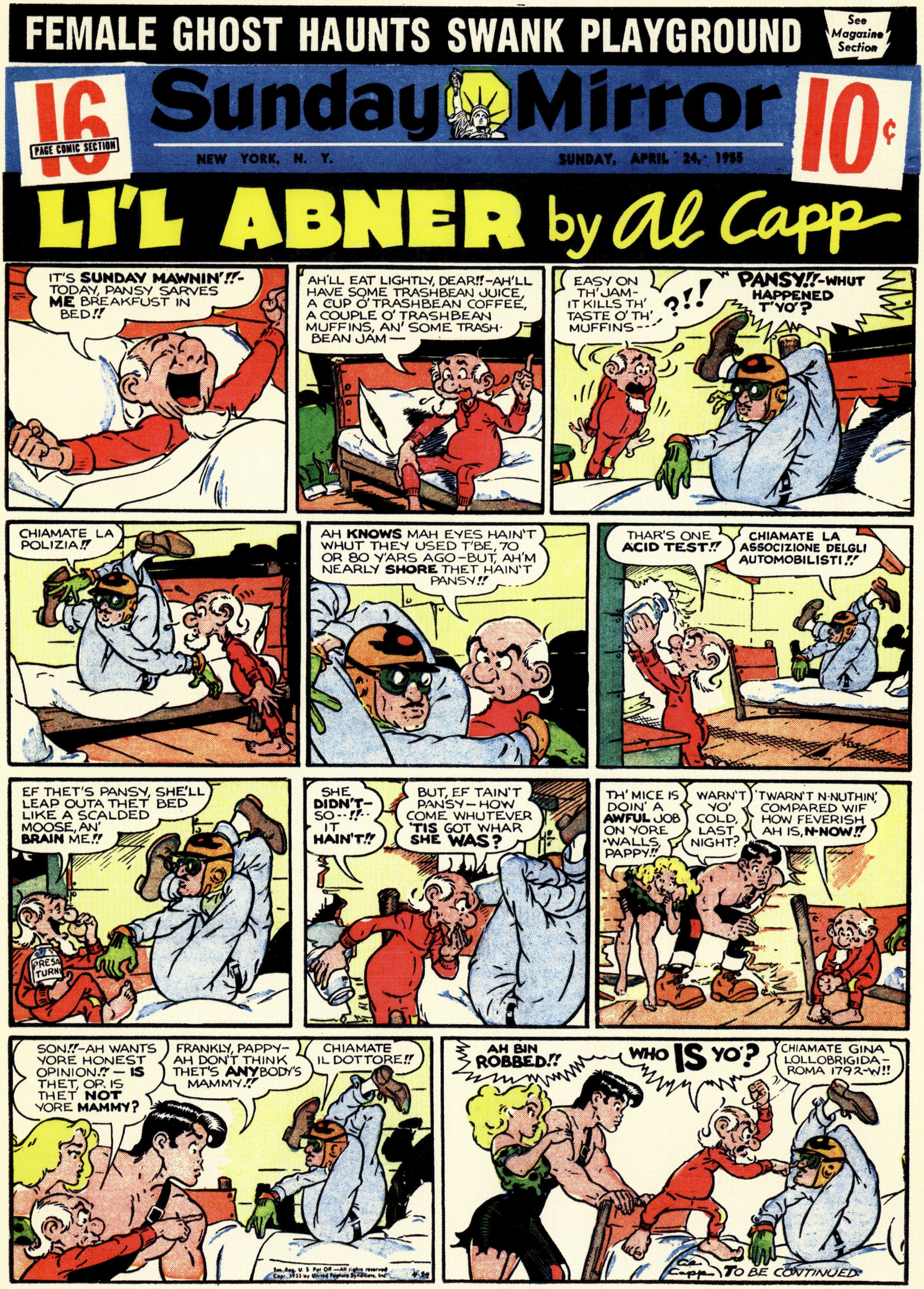
FEMALE GHOST HAUNTS SWANK PLAYGROUND
See Magazine Section
16
PAGE COMIC SECTION
Sunday Mirror
NEW YORK, N. Y.
SUNDAY, APRIL 24, 1955
10¢
LI'L ABNER by Al Capp
IT'S SUNDAY MAWNIN'!!- TODAY, PANSY SARVES ME BREAKFUST IN BED!!
AH'LL EAT LIGHTLY, DEAR!!-AH'LL HAVE SOME TRASHBEAN JUICE, A CUP O'TRASHBEAN COFFEE, A COUPLE O'TRASHBEAN MUFFINS, AN' SOME TRASH-BEAN JAM —
EASY ON TH' JAM- IT KILLS TH' TASTE O' TH' MUFFINS---
?!!
PANSY!!-WHUT HAPPENED T'YO'?
CHIAMATE LA POLIZIA!!
AH KNOWS MAH EYES HAIN'T WHUT THEY USED T'BE, 70 OR 80 Y'ARS AGO-BUT, AH'M NEARLY SHORE THET HAIN'T PANSY!!
THAR'S ONE ACID TEST!!
CHIAMATE LA ASSOCIZIONE DELGLI AUTOMOBILISTI!!
EF THET'S PANSY, SHE'LL LEAP OUTA THET BED LIKE A SCALDED MOOSE, AN' BRAIN ME!!
PRESA TURNI
SHE DIDN'T- SO--!!- IT HAIN'T!!
BUT, EF TAIN'T PANSY—HOW COME WHUTEVER 'TIS GOT WHAR SHE WAS?
TH' MICE IS DOIN' A AWFUL JOB ON YORE WALLS, PAPPY!!
WARN'T YO' COLD, LAST NIGHT?
'TWARN'T N-NUTHIN', COMPARED WIF HOW FEVERISH AH IS, N-NOW!!
SON!!-AH WANTS YORE HONEST OPINION!!— IS THET, OR IS THET NOT YORE MAMMY?
FRANKLY, PAPPY- AH DON'T THINK THET'S ANYBODY'S MAMMY!!
CHIAMATE IL DOTTORE!!
AH BIN ROBBED!!
WHO IS YO'?
CHIAMATE GINA LOLLOBRIGIDA- ROMA 1792-W!!
Al Capp
TO BE CONTINUED.

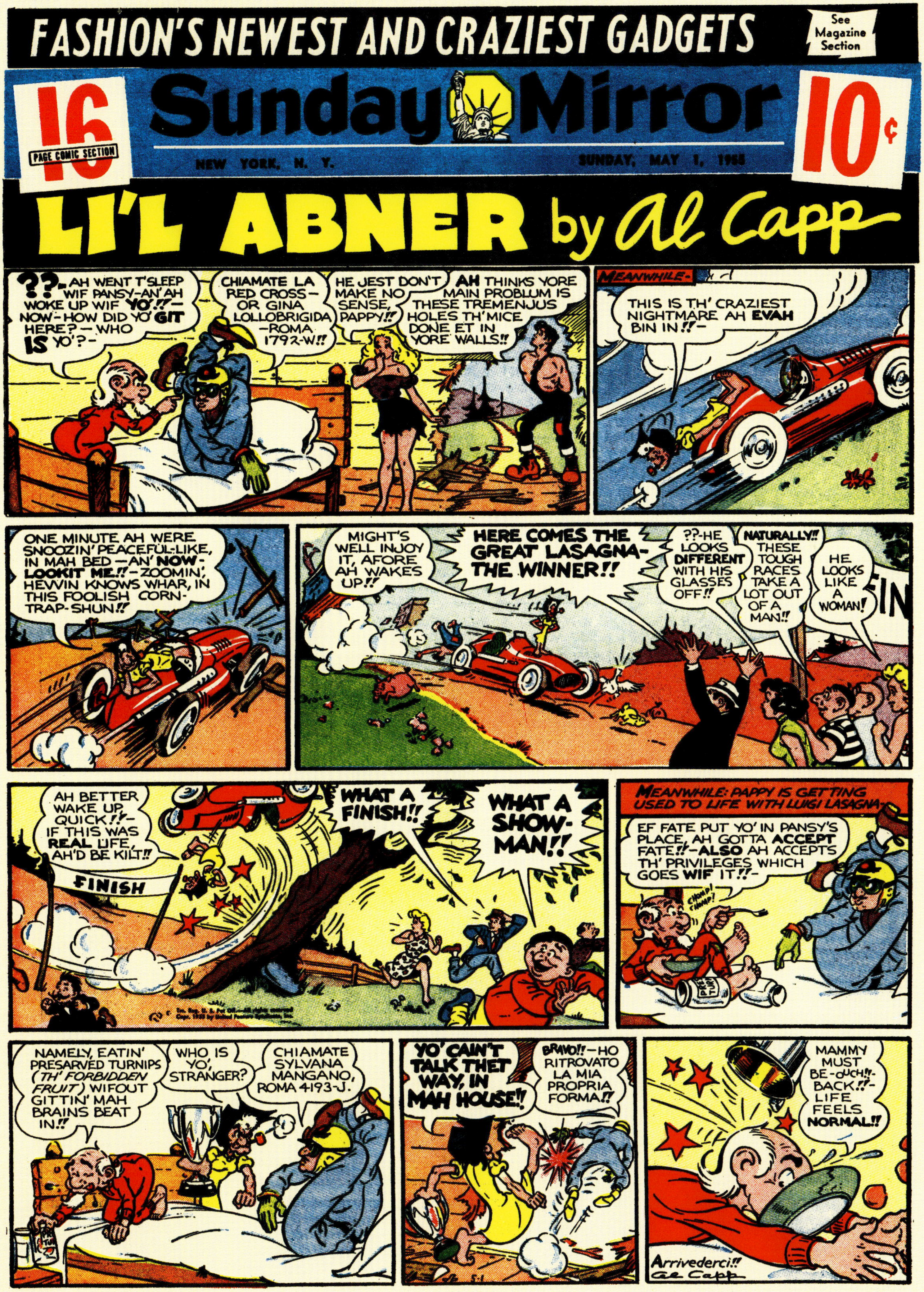

FASHION'S NEWEST AND CRAZIEST GADGETS
See Magazine Section
16
PAGE COMIC SECTION
Sunday Mirror
10¢
NEW YORK, N. Y.
SUNDAY, MAY 1, 1955
LI'L ABNER by Al Capp
??-AH WENT T'SLEEP WIF PANSY-AN' AH WOKE UP WIF YO'!!-NOW-HOW DID YO' GIT HERE?-WHO IS YO'?-
CHIAMATE LA RED CROSS-OR GINA LOLLOBRIGIDA-ROMA 1792-W!!
HE JEST DON'T MAKE NO SENSE, PAPPY!!
AH THINKS YORE MAIN PROBLUM IS THESE TREMENJUS HOLES TH' MICE DONE ET IN YORE WALLS!!
MEANWHILE-
THIS IS TH' CRAZIEST NIGHTMARE AH EVAH BIN IN!!-
ONE MINUTE AH WERE SNOOZIN' PEACEFUL-LIKE, IN MAH BED-AN' NOW-LOOKIT ME!!-ZOOMIN', HEVVIN KNOWS WHAR, IN THIS FOOLISH CORN-TRAP-SHUN!!
MIGHT'S WELL INJOY IT, AFORE AH WAKES UP!!
HERE COMES THE GREAT LASAGNA-THE WINNER!!
??-HE LOOKS DIFFERENT WITH HIS GLASSES OFF!!
NATURALLY!! THESE TOUGH RACES TAKE A LOT OUT OF A MAN!!
HE LOOKS LIKE A WOMAN!
FIN
AH BETTER WAKE UP QUICK!!-IF THIS WAS REAL LIFE, AH'D BE KILT!!
FINISH
WHAT A FINISH!!
WHAT A SHOW-MAN!!
MEANWHILE: PAPPY IS GETTING USED TO LIFE WITH LUIGI LASAGNA-
EF FATE PUT YO' IN PANSY'S PLACE, AH GOTTA ACCEPT FATE!!-ALSO AH ACCEPTS TH' PRIVILEGES WHICH GOES WIF IT!!-
CHOMP! CHOMP!
NAMELY, EATIN' PRESARVED TURNIPS (TH' FORBIDDEN FRUIT) WIFOUT GITTIN' MAH BRAINS BEAT IN!!
WHO IS YO', STRANGER?
CHIAMATE SYLVANA MANGANO, ROMA 4193-J.
YO' CAIN'T TALK THET WAY IN MAH HOUSE!!
BRAVO!!-HO RITROVATO LA MIA PROPRIA FORMA!!
MAMMY MUST BE-OUCH!!-BACK!!-LIFE FEELS NORMAL!!
Arrivederci!!
Al Capp

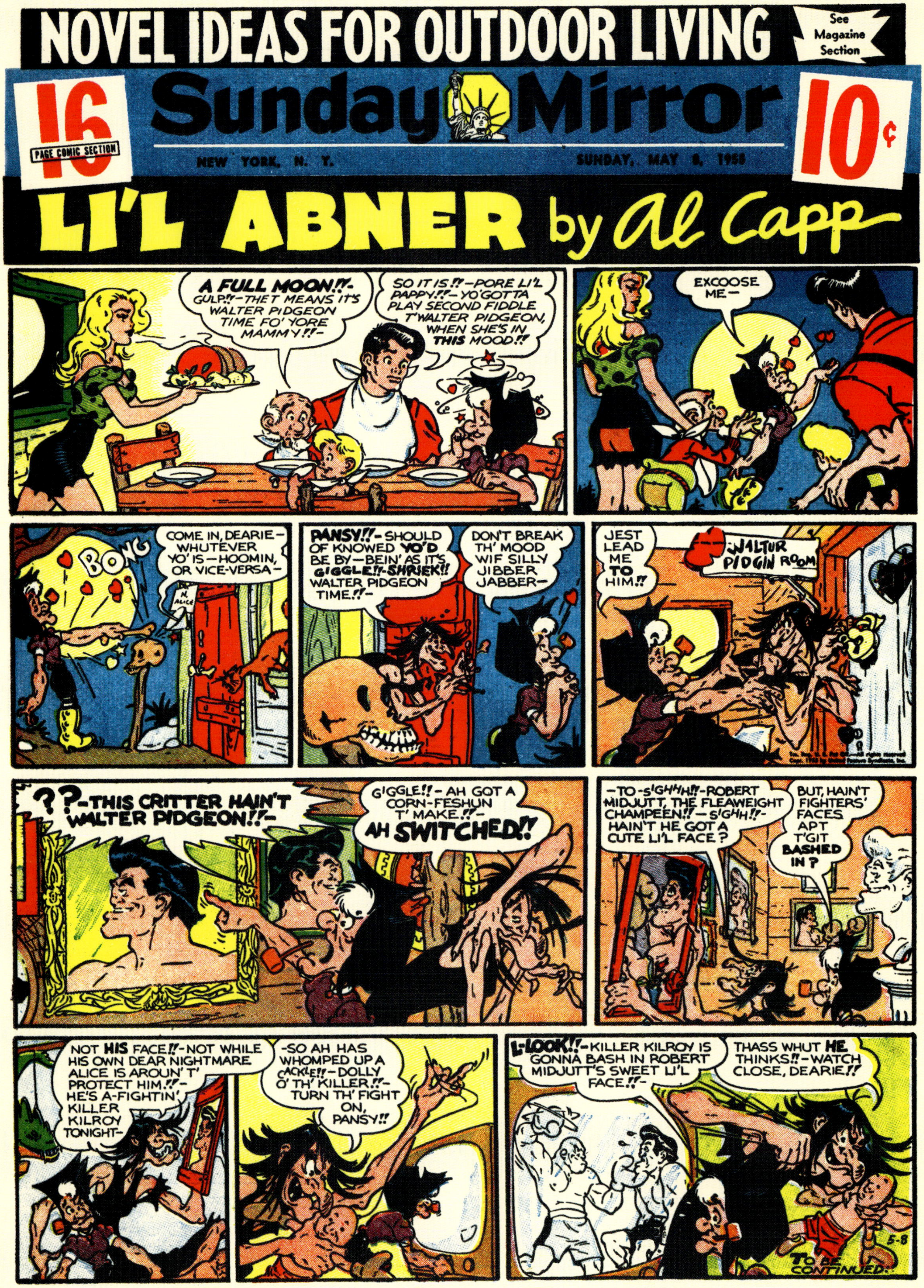

NOVEL IDEAS FOR OUTDOOR LIVING
See Magazine Section
16 PAGE COMIC SECTION
Sunday Mirror
10¢
NEW YORK, N. Y.
SUNDAY, MAY 8, 1955
LI'L ABNER by Al Capp
A FULL MOON!!- GULP!!- THET MEANS IT'S WALTER PIDGEON TIME FO' YORE MAMMY!!-
SO IT IS!!- PORE LI'L PAPPY!!- YO'GOTTA PLAY SECOND FIDDLE T'WALTER PIDGEON, WHEN SHE'S IN THIS MOOD!!-
EXCOOSE ME-
BONG
COME IN, DEARIE- WHUTEVER YO' IS- HOOMIN, OR VICE-VERSA-
N. ALICE
PANSY!!- SHOULD OF KNOWED YO'D BE BY- BEIN' AS IT'S GIGGLE!!- SHRIEK!! WALTER PIDGEON TIME.!!-
DON'T BREAK TH' MOOD WIF SILLY JIBBER JABBER-
JEST LEAD ME TO HIM.!!
WALTUR PIDGIN ROOM
??- THIS CRITTER HAIN'T WALTER PIDGEON!!-
GIGGLE!!- AH GOT A CORN-FESHUN T' MAKE.!!- AH SWITCHED!!
-TO- SIGHHH!!- ROBERT MIDJUTT, THE FLEAWEIGHT CHAMPEEN!!- SIGHH!!- HAIN'T HE GOT A CUTE LI'L FACE?
BUT, HAIN'T FIGHTERS' FACES APT T'GIT BASHED IN?
NOT HIS FACE!!- NOT WHILE HIS OWN DEAR NIGHTMARE ALICE IS AROUN' T' PROTECT HIM.!!- HE'S A-FIGHTIN' KILLER KILROY TONIGHT-
-SO AH HAS WHOMPED UP A CACKLE!!- DOLLY O' TH' KILLER.!!- TURN TH' FIGHT ON, PANSY!!
L-LOOK!!- KILLER KILROY IS GONNA BASH IN ROBERT MIDJUTT'S SWEET LI'L FACE.!!-
THASS WHUT HE THINKS!!- WATCH CLOSE, DEARIE!!
5-8
TO BE CONTINUED.

THESE ARE OUR ARMS FOR ARMED FORCES DAY
See Magazine Section
16
PAGE COMIC SECTION
Sunday Mirror
10¢
NEW YORK, N. Y.
SUNDAY, MAY
LI'L ABNER by Al Capp
L-LOOK!!-KILLER KILROY'S GONNA BASH IN ROBERT MIDJUTT'S SWEET LI'L FACE!!
CACKLE!!-THASS WHUT HE THINKS!!-WATCH CLOSE, DEARIE!!-
BOP!
AT THAT INSTANT!!-1,000 MILES AWAY-MADISON SQUARE GARDEN IS ELECTRIFIED!!-
KILROY FLOPPED!! JUST AS HE WAS ABOUT TO K.O. MIDJUTT!!
I DIDN'T SEE THE PUNCH!!
FAKE!!
I DEMAND A COMPLETE MEDICAL REPORT, DOCTOR!!
COMMISSIONER!!-THIS IS THE MOST KNOCKED-OUT FIGHTER I'VE EVER SEEN!!-
TH' WINNAH!!
(??-THIS IS INCREDITABLE!! I D-DON'T KNOW HOW I DONE IT!!-)
LET'S CELEBRATE!! I DATED TWO DOLLS FROM THE COPABANANA GET INTO YOUR TUX!!
(-I JUST CAN'T REMEMBER WHAT I DONE!!-)
IT MUSTA BIN MAGIC!!
RIGHT, DEARIE!!-THAT OLD BLACK MAGIC, THAT AH KNOWS SO WELL!!
-AN' I DONE IT FO' YO', BECUZ AH IS UNDER YORE SPELL!!
GET LOST, YOU OLD CREEP!!-WE GOT DATES, WITH A COUPLE O' REAL DOLLS!!-
CACKLE!!-SPEAKIN' O' DOLLS-AH GOT ONE, HERE!!-
??-IT LOOKS LIKE ME!!
ZZIP!
-AN' IT'S GONNA FEEL LIKE YO'!!-HERE'S HOW AH DONE IT, MIDJUTT!!
BAP!!
BAP!!
5-15
YOU'RE TH' MOST WONDERFUL GIRL IN THE WHOLE WORLD!!
D-DOES YO' REALLY AN' TRULY LOVE ME?
TO BE CONTINUED:

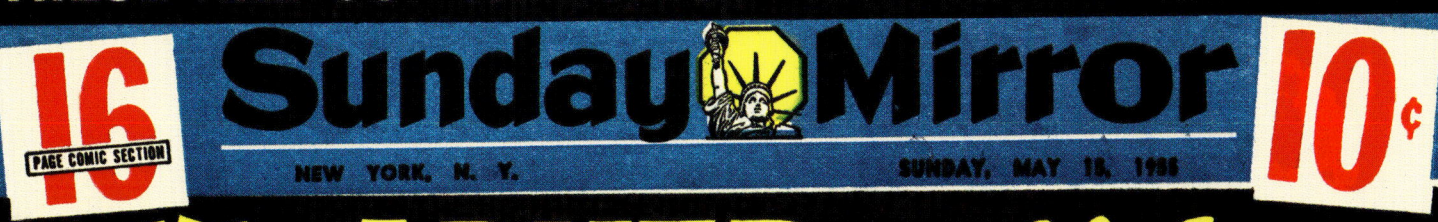

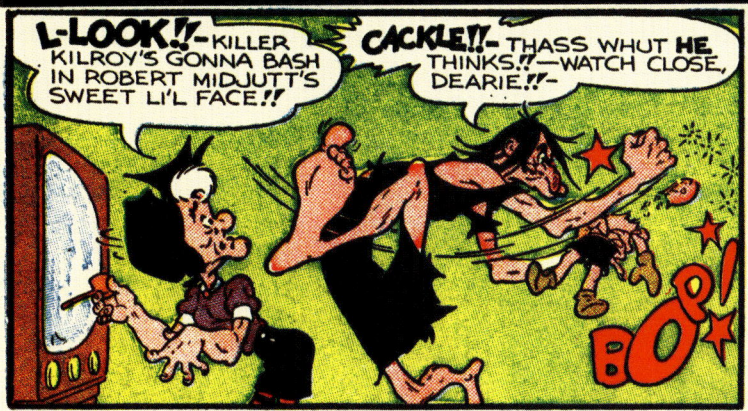

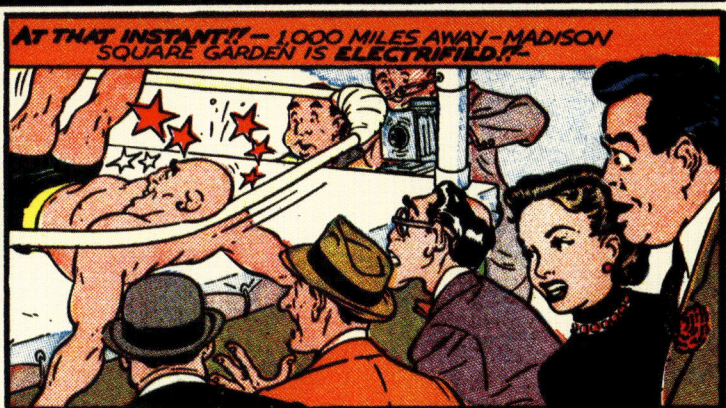

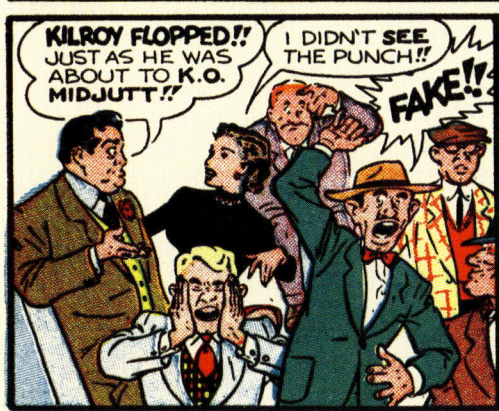

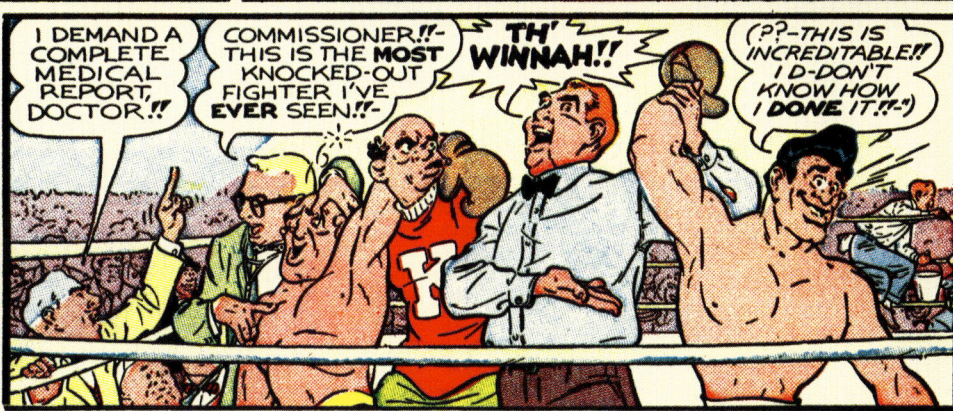

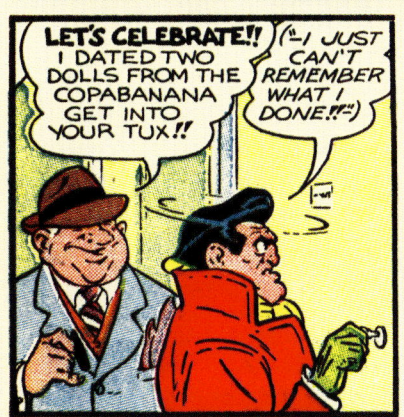

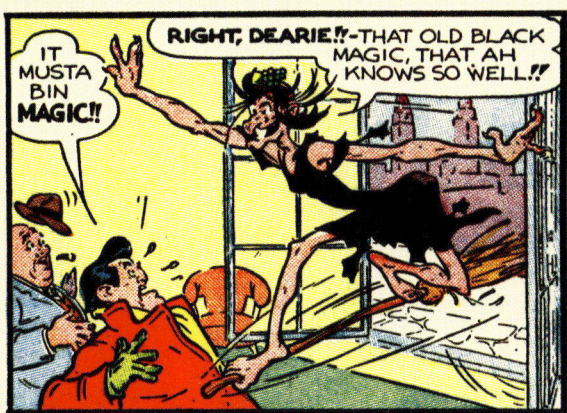

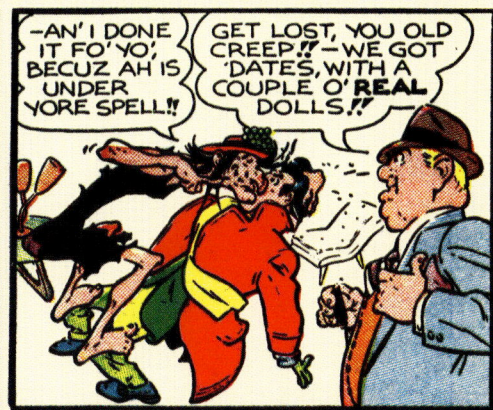

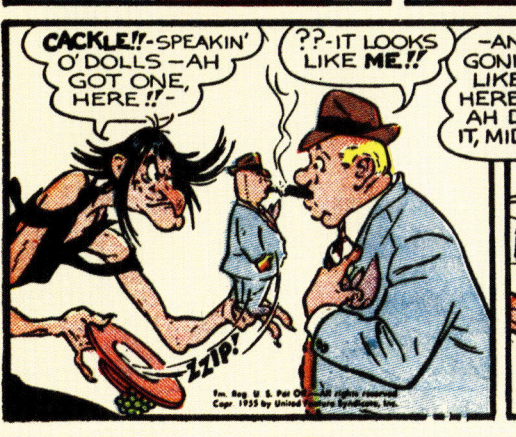

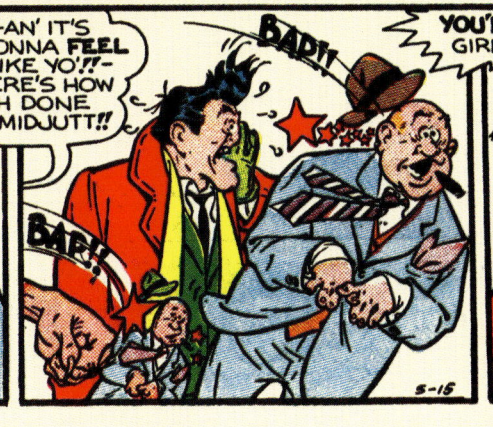

HORRORS! IN THE EX-TUNNEL OF LOVE
See Magazine Section
16
PAGE COMIC SECTION
Sunday Mirror
NEW YORK, N. Y.
SUNDAY, MAY 22, 1955
10¢
LI'L ABNER by Al Capp
??-YOU WON ALL MY FIGHTS FOR ME, MISS -ER- ??- I DIDN'T GET YOUR NAME—
NIGHTMARE ALICE IS THE NAME —AN' HEXIN' IS MAH GAME!!-
AH-BLUSH!!-FELL FO' YO', TH' FUST TIME AH SEEN YO' ON TELLY-VISION!!-
'TWERE WHEN YO' WAS JEST STARTIN' OUT—
OH, YEAH!!-I WON THAT FOIST BOUT, UNEXPECTED-LIKE!! THE OTHER BOY WAS FRACTURIN' ME—
WHEN-SUDDENLY-HE LETS OUT A HEART-RENDERIN' SHRIEK-AN' ZOOMS!!-
FUNNY THING WAS- I DON'T REMEMBER TH' PUNCH!!
BLUSH!!-AH DO!!-IT WAS A CIGAR-BUTT, TO TH' SOLAR PLEXUS -LIKE THIS!!-
AAKK!!
P-PLEASE, LADY!! D-DON'T DEMONSTRATE WITH MY DOLLY!!
ALL THROUGH YORE CAREER, SWEET ROBERT MIDJUTT- AH BIN WINNIN' YORE FIGHTS!!
??-YOU MEAN-??-
Tm. Reg. U. S. Pat Off.—All rights reserved
Copr. 1955 by United Feature Syndicate, Inc.
RIGHT!!-YO' CAIN'T LICK A ONE-CENT STAMP!!-BUT DON'T WORRY!!- STICK WIF ME, AN' YO'LL BE CHAMP!!
S-STICK WITH-SHUDDER!!- YOU?-WHAT DO YOU M-MEAN?
(-CANTCHA SEE WHAT SHE MEANS? TH' OLD CREEP LOVES YOU!!-I ADMIT SHE'S NOT EXACTLY THE TYPE OF TOMATO ONE DREAMS ABOUT-EXCEPT AFTER ONE HAS ET UNWISELY!!-)
BUT, SHE GOT TALENT!! JUST STRING HER ALONG -AN' YOU'LL BE RICH, AN' FAMOUS-AN' WHAT'S EVEN MORE IMPORTANT -SO WILL I-
5-22
OKAY!!-I'LL GO ALONG WITH IT!!-BUT I JUST GOTTA GET SOME TIME OFF TO SEE JOE!!-
RIGHT!!- JOE IS TH' MOST IMPORTANT THING IN YOUR LIFE!!
WHO IS "JOE"?

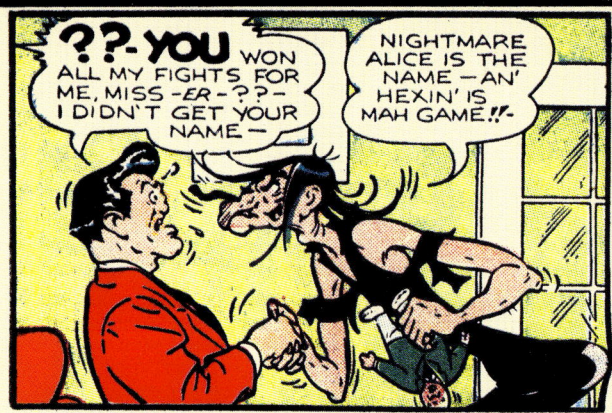

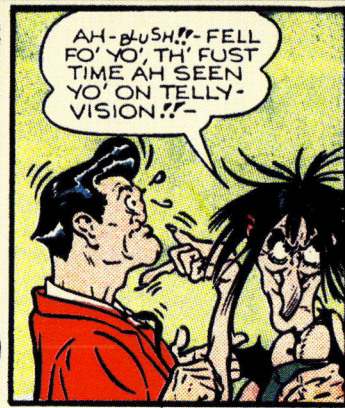

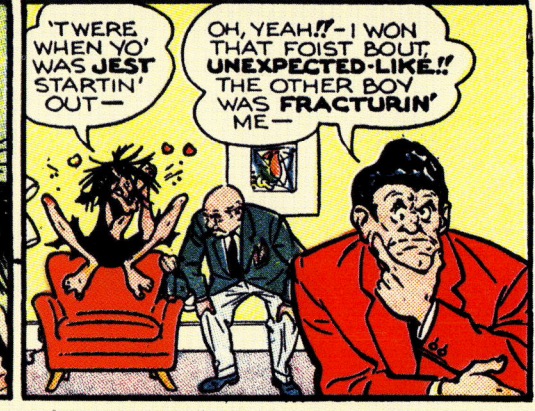

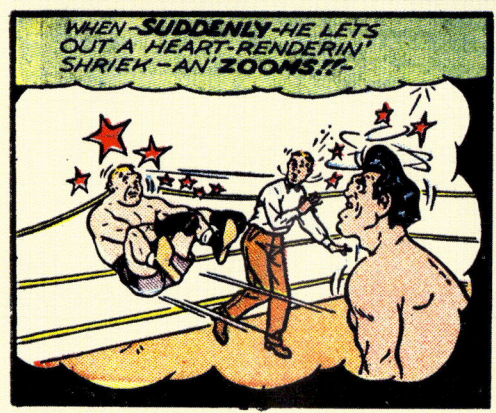

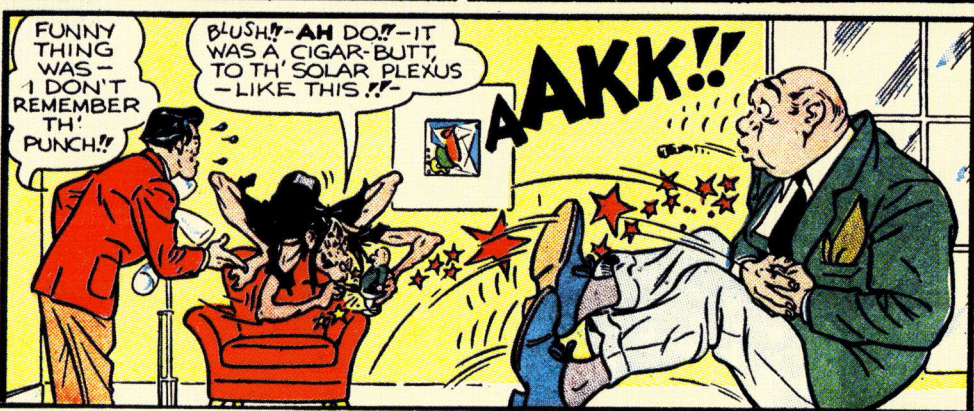

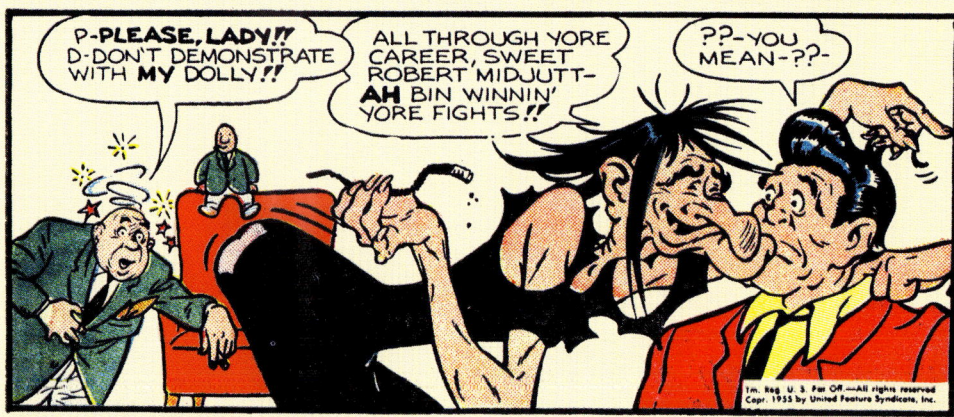

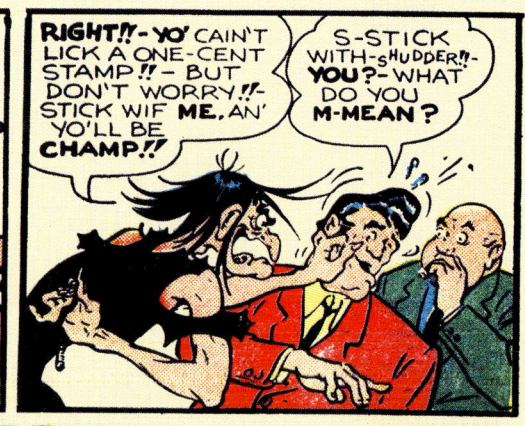

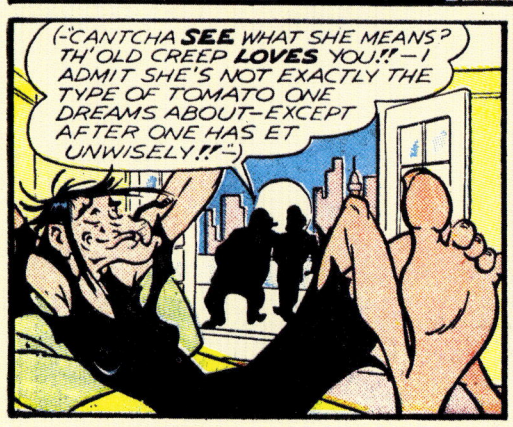

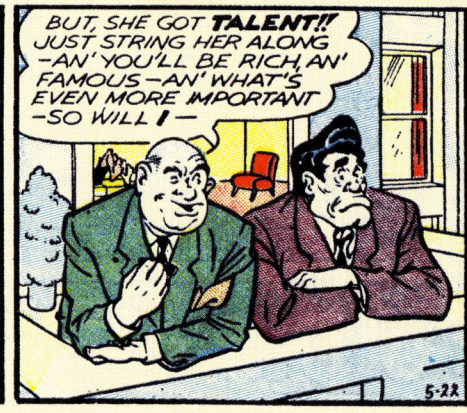

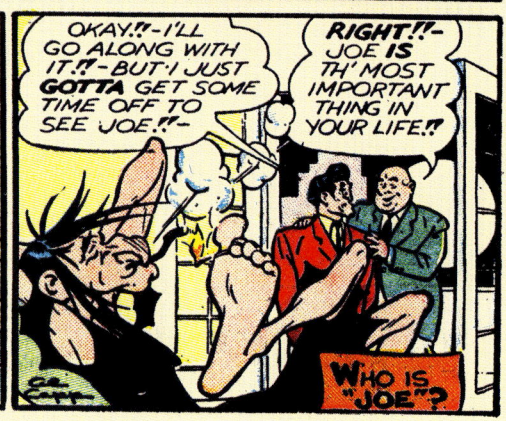

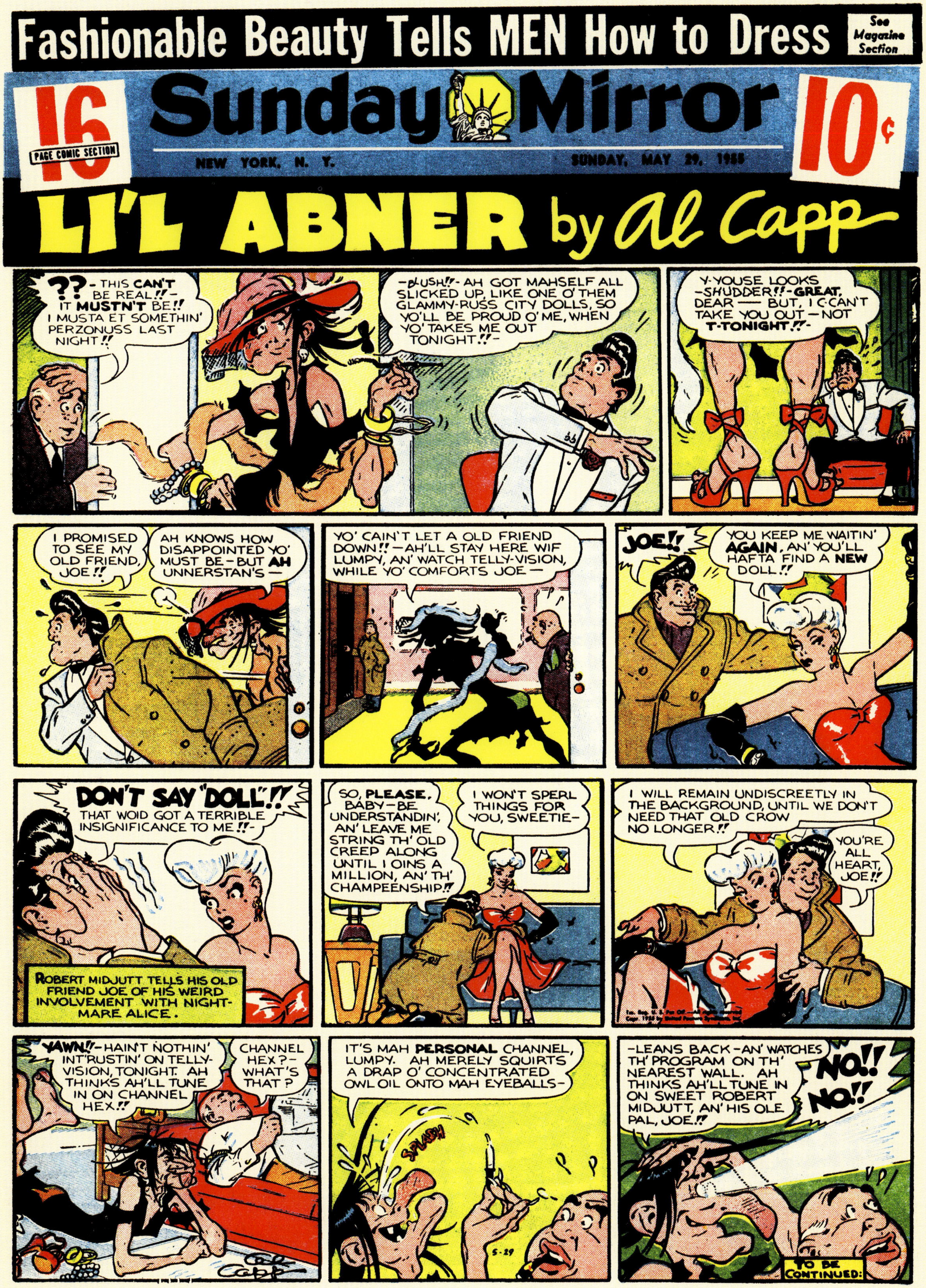
Fashionable Beauty Tells MEN How to Dress
See Magazine Section
16 PAGE COMIC SECTION
Sunday Mirror
10¢
NEW YORK, N. Y.
SUNDAY, MAY 29, 1955
LI'L ABNER by Al Capp
??-THIS CAN'T BE REAL!!-IT MUSTN'T BE!! I MUSTA ET SOMETHIN' PERZONUSS LAST NIGHT!!
-BLUSH!!-AH GOT MAHSELF ALL SLICKED UP, LIKE ONE O' THEM GLAMMY-RUSS CITY DOLLS, SO YO'LL BE PROUD O' ME, WHEN YO' TAKES ME OUT TONIGHT!!-
Y-YOUSE LOOKS -SHUDDER!!-GREAT, DEAR — BUT, I C-CAN'T TAKE YOU OUT — NOT T-TONIGHT!!-
I PROMISED TO SEE MY OLD FRIEND, JOE!!
AH KNOWS HOW DISAPPOINTED YO' MUST BE-BUT AH UNNERSTAN'S —
YO' CAIN'T LET A OLD FRIEND DOWN!!—AH'LL STAY HERE WIF LUMPY, AN' WATCH TELLY-VISION, WHILE YO' COMFORTS JOE —
JOE!!
YOU KEEP ME WAITIN' AGAIN, AN' YOU'LL HAFTA FIND A NEW DOLL!!
DON'T SAY "DOLL"!! THAT WOID GOT A TERRIBLE INSIGNIFICANCE TO ME!!-
ROBERT MIDJUTT TELLS HIS OLD FRIEND JOE OF HIS WEIRD INVOLVEMENT WITH NIGHT-MARE ALICE.
SO, PLEASE, BABY—BE UNDERSTANDIN', AN' LEAVE ME STRING TH' OLD CREEP ALONG UNTIL I OINS A MILLION, AN' TH' CHAMPEENSHIP!!
I WON'T SPERL THINGS FOR YOU, SWEETIE-
I WILL REMAIN UNDISCREETLY IN THE BACKGROUND, UNTIL WE DON'T NEED THAT OLD CROW NO LONGER!!
YOU'RE ALL HEART, JOE!!
YAWN!!-HAIN'T NOTHIN' INT'RUSTIN' ON TELLY-VISION, TONIGHT. AH THINKS AH'LL TUNE IN ON CHANNEL HEX!!
CHANNEL HEX?-WHAT'S THAT?
IT'S MAH PERSONAL CHANNEL, LUMPY. AH MERELY SQUIRTS A DRAP O' CONCENTRATED OWL OIL ONTO MAH EYEBALLS-
SPLASH
5-29
-LEANS BACK-AN' WATCHES TH' PROGRAM ON TH' NEAREST WALL. AH THINKS AH'LL TUNE IN ON SWEET ROBERT MIDJUTT, AN' HIS OLE PAL, JOE!!
NO!! NO!!
TO BE CONTINUED!
Al Capp

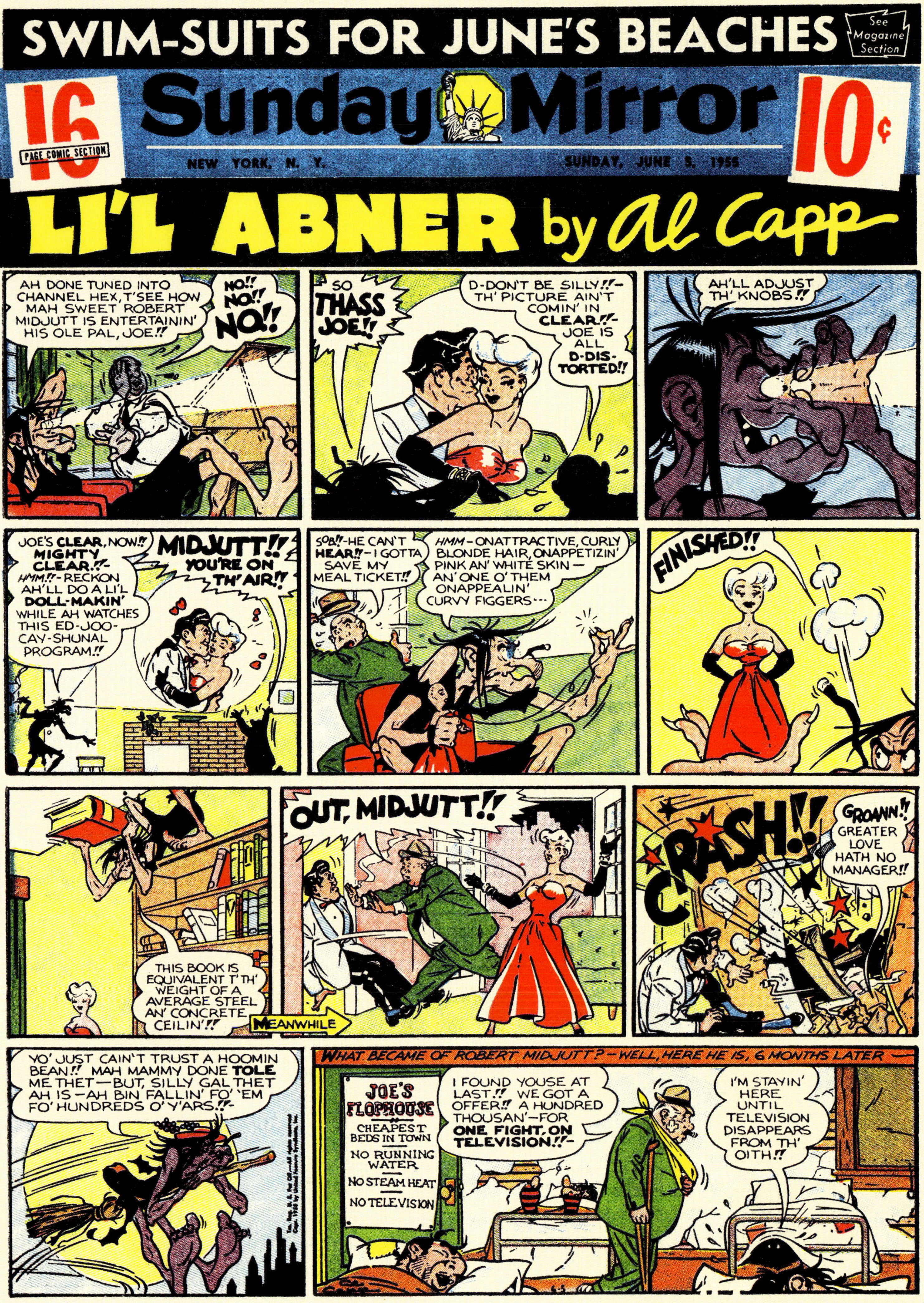

SWIM-SUITS FOR JUNE'S BEACHES
See Magazine Section
16 PAGE COMIC SECTION
Sunday Mirror
10¢
NEW YORK, N. Y.
SUNDAY, JUNE 5, 1955
LI'L ABNER by Al Capp
AH DONE TUNED INTO CHANNEL HEX, T'SEE HOW MAH SWEET ROBERT MIDJUTT IS ENTERTAININ' HIS OLE PAL, JOE.!!
NO!! NO!! NO!!
SO THASS JOE!!
D-DON'T BE SILLY!!– TH' PICTURE AIN'T COMIN' IN CLEAR!!– JOE IS ALL D-DIS-TORTED!!
AH'LL ADJUST TH' KNOBS.!!
JOE'S CLEAR, NOW!! MIGHTY CLEAR.!!– HMM!!– RECKON AH'LL DO A LI'L DOLL-MAKIN' WHILE AH WATCHES THIS ED-JOO-CAY-SHUNAL PROGRAM!!
MIDJUTT!! YOU'RE ON TH' AIR!!
SOB!!– HE CAN'T HEAR!!– I GOTTA SAVE MY MEAL TICKET!!
HMM – ONATTRACTIVE, CURLY BLONDE HAIR, ONAPPETIZIN' PINK AN' WHITE SKIN – AN' ONE O' THEM ONAPPEALIN' CURVY FIGGERS---
FINISHED!!
THIS BOOK IS EQUIVALENT T' TH' WEIGHT OF A AVERAGE STEEL AN' CONCRETE CEILIN'!!
MEANWHILE
OUT, MIDJUTT!!
CRASH!!
GROANN!! GREATER LOVE HATH NO MANAGER!!
YO' JUST CAIN'T TRUST A HOOMIN BEAN!! MAH MAMMY DONE TOLE ME THET – BUT, SILLY GAL THET AH IS – AH BIN FALLIN' FO' 'EM FO' HUNDREDS O' Y'ARS!!–
WHAT BECAME OF ROBERT MIDJUTT? – WELL, HERE HE IS, 6 MONTHS LATER –
JOE'S FLOPHOUSE
CHEAPEST BEDS IN TOWN
NO RUNNING WATER
NO STEAM HEAT
NO TELEVISION
I FOUND YOUSE AT LAST!! WE GOT A OFFER!! A HUNDRED THOUSAN' – FOR ONE FIGHT, ON TELEVISION!!–
I'M STAYIN' HERE UNTIL TELEVISION DISAPPEARS FROM TH' OITH!!

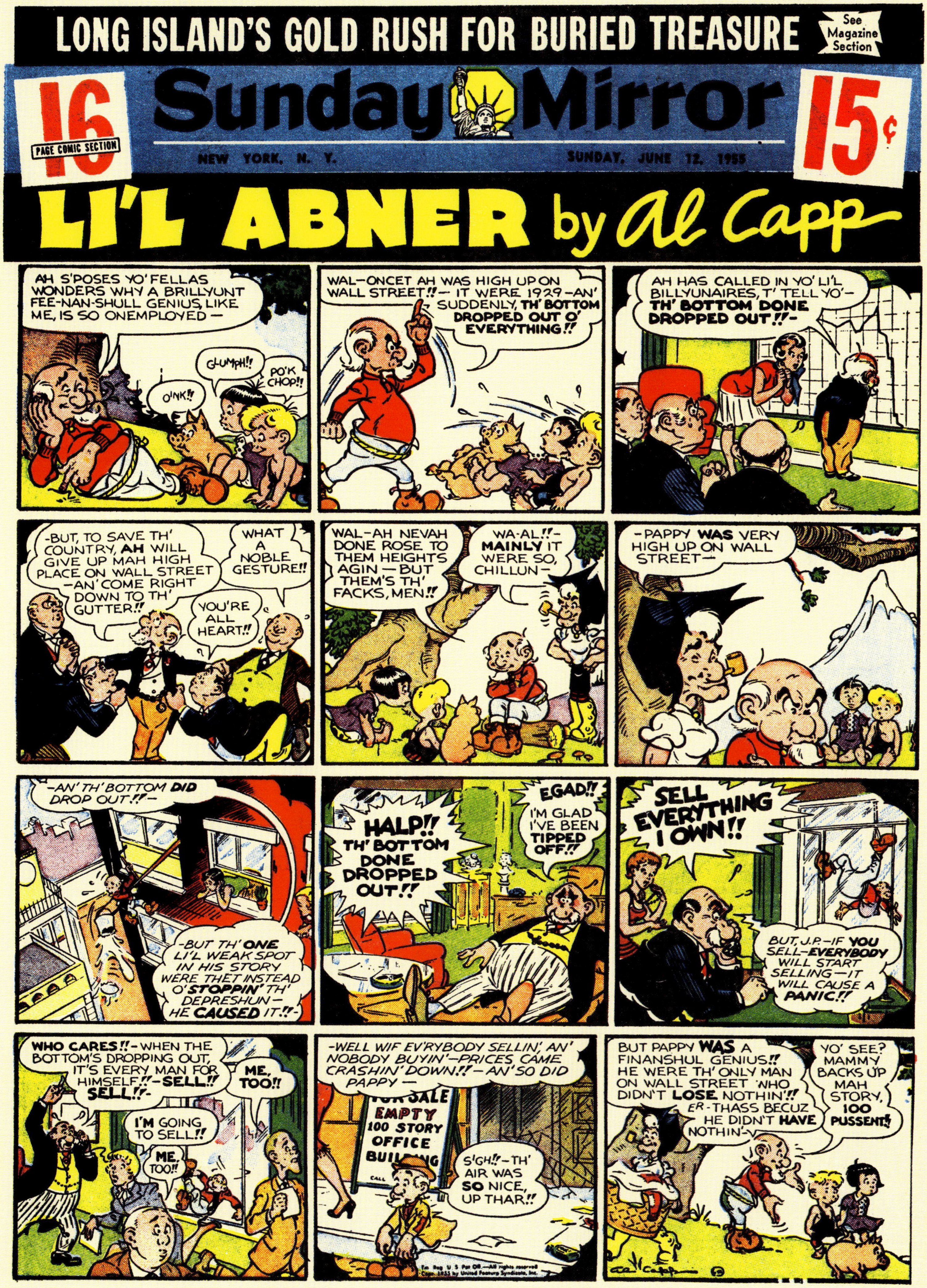
LONG ISLAND'S GOLD RUSH FOR BURIED TREASURE
See Magazine Section
16
PAGE COMIC SECTION
Sunday Mirror
NEW YORK, N. Y.
SUNDAY, JUNE 12, 1955
15¢
LI'L ABNER by Al Capp
AH S'POSES YO' FELLAS WONDERS WHY A BRILLYUNT FEE-NAN-SHULL GENIUS, LIKE ME, IS SO ONEMPLOYED —
GLUMPH!!
PO'K CHOP!!
OINK!!
WAL—ONCET AH WAS HIGH UP ON WALL STREET!!— IT WERE 1929—AN' SUDDENLY, TH' BOTTOM DROPPED OUT O' EVERYTHING!!
AH HAS CALLED IN YO' LI'L BILLYUNAIRES, T' TELL YO'— TH' BOTTOM DONE DROPPED OUT!!—
—BUT, TO SAVE TH' COUNTRY, AH WILL GIVE UP MAH HIGH PLACE ON WALL STREET —AN' COME RIGHT DOWN TO TH' GUTTER!!
WHAT A NOBLE GESTURE!!
YOU'RE ALL HEART!!
WAL—AH NEVAH DONE ROSE TO THEM HEIGHTS AGIN — BUT THEM'S TH' FACKS, MEN!!
WA-AL!!— MAINLY IT WERE SO, CHILLUN—
—PAPPY WAS VERY HIGH UP ON WALL STREET—
—AN' TH' BOTTOM DID DROP OUT!!—
—BUT TH' ONE LI'L WEAK SPOT IN HIS STORY WERE THET INSTEAD O' STOPPIN' TH' DEPRESHUN— HE CAUSED IT!!—
HALP!! TH' BOTTOM DONE DROPPED OUT!!
EGAD!! I'M GLAD I'VE BEEN TIPPED OFF!!
SELL EVERYTHING I OWN!!
BUT, J.P.—IF YOU SELL—EVERYBODY WILL START SELLING—IT WILL CAUSE A PANIC!!
WHO CARES!!—WHEN THE BOTTOM'S DROPPING OUT, IT'S EVERY MAN FOR HIMSELF!!—SELL!! SELL!!—
ME, TOO!!
I'M GOING TO SELL!!
ME, TOO!!
—WELL WIF EV'RYBODY SELLIN', AN' NOBODY BUYIN'—PRICES CAME CRASHIN' DOWN!!—AN' SO DID PAPPY —
FOR SALE EMPTY 100 STORY OFFICE BUILDING
S'GH!!—TH' AIR WAS SO NICE, UP THAR!!
BUT PAPPY WAS A FINANSHUL GENIUS!! HE WERE TH' ONLY MAN ON WALL STREET WHO DIDN'T LOSE NOTHIN'!!
ER—THASS BECUZ HE DIDN'T HAVE NOTHIN'—
YO' SEE? MAMMY BACKS UP MAH STORY, 100 PUSSENT!!

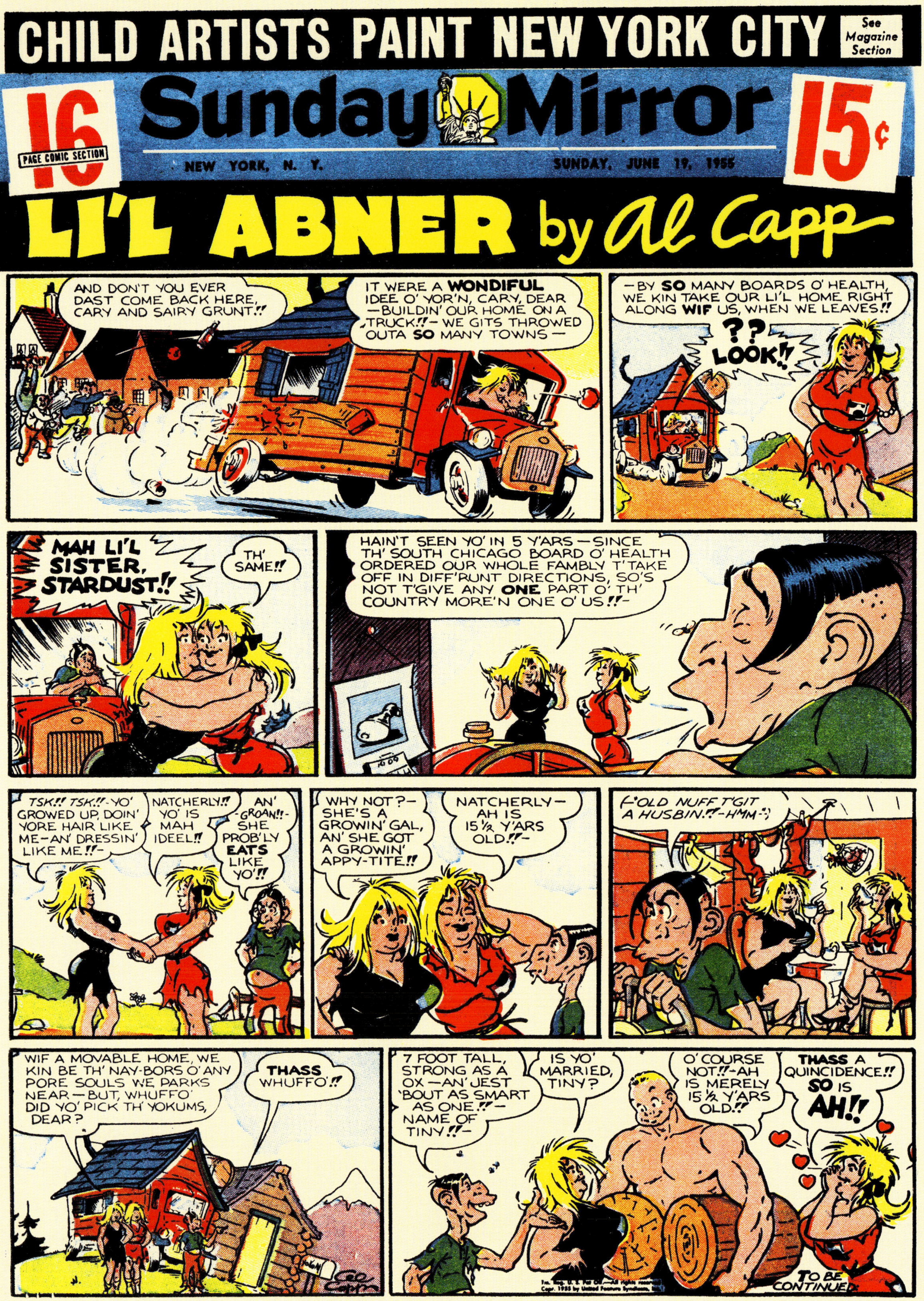
CHILD ARTISTS PAINT NEW YORK CITY
See Magazine Section
16
PAGE COMIC SECTION
Sunday Mirror
NEW YORK, N. Y.
SUNDAY, JUNE 19, 1955
15¢
LI'L ABNER by Al Capp
AND DON'T YOU EVER DAST COME BACK HERE, CARY AND SAIRY GRUNT!!
IT WERE A WONDIFUL IDEE O' YOR'N, CARY, DEAR —BUILDIN' OUR HOME ON A TRUCK!!— WE GITS THROWED OUTA SO MANY TOWNS —
—BY SO MANY BOARDS O' HEALTH, WE KIN TAKE OUR LI'L HOME RIGHT ALONG WIF US, WHEN WE LEAVES!!
??
LOOK!!
MAH LI'L SISTER, STARDUST!!
TH' SAME!!
HAIN'T SEEN YO' IN 5 Y'ARS — SINCE TH' SOUTH CHICAGO BOARD O' HEALTH ORDERED OUR WHOLE FAMBLY T'TAKE OFF IN DIFF'RUNT DIRECTIONS, SO'S NOT T'GIVE ANY ONE PART O' TH' COUNTRY MORE'N ONE O' US!!—
TSK!! TSK!!-YO' GROWED UP, DOIN' YORE HAIR LIKE ME-AN' DRESSIN' LIKE ME!!—
NATCHERLY!! YO' IS MAH IDEEL!!
AN' -GROAN!!- SHE PROB'LY EATS LIKE YO'!!
WHY NOT?— SHE'S A GROWIN' GAL, AN' SHE GOT A GROWIN' APPY-TITE!!
NATCHERLY— AH IS 15½ Y'ARS OLD!!—
(-OLD NUFF T'GIT A HUSBIN.!!-HMM-)
WIF A MOVABLE HOME, WE KIN BE TH' NAY-BORS O' ANY PORE SOULS WE PARKS NEAR — BUT, WHUFFO' DID YO' PICK TH' YOKUMS, DEAR?
THASS WHUFFO'!!
7 FOOT TALL, STRONG AS A OX — AN' JEST 'BOUT AS SMART AS ONE!!— NAME OF TINY!!—
IS YO' MARRIED, TINY?
O' COURSE NOT!!-AH IS MERELY 15½ Y'ARS OLD!!
THASS A QUINCIDENCE!! SO IS AH!!
TO BE CONTINUED

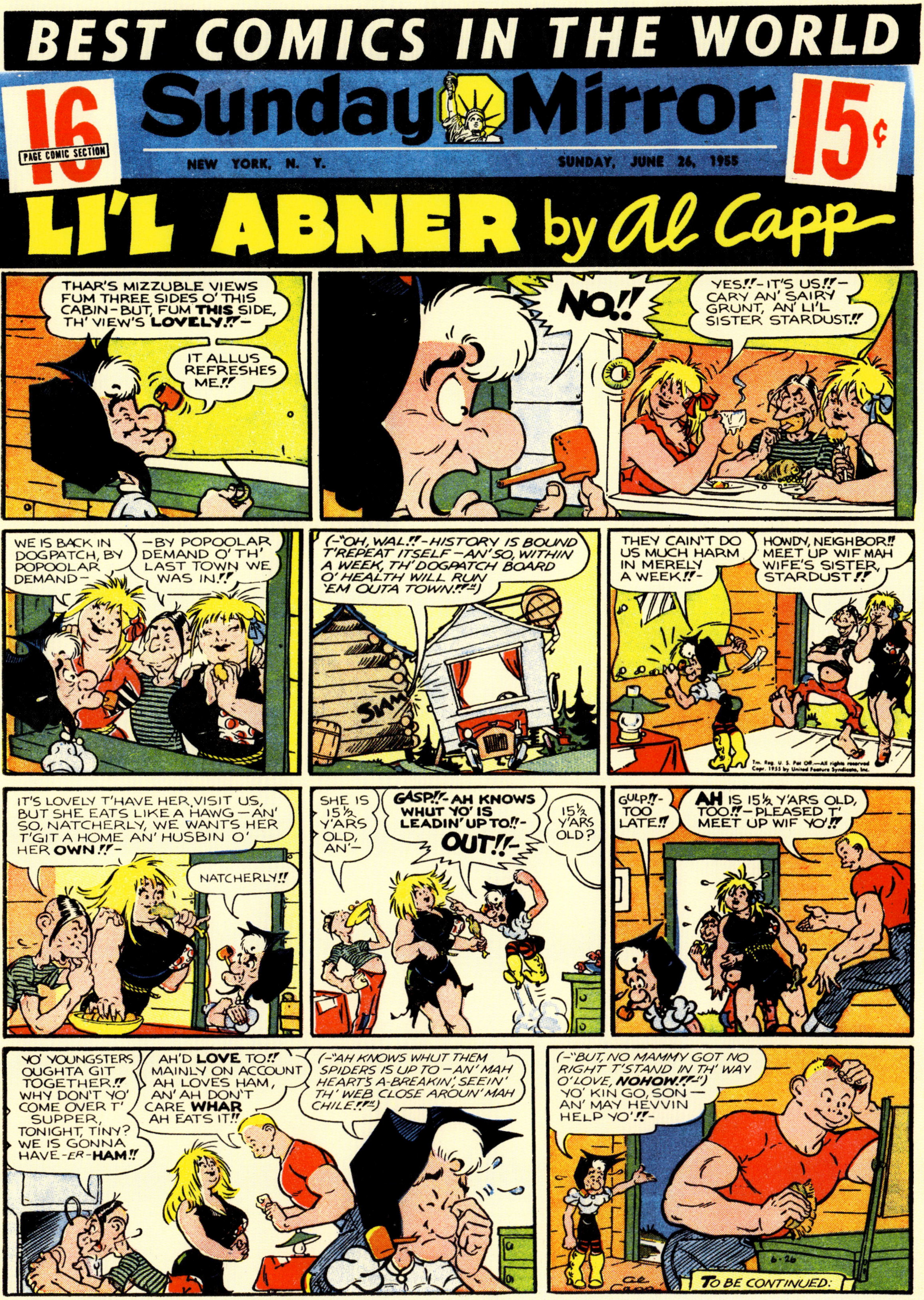

BEST COMICS IN THE WORLD
16
PAGE COMIC SECTION
Sunday Mirror
15¢
NEW YORK, N. Y.
SUNDAY, JUNE 26, 1955
LI'L ABNER by Al Capp
THAR'S MIZZUBLE VIEWS FUM THREE SIDES O' THIS CABIN—BUT, FUM THIS SIDE, TH' VIEW'S LOVELY!!—
IT ALLUS REFRESHES ME!!
NO!!
YES!!—IT'S US!!—CARY AN' SAIRY GRUNT, AN' LI'L SISTER STARDUST!!
WE IS BACK IN DOGPATCH, BY POPOOLAR DEMAND—
—BY POPOOLAR DEMAND O' TH' LAST TOWN WE WAS IN!!
(—"OH, WAL!!—HISTORY IS BOUND T'REPEAT ITSELF—AN' SO, WITHIN A WEEK, TH' DOGPATCH BOARD O' HEALTH WILL RUN 'EM OUTA TOWN!!"—)
SLAM
THEY CAIN'T DO US MUCH HARM IN MERELY A WEEK!!—
HOWDY, NEIGHBOR!! MEET UP WIF MAH WIFE'S SISTER, STARDUST!!
Tm. Reg. U. S. Pat. Off.—All rights reserved Copr. 1955 by United Feature Syndicate, Inc.
IT'S LOVELY T'HAVE HER VISIT US, BUT SHE EATS LIKE A HAWG—AN' SO, NATCHERLY, WE WANTS HER T'GIT A HOME AN' HUSBIN O' HER OWN!!—
NATCHERLY!!
SHE IS 15½ Y'ARS OLD, AN'—
GASP!!—AH KNOWS WHUT YO' IS LEADIN' UP TO!!—
OUT!!—
15½ Y'ARS OLD?
GULP!!—TOO LATE!!
AH IS 15½ Y'ARS OLD, TOO!!—PLEASED T' MEET UP WIF YO'!!
YO' YOUNGSTERS OUGHTA GIT TOGETHER!! WHY DON'T YO' COME OVER T' SUPPER, TONIGHT, TINY? WE IS GONNA HAVE-ER-HAM!!
AH'D LOVE TO!! MAINLY ON ACCOUNT AH LOVES HAM, AN' AH DON'T CARE WHAR AH EATS IT!!
(—"AH KNOWS WHUT THEM SPIDERS IS UP TO—AN' MAH HEART'S A-BREAKIN', SEEIN' TH' WEB CLOSE AROUN' MAH CHILE!!"—)
(—"BUT, NO MAMMY GOT NO RIGHT T'STAND IN TH' WAY O'LOVE, NOHOW!!"—) YO' KIN GO, SON—AN' MAY HEVVIN HELP YO'!!—
6-26
TO BE CONTINUED:

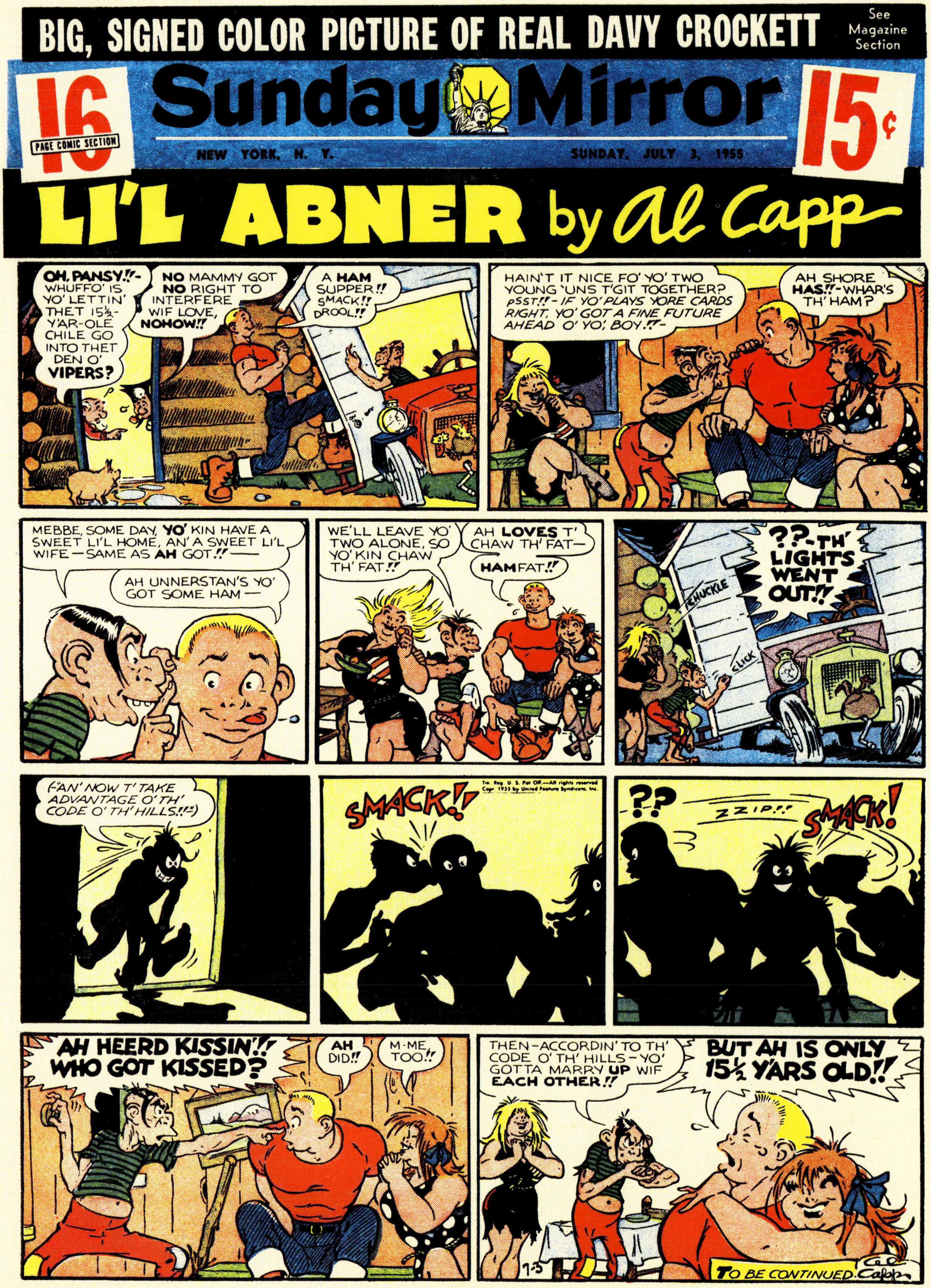

BIG, SIGNED COLOR PICTURE OF REAL DAVY CROCKETT
See Magazine Section
16
PAGE COMIC SECTION
Sunday Mirror
15¢
NEW YORK, N. Y.
SUNDAY, JULY 3, 1955
LI'L ABNER by Al Capp
OH, PANSY!!- WHUFFO' IS YO' LETTIN' THET 15½-Y'AR-OLE CHILE GO INTO THET DEN O' VIPERS?
NO MAMMY GOT NO RIGHT TO INTERFERE WIF LOVE, NOHOW!!
A HAM SUPPER!! SMACK!! DROOL!!
HAIN'T IT NICE FO' YO' TWO YOUNG 'UNS T'GIT TOGETHER? PSST!!- IF YO' PLAYS YORE CARDS RIGHT, YO' GOT A FINE FUTURE AHEAD O' YO', BOY!!-
AH SHORE HAS!!- WHAR'S TH' HAM?
MEBBE, SOME DAY, YO' KIN HAVE A SWEET LI'L HOME, AN' A SWEET LI'L WIFE — SAME AS AH GOT!! —
AH UNNERSTAN'S YO' GOT SOME HAM —
WE'LL LEAVE YO' TWO ALONE, SO YO' KIN CHAW TH' FAT!!
AH LOVES T' CHAW TH' FAT—
HAMFAT!!
??-TH' LIGHTS WENT OUT!!
CHUCKLE
CLICK
(-AN' NOW T' TAKE ADVANTAGE O' TH' CODE O' TH' HILLS!!-)
SMACK!!
??
ZZIP!!
SMACK!
AH HEERD KISSIN'!! WHO GOT KISSED?
AH DID!!
M-ME, TOO!!
THEN-ACCORDIN' TO TH' CODE O' TH' HILLS—YO' GOTTA MARRY UP WIF EACH OTHER!!
BUT AH IS ONLY 15½ Y'ARS OLD!!
7-3
TO BE CONTINUED
Capp

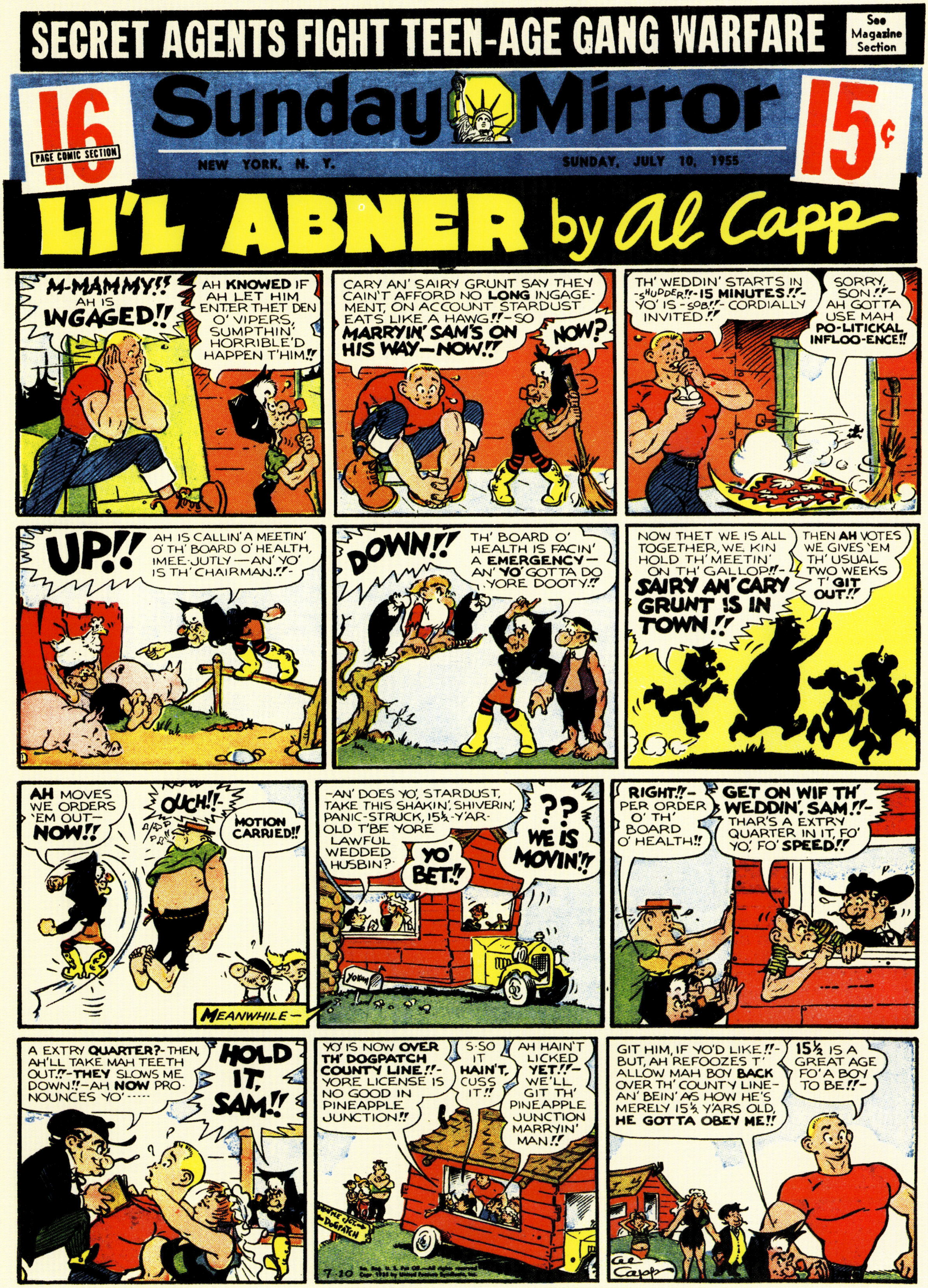
SECRET AGENTS FIGHT TEEN-AGE GANG WARFARE
See Magazine Section
16
PAGE COMIC SECTION
Sunday Mirror
NEW YORK, N. Y.
SUNDAY, JULY 10, 1955
15¢
LI'L ABNER by Al Capp
M-MAMMY!! AH IS INGAGED!!
AH KNOWED IF AH LET HIM ENTER THET DEN O' VIPERS, SUMPTHIN' HORRIBLE'D HAPPEN T'HIM!!
CARY AN' SAIRY GRUNT SAY THEY CAIN'T AFFORD NO LONG INGAGEMENT, ON ACCOUNT STARDUST EATS LIKE A HAWG!!-SO MARRYIN' SAM'S ON HIS WAY—NOW!!
NOW?
TH' WEDDIN' STARTS IN -SHUDDER!!- 15 MINUTES!!- YO' IS -SOB!!- CORDIALLY INVITED!!
SORRY, SON!!- AH GOTTA USE MAH PO-LITICKAL INFLOO-ENCE!!
UP!!
AH IS CALLIN' A MEETIN' O' TH' BOARD O' HEALTH, IMEE-JUTLY —AN' YO' IS TH' CHAIRMAN!!-
DOWN!!
TH' BOARD O' HEALTH IS FACIN' A EMERGENCY— AN' YO' GOTTA DO YORE DOOTY!!
NOW THET WE IS ALL TOGETHER, WE KIN HOLD TH' MEETIN' ON TH' GALLOP!!- SAIRY AN' CARY GRUNT IS IN TOWN!!
THEN AH VOTES WE GIVES 'EM TH' USUAL TWO WEEKS T' GIT OUT!!
AH MOVES WE ORDERS 'EM OUT— NOW!!
OUCH!!-
MOTION CARRIED!!
MEANWHILE—
-AN' DOES YO', STARDUST, TAKE THIS SHAKIN', SHIVERIN', PANIC-STRUCK, 15½-YAR-OLD T'BE YORE LAWFUL WEDDED HUSBIN?
YO' BET!!
?? WE IS MOVIN'!!
YOKUM
RIGHT!!- PER ORDER O' TH' BOARD O' HEALTH!!
GET ON WIF TH' WEDDIN', SAM!!- THAR'S A EXTRY QUARTER IN IT, FO' YO', FO' SPEED!!
A EXTRY QUARTER?- THEN, AH'LL TAKE MAH TEETH OUT!!- THEY SLOWS ME DOWN!!- AH NOW PRONOUNCES YO'-----
HOLD IT, SAM!!
YO' IS NOW OVER TH' DOGPATCH COUNTY LINE!!- YORE LICENSE IS NO GOOD IN PINEAPPLE JUNCTION!!
S-SO IT HAIN'T, CUSS IT!!
AH HAIN'T LICKED YET!!- WE'LL GIT TH' PINEAPPLE JUNCTION MARRYIN' MAN!!
7-10
GIT HIM, IF YO'D LIKE!!- BUT, AH REFOOZES T' ALLOW MAH BOY BACK OVER TH' COUNTY LINE- AN' BEIN' AS HOW HE'S MERELY 15½ Y'ARS OLD, HE GOTTA OBEY ME!!
15½ IS A GREAT AGE FO' A BOY TO BE!!-
Al Capp

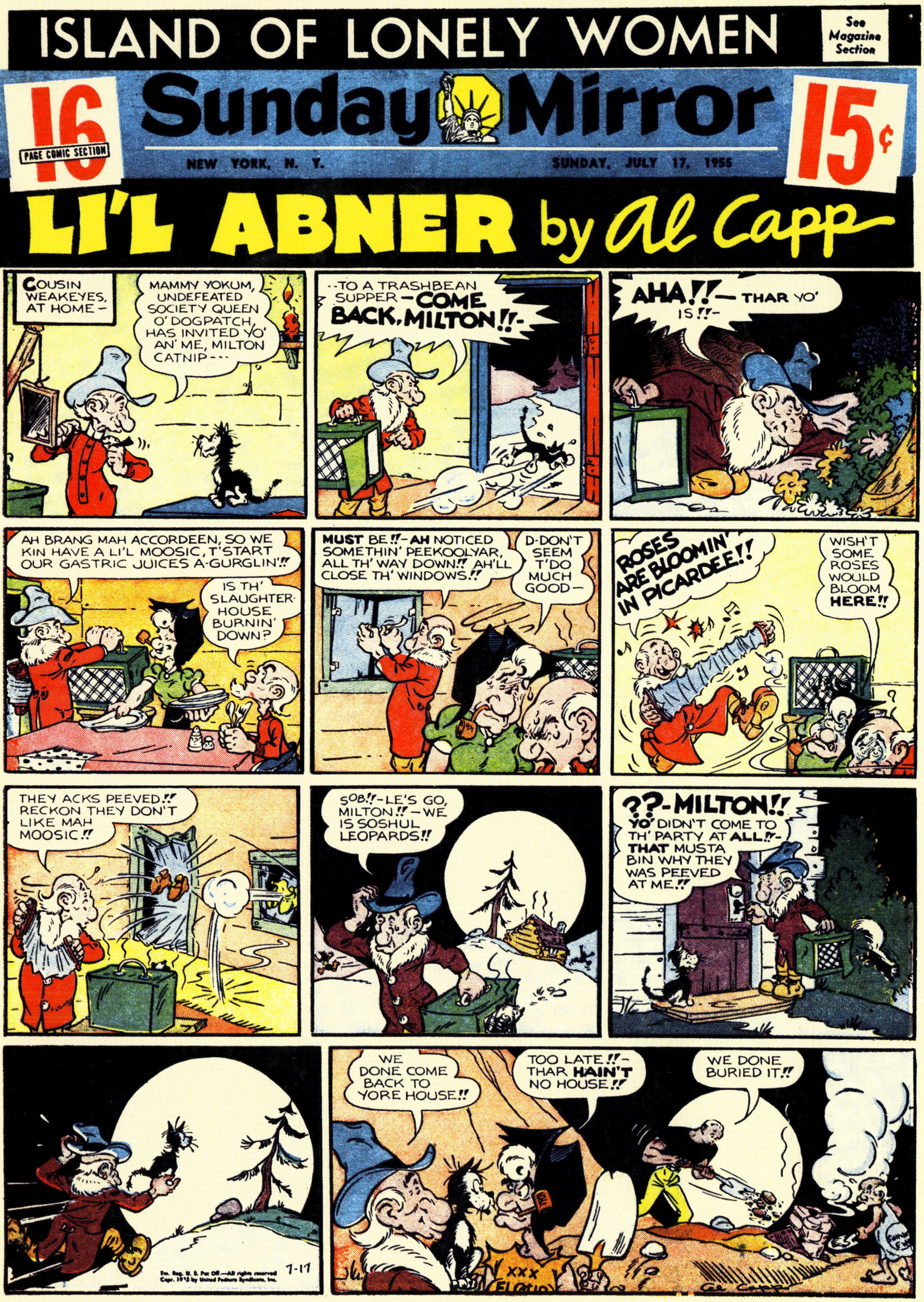
ISLAND OF LONELY WOMEN
See Magazine Section
16
PAGE COMIC SECTION
Sunday Mirror
NEW YORK, N. Y.
SUNDAY, JULY 17, 1955
15¢
LI'L ABNER by Al Capp
COUSIN WEAKEYES, AT HOME —
MAMMY YOKUM, UNDEFEATED SOCIETY QUEEN O' DOGPATCH, HAS INVITED YO' AN' ME, MILTON CATNIP - - -
- -TO A TRASHBEAN SUPPER —COME BACK, MILTON!! -
AHA!! — THAR YO' IS!! -
AH BRANG MAH ACCORDEEN, SO WE KIN HAVE A LI'L MOOSIC, T'START OUR GASTRIC JUICES A-GURGLIN'!!
IS TH' SLAUGHTER-HOUSE BURNIN' DOWN?
MUST BE!! - AH NOTICED SOMETHIN' PEEKOOLYAR, ALL TH' WAY DOWN!! AH'LL CLOSE TH' WINDOWS!!
D-DON'T SEEM T'DO MUCH GOOD —
ROSES ARE BLOOMIN' IN PICARDEE!!
WISH'T SOME ROSES WOULD BLOOM HERE!!
THEY ACKS PEEVED!! RECKON THEY DON'T LIKE MAH MOOSIC!!
SOB!! - LE'S GO, MILTON!! — WE IS SOSHUL LEOPARDS!!
??- MILTON!! YO' DIDN'T COME TO TH' PARTY AT ALL!! - THAT MUSTA BIN WHY THEY WAS PEEVED AT ME.!!
7-17
WE DONE COME BACK TO YORE HOUSE!!
TOO LATE!! - THAR HAIN'T NO HOUSE!!
WE DONE BURIED IT!!

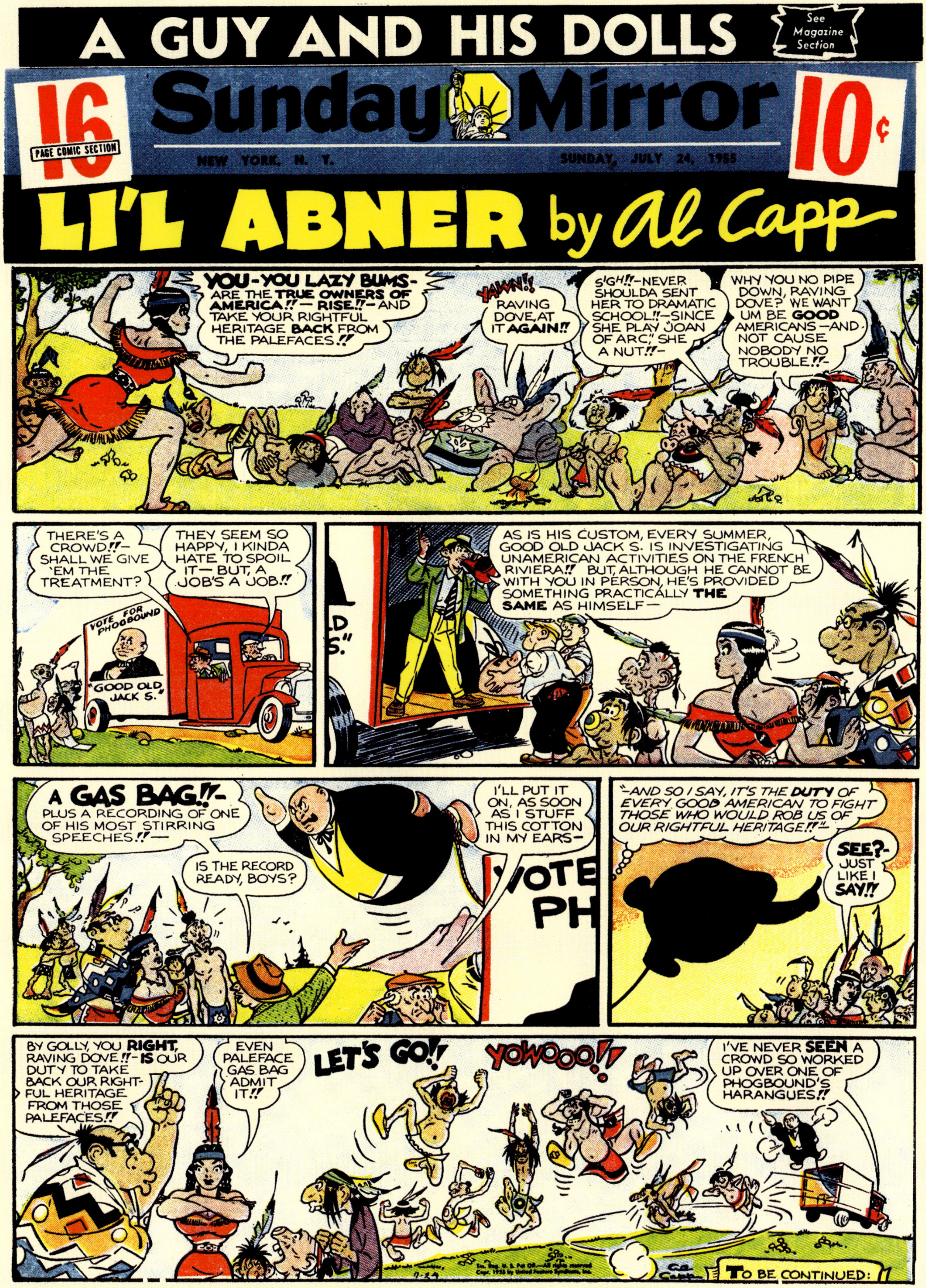
A GUY AND HIS DOLLS
See Magazine Section
16
PAGE COMIC SECTION
Sunday Mirror
NEW YORK, N. Y.
SUNDAY, JULY 24, 1955
10¢
LI'L ABNER by Al Capp
YOU-YOU LAZY BUMS-ARE THE TRUE OWNERS OF AMERICA!!-RISE!!-AND TAKE YOUR RIGHTFUL HERITAGE BACK FROM THE PALEFACES!!
YAWN!!
RAVING DOVE, AT IT AGAIN!!
SIGH!!-NEVER SHOULDA SENT HER TO DRAMATIC SCHOOL!!-SINCE SHE PLAY "JOAN OF ARC," SHE A NUT!!-
WHY YOU NO PIPE DOWN, RAVING DOVE? WE WANT UM BE GOOD AMERICANS-AND NOT CAUSE NOBODY NO TROUBLE!!-
THERE'S A CROWD!!-SHALL WE GIVE 'EM THE TREATMENT?
THEY SEEM SO HAPPY, I KINDA HATE TO SPOIL IT-BUT, A JOB'S A JOB!!
VOTE FOR PHOGBOUND
"GOOD OLD JACK S."
AS IS HIS CUSTOM, EVERY SUMMER, GOOD OLD JACK S. IS INVESTIGATING UNAMERICAN ACTIVITIES ON THE FRENCH RIVIERA!! BUT, ALTHOUGH HE CANNOT BE WITH YOU IN PERSON, HE'S PROVIDED SOMETHING PRACTICALLY THE SAME AS HIMSELF-
A GAS BAG!!-PLUS A RECORDING OF ONE OF HIS MOST STIRRING SPEECHES!!-
IS THE RECORD READY, BOYS?
I'LL PUT IT ON, AS SOON AS I STUFF THIS COTTON IN MY EARS-
VOTE PH
-AND SO I SAY, IT'S THE DUTY OF EVERY GOOD AMERICAN TO FIGHT THOSE WHO WOULD ROB US OF OUR RIGHTFUL HERITAGE!!-
SEE?-JUST LIKE I SAY!!
BY GOLLY, YOU RIGHT, RAVING DOVE!!-IS OUR DUTY TO TAKE BACK OUR RIGHTFUL HERITAGE FROM THOSE PALEFACES!!
EVEN PALEFACE GAS BAG ADMIT IT!!
LET'S GO!!
YOWOOO!!
I'VE NEVER SEEN A CROWD SO WORKED UP OVER ONE OF PHOGBOUND'S HARANGUES!!
TO BE CONTINUED:

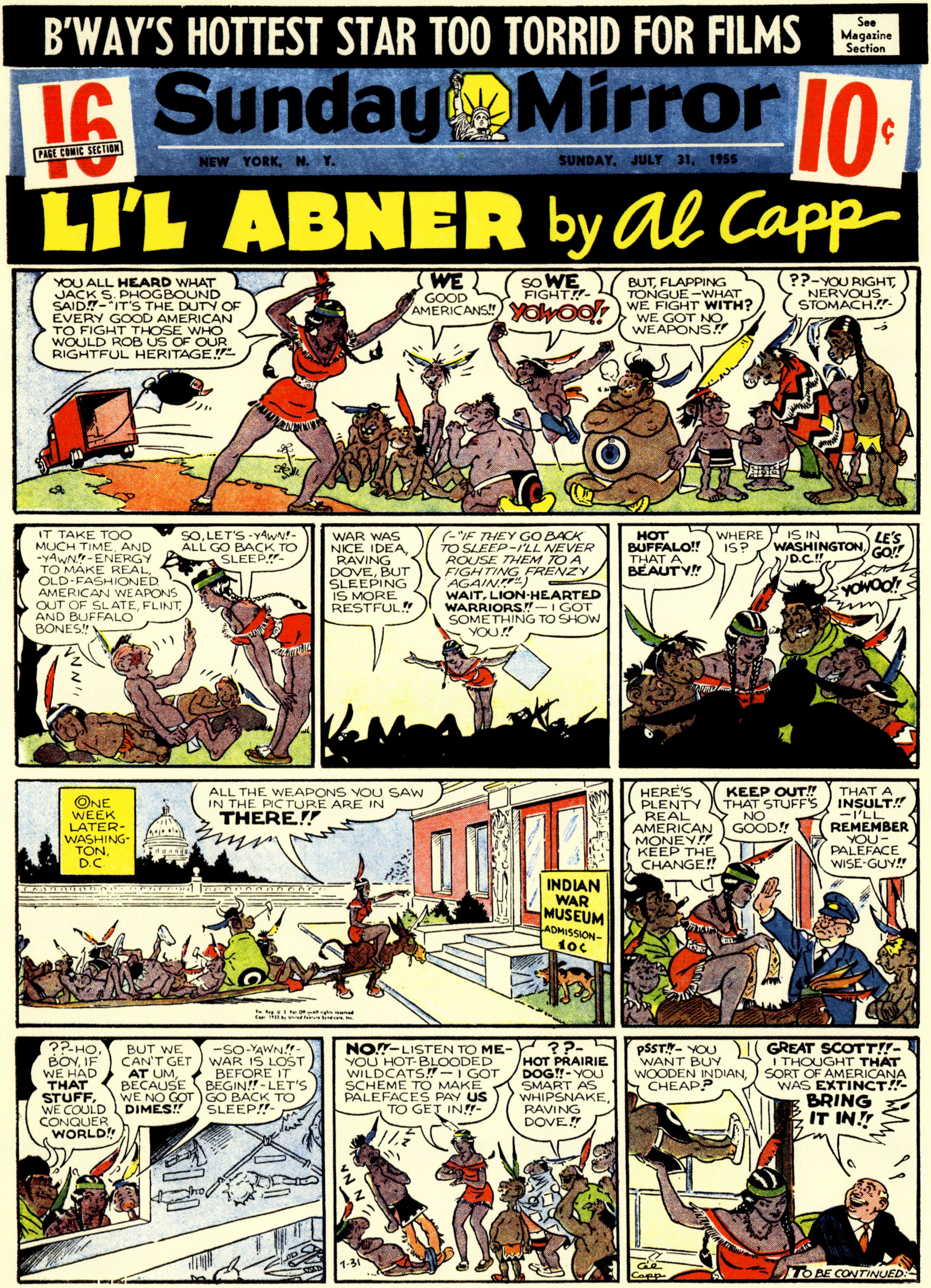

B'WAY'S HOTTEST STAR TOO TORRID FOR FILMS
See Magazine Section
16
PAGE COMIC SECTION
Sunday Mirror
NEW YORK, N. Y.
SUNDAY, JULY 31, 1955
10¢
LI'L ABNER by Al Capp
YOU ALL HEARD WHAT JACK S. PHOGBOUND SAID!!–"IT'S THE DUTY OF EVERY GOOD AMERICAN TO FIGHT THOSE WHO WOULD ROB US OF OUR RIGHTFUL HERITAGE!!"–
WE GOOD AMERICANS!!
SO WE FIGHT!!–
YOWOO!!
BUT, FLAPPING TONGUE–WHAT WE FIGHT WITH? WE GOT NO WEAPONS!!
??–YOU RIGHT, NERVOUS STOMACH!!–
IT TAKE TOO MUCH TIME, AND –YAWN!!–ENERGY TO MAKE REAL, OLD-FASHIONED AMERICAN WEAPONS OUT OF SLATE, FLINT, AND BUFFALO BONES!!
SO, LET'S –YAWN!!– ALL GO BACK TO SLEEP!!–
WAR WAS NICE IDEA, RAVING DOVE, BUT SLEEPING IS MORE RESTFUL!!
(–"IF THEY GO BACK TO SLEEP–I'LL NEVER ROUSE THEM TO A FIGHTING FRENZY AGAIN!!"–)
WAIT, LION-HEARTED WARRIORS!!–I GOT SOMETHING TO SHOW YOU!!
HOT BUFFALO!! THAT A BEAUTY!!
WHERE IS?
IS IN WASHINGTON, D.C.!!
LE'S GO!!
YOWOO!!
ONE WEEK LATER–WASHINGTON, D.C.
ALL THE WEAPONS YOU SAW IN THE PICTURE ARE IN THERE!!
INDIAN WAR MUSEUM
ADMISSION–10¢
HERE'S PLENTY REAL AMERICAN MONEY!! KEEP THE CHANGE!!
KEEP OUT!! THAT STUFF'S NO GOOD!!
THAT A INSULT!!–I'LL REMEMBER YOU–PALEFACE WISE-GUY!!
??–HO, BOY, IF WE HAD THAT STUFF, WE COULD CONQUER WORLD!!
BUT WE CAN'T GET AT UM, BECAUSE WE NO GOT DIMES!!
–SO–YAWN!!– WAR IS LOST BEFORE IT BEGIN!!–LET'S GO BACK TO SLEEP!!–
NO!!–LISTEN TO ME–YOU HOT-BLOODED WILDCATS!!–I GOT SCHEME TO MAKE PALEFACES PAY US TO GET IN!!–
??–HOT PRAIRIE DOG!!–YOU SMART AS WHIPSNAKE, RAVING DOVE!!
PSST!!–YOU WANT BUY WOODEN INDIAN, CHEAP?
GREAT SCOTT!!–I THOUGHT THAT SORT OF AMERICANA WAS EXTINCT!!–BRING IT IN!!
Al Capp
TO BE CONTINUED.

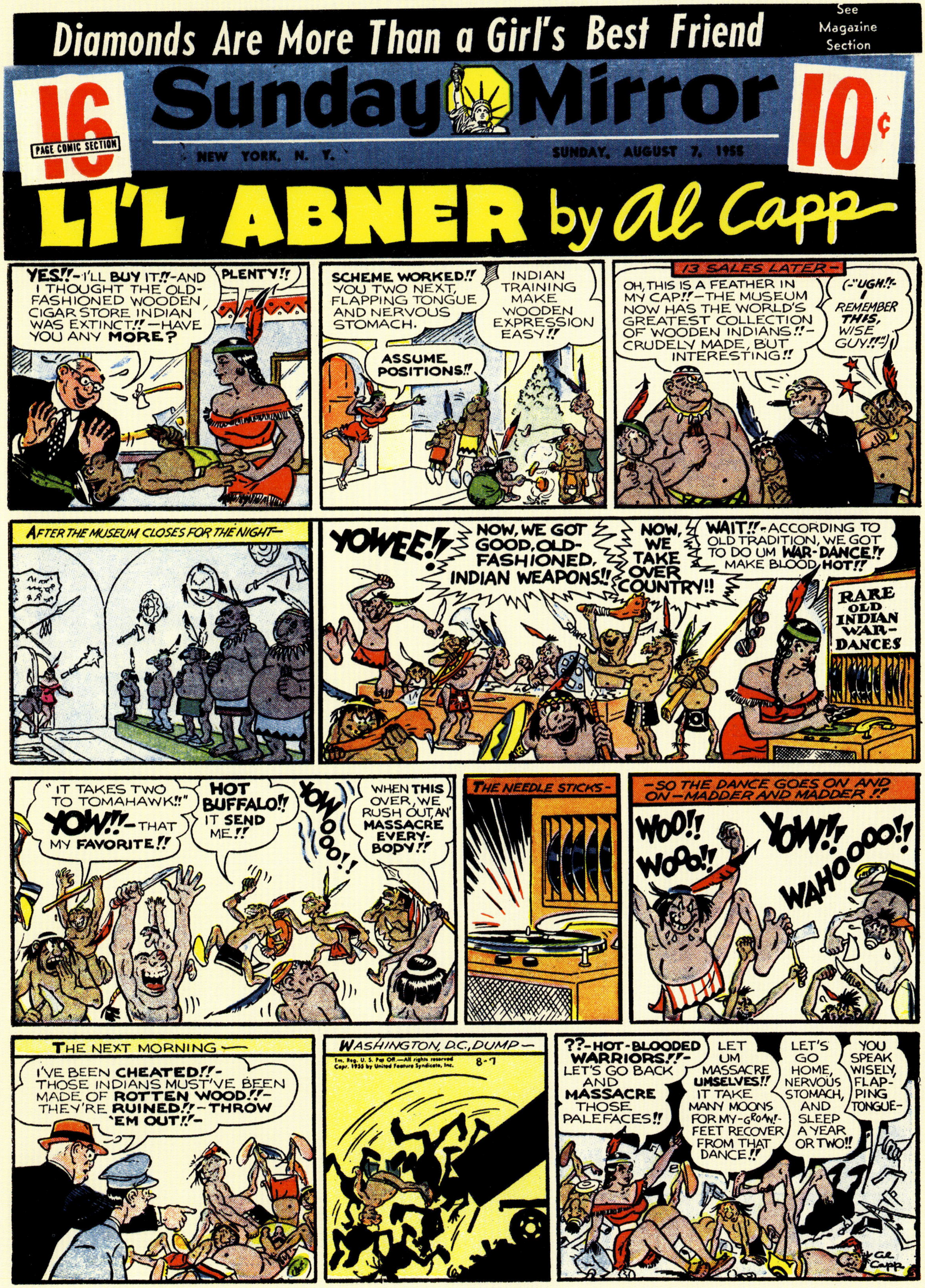

Diamonds Are More Than a Girl's Best Friend
See Magazine Section
16
PAGE COMIC SECTION
Sunday Mirror
NEW YORK, N. Y.
SUNDAY, AUGUST 7, 1955
10¢
LI'L ABNER by Al Capp
YES!!-I'LL BUY IT!!-AND I THOUGHT THE OLD-FASHIONED WOODEN CIGAR STORE INDIAN WAS EXTINCT!!-HAVE YOU ANY MORE?
PLENTY!!
SCHEME WORKED!!-YOU TWO NEXT, FLAPPING TONGUE AND NERVOUS STOMACH.
INDIAN TRAINING MAKE WOODEN EXPRESSION EASY!!
ASSUME POSITIONS!!
13 SALES LATER-
OH, THIS IS A FEATHER IN MY CAP!!-THE MUSEUM NOW HAS THE WORLD'S GREATEST COLLECTION OF WOODEN INDIANS!!-CRUDELY MADE, BUT INTERESTING!!
("UGH!!-I REMEMBER THIS, WISE GUY!!")
AFTER THE MUSEUM CLOSES FOR THE NIGHT-
YOWEE!!
NOW, WE GOT GOOD, OLD-FASHIONED, INDIAN WEAPONS!!
NOW, WE TAKE OVER COUNTRY!!
WAIT!!-ACCORDING TO OLD TRADITION, WE GOT TO DO UM WAR-DANCE!! MAKE BLOOD HOT!!
RARE OLD INDIAN WAR-DANCES
"IT TAKES TWO TO TOMAHAWK!!"
YOW!!-THAT MY FAVORITE!!
HOT BUFFALO!! IT SEND ME.!!
YOWOOO!!
WHEN THIS OVER, WE RUSH OUT, AN' MASSACRE EVERY-BODY!!
THE NEEDLE STICKS-
-SO THE DANCE GOES ON AND ON-MADDER AND MADDER!!
WOO!!
WOOO!!
YOW!!
WAHOOOOO!!
THE NEXT MORNING-
I'VE BEEN CHEATED!!-THOSE INDIANS MUST'VE BEEN MADE OF ROTTEN WOOD!!-THEY'RE RUINED!!-THROW 'EM OUT!!-
WASHINGTON, D.C., DUMP-
Tm. Reg. U. S. Pat Off.—All rights reserved Copr. 1955 by United Feature Syndicate, Inc.
8-7
??-HOT-BLOODED WARRIORS!!-LET'S GO BACK AND MASSACRE THOSE PALEFACES!!
LET UM MASSACRE UMSELVES!!-IT TAKE MANY MOONS FOR MY-GROAN!-FEET RECOVER FROM THAT DANCE!!
LET'S GO HOME, NERVOUS STOMACH, AND SLEEP A YEAR OR TWO!!
YOU SPEAK WISELY, FLAP-PING TONGUE-
Al Capp

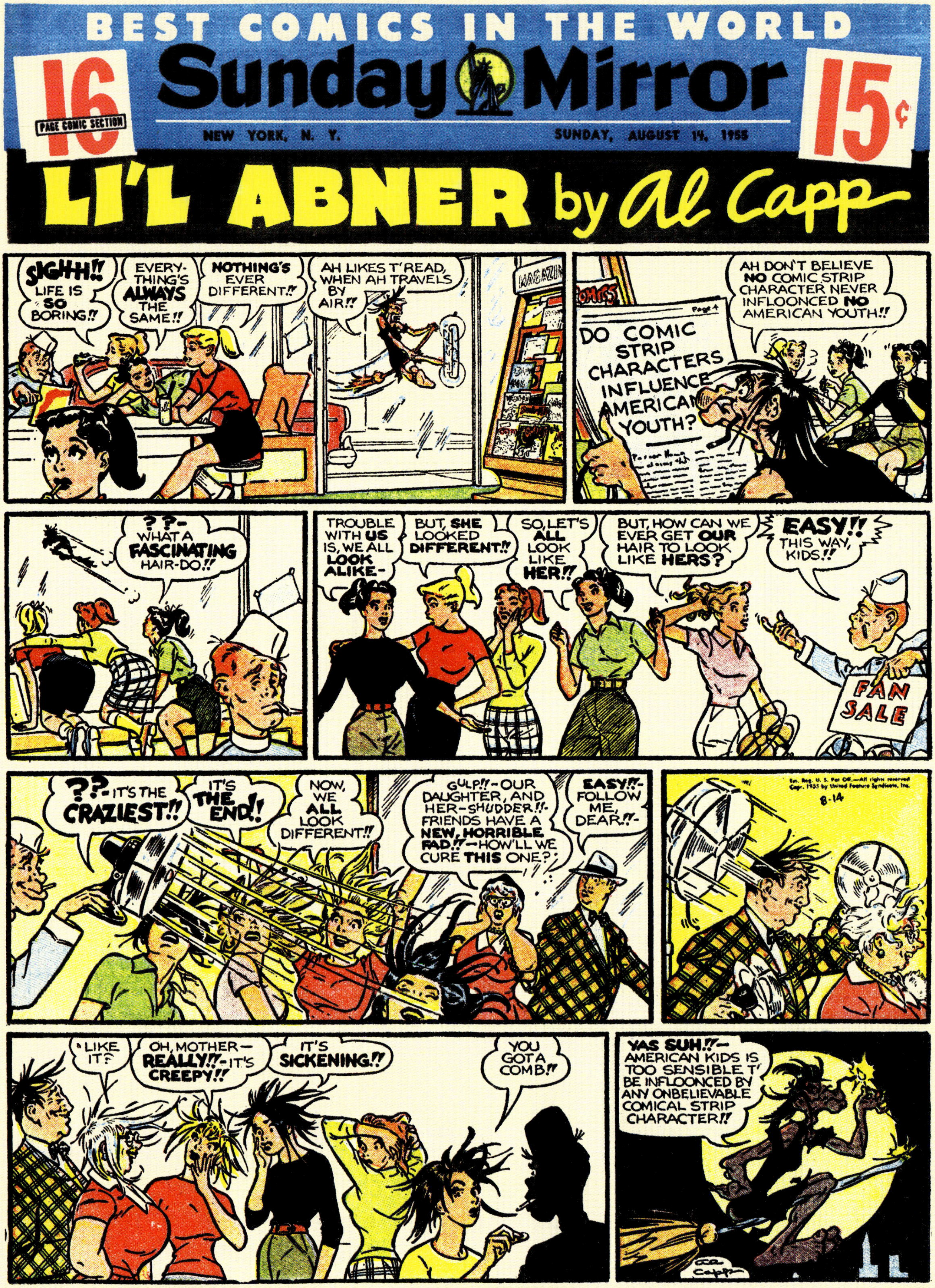

BEST COMICS IN THE WORLD
16 PAGE COMIC SECTION
Sunday Mirror
15¢
NEW YORK, N. Y.
SUNDAY, AUGUST 14, 1955
LI'L ABNER by Al Capp
SIGHHH!! LIFE IS SO BORING!!
EVERY-THING'S ALWAYS THE SAME!!
NOTHING'S EVER DIFFERENT!!
AH LIKES T'READ, WHEN AH TRAVELS BY AIR!!
MAGAZIN
COMICS
AH DON'T BELIEVE NO COMIC STRIP CHARACTER NEVER INFLOONCED NO AMERICAN YOUTH!!
DO COMIC STRIP CHARACTERS INFLUENCE AMERICAN YOUTH?
??- WHAT A FASCINATING HAIR-DO!!
TROUBLE WITH US IS, WE ALL LOOK ALIKE-
BUT, SHE LOOKED DIFFERENT!!
SO, LET'S ALL LOOK LIKE HER!!
BUT, HOW CAN WE EVER GET OUR HAIR TO LOOK LIKE HERS?
EASY!! THIS WAY, KIDS!!
FAN SALE
??- IT'S THE CRAZIEST!!
IT'S THE END!!
NOW, WE ALL LOOK DIFFERENT!!
GULP!!- OUR DAUGHTER, AND HER- SHUDDER!!- FRIENDS HAVE A NEW, HORRIBLE FAD!!- HOW'LL WE CURE THIS ONE?
EASY!!- FOLLOW ME, DEAR!!-
8-14
LIKE IT?
OH, MOTHER- REALLY!!- IT'S CREEPY!!
IT'S SICKENING!!
YOU GOT A COMB!!
YAS SUH!!- AMERICAN KIDS IS TOO SENSIBLE T' BE INFLOONCED BY ANY ONBELIEVABLE COMICAL STRIP CHARACTER!!
Al Capp

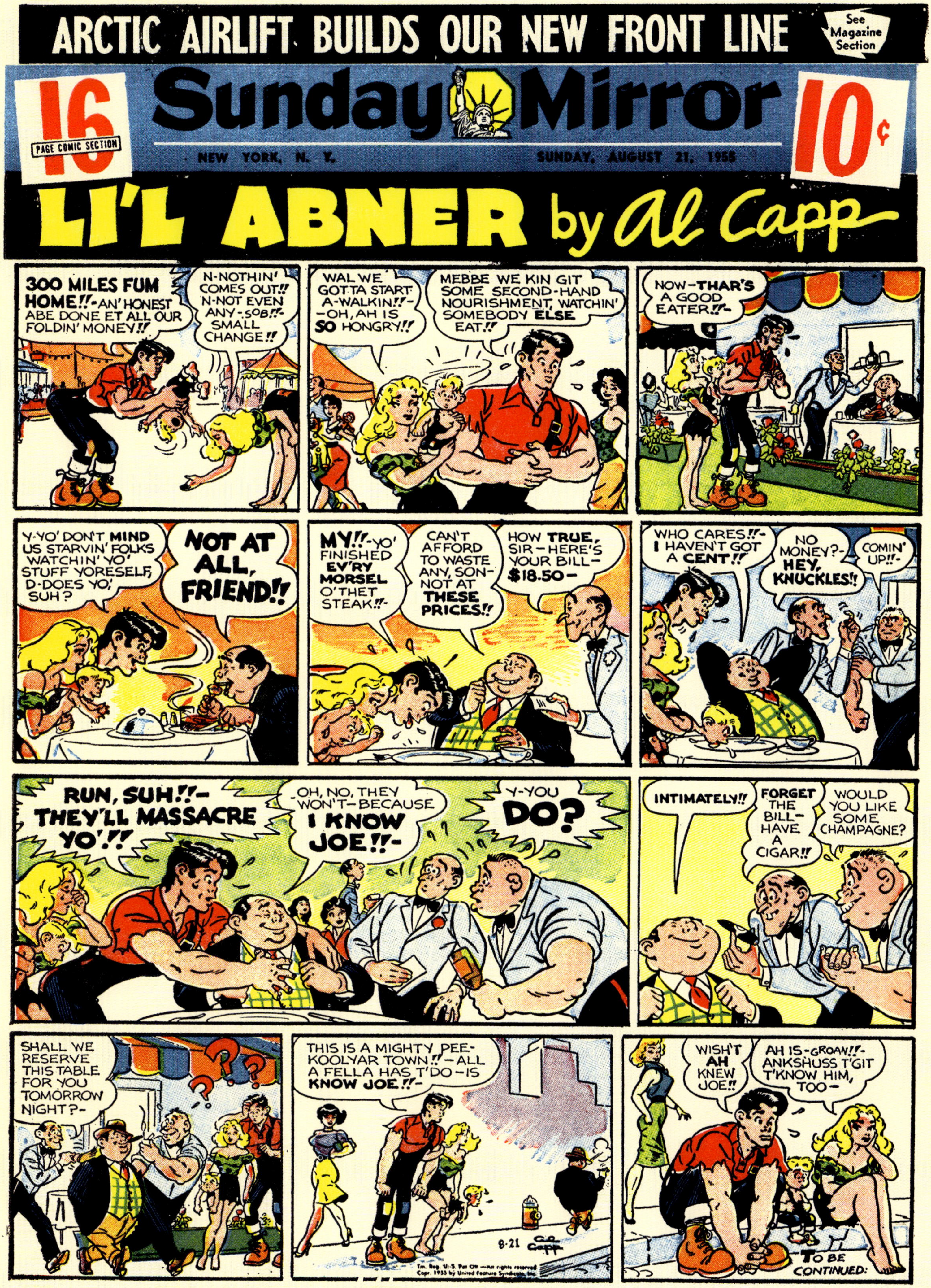
ARCTIC AIRLIFT BUILDS OUR NEW FRONT LINE
See Magazine Section
16 PAGE COMIC SECTION
Sunday Mirror
10¢
NEW YORK, N. Y.
SUNDAY, AUGUST 21, 1955
LI'L ABNER by Al Capp
300 MILES FUM HOME!!-AN' HONEST ABE DONE ET ALL OUR FOLDIN' MONEY!!
N-NOTHIN' COMES OUT!! N-NOT EVEN ANY-SOB!!- SMALL CHANGE!!
WAL WE GOTTA START A-WALKIN!!- -OH, AH IS SO HONGRY!!
MEBBE WE KIN GIT SOME SECOND-HAND NOURISHMENT, WATCHIN' SOMEBODY ELSE EAT!!
NOW-THAR'S A GOOD EATER!!-
Y-YO' DON'T MIND US STARVIN' FOLKS WATCHIN' YO' STUFF YORESELF, D-DOES YO', SUH?
NOT AT ALL, FRIEND!!
MY!!-YO' FINISHED EV'RY MORSEL O'THET STEAK!!-
CAN'T AFFORD TO WASTE ANY, SON-NOT AT THESE PRICES!!
HOW TRUE, SIR-HERE'S YOUR BILL-$18.50-
WHO CARES!!- I HAVEN'T GOT A CENT!!
NO MONEY?- HEY, KNUCKLES!!
COMIN' UP!!-
RUN, SUH!!- THEY'LL MASSACRE YO'!!
OH, NO, THEY WON'T-BECAUSE I KNOW JOE!!-
Y-YOU DO?
INTIMATELY!!
FORGET THE BILL-HAVE A CIGAR!!
WOULD YOU LIKE SOME CHAMPAGNE?
SHALL WE RESERVE THIS TABLE FOR YOU TOMORROW NIGHT?-
THIS IS A MIGHTY PEE-KOOLYAR TOWN!!-ALL A FELLA HAS T'DO-IS KNOW JOE!!-
8-21
WISH'T AH KNEW JOE!!
AH IS-GROAN!!-ANKSHUSS T'GIT T'KNOW HIM, TOO-
TO BE CONTINUED:

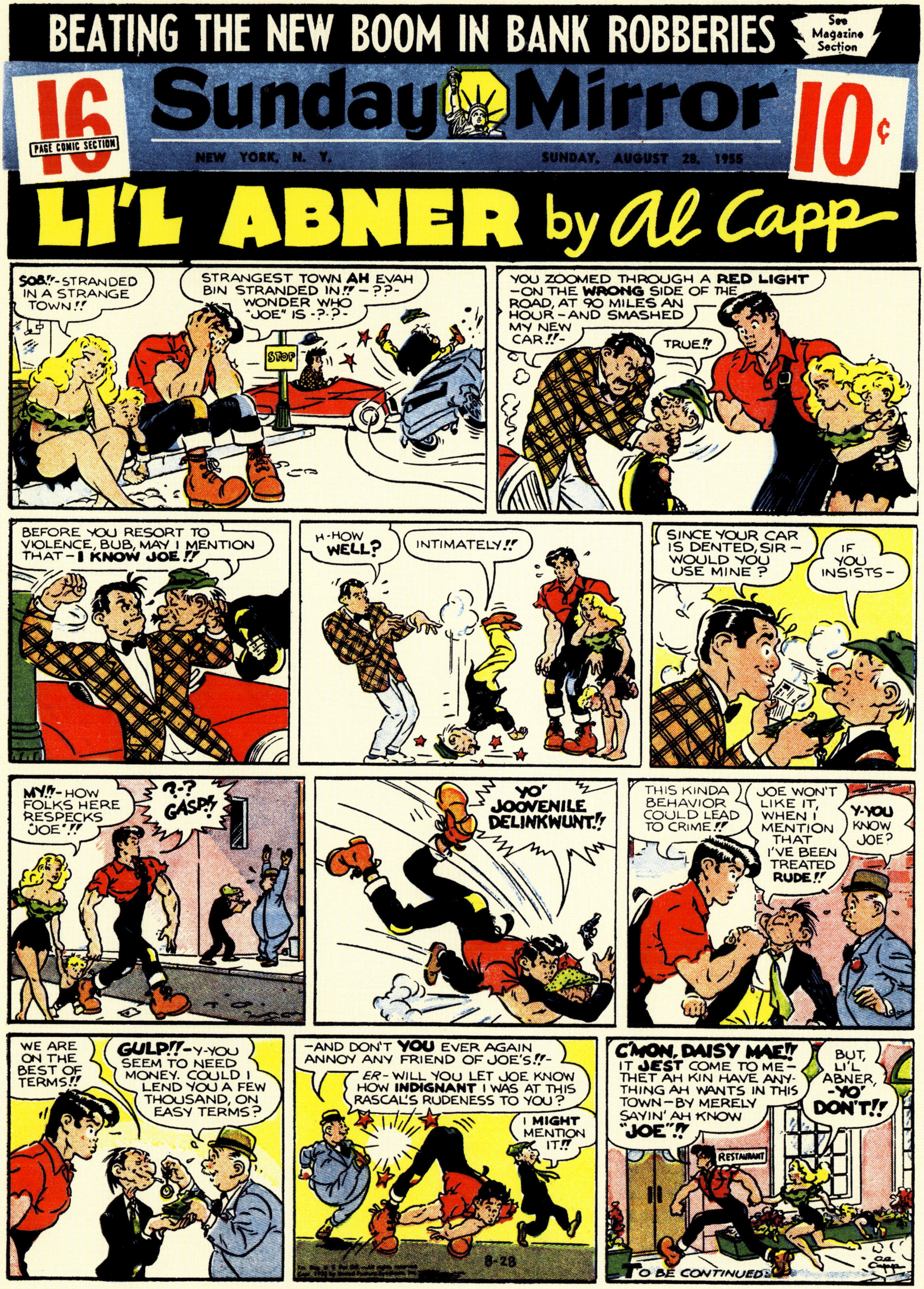
BEATING THE NEW BOOM IN BANK ROBBERIES
See Magazine Section
16
PAGE COMIC SECTION
Sunday Mirror
NEW YORK, N. Y.
SUNDAY, AUGUST 28, 1955
10¢
LI'L ABNER by Al Capp
SOB!!-STRANDED IN A STRANGE TOWN!!
STRANGEST TOWN AH EVAH BIN STRANDED IN!! - ??- WONDER WHO "JOE" IS -?-?-
STOP
YOU ZOOMED THROUGH A RED LIGHT -ON THE WRONG SIDE OF THE ROAD, AT 90 MILES AN HOUR - AND SMASHED MY NEW CAR!!-
TRUE!!
BEFORE YOU RESORT TO VIOLENCE, BUB, MAY I MENTION THAT - I KNOW JOE!!
H-HOW WELL?
INTIMATELY!!
SINCE YOUR CAR IS DENTED, SIR - WOULD YOU USE MINE?
IF YOU INSISTS-
MY!!-HOW FOLKS HERE RESPECKS "JOE"!!
?-? GASP!!
YO' JOOVENILE DELINKWUNT!!
THIS KINDA BEHAVIOR COULD LEAD TO CRIME!!
JOE WON'T LIKE IT, WHEN I MENTION THAT I'VE BEEN TREATED RUDE!!
Y-YOU KNOW JOE?
WE ARE ON THE BEST OF TERMS!!
GULP!!-Y-YOU SEEM TO NEED MONEY. COULD I LEND YOU A FEW THOUSAND, ON EASY TERMS?
-AND DON'T YOU EVER AGAIN ANNOY ANY FRIEND OF JOE'S!!-
ER-WILL YOU LET JOE KNOW HOW INDIGNANT I WAS AT THIS RASCAL'S RUDENESS TO YOU?
I MIGHT MENTION IT!!
8-28
C'MON, DAISY MAE!! IT JEST COME TO ME - THET AH KIN HAVE ANY-THING AH WANTS IN THIS TOWN - BY MERELY SAYIN' AH KNOW "JOE"!!
BUT, LI'L ABNER, -YO' DON'T!!
RESTAURANT
TO BE CONTINUED
Al Capp

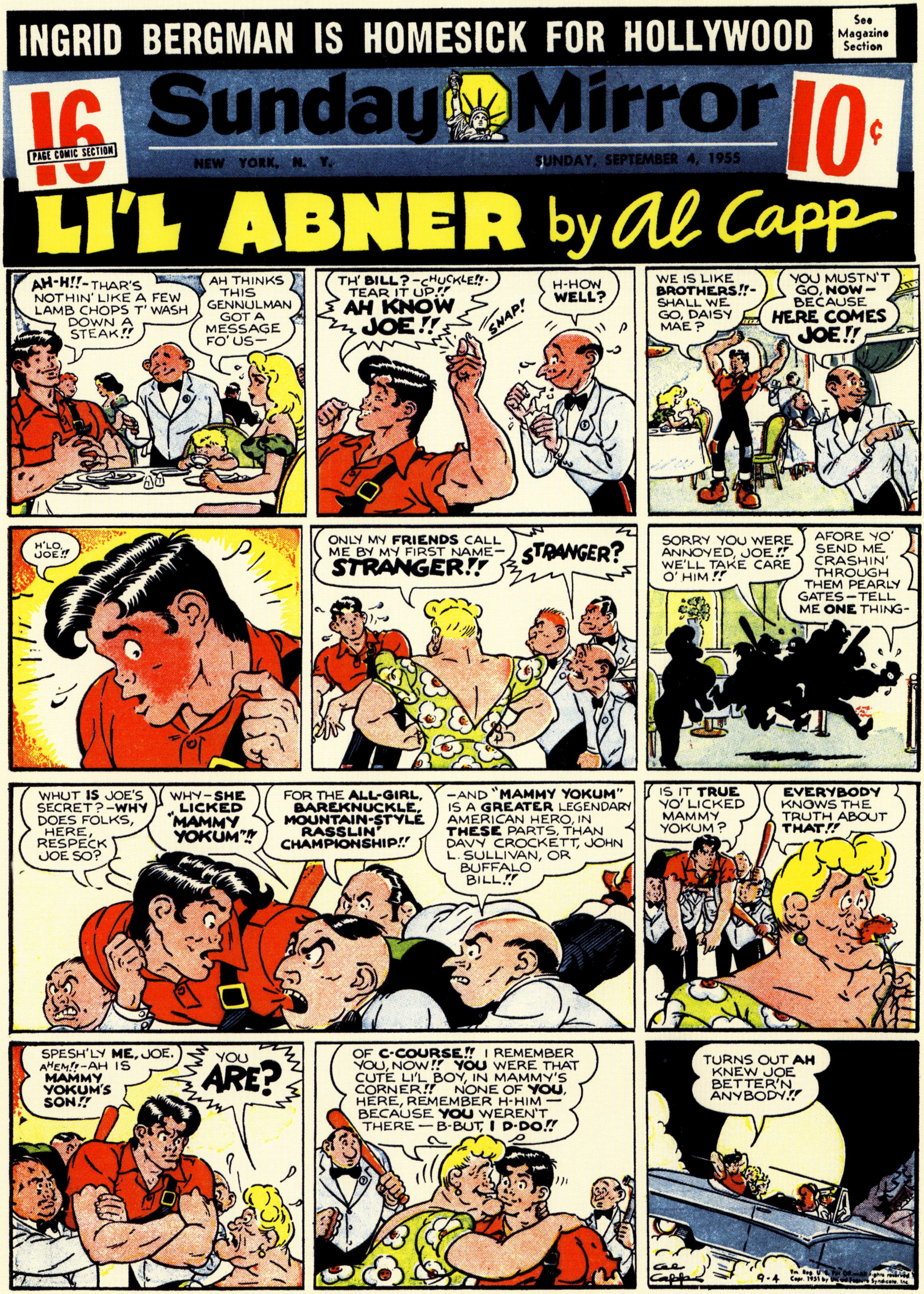
INGRID BERGMAN IS HOMESICK FOR HOLLYWOOD
See Magazine Section
16 PAGE COMIC SECTION
Sunday Mirror
10¢
NEW YORK, N. Y.
SUNDAY, SEPTEMBER 4, 1955
LI'L ABNER by Al Capp
AH-H!!-THAR'S NOTHIN' LIKE A FEW LAMB CHOPS T' WASH DOWN A STEAK!!
AH THINKS THIS GENNULMAN GOT A MESSAGE FO' US—
TH' BILL? -CHUCKLE!!- TEAR IT UP!! AH KNOW JOE!!
SNAP!
H-HOW WELL?
WE IS LIKE BROTHERS!!- SHALL WE GO, DAISY MAE?
YOU MUSTN'T GO, NOW— BECAUSE HERE COMES JOE!!
H'LO, JOE!!
ONLY MY FRIENDS CALL ME BY MY FIRST NAME— STRANGER!!
STRANGER?
SORRY YOU WERE ANNOYED, JOE!! WE'LL TAKE CARE O' HIM!!
AFORE YO' SEND ME CRASHIN' THROUGH THEM PEARLY GATES—TELL ME ONE THING—
WHUT IS JOE'S SECRET?-WHY DOES FOLKS, HERE, RESPECK JOE SO?
WHY—SHE LICKED "MAMMY YOKUM"!!
FOR THE ALL-GIRL, BAREKNUCKLE, MOUNTAIN-STYLE RASSLIN' CHAMPIONSHIP!!
—AND "MAMMY YOKUM" IS A GREATER LEGENDARY AMERICAN HERO, IN THESE PARTS, THAN DAVY CROCKETT, JOHN L. SULLIVAN, OR BUFFALO BILL!!
IS IT TRUE YO' LICKED MAMMY YOKUM?
EVERYBODY KNOWS THE TRUTH ABOUT THAT!!
SPESH'LY ME, JOE. AHEM!!-AH IS MAMMY YOKUM'S SON!!
YOU ARE?
OF C-COURSE!! I REMEMBER YOU, NOW!! YOU WERE THAT CUTE LI'L BOY, IN MAMMY'S CORNER!! NONE OF YOU, HERE, REMEMBER H-HIM— BECAUSE YOU WEREN'T THERE—B-BUT, I D-DO!!
TURNS OUT AH KNEW JOE BETTER'N ANYBODY!!
Al Capp
9-4

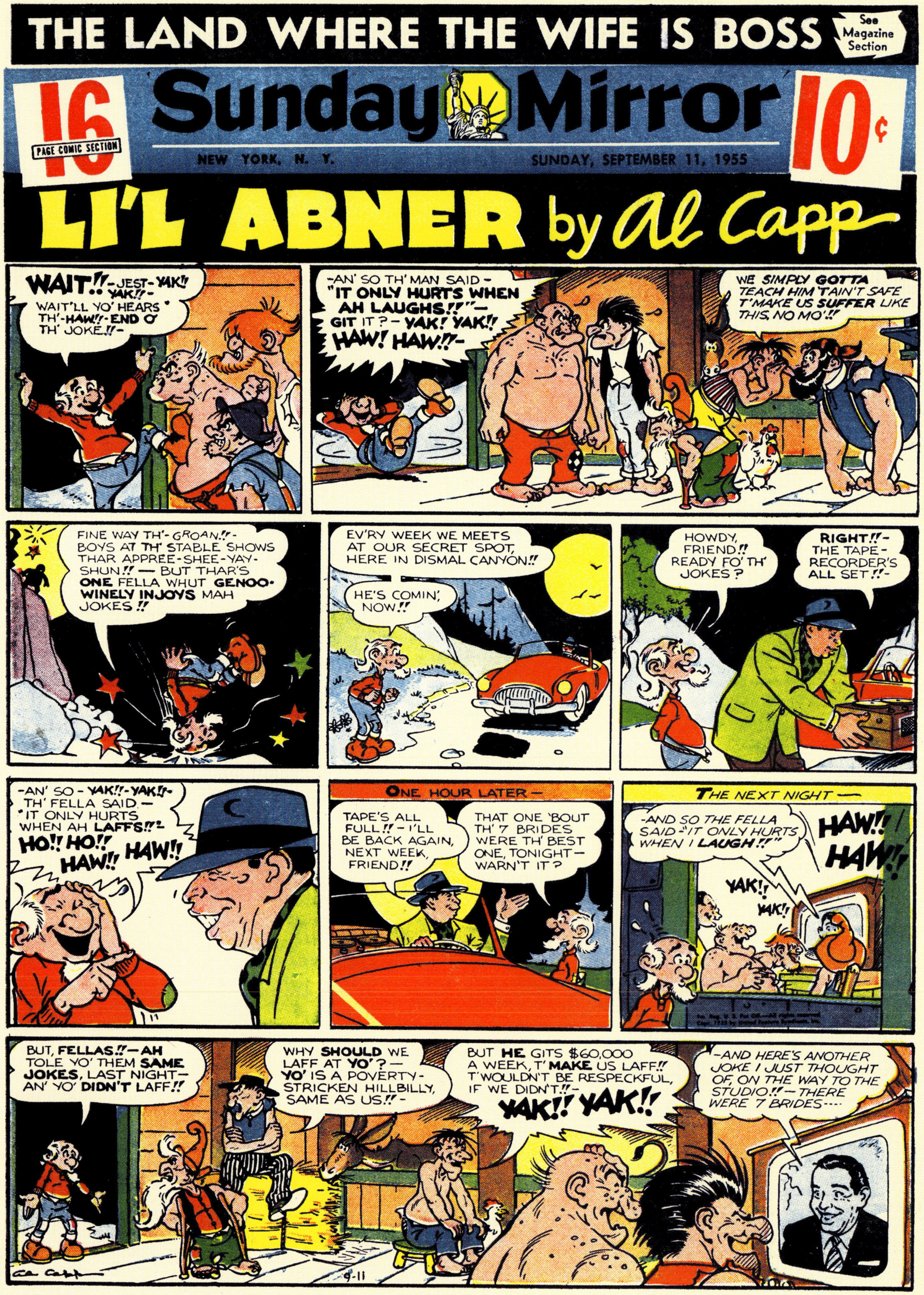
THE LAND WHERE THE WIFE IS BOSS
See Magazine Section
16
PAGE COMIC SECTION
Sunday Mirror
10¢
NEW YORK, N. Y.
SUNDAY, SEPTEMBER 11, 1955
LI'L ABNER by Al Capp
WAIT!!-JEST-YAK!! YAK!!- WAIT'LL YO' HEARS TH'-HAW!!-END O' TH' JOKE.!!-
-AN' SO TH' MAN SAID- "IT ONLY HURTS WHEN AH LAUGHS!!"- GIT IT?-YAK! YAK!! HAW! HAW!!-
WE SIMPLY GOTTA TEACH HIM 'TAIN'T SAFE T'MAKE US SUFFER LIKE THIS, NO MO'!!
FINE WAY TH'-GROAN!!- BOYS AT TH' STABLE SHOWS THAR APPREE-SHEE-YAY-SHUN!! — BUT THAR'S ONE FELLA WHUT GENOO-WINELY INJOYS MAH JOKES!!
EV'RY WEEK WE MEETS AT OUR SECRET SPOT, HERE IN DISMAL CANYON!!
HE'S COMIN', NOW!!
HOWDY, FRIEND!! READY FO' TH' JOKES?
RIGHT!!- THE TAPE-RECORDER'S ALL SET!!-
-AN' SO-YAK!!-YAK!!- TH' FELLA SAID- "IT ONLY HURTS WHEN AH LAFFS!!"-
HO!! HO!! HAW!! HAW!!
ONE HOUR LATER—
TAPE'S ALL FULL!!-I'LL BE BACK AGAIN, NEXT WEEK, FRIEND!!
THAT ONE 'BOUT TH' 7 BRIDES WERE TH' BEST ONE, TONIGHT— WARN'T IT?
THE NEXT NIGHT—
-AND SO THE FELLA SAID-"IT ONLY HURTS WHEN I LAUGH!!"
HAW!! HAW!!
YAK!! YAK!!
BUT, FELLAS!!—AH TOLE YO' THEM SAME JOKES, LAST NIGHT— AN' YO' DIDN'T LAFF!!
WHY SHOULD WE LAFF AT YO'?— YO' IS A POVERTY-STRICKEN HILLBILLY, SAME AS US!!-
BUT HE GITS $60,000 A WEEK, T'MAKE US LAFF!! T'WOULDN'T BE RESPECKFUL, IF WE DIDN'T!!-
YAK!! YAK!!
-AND HERE'S ANOTHER JOKE I JUST THOUGHT OF, ON THE WAY TO THE STUDIO!!—THERE WERE 7 BRIDES----
AL CAPP
9-11

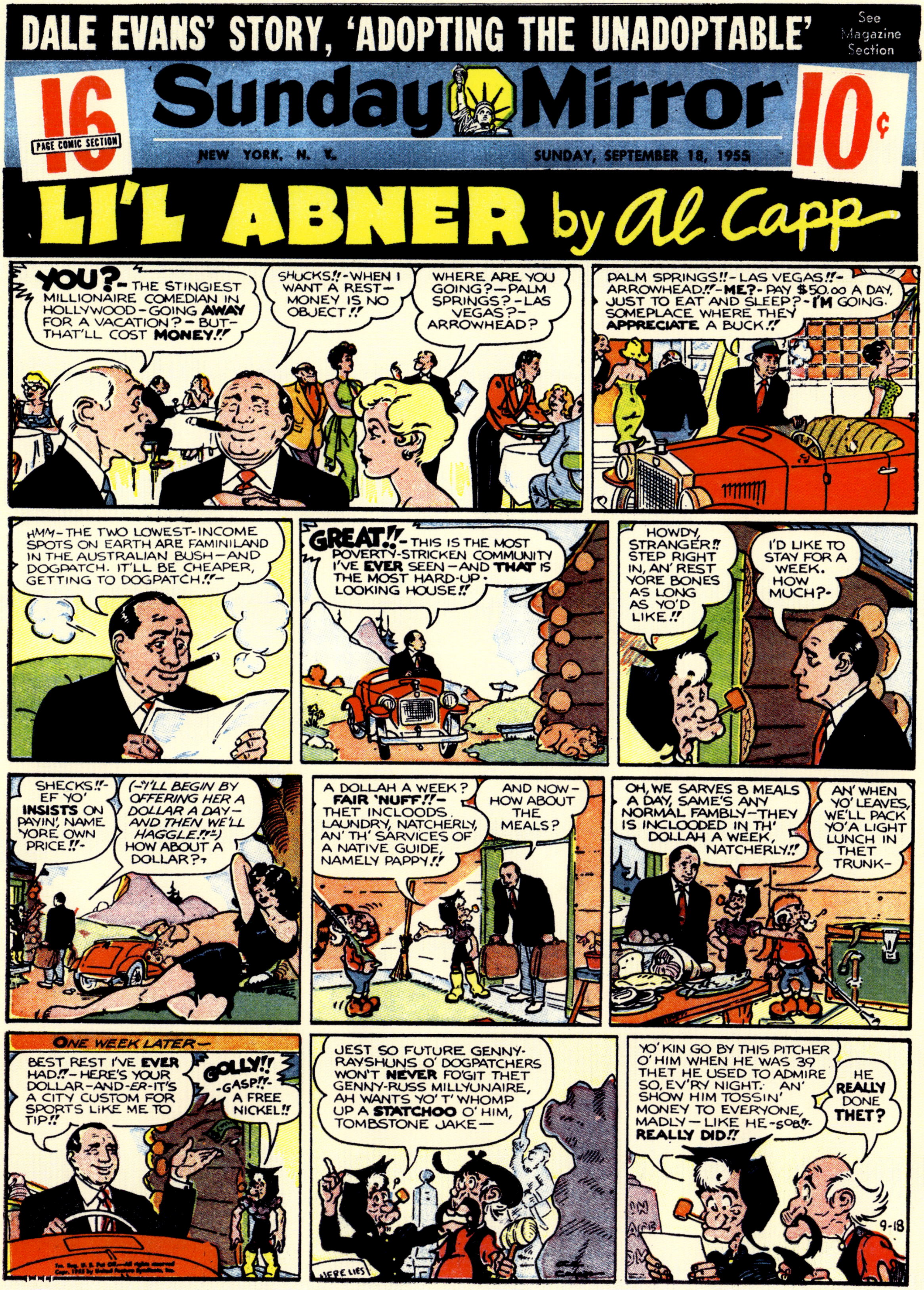

DALE EVANS' STORY, 'ADOPTING THE UNADOPTABLE'
See Magazine Section
16
PAGE COMIC SECTION
Sunday Mirror
10¢
NEW YORK, N. Y.
SUNDAY, SEPTEMBER 18, 1955
LI'L ABNER by Al Capp
YOU?- THE STINGIEST MILLIONAIRE COMEDIAN IN HOLLYWOOD - GOING AWAY FOR A VACATION? - BUT- THAT'LL COST MONEY!!
SHUCKS!!- WHEN I WANT A REST- MONEY IS NO OBJECT!!
WHERE ARE YOU GOING?— PALM SPRINGS? - LAS VEGAS?- ARROWHEAD?
PALM SPRINGS!!- LAS VEGAS!!- ARROWHEAD!!- ME?- PAY $50.00 A DAY, JUST TO EAT AND SLEEP?- I'M GOING, SOMEPLACE WHERE THEY APPRECIATE A BUCK!!
HMM- THE TWO LOWEST-INCOME SPOTS ON EARTH ARE FAMINILAND IN THE AUSTRALIAN BUSH — AND DOGPATCH. IT'LL BE CHEAPER, GETTING TO DOGPATCH!!-
GREAT!!- THIS IS THE MOST POVERTY-STRICKEN COMMUNITY I'VE EVER SEEN — AND THAT IS THE MOST HARD-UP-LOOKING HOUSE!!
HOWDY, STRANGER!! STEP RIGHT IN, AN' REST YORE BONES AS LONG AS YO'D LIKE!!
I'D LIKE TO STAY FOR A WEEK. HOW MUCH?-
SHECKS!!- EF YO' INSISTS ON PAYIN', NAME YORE OWN PRICE!!-
(-"I'LL BEGIN BY OFFERING HER A DOLLAR A DAY- AND THEN WE'LL HAGGLE!!"-) HOW ABOUT A DOLLAR?-
A DOLLAH A WEEK? FAIR 'NUFF!!- THET INCLOODS LAUNDRY, NATCHERLY, AN' TH' SARVICES OF A NATIVE GUIDE, NAMELY PAPPY!!
AND NOW- HOW ABOUT THE MEALS?
OH, WE SARVES 8 MEALS A DAY, SAME'S ANY NORMAL FAMBLY— THEY IS INCLOODED IN TH' DOLLAH A WEEK, NATCHERLY!!
AN' WHEN YO' LEAVES, WE'LL PACK YO' A LIGHT LUNCH IN THET TRUNK-
ONE WEEK LATER—
BEST REST I'VE EVER HAD!!- HERE'S YOUR DOLLAR- AND- ER- IT'S A CITY CUSTOM FOR SPORTS LIKE ME TO TIP!!
GOLLY!! -GASP!!- A FREE NICKEL!!
JEST SO FUTURE GENNY-RAYSHUNS O' DOGPATCHERS WON'T NEVER FO'GIT THET GENNY-RUSS MILLYUNAIRE, AH WANTS YO' T' WHOMP UP A STATCHOO O' HIM, TOMBSTONE JAKE—
HERE LIES
YO' KIN GO BY THIS PITCHER O' HIM WHEN HE WAS 39 THET HE USED TO ADMIRE SO, EV'RY NIGHT. AN' SHOW HIM TOSSIN' MONEY TO EVERYONE, MADLY — LIKE HE -SOB!!- REALLY DID!!
HE REALLY DONE THET?
9-18

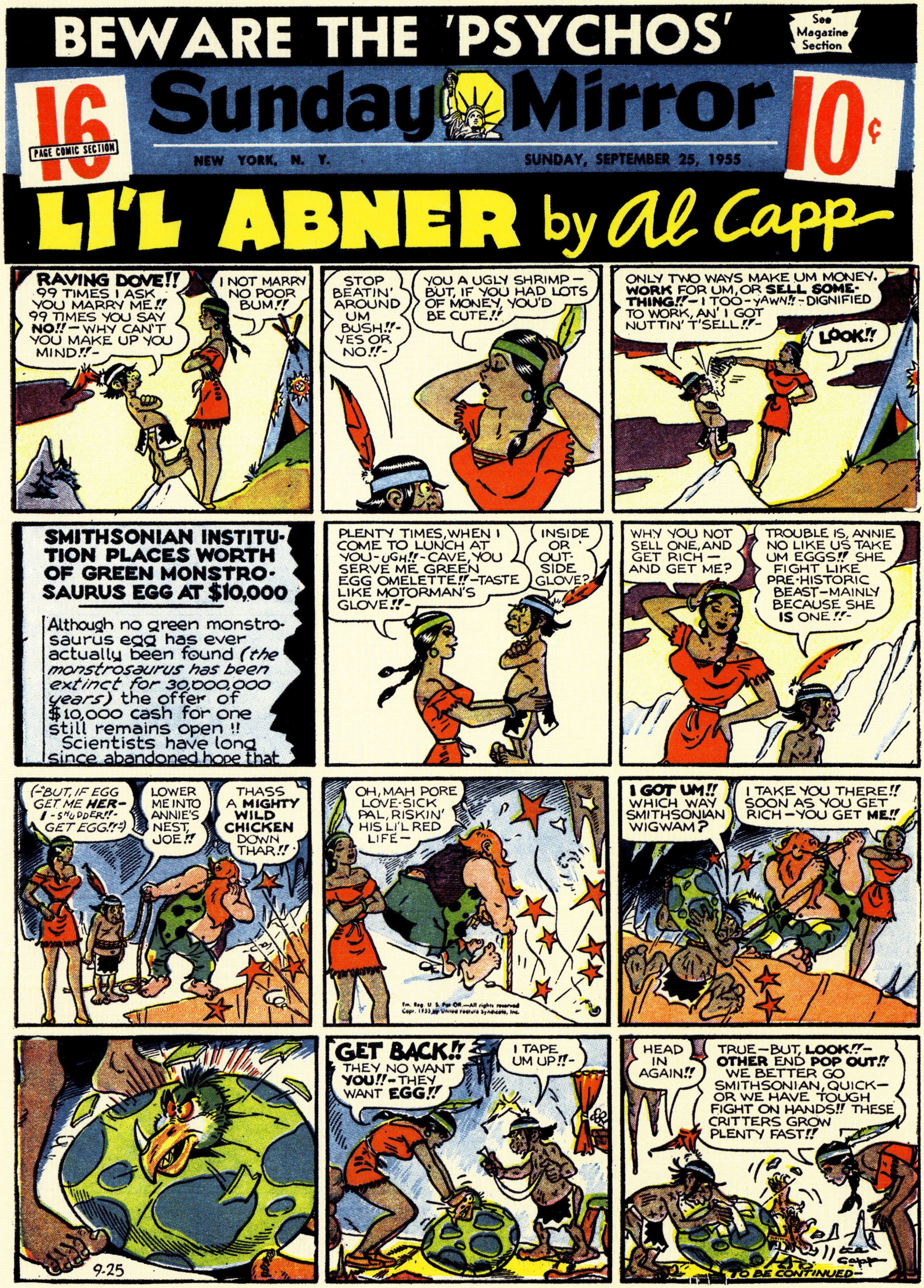
BEWARE THE 'PSYCHOS'
See Magazine Section
16 PAGE COMIC SECTION
Sunday Mirror
NEW YORK, N. Y.
SUNDAY, SEPTEMBER 25, 1955
10¢
LI'L ABNER by Al Capp
RAVING DOVE!! 99 TIMES I ASK YOU MARRY ME!! 99 TIMES YOU SAY NO!!—WHY CAN'T YOU MAKE UP YOU MIND!!-
I NOT MARRY NO POOR BUM!!
STOP BEATIN' AROUND UM BUSH!!-YES OR NO!!-
YOU A UGLY SHRIMP—BUT, IF YOU HAD LOTS OF MONEY, YOU'D BE CUTE!!
ONLY TWO WAYS MAKE UM MONEY. WORK FOR UM, OR SELL SOME-THING!!—I TOO-YAWN!!-DIGNIFIED TO WORK, AN' I GOT NUTTIN' T'SELL!!-
LOOK!!
SMITHSONIAN INSTITU-TION PLACES WORTH OF GREEN MONSTRO-SAURUS EGG AT $10,000
Although no green monstro-saurus egg has ever actually been found (the monstrosaurus has been extinct for 30,000,000 years) the offer of $10,000 cash for one still remains open !! Scientists have long since abandoned hope that
PLENTY TIMES, WHEN I COME TO LUNCH AT YOU-UGH!!-CAVE, YOU SERVE ME GREEN EGG OMELETTE!!—TASTE LIKE MOTORMAN'S GLOVE!!-
INSIDE OR OUT-SIDE GLOVE?
WHY YOU NOT SELL ONE, AND GET RICH—AND GET ME?
TROUBLE IS, ANNIE NO LIKE US TAKE UM EGGS!! SHE FIGHT LIKE PRE-HISTORIC BEAST—MAINLY BECAUSE SHE IS ONE!!-
(—BUT, IF EGG GET ME HER—I-SHUDDER!!-GET EGG!!-)
LOWER ME INTO ANNIE'S NEST, JOE!!
THASS A MIGHTY WILD CHICKEN DOWN THAR!!-
OH, MAH PORE LOVE-SICK PAL, RISKIN' HIS LI'L RED LIFE—
Tm. Reg. U.S. Pat. Off.—All rights reserved Copr. 1955 by United Feature Syndicate, Inc.
I GOT UM!! WHICH WAY SMITHSONIAN WIGWAM?
I TAKE YOU THERE!! SOON AS YOU GET RICH—YOU GET ME!!
9-25
GET BACK!! THEY NO WANT YOU!!—THEY WANT EGG!!
I TAPE UM UP!!-
HEAD IN AGAIN!!
TRUE—BUT, LOOK!!—OTHER END POP OUT!! WE BETTER GO SMITHSONIAN, QUICK—OR WE HAVE TOUGH FIGHT ON HANDS!! THESE CRITTERS GROW PLENTY FAST!!
CAPP
TO BE CONTINUED—

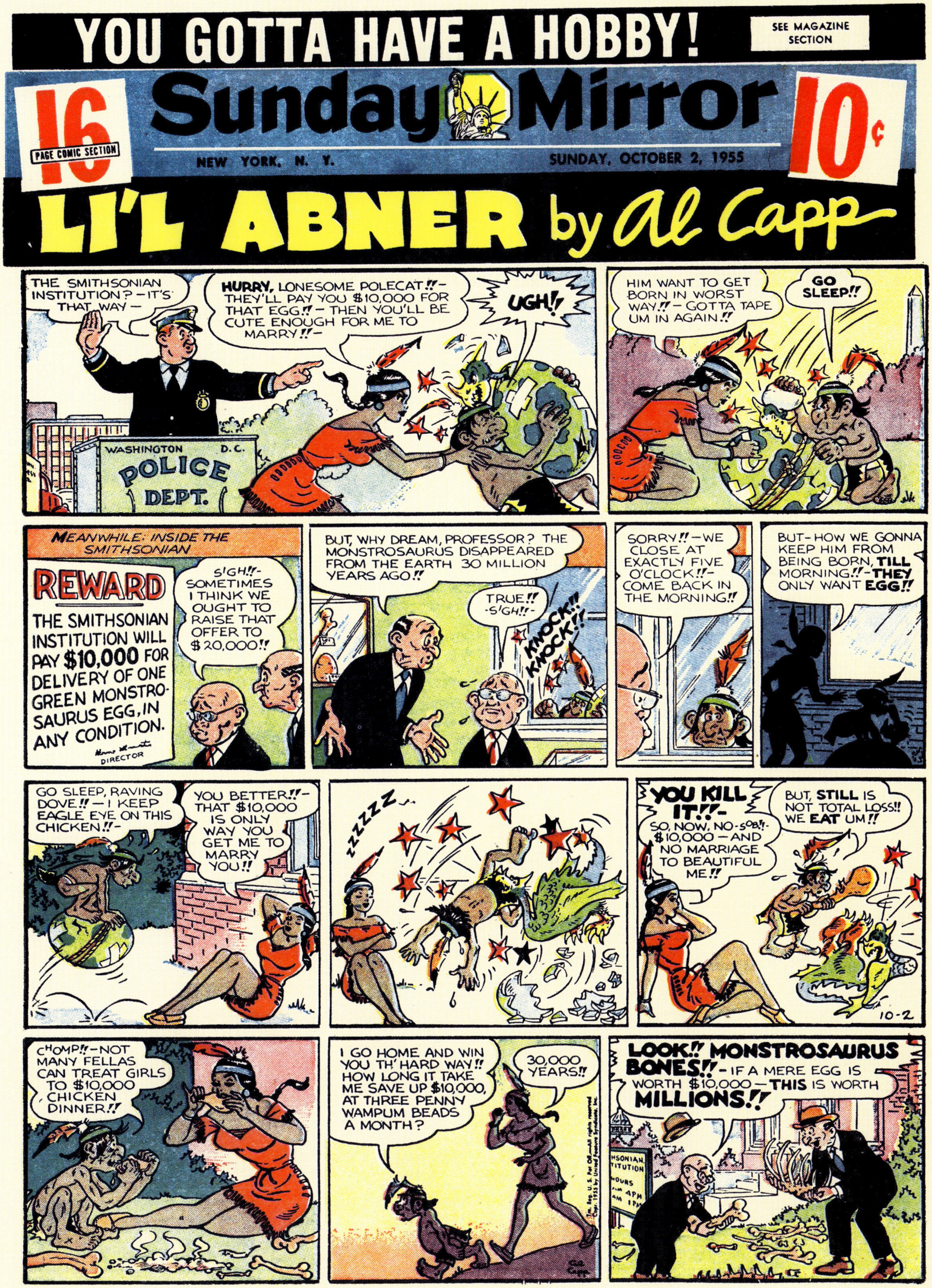

YOU GOTTA HAVE A HOBBY!
SEE MAGAZINE SECTION
16 PAGE COMIC SECTION
Sunday Mirror
NEW YORK, N. Y.
SUNDAY, OCTOBER 2, 1955
10¢
LI'L ABNER by al Capp
THE SMITHSONIAN INSTITUTION? —IT'S THAT WAY —
HURRY, LONESOME POLECAT!! — THEY'LL PAY YOU $10,000 FOR THAT EGG!! — THEN YOU'LL BE CUTE ENOUGH FOR ME TO MARRY!! —
UGH!!
WASHINGTON D.C. POLICE DEPT.
HIM WANT TO GET BORN IN WORST WAY!! — GOTTA TAPE UM IN AGAIN!!
GO SLEEP!!
MEANWHILE: INSIDE THE SMITHSONIAN
REWARD
THE SMITHSONIAN INSTITUTION WILL PAY $10,000 FOR DELIVERY OF ONE GREEN MONSTROSAURUS EGG, IN ANY CONDITION.
DIRECTOR
SIGH!! — SOMETIMES I THINK WE OUGHT TO RAISE THAT OFFER TO $20,000!!
BUT, WHY DREAM, PROFESSOR? THE MONSTROSAURUS DISAPPEARED FROM THE EARTH 30 MILLION YEARS AGO!!
TRUE!! -SIGH!! -
KNOCK!! KNOCK!!
SORRY!! —WE CLOSE AT EXACTLY FIVE O'CLOCK!! — COME BACK IN THE MORNING!!
BUT- HOW WE GONNA KEEP HIM FROM BEING BORN, TILL MORNING!! — THEY ONLY WANT EGG!!
GO SLEEP, RAVING DOVE!! — I KEEP EAGLE EYE ON THIS CHICKEN!! —
YOU BETTER!! — THAT $10,000 IS ONLY WAY YOU GET ME TO MARRY YOU!!
ZZZZZZ
YOU KILL IT!! — SO, NOW, NO- SOB!! - $10,000 — AND NO MARRIAGE TO BEAUTIFUL ME!!
BUT, STILL IS NOT TOTAL LOSS!! WE EAT UM!!
10-2
CHOMP!! — NOT MANY FELLAS CAN TREAT GIRLS TO $10,000 CHICKEN DINNER!!
I GO HOME AND WIN YOU TH' HARD WAY!! HOW LONG IT TAKE ME SAVE UP $10,000, AT THREE PENNY WAMPUM BEADS A MONTH?
30,000 YEARS!!
LOOK!! MONSTROSAURUS BONES!! — IF A MERE EGG IS WORTH $10,000 — THIS IS WORTH MILLIONS!!

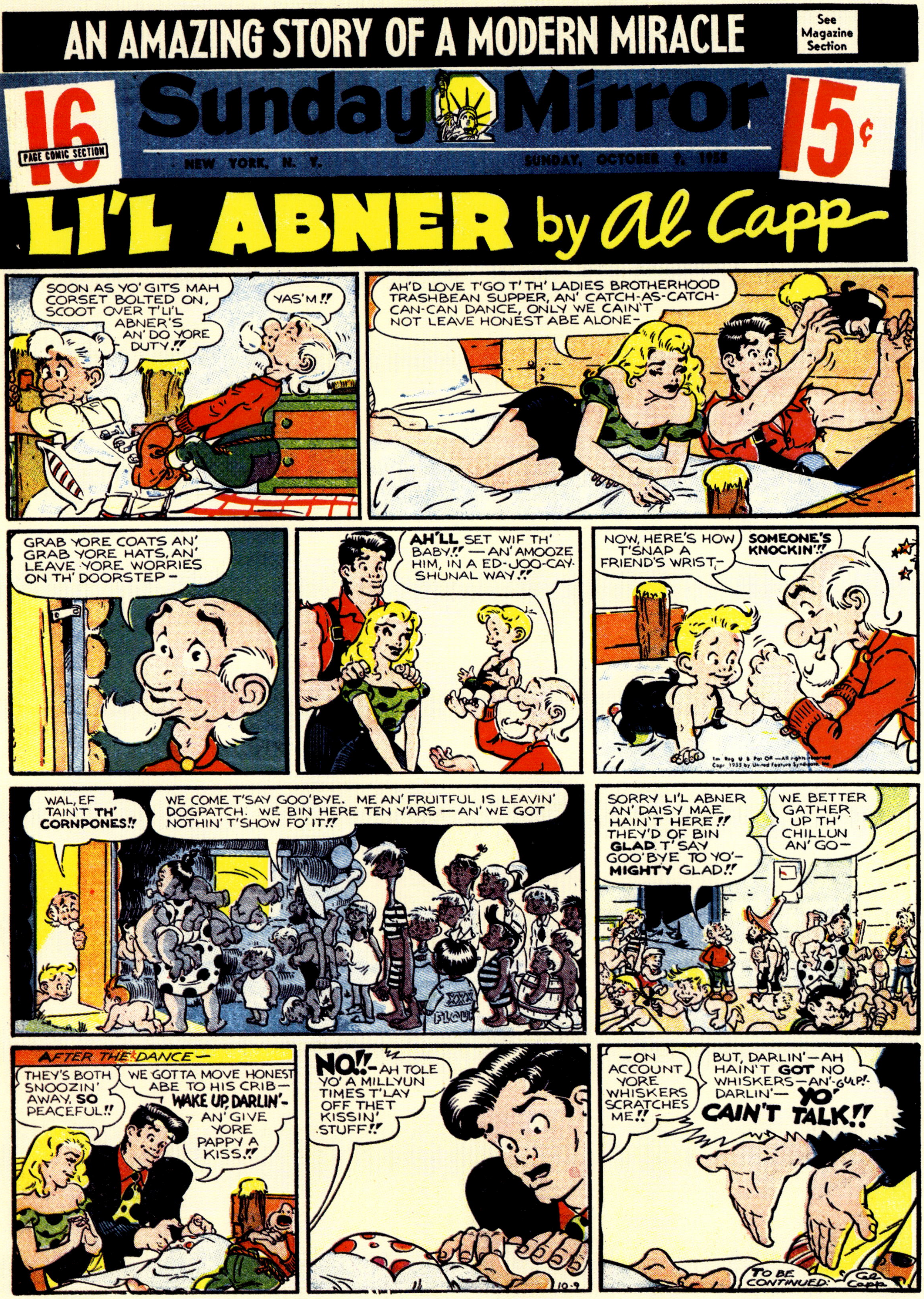

AN AMAZING STORY OF A MODERN MIRACLE
See Magazine Section
16 PAGE COMIC SECTION
Sunday Mirror
15¢
NEW YORK, N. Y.
SUNDAY, OCTOBER 9, 1955
LI'L ABNER by Al Capp
SOON AS YO' GITS MAH CORSET BOLTED ON, SCOOT OVER T'LI'L ABNER'S AN' DO YORE DUTY!!
YAS'M!!
AH'D LOVE T'GO T'TH' LADIES BROTHERHOOD TRASHBEAN SUPPER, AN' CATCH-AS-CATCH-CAN-CAN DANCE, ONLY WE CAIN'T NOT LEAVE HONEST ABE ALONE–
GRAB YORE COATS AN' GRAB YORE HATS, AN' LEAVE YORE WORRIES ON TH' DOORSTEP–
AH'LL SET WIF TH' BABY!! – AN' AMOOZE HIM, IN A ED-JOO-CAY-SHUNAL WAY!!
NOW, HERE'S HOW T'SNAP A FRIEND'S WRIST,–
SOMEONE'S KNOCKIN'!!
WAL, EF TAIN'T TH' CORNPONES!!
WE COME T'SAY GOO'BYE. ME AN' FRUITFUL IS LEAVIN' DOGPATCH. WE BIN HERE TEN Y'ARS – AN' WE GOT NOTHIN' T'SHOW FO' IT!!
SORRY LI'L ABNER AN' DAISY MAE HAIN'T HERE!! THEY'D OF BIN GLAD T'SAY GOO'BYE TO YO'– MIGHTY GLAD!!
WE BETTER GATHER UP TH' CHILLUN AN' GO–
AFTER THE DANCE–
THEY'S BOTH SNOOZIN' AWAY, SO PEACEFUL!!
WE GOTTA MOVE HONEST ABE TO HIS CRIB– WAKE UP, DARLIN'– AN' GIVE YORE PAPPY A KISS!!
NO!!–AH TOLE YO' A MILLYUN TIMES T'LAY OFF THET KISSIN' STUFF!!
–ON ACCOUNT YORE WHISKERS SCRATCHES ME!!
BUT, DARLIN'–AH HAIN'T GOT NO WHISKERS–AN'–GULP!– DARLIN'– YO' CAIN'T TALK!!
TO BE CONTINUED

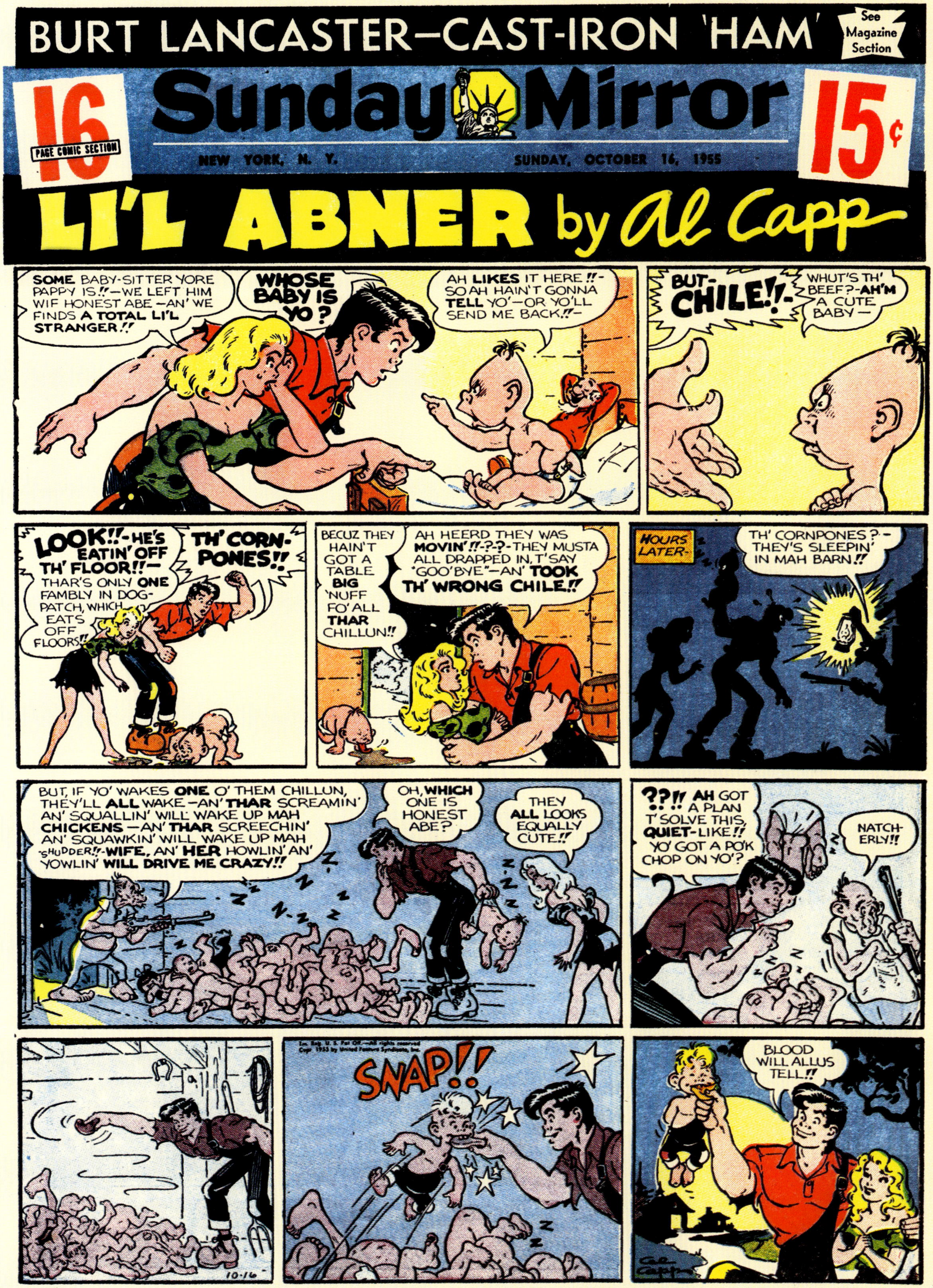

BURT LANCASTER—CAST-IRON 'HAM'
See Magazine Section
16 PAGE COMIC SECTION
Sunday Mirror
15¢
NEW YORK, N. Y.
SUNDAY, OCTOBER 16, 1955
LI'L ABNER by Al Capp
SOME BABY-SITTER YORE PAPPY IS!!—WE LEFT HIM WIF HONEST ABE—AN' WE FINDS A TOTAL LI'L STRANGER!!
WHOSE BABY IS YO?
AH LIKES IT HERE!!—SO AH HAIN'T GONNA TELL YO'—OR YO'LL SEND ME BACK!!—
BUT-CHILE!!—
WHUT'S TH' BEEF?-AH'M A CUTE BABY—
LOOK!!-HE'S EATIN' OFF TH' FLOOR!!—THAR'S ONLY ONE FAMBLY IN DOG-PATCH, WHICH EATS OFF FLOORS!!
TH' CORN-PONES!!
BECUZ THEY HAIN'T GOT A TABLE BIG 'NUFF FO' ALL THAR CHILLUN!!
AH HEERD THEY WAS MOVIN'!!-?-?-THEY MUSTA ALL DRAPPED IN, T'SAY "GOO'BYE"—AN' TOOK TH' WRONG CHILE!!
HOURS LATER-
TH' CORNPONES?—THEY'S SLEEPIN' IN MAH BARN!!
BUT, IF YO' WAKES ONE O' THEM CHILLUN, THEY'LL ALL WAKE—AN' THAR SCREAMIN' AN' SQUALLIN' WILL WAKE UP MAH CHICKENS—AN' THAR SCREECHIN' AN' SQUAWKIN' WILL WAKE UP MAH -SHUDDER!!- WIFE, AN' HER HOWLIN' AN' YOWLIN' WILL DRIVE ME CRAZY!!
OH, WHICH ONE IS HONEST ABE?
THEY ALL LOOKS EQUALLY CUTE!!
??!! AH GOT A PLAN T'SOLVE THIS, QUIET-LIKE!! YO' GOT A PO'K CHOP ON YO'?
NATCH-ERLY!!
10-16
SNAP!!
BLOOD WILL ALLUS TELL!!

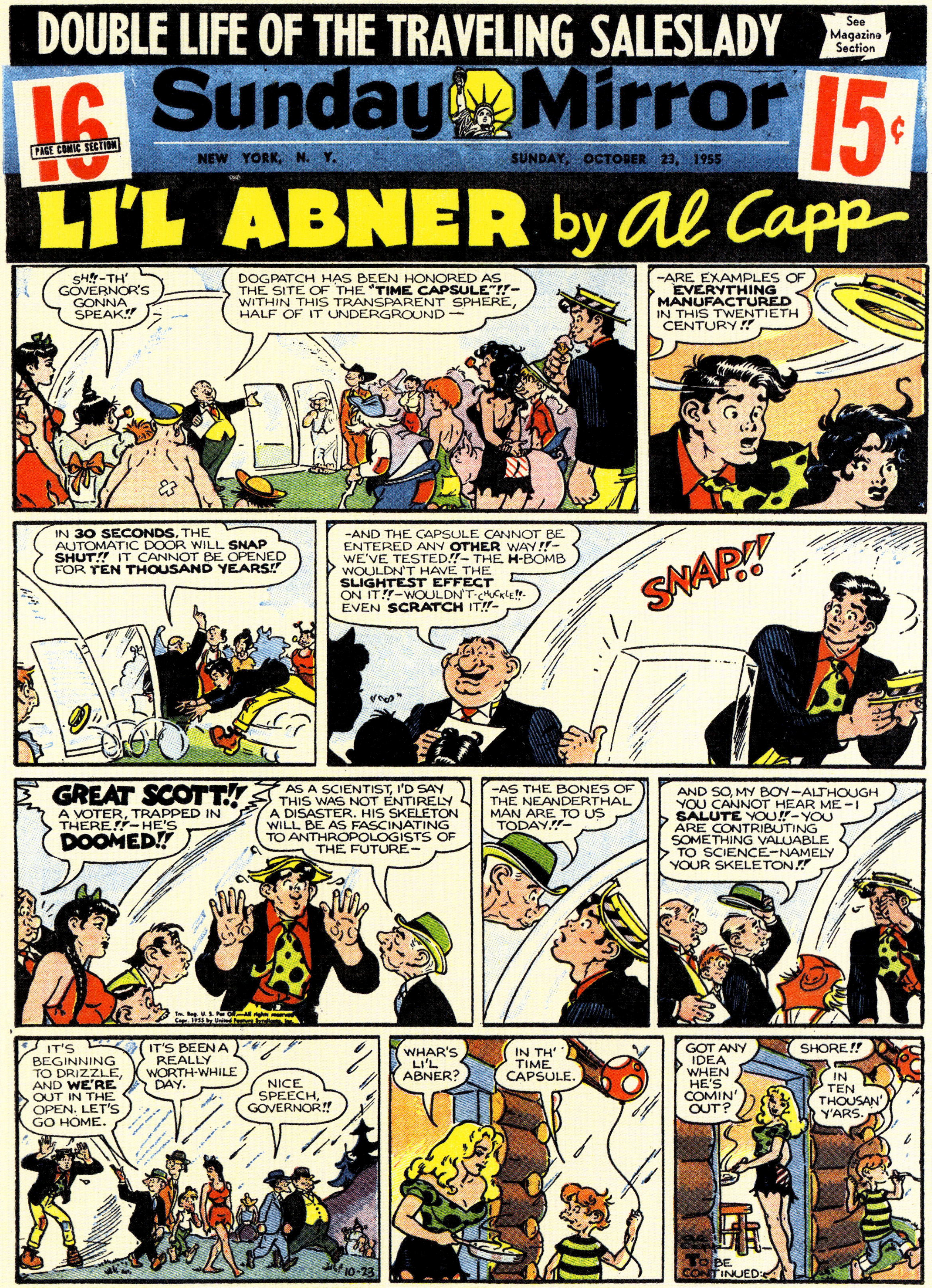

DOUBLE LIFE OF THE TRAVELING SALESLADY
See Magazine Section
16 PAGE COMIC SECTION
Sunday Mirror
15¢
NEW YORK, N. Y.
SUNDAY, OCTOBER 23, 1955
LI'L ABNER by Al Capp
SH!!-TH' GOVERNOR'S GONNA SPEAK!!
DOGPATCH HAS BEEN HONORED AS THE SITE OF THE "TIME CAPSULE"!!- WITHIN THIS TRANSPARENT SPHERE, HALF OF IT UNDERGROUND —
-ARE EXAMPLES OF EVERYTHING MANUFACTURED IN THIS TWENTIETH CENTURY!!
IN 30 SECONDS, THE AUTOMATIC DOOR WILL SNAP SHUT!! IT CANNOT BE OPENED FOR TEN THOUSAND YEARS!!
-AND THE CAPSULE CANNOT BE ENTERED ANY OTHER WAY!!- WE'VE TESTED!!- THE H-BOMB WOULDN'T HAVE THE SLIGHTEST EFFECT ON IT!!-WOULDN'T-CHUCKLE!!- EVEN SCRATCH IT!!-
SNAP!!
GREAT SCOTT!! A VOTER, TRAPPED IN THERE!!-HE'S DOOMED!!
AS A SCIENTIST, I'D SAY THIS WAS NOT ENTIRELY A DISASTER. HIS SKELETON WILL BE AS FASCINATING TO ANTHROPOLOGISTS OF THE FUTURE-
-AS THE BONES OF THE NEANDERTHAL MAN ARE TO US TODAY!!-
AND SO, MY BOY-ALTHOUGH YOU CANNOT HEAR ME-I SALUTE YOU!!-YOU ARE CONTRIBUTING SOMETHING VALUABLE TO SCIENCE-NAMELY YOUR SKELETON!!
IT'S BEGINNING TO DRIZZLE, AND WE'RE OUT IN THE OPEN. LET'S GO HOME.
IT'S BEEN A REALLY WORTH-WHILE DAY.
NICE SPEECH, GOVERNOR!!
10-23
WHAR'S LI'L ABNER?
IN TH' TIME CAPSULE.
GOT ANY IDEA WHEN HE'S COMIN' OUT?
SHORE!!
IN TEN THOUSAN' Y'ARS.
TO BE CONTINUED

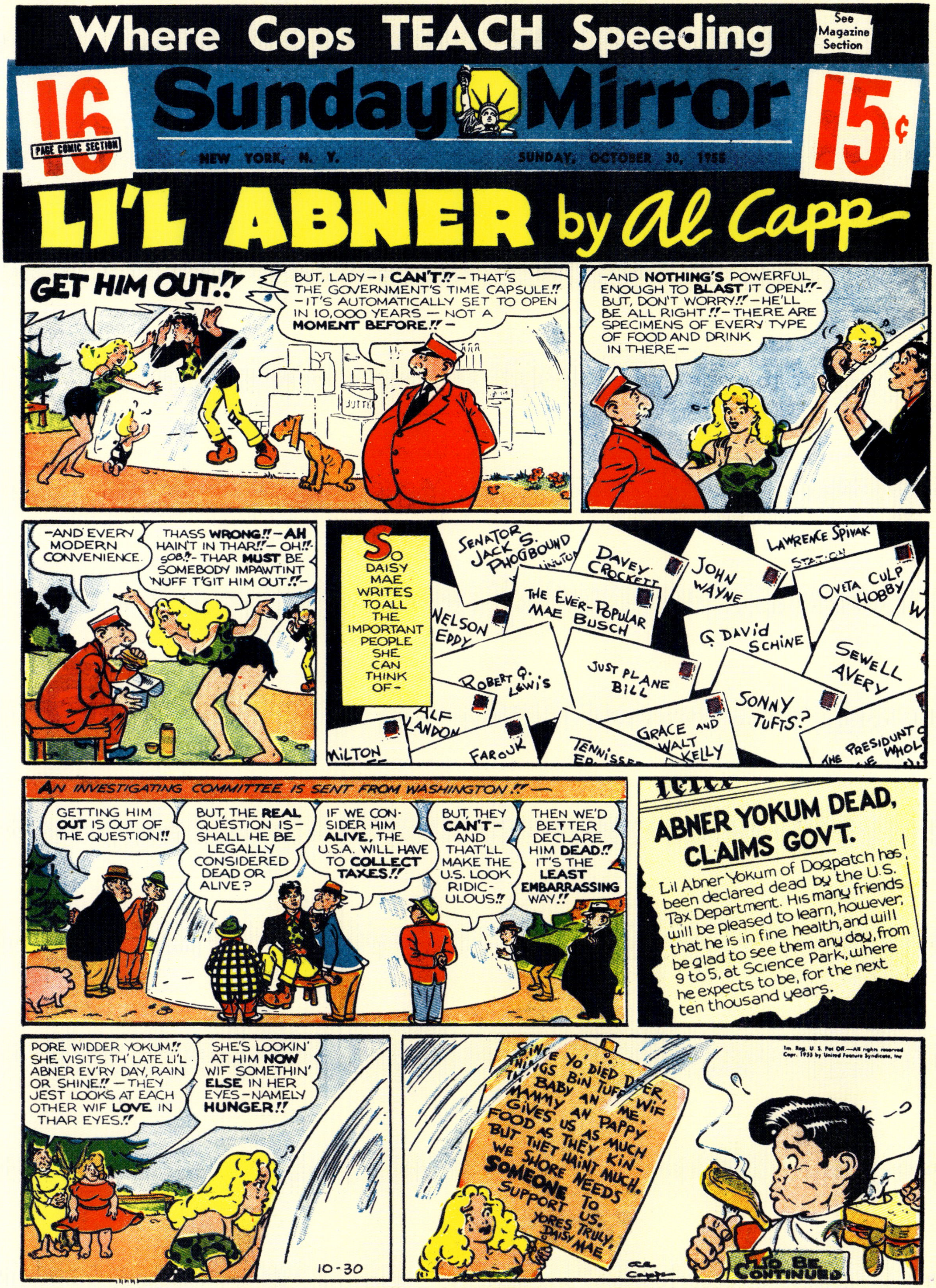

Where Cops TEACH Speeding
See Magazine Section
16 PAGE COMIC SECTION
Sunday Mirror
15¢
NEW YORK, N. Y.
SUNDAY, OCTOBER 30, 1955
LI'L ABNER by Al Capp
GET HIM OUT!!
BUT, LADY – I CAN'T!! – THAT'S THE GOVERNMENT'S TIME CAPSULE!! – IT'S AUTOMATICALLY SET TO OPEN IN 10,000 YEARS – NOT A MOMENT BEFORE!! –
–AND NOTHING'S POWERFUL ENOUGH TO BLAST IT OPEN!! – BUT, DON'T WORRY!! – HE'LL BE ALL RIGHT!! – THERE ARE SPECIMENS OF EVERY TYPE OF FOOD AND DRINK IN THERE –
–AND EVERY MODERN CONVENIENCE.
THASS WRONG!! – AH HAIN'T IN THAR!! – OH!! SOB!! – THAR MUST BE SOMEBODY IMPAWTINT 'NUFF T'GIT HIM OUT!! –
SO DAISY MAE WRITES TO ALL THE IMPORTANT PEOPLE SHE CAN THINK OF –
SENATOR JACK S. PHOGBOUND
DAVEY CROCKETT
JOHN WAYNE
LAWRENCE SPIVAK
OVETA CULP HOBBY
NELSON EDDY
THE EVER-POPULAR MAE BUSCH
G. DAVID SCHINE
SEWELL AVERY
ROBERT Q. LEWIS
JUST PLANE BILL
SONNY TUFTS?
ALF LANDON
MILTON
FAROUK
GRACE AND WALT KELLY
THE PRESIDUNT
AN INVESTIGATING COMMITTEE IS SENT FROM WASHINGTON!! —
GETTING HIM OUT IS OUT OF THE QUESTION!!
BUT, THE REAL QUESTION IS – SHALL HE BE LEGALLY CONSIDERED DEAD OR ALIVE?
IF WE CONSIDER HIM ALIVE, THE U.S.A. WILL HAVE TO COLLECT TAXES!!
BUT, THEY CAN'T – AND THAT'LL MAKE THE U.S. LOOK RIDICULOUS!!
THEN WE'D BETTER DECLARE HIM DEAD!! IT'S THE LEAST EMBARRASSING WAY!!
ABNER YOKUM DEAD, CLAIMS GOVT.
Li'l Abner Yokum of Dogpatch has been declared dead by the U.S. Tax Department. His many friends will be pleased to learn, however, that he is in fine health, and will be glad to see them any day, from 9 to 5, at Science Park, where he expects to be, for the next ten thousand years.
PORE WIDDER YOKUM!! SHE VISITS TH' LATE LI'L ABNER EV'RY DAY, RAIN OR SHINE!! – THEY JEST LOOKS AT EACH OTHER WIF LOVE IN THAR EYES!!
SHE'S LOOKIN' AT HIM NOW WIF SOMETHIN' ELSE IN HER EYES – NAMELY HUNGER!!
10-30
SINCE YO' DIED DEER, THINGS BIN TUFF WIF TH' BABY AN' ME. MAMMY AN PAPPY GIVES US AS MUCH FOOD AS THEY KIN – BUT THET HAINT MUCH. WE SHORE NEEDS SOMEONE TO SUPPORT US. YORES TRULY, DAISY MAE
Tm. Reg. U. S. Pat Off. — All rights reserved Copr. 1955 by United Feature Syndicate, Inc
Al Capp
TO BE CONTINUED

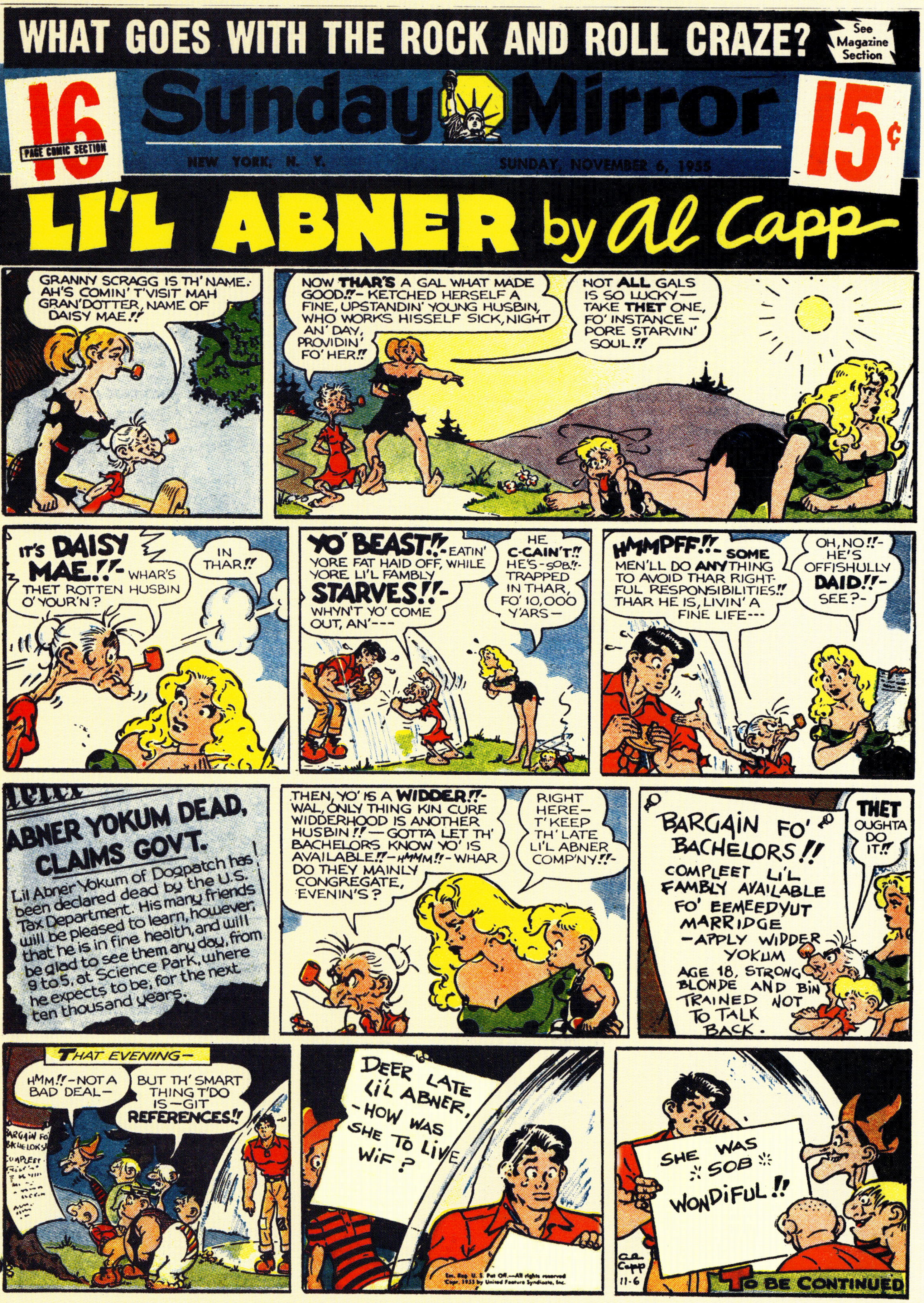
WHAT GOES WITH THE ROCK AND ROLL CRAZE?
See Magazine Section
16
PAGE COMIC SECTION
Sunday Mirror
NEW YORK, N. Y.
SUNDAY, NOVEMBER 6, 1955
15¢
LI'L ABNER by Al Capp
GRANNY SCRAGG IS TH' NAME. AH'S COMIN' T'VISIT MAH GRAN'DOTTER, NAME OF DAISY MAE.!!
NOW THAR'S A GAL WHAT MADE GOOD.!!– KETCHED HERSELF A FINE, UPSTANDIN' YOUNG HUSBIN, WHO WORKS HISSELF SICK, NIGHT AN' DAY, PROVIDIN' FO' HER.!!
NOT ALL GALS IS SO LUCKY– TAKE THET ONE, FO' INSTANCE – PORE STARVIN' SOUL.!!
IT'S DAISY MAE.!!– WHAR'S THET ROTTEN HUSBIN O' YOUR'N?
IN THAR.!!
YO' BEAST!!– EATIN' YORE FAT HAID OFF, WHILE YORE LI'L FAMBLY STARVES!!– WHYN'T YO' COME OUT, AN'---
HE C-CAIN'T!! HE'S–SOB!!– TRAPPED IN THAR, FO' 10,000 Y'ARS–
HMMPFF!!– SOME MEN'LL DO ANYTHING TO AVOID THAR RIGHT-FUL RESPONSIBILITIES!! THAR HE IS, LIVIN' A FINE LIFE---
OH, NO!!– HE'S OFFISHULLY DAID!!– SEE?–
ABNER YOKUM DEAD, CLAIMS GOVT.
Lil Abner Yokum of Dogpatch has been declared dead by the U.S. Tax Department. His many friends will be pleased to learn, however, that he is in fine health, and will be glad to see them any day, from 9 to 5, at Science Park, where he expects to be, for the next ten thousand years.
THEN, YO' IS A WIDDER!!– WAL, ONLY THING KIN CURE WIDDERHOOD IS ANOTHER HUSBIN!!– GOTTA LET TH' BACHELORS KNOW YO' IS AVAILABLE!!– HMMM!!– WHAR DO THEY MAINLY CONGREGATE, EVENIN'S?
RIGHT HERE– T'KEEP TH' LATE LI'L ABNER COMP'NY!!–
BARGAIN FO' BACHELORS!! COMPLEET LI'L FAMBLY AVAILABLE FO' EEMEEDYUT MARRIDGE –APPLY WIDDER YOKUM AGE 18, STRONG BLONDE AND BIN TRAINED NOT TO TALK BACK.
THET OUGHTA DO IT.!!
THAT EVENING–
HMM!!– NOT A BAD DEAL–
BUT TH' SMART THING T'DO IS–GIT REFERENCES!!
DEER LATE LI'L ABNER, –HOW WAS SHE TO LIVE WIF?
SHE WAS SOB WONDIFUL!!
TO BE CONTINUED

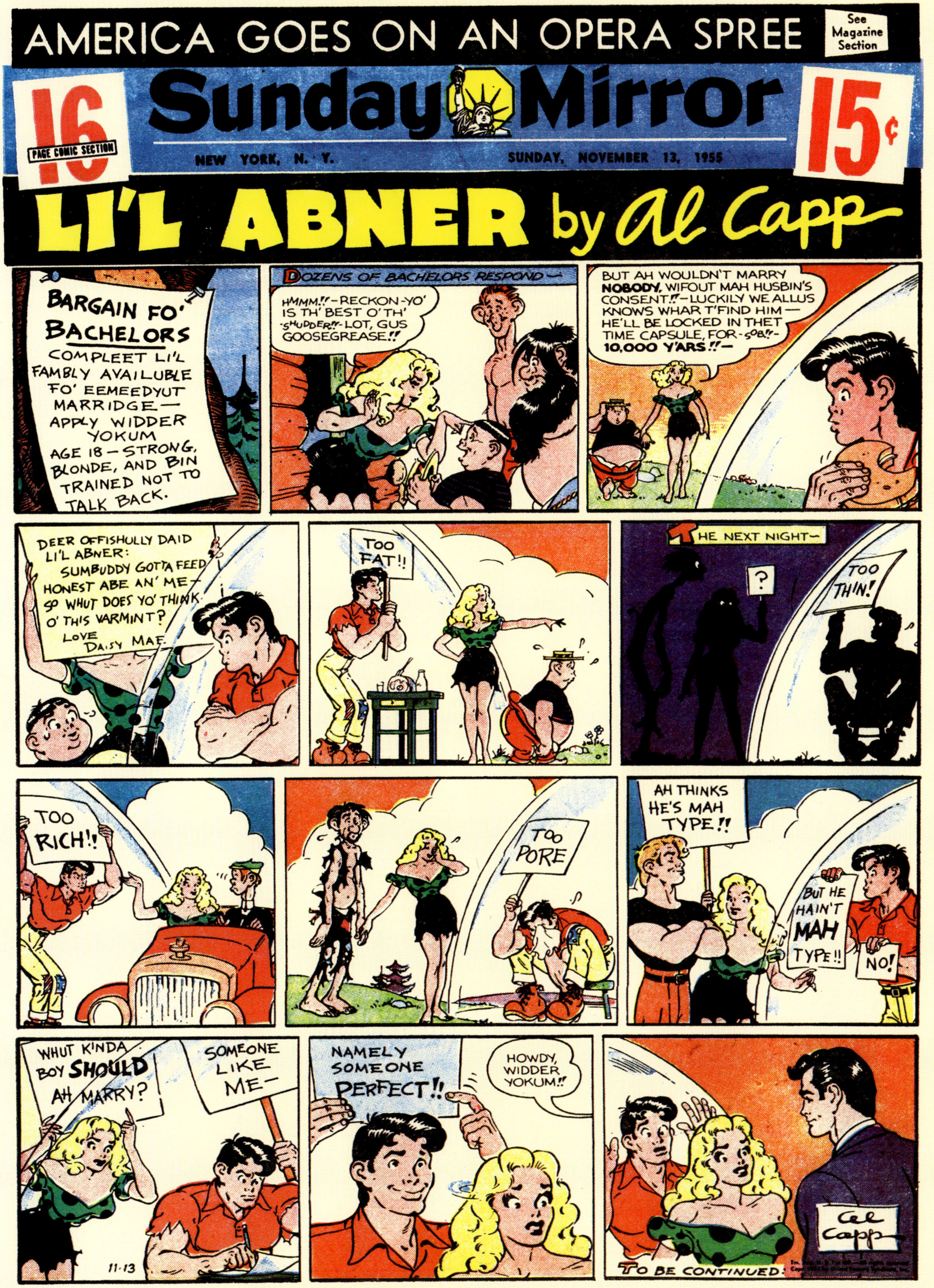
AMERICA GOES ON AN OPERA SPREE
See Magazine Section
16 PAGE COMIC SECTION
Sunday Mirror
15¢
NEW YORK, N. Y.
SUNDAY, NOVEMBER 13, 1955
LI'L ABNER by Al Capp
BARGAIN FO' BACHELORS
COMPLEET LI'L FAMBLY AVAILUBLE FO' EEMEEDYUT MARRIDGE— APPLY WIDDER YOKUM AGE 18—STRONG, BLONDE, AND BIN TRAINED NOT TO TALK BACK.
DOZENS OF BACHELORS RESPOND—
HMMM!!—RECKON-YO' IS TH' BEST O'TH' SHUDDER!!-LOT, GUS GOOSEGREASE!!
BUT AH WOULDN'T MARRY NOBODY, WIFOUT MAH HUSBIN'S CONSENT!!—LUCKILY WE ALLUS KNOWS WHAR T'FIND HIM— HE'LL BE LOCKED IN THET TIME CAPSULE, FOR-SOB!!- 10,000 Y'ARS!!—
DEER OFFISHULLY DAID LI'L ABNER: SUMBUDDY GOTTA FEED HONEST ABE AN' ME— SO WHUT DOES YO' THINK O' THIS VARMINT? LOVE DAISY MAE.
TOO FAT!!
THE NEXT NIGHT—
?
TOO THIN!
TOO RICH!!
TOO PORE
AH THINKS HE'S MAH TYPE!!
BUT HE HAIN'T MAH TYPE!!
NO!
WHUT KINDA BOY SHOULD AH MARRY?
SOMEONE LIKE ME—
11-13
NAMELY SOMEONE PERFECT!!
HOWDY, WIDDER YOKUM!!
Al Capp
TO BE CONTINUED.

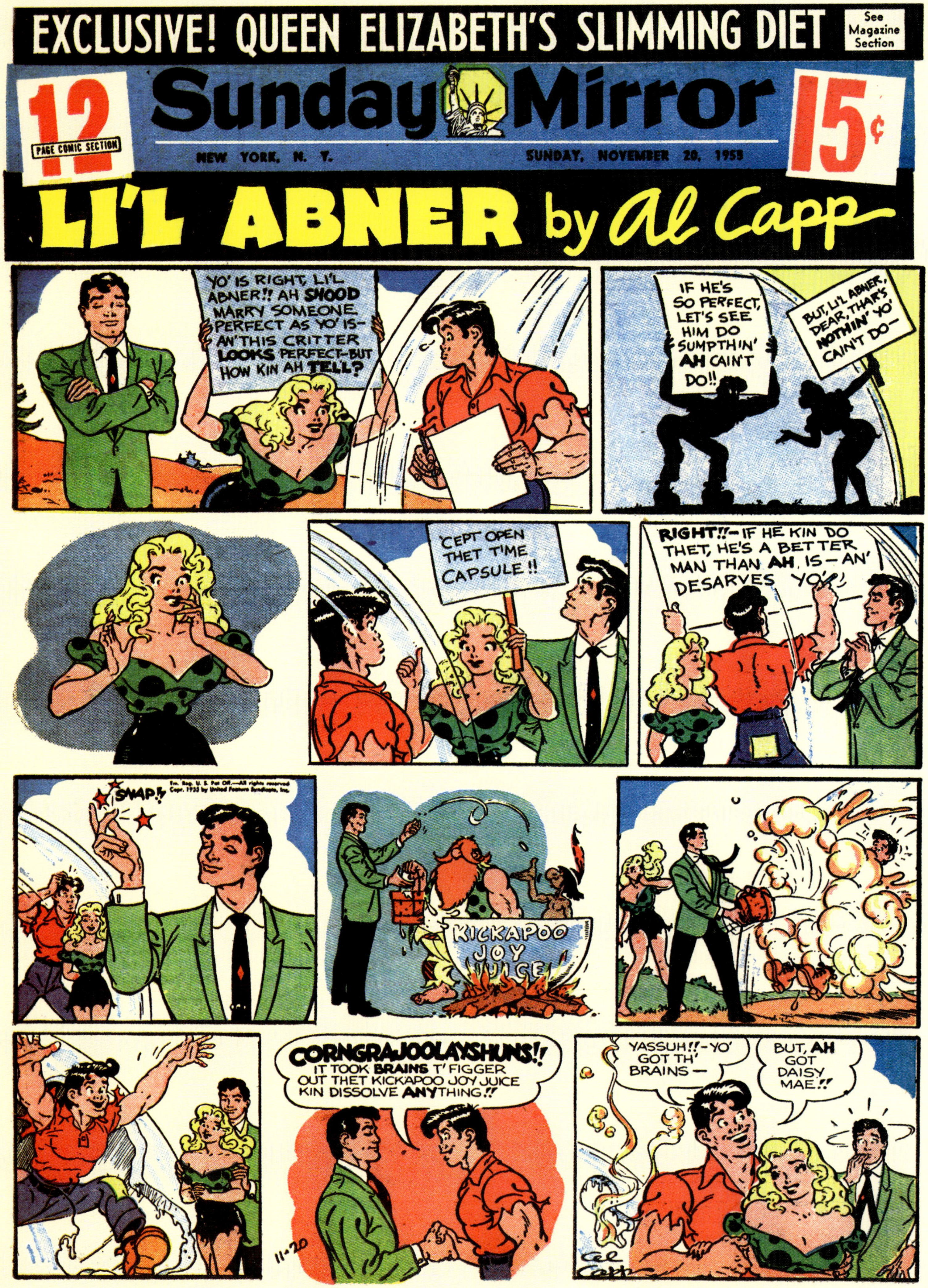
EXCLUSIVE! QUEEN ELIZABETH'S SLIMMING DIET
See Magazine Section
12 PAGE COMIC SECTION
Sunday Mirror
NEW YORK, N. Y.
SUNDAY, NOVEMBER 20, 1955
15¢
LI'L ABNER by Al Capp
YO' IS RIGHT, LI'L ABNER!! AH SHOOD MARRY SOMEONE PERFECT AS YO' IS– AN' THIS CRITTER LOOKS PERFECT–BUT HOW KIN AH TELL?
IF HE'S SO PERFECT, LET'S SEE HIM DO SUMPTHIN' AH CAIN'T DO!!
BUT, LI'L ABNER, DEAR, THAR'S NOTHIN' YO' CAIN'T DO–
'CEPT OPEN THET TIME CAPSULE!!
RIGHT!!–IF HE KIN DO THET, HE'S A BETTER MAN THAN AH, IS–AN' DESARVES YO'!!
SNAP!!
Tm. Reg. U. S. Pat. Off.—All rights reserved Copr. 1955 by United Feature Syndicate, Inc.
KICKAPOO JOY JUICE
CORNGRAJOOLAYSHUNS!! IT TOOK BRAINS T' FIGGER OUT THET KICKAPOO JOY JUICE KIN DISSOLVE ANYTHING!!
YASSUH!!–YO' GOT TH' BRAINS–
BUT, AH GOT DAISY MAE!!
11-20
Al Capp

Annotations for Al Capp's LI'L ABNER: The Frazetta Sundays, Volume 1 (1954-55)

November 15, 1953. Page 15. "Th' Comin' of th' Wrecker!" (1 of 15). 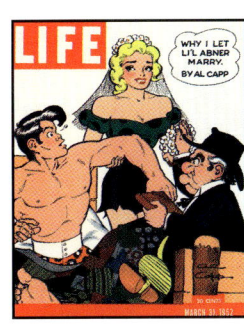 Li'l Abner creator **Al Capp** generally kept his Sunday continuities brief. Two to four sequences are typical, and many Sundays are self-contained. The story commencing here is unusual in that it stretches over fifteen Sundays. Because the **"Wrecker"** story does not end till the February 21st installment, we are including the end of 1953 episodes in this 1954-55 volume for the sake of completeness.

The pig sharing the dining table with **Pappy Yokum** in panel two is **Salomey**, the last survivor of the *Hammus Alabammus* species, who is treated as a full member of the Yokum family. The presence of ten-week-old infant **Honest Abe** is a reminder that, after eighteen years of **Daisy Mae Scragg** relentlessly chasing confirmed bachelor **Li'l Abner Yokum**, the couple married March 29, 1952. The event was of such cultural significance that the ceremony made the cover of *Life* magazine. **Honest Abe** followed on August 27, 1953.

Sensing danger to her marriage, the generally compliant **Daisy Mae** is very assertive in this episode as she and her mother-in-law **Mammy Yokum** convene an emergency meeting of the **Dogpatch Ladies Brotherhood** (the paradoxical name is pure **Capp**). The motley line of women entering the meeting in the third tier is a typical Dogpatch profile. The hillbilly hamlet's female inhabitants come in just two varieties: they are either gorgeous or uncommonly hideous. When **Frank Frazetta** joins Capp's staff later in 1954, the extremes are only intensified. With the exception of **Li'l Abner** and his surgically enhanced brother (see 6/19/55), *all* the Dogpatch men are homely.

 **November 22, 1953.** Page 16. "Th' Wrecker on a War Path" (2 of 15). Making a cameo appearance in the second panel (smoking a pipe at right) is **Moonbeam McSwine**. Though one of Dogpatch's certified knockouts, **Moonbeam's** personal hygiene is non-existent. (See the episode beginning 11/7/54.)

November 29, 1953. Page 17. "The Men are Safe...in Jail" (3 of 15).  Three weeks into the story we have not yet seen **th' Wrecker**. The only hint from **Capp**, a certified master of suspense, is the cast shadow in the final panel, and that menacing shadowy figure certainly seems to have horns.

December 6, 1953. Page 18. "Refugees" (4 of 15).  The "horned" figure is revealed as a red herring and the tension is extended another week.

December 13, 1953. Page 19. "Th' Wrecker is Revealed!" (5 of 15). We've been led to believe that **th' Wrecker** is the ultimate sexpot. So when a relatively plain  and shy young woman confesses her identity, the mystery of her power over men only deepens. **Capp** is reeling us in. A silent sidebar of the seemingly scrawny **Mammy** routinely pulverizing a grizzly does not even interrupt the dialogue. Regular readers understand that **Mammy's** strength and fighting abilities are legendary.

December 20, 1953. Page 20. "Plain as a Turnip" (6 of 15). Mammy's judgment is usually flawless, so when she is confident **th' Wrecker** intends no ill, we are further mystified by the trail of broken marriages in every town leading to Dogpatch.

 **December 27, 1953.** Page 21. "Lucifer Rising" (7 of 15). Docile **Pappy Yokum** is not known to have a wandering eye, so how does **th' Wrecker** reduce him to howling like a wolf?

January 3, 1954. Page 22. "Yo' Gotta be a Man to Understand" (8 of 15). The latest victim of **th' Wrecker**, straight-laced **Norman P. McNormal**, is probably inspired by the **Reverend Norman Vincent Peale**, a dispenser of positive thinking advice in  vehicles like *Guideposts* and *Reader's Digest* in the 1950s. He would have been regarded as one of the more "normal" men of his era.

January 10, 1954. Page 23. "Tricky Varmint" (9 of 15).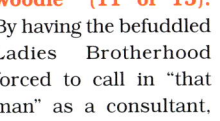

January 17, 1954. Page 24. "Earth's Strangest Forms of Life" (10 of 15).

January 24, 1954. Page 25. "Petrified Woodie" (11 of 15). By having the befuddled Ladies Brotherhood forced to call in "that man" as a consultant,  **Capp** creates a mystery within a mystery.

January 31, 1954. Page 26. "C. C. Yokum" (12 of 15). While coldly inhuman C. C. —"Complete Control"—Yokum is completely unmoved when **Mammy** shows him a **Marilyn Monroe** calendar, red-blooded American men in 1954 are captivated by the actress's celebrated nude calendar pose, repeated in the debut issue of *Playboy* (December 1953). **Rita Hayworth**, whose measurements also fail to arouse C. C., was regarded by many as the most beautiful woman in the world. Doubting Thomases should view her in the film *Gilda*.

February 7, 1954. Page 27. "No Reaction" (13 of 15).

February 14, 1954. Page 28. "C. C. Explains the Secret of th' Wrecker" (14 of 15).  With two final clues—the "wall" test and C. C.'s final panel comment—**Capp** sadistically prolongs the mystery of **th' Wrecker's** extraordinary power for one more long week.

February 21, 1954. Page 29. "Getting to the Bottom of Things" (15 of 15). Fifteen weeks after the story's inception we learn the startling truth: women look at other women's faces, but men look at women's bottoms. It was **th'**

Wrecker's spectacular "hula-hula walk" that drove the weaker sex crazy. **Mammy's** final advice to **th' Wrecker** (after "readjusting" her naughty spine) is that she should capture a husband the "ole-fashioned Dogpatch way—by trickery an' force!!" **Mammy** speaks from first-hand experience, as we see revealed just four episodes down the road (3/21/54).

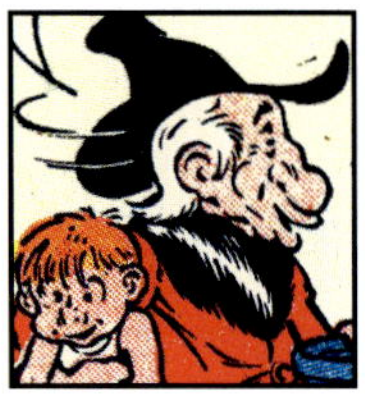

February 28, 1954. Page 30. **"Bucktooth on the Loose" (1 of 1).** **Capp** breaks the rhythm of an exceptionally long Sunday continuity with a one-shot featuring **Cousin Weakeyes Yokum**. The stumbling, visually impaired **Weakeyes**, a **Mr. Magoo** type, was a frequently utilized cast member. Walking off a cliff at the end of a sequence was one of his hallmarks.

March 7, 1954. Page 31. **"Great Idea for a TV Show" (1 of 3).** Soda jerk **Alf Egbert's** successful brother **Ralph** is based on **Ralph Edwards**, host of NBC's popular

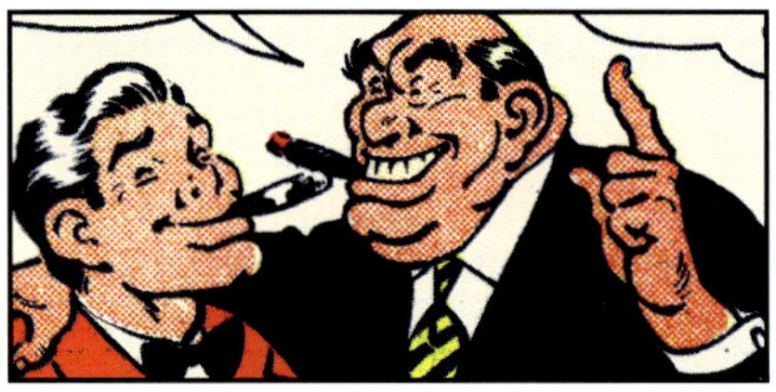

"This Is Your Life," which debuted on TV in October 1952 after several years as a radio hit. The premise: A celebrity would be lured to the studio on a pretense, then **Edwards** would proclaim "This is Your Life!" and, with cameras rolling, a stream of relatives and old friends would recount incidents from the celeb's life and career. When the TV exec here proclaims, "Find me the *happiest married couple in America!!*" we know a pair of **Yokums** will be involved.

March 14, 1954. Page 32. **"This Is Your Wife" (2 of 3).** We learn to our surprise that **Lucifer (Pappy) Yokum**, "a mizzuble-lookin' li'l rat" even when young, actually had suitors back in 1902.

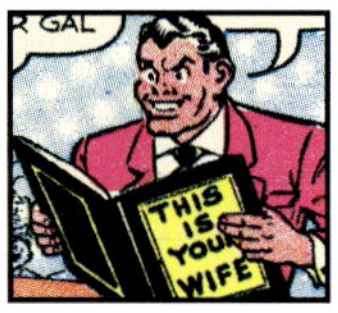
THIS IS YOUR WIFE

March 21, 1954. Page 33. **"The Secret of Miss Turnip of 1903" (3 of 3).** "Th' greatest attrack-shun us wives got is *mystery*!! An' th' *biggest* mystery t' most men is how we ever got 'em to marry us!!" This homespun aphorism is typical **Mammy**. The

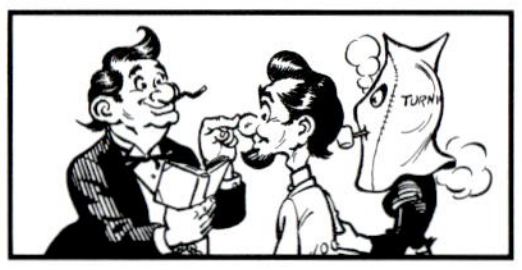

strip may be named after her firstborn, but she is the heart and soul of "Li'l Abner." When **Al Capp** retired in 1977, *The Boston Phoenix* asked him who his favorite character was. His answer: "Mammy…a charming little creature, so arrogant and self-righteous and so totally unaware of it."

March 28, 1954. Page 34. **"The Most Impawtint Man on Earth" (1 of 12).** Bodyguard *Abijah Gooch* and *Li'l Abner* go way back in the strip's history. **Gooch** appeared in just the seventh strip, in

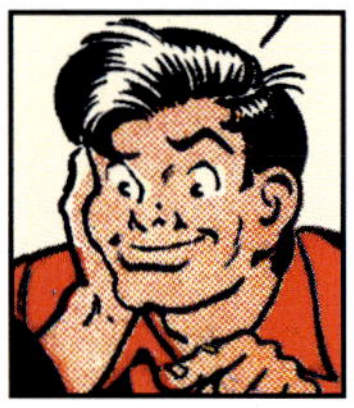

1934, the recipient of Abner's first punch. Horn-rimmed **Dave Garroway** was the first host of the *Today* show, network television's longest-running daytime series. **King Farouk**, who abdicated his throne in 1952, was Egypt's last reigning monarch. Baritone **Nelson Eddy**, a frequent butt of **Capp** jokes, starred in numerous schmaltzy film roles and duets with **Jeanette MacDonald. H. V. Kaltenborn** was a noted radio broadcaster and sometime TV game show panelist. **The Cisco Kid** (actor **Duncan Renaldo**) was a TV cowboy (1950-55) kept popular by years of reruns. But none of these sterling candidates, not even **Winston Churchill**, qualify as "th' most impawtint man on earth."

April 4, 1954. Page 35. **"Unquestionin' Obediance" (2 of 12).** Billionaire **General Bashington Bullmoose** is revealed as the most important man on Earth. **Charles E. Wilson**, former head of America's largest corporation **General Motors**, is the source of **Bullmoose's** oft-quoted mantra, "What's good for **General Bullmoose** is good for everybody!" **Wilson**, who became Secretary of Defense in the **Eisenhower** administration, famously told a congressional committee in 1952, "What is good for the country is good for General Motors, and what is good for General Motors is good for the

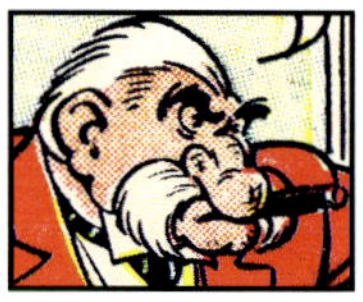

country." **Wilson** "created the character for me," **Al Capp** noted in 1955. Though **Capp** is more remembered today for his latter day right-wing political views, in the 1950s he was a true liberal who frequently lampooned the excesses of big business, as epitomized by über-capitalist **Bullmoose**.

April 11, 1954. Page 36. **"A Hearty Dinner" (3 of 12).**

April 18, 1954. Page 37. **"Five Billion Dollars' Worth of Bad Dogfood" (4 of 12).** The U.S. was conducting nuclear bomb tests on uninhabited Pacific atolls during this time, so it was not such a satiric

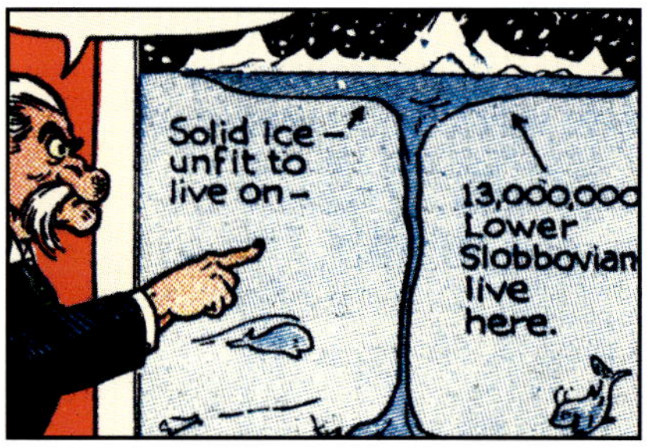
Solid Ice – unfit to live on –
13,000,000 Lower Slobbovians live here.

stretch to liberate **Lower Slobbovia** by similar means. Junketing **Senator Jack S. Phogbound**, whose constituency includes Dogpatch, is not surprisingly complicit. **Bullmoose's** ascetic and time-efficient habits of avoiding real food (last week) and sleeping on beds of ice make his lifestyle, ironically, comparable to that of an ordinary Slobbovian.

April 25, 1954. Page 38. **"Continental Drift" (5 of 12).** The dreadfully backward frozen wasteland of **Lower Slobbovia**, based loosely on Siberia and Outer Mongolia, appears periodically as a plot

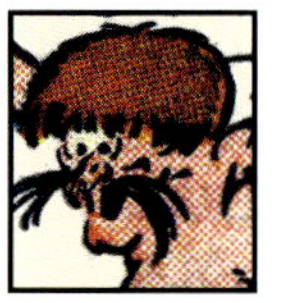

element in "Li'l Abner." The black cloud hanging over the free-floating continent in panel 5 is reminiscent of the rain cloud hanging over another recurring character, super-jinx **Joe Btfsplk**.

May 2, 1954. Page 39. **"Approaching the Hew Hess Hay" (6 of 12).** The Dutch girl's "Oh Mein Papa!" expression may appear to be a throwaway line, but in 1954 it was a nod to crooner **Eddie Fisher's** chart-busting hit. In the commie paranoia of the early '50s, Marxist menace emanates from **Liddle Noodnik's** greeting poem, "We got nuttin', You got lots—so we'll divide it all in equal pots!!"

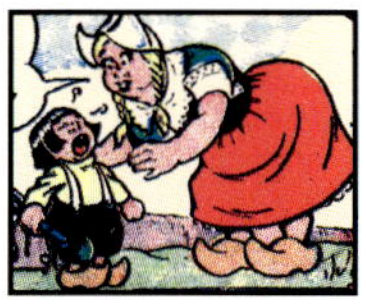

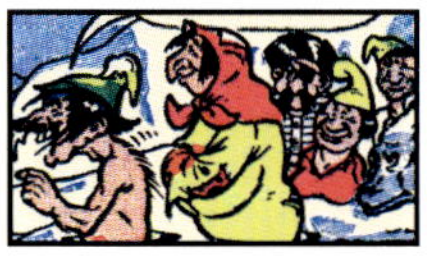

May 9, 1954. Page 40. **"Introducing the Bald Iggle" (7 of 12).** The "unemployed… ragged bums" and welfare cases invading Florida's gold coast are strangely prescient of much later headlines involving Cuban boat people and Haitians.

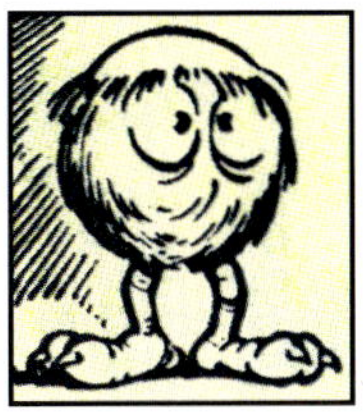

May 16, 1954. Page 41. **"The Living Lie Detector" (8 of 12).** Slobbovia's national symbol, the **Bald Iggle**, is the latest in a series of unusual **Al Capp** creatures that promise to be the salvation of humanity but prove to be more bane than boon. The miraculous **Shmoo** (1948), his most celebrated invention, provides owners with an unlimited source of sustenance, but ultimately threatens the social fabric. The **Kigmy** (1949) happily absorbs a person's pent-up aggression, but ends up turning the tables. The **Bald Iggle's** grand purpose—inspiring the truth—also backfires on humanity. As **Jack Nicholson** would say, "The truth? You can't handle the truth!!"

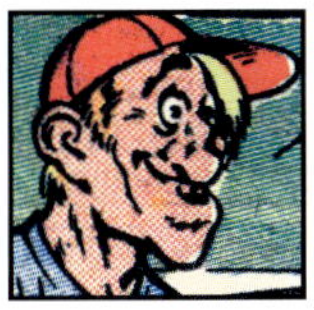

May 23, 1954. Page 42. **"Truth in Media" (9 of 12).** Many of **Al Capp's** comic ideas show up later, coincidentally or not, in other media. *The Beverly Hillbillies* represent perhaps the most egregious swipe. Here the compulsion to tell the truth, with tragi-comic consequences, is mirrored years later in the Jim Carrey film *Liar Liar*.

May 30, 1954. Page 43. **"Truth in Politics" (10 of 12).**

June 6, 1954. Page 44. **"Truth in Fashion and Justice" (11 of 12).**

June 13, 1954. Page 45. **"Insulting the National Umblum" (12 of 12).** Though this Sunday strip might seem to signal the end of the **Bald Iggle**, it was not. Like the **Shmoo** before him, the **Iggle** was too good to retire. A 1956 **Bald Iggle** daily adventure was collected into book format by Simon & Schuster, with gushing cover blurbs from **John Steinbeck**, *Time*, *Newsweek*, and *Harper's*.

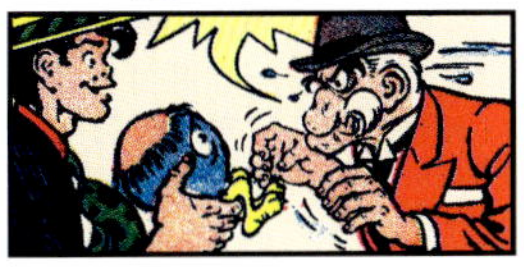

June 20, 1954. Page 46. **"Life Insurance" (1 of 4).** Inseparable pals **Lonesome Polecat** (the diminutive native American) and his bosom buddy **Hairless Joe** (the hirsute Caucasian) are cave-dwelling Dogpatch denizens who appear throughout most of "Li'l Abner's" long history. They are best known for concocting vats of their ultra-potent moonshine **"Kickapoo Joy Juice,"** a tonic with many powers (and which for many years was the namesake of a decidedly less potent licensed soda drink).

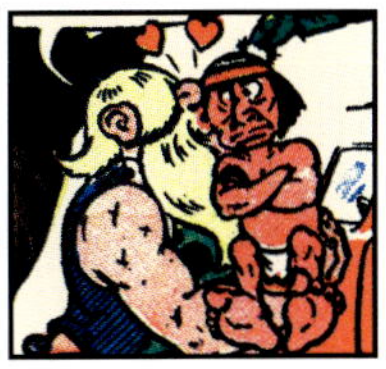

June 27, 1954. Page 47. **"Friends till Death do Us Part" (2 of 4).**

July 4, 1954. Page 48. **"Bosom Buddy or Bosomy Wife?" (3 of 4).**

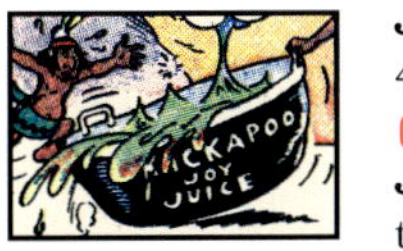
KICKAPOO JOY JUICE

July 11, 1954. Page 49. **"Insurance Fraud" (4 of 4).** **Hairless Joe's** virtual resurrection demonstrates the amazing regenerative powers of **Kickapoo Joy Juice** and the power of male bonding trumps a beautiful woman.

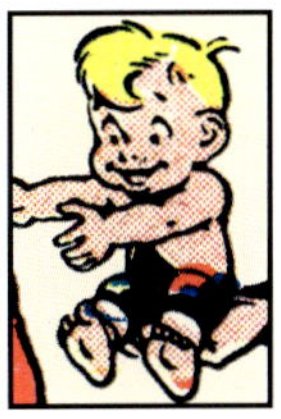

July 18, 1954. Page 50. **"Pappy's Flights of Fancy" (1 of 2).** One of **Capp's** periodic plot devices was to have **Pappy Yokum** claim credit for a historic or noble moment and then to be deflated.

July 25, 1954. Page 51. **"Humoring th' Chillun" (2 of 2).** Readers waiting a week between Sunday strips tend to have short memories, which is why **Al Capp** often provides a brief "recap" at the start of each connected episode. Given such short memories, it is also tempting to sometimes "recycle" art to cut corners. Panel 3 is an example of

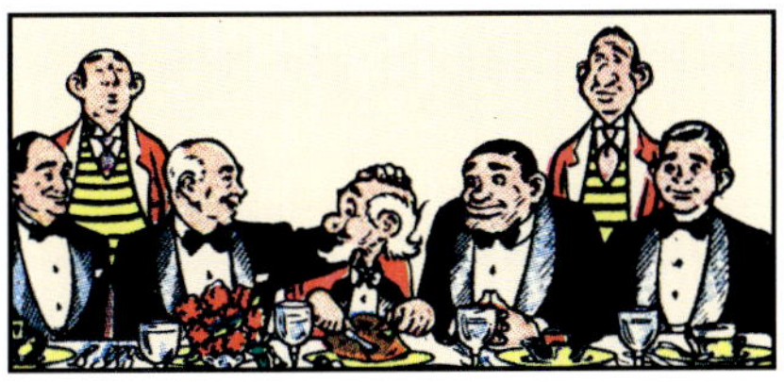

the frugal **Capp** doing so. This graphic is identical to—a photostat of—the previous week's panel 3. Unlike last week, however, **Mammy** grants **Pappy** a rare bit of latitude.

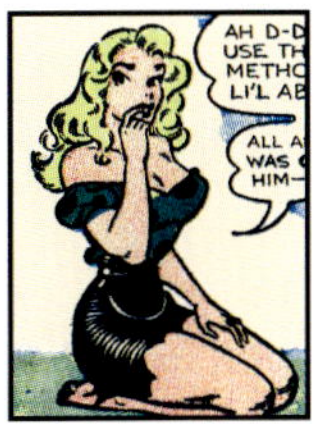

August 1, 1954. Page 52. **"Wife Magazine's Secrets of a Happy Marriage" (1 of 1).** Two decades before the women's liberation movement begins to flourish, **Al Capp** tweaks a female journalist espousing "modern scientific methods" of catching and training husbands while he simultaneously makes virtually every panel a pinup of **Daisy Mae**. This overtly sexy layout compares to the memorable 1/8/56 **Marilyn Monroe** Sunday (see Volume 2).

August 8, 1954. Page 53. **"Pappy's New Suit" (1 of 3).**

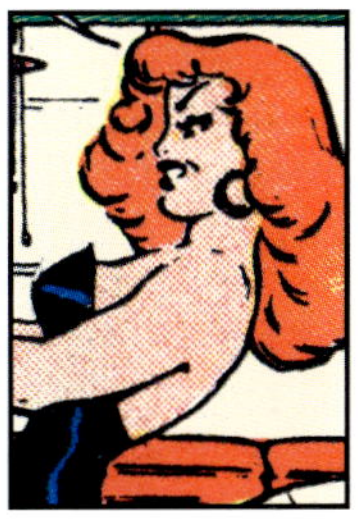

August 15, 1954. Page 54. **"The Tigress' Lair" (2 of 3).** The distinctive rendering of **The Tigress** in the bottom tier provides the first unmistakable evidence of **Frank Frazetta's** hand in the Sunday strips. His work on "Li'l Abner" was simultaneously appearing in the daily "Li'l Abner" strip, culminating in the legendary *Wild Ones* parody featuring a motorcycle hood named **Frankie** in the **Marlon Brando** role.

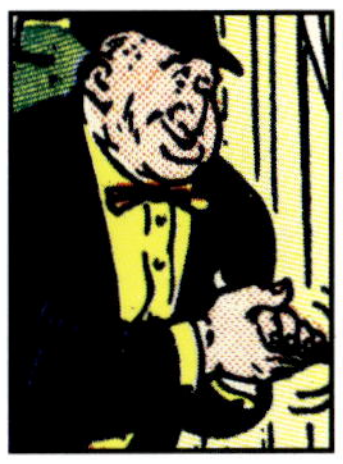

August 22, 1954. Page 55. **"Taming of the Tigress" (3 of 3).** The hoodlum **One-Shot Frankie** is ostensibly named for his shooting prowess, but two in-jokes are at play. He is undoubtedly named after **Al Capp's** new assistant, **Frank Frazetta**, who is simultaneously the namesake of a motorcyclist in the concurrent daily adventure. Secondly, this episode's **Frankie** makes a single appearance. In fact, he's limited to a single panel. In comic strip parlance, that makes him literally a "one-shot." Meanwhile, feeble-minded **Pappy Yokum** survives while his doppelganger cousin bites the dust.

August 29, 1954. Page 56. **"Harvard Lowers its Standards" (1 of 7).** Trademark **Frank Frazetta** women, like the blonde government secretary, will be visual hallmarks of "Li'l Abner" into 1961. **Harvard University** frequently plays into "Li'l Abner" adventures because **Al Capp's** home was in Cambridge, MA and his studio was in Boston. The mule-riding mailman delivering Harvard scholarships to **Lonesome Polecat** and **Hairless Joe** is a familiar-looking cast

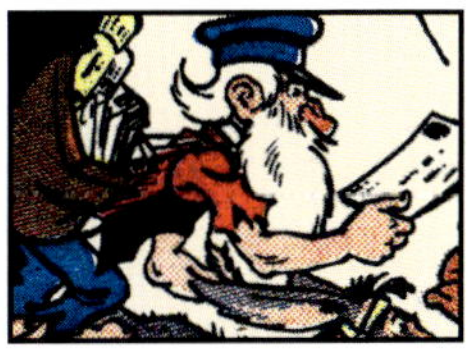

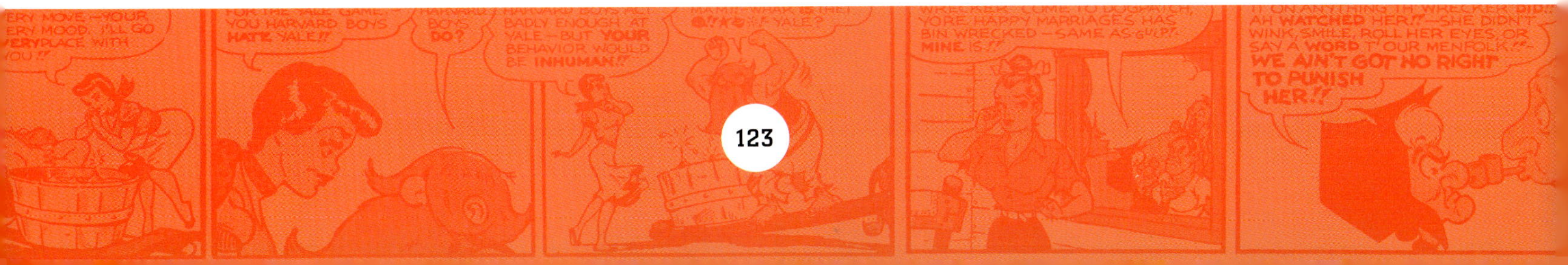

member. Whenever a letter (or newspaper containing "Fearless Fosdick") is delivered, he is the one delivering it, but even most long-time readers don't know his name. He's **Eddie McSkunk** and the name of his mount is **The U.S. Mule**.

September 5, 1954. Page 57. **"Studying the Sub-Human" (2 of 7).**

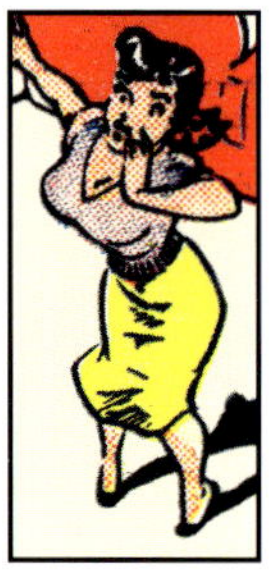

As Capp's motley cast travels to Yale University and New Haven, CT, he brings them to his birthplace. **Capp** lost his left leg in a trolley accident in New Haven at the age of 9 in 1919. Interestingly, anthropologist **Ondine Onusual** was identified in the previous week's teaser tag as **"Ondine Van Stakt."** Was the quick change to a non-risqué name the result of syndicate pressure or simply sloppy editing?

September 12, 1954. Page 58. **"A Diner, Not a Dinner" (3 of 7).**

September 19, 1954. Page 59. **"Harvard Beats Yale" (4 of 7).**

September 26, 1954. Page 60. **"Hairless Joe in Love?" (5 of 7).**

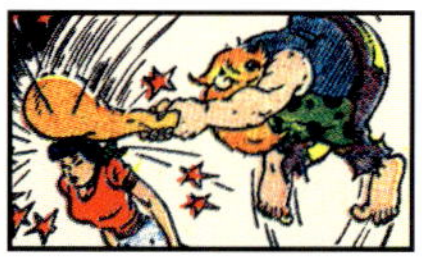

One of the cartooning profession's oldest visual clichés is the club-wielding caveman who demonstrates his love for his mate by bashing her into submission. **Capp** seemingly adopts the trite gag. But next week **Hairless Joe**, whose testosterone level is ordinarily much lower than his scrawny pal **Lonesome Polecat**, returns to character, unaroused by the comely anthropologist.

October 3, 1954. Page 61. **"Go Easy with the Punch" (6 of 7).**

October 10, 1954. Page 62. **"Boston Society Party" (7 of 7).** The seven-part

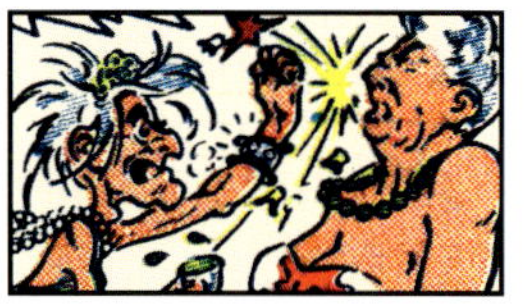

adventure climaxes with a common **Al Capp** truism. Like Dorothy returning to Kansas, Dogpatchers always come home. Those who venture from the security of their simple hillbilly haven find life in New York, Boston, and other exotic locales to be variously too uncivilized, too crooked or, in the case of our Harvard drop-outs, simply too dangerous.

October 17, 1954. Page 63. **"Loverboynik" (1 of 3).** In the early 1950s, long before his ostentatious Las Vegas persona, and long before his public outing and grim decline, the

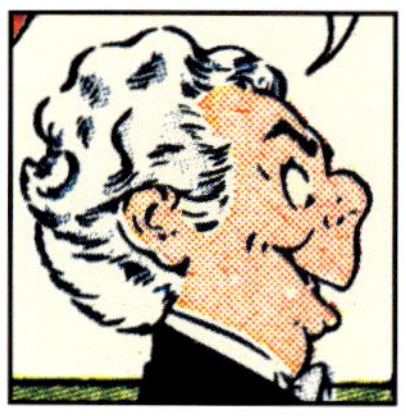

flamboyant pianist **Liberace** was a successful TV star. His boyish charm, wavy hair, and dimples drove mostly middle-aged women wild. **Liberace** also stressed his closeness to his mother, which clearly annoyed **Al Capp**. At an October 1955 speaking engagement **Capp** said, "I got the idea from a series of articles several newspapers were running on how much a certain piano player loved his mother. Most people love their mothers for free, so I decided to do **Loverboynik**." By having **Loverboynik** want his piano polished by **Li'l Abner**, not tuned, **Capp** aims his satire at the essence of style over substance.

October 24, 1954. Page 64. **"The World Tour" (2 of 3).** Acknowledging the intense loyalty of **Liberace's** audience, **Al Capp** precedes this week's episode with a tongue-in-cheek disclaimer.

October 31, 1954. Page 65. **"Hammy Performer" (3 of 3).** "I Don't Want to Set the World on Fire" [...I just want to start a flame in your heart] was a hit song by **The Inkspots**. The **Dogpatch Ham**, the

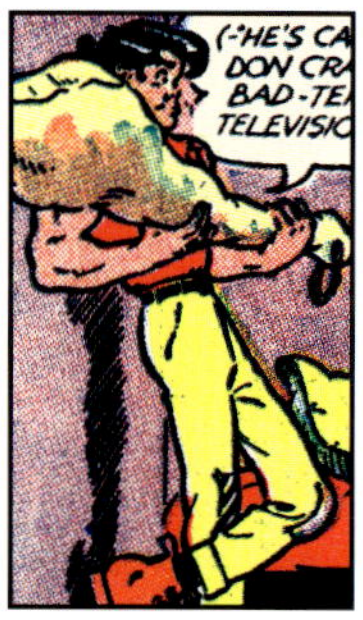

ultimate in "food to go," made numerous appearances in the strip over the years. A particularly phallic version of the ham accompanied **Daisy Mae** and **Li'l Abner** on their 1952 honeymoon. **Capp** ordinarily kept his Sunday continuities completely separate from the dailies, but a parallel **Loverboynik** episode ran concurrently in the dailies beginning October 30, 1954, as part of the annual November **Sadie Hawkins Day Race**.

November 7, 1954. Page 66. **"Dirty and Innercent" (1 of 4).**

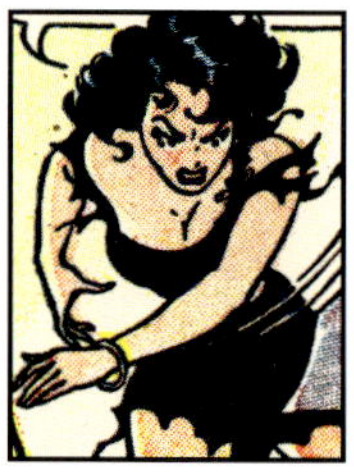

Longtime readers of "Li'l Abner" recognize gorgeous pipe-smoking **Moonbeam McSwine** as a Dogpatch fixture. She is often pictured wallowing with her beloved hogs, whose company she prefers to men. Even by Dogpatch's low standards, her hygiene is regarded as poor.

November 14, 1954. Page 67. **"The Ol' Switcheroo" (2 of 4). Henry Cabbage Cod** (like **Henrietta** in the 10/3/54 Sunday) is a play on **Henry Cabot Lodge**, a prominent New England statesman and blueblood. **Henry Cabot Lodge, Jr.** was a Senator from Capp's home state of Massachusetts

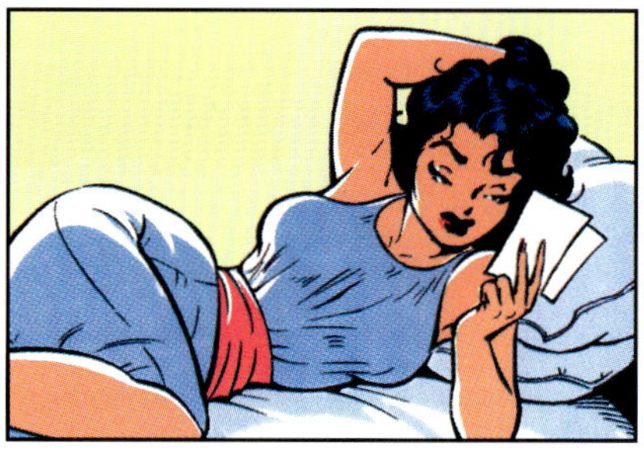

till 1952 and **Richard Nixon's** running mate in their failed 1960 presidential bid. **Lawrence Oliverwurst's** name is a spoof on British actor **Sir Lawrence Olivier**. Liverwurst is, of course, a sausage.

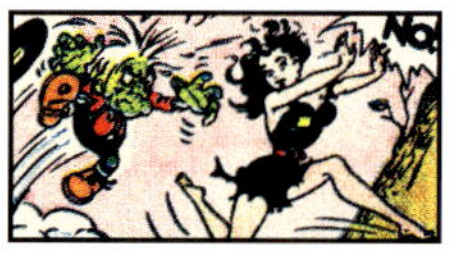
NO!

November 21, 1954. Page 68. **"Out of Control" (3 of 4).** When we last saw **C. C. Yokum** he was the only male who could resist **th' Wrecker's** salacious bump and grind (2/7/54). But even cold-blooded **"Complete Control"** has a libidinal weakness: a "clean" **Moonbeam McSwine**.

November 28, 1954. Page 69. **"The Bum's Rush" (4 of 4).**

December 5, 1954. Page 70. **"Introducing Druthers" (1 of 9).** The A-bomb (atomic) was used during World War II and the first H-bomb tests made headlines in 1953. In **Al Capp's** world, the U.S. government has no problem testing its new "X-bomb" on Dogpatch's outskirts, testimony to *just* how remote and backward the hamlet is. Only Lower Slobbovia suffers similar indignities (4/18/54 Sunday).

December 12, 1954. Page 71. **"Druthering Heights" (2 of 9).**

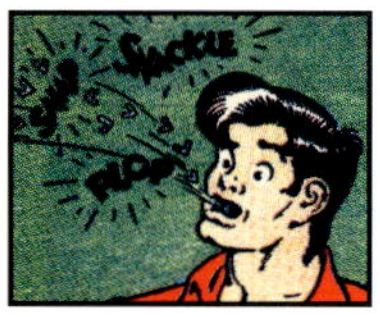

Emily Bronte's popular novel *Wuthering Heights* was written in 1847. **Ernest Hummingbird's** name, though nothing else, is a play on **Ernest Hemingway**.

December 19, 1954. Page 72. **"Too Evil for Harvard, Too Smart for Business" (3 of 9).**

December 26, 1954. Page 73. **"Opportunity Strikes" (4 of 9).** When evil entrepreneur **Hummingbird** says, "I'd druther eat these than do anything!" it conjures another context of **Peter Palmer** (**Li'l Abner**) singing, "If I had my druthers, I'd druther have my druthers than do any thing at all," in the 1956 *Li'l Abner* Broadway musical and subsequent film adaptation.

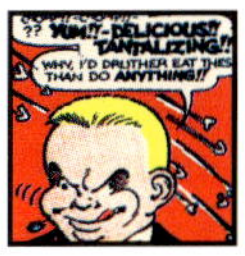
?? YUM!!-DELICIOUS!! TANTALIZING!!
WHY, I'D DRUTHER EAT THESE THAN DO ANYTHING!!

January 2, 1955. Page 74. **"Mammy's Fatal Contract" (5 of 9).**

January 9, 1955. Page 75. **"America Goes Druthers Mad!" (6 of 9).** **Mammy Yokum** speaks to **General Bullmoose** on Dogpatch's single antiquated phone, located at the general store owned by **Soft-Hearted John**.

January 16, 1955. Page 76. **"He'd Druther Charge More" (7 of 9).** Suddenly popular young collector Shorty is offered multiple images of **Ted Williams** (Boston Red Sox star), **Robert Montgomery** (movie star), and **Rocky Marciano** (boxing champ) for his **Mammy Yokum** box covers. The point of her popularity is well taken, even if the law of supply and demand is not (the other boys can buy Druthers for a penny a box too).

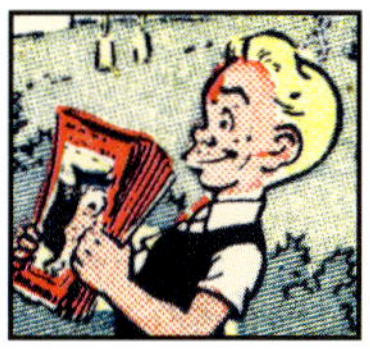

January 23, 1954. Page 77. **"Mammy Reviled" (8 of 9).**

January 30, 1955. Page 78. **"March on Dogpatch" (9 of 9).**

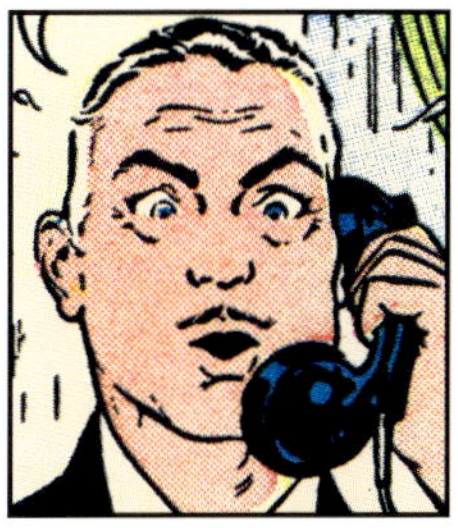

February 6, 1955. Page 79. **"Moontwinkle Cloth" (1 of 4).** Down-and-out couturier **Hernando Slideaway's** name is taken from the top ten hit, "Hernando's Hideaway." In 1954 it was evidently still acceptable for **Slideaway** or his creator to call inhabitants of "darkest" Africa "savages." These savages, nonetheless, demonstrate better fashion taste than the "primitive" women of Dogpatch.

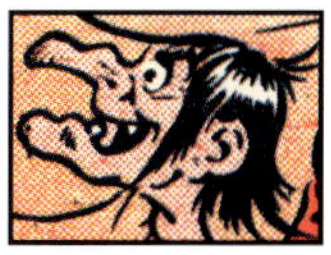

February 13, 1955. Page 80. **"Bat Brains and Lizard Livers" (2 of 4).** Dogpatch's resident witch **Nightmare Alice** is another recurring cast member. **Al Capp** said that he named her after the 1947 carnival film *Nightmare Alley*.

February 20, 1954. Page 81. **"A Hoomin Tongue" (3 of 4).**

February 27, 1954. Page 82. **"King of Sack Dresses" (4 of 4).**

March 6, 1955. Page 83. **"Sole Searching" (1 of 3).** The Dogpatch mother holding several children with bare butts in the panel 4 audience is **Fruitful Cornpone**. She's a recurring character, almost always seen carrying a haggle of children under both arms. In a memorable 1953 panel she hangs no less than nine of her naked kids on a tree like wash on a clothesline while she midwifes the birth of **"Mysterious" (Honest Abe) Yokum**. In the 10/16/55 Sunday later in this volume her children form a heaping flesh pile. In a notoriously conservative business where even many years later **Mort** ("Beetle Bailey") **Walker** was not allowed to draw a navel on his **Miss Buxley** character, **Al Capp** brashly pushed the limits of syndicated comics in countless ways.

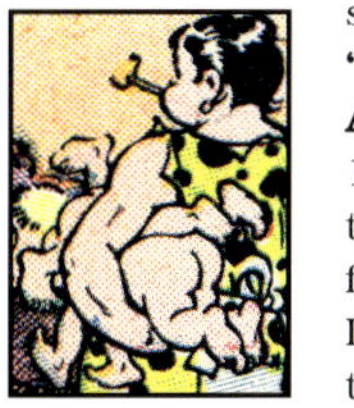

March 13, 1954. Page 84. **"How Tragic is My Breakfast" (2 of 3).**

March 20, 1955. Page 85. **"Smiles" (3 of 3).** There's a subtle joke in the opening announcement. Having had his pocket picked by the crooked toes of a barefoot audience member in the 3/6/55 Sunday, itinerant lecturer **Professor Fleasong** is quick to add "Shoes Compulsory" to his "Smiles" lecture handbill. And speaking of jokes, in the 4th panel **Fleasong** authoritatively asserts that the "world's most depressin' smile" is that of "someone who is listenin' to a joke they don't git!! This type o' smile is frequently found on mothers an' wives." Two years earlier **Al Capp** expanded considerably on this theme. He wrote an article for *Compact: The Pocket Magazine for Young People* called "Girls Have No Sense of Humor." This deliberately provocative piece cited his wife **Catherine** and daughters **Cathie** and **Julie** as examples of his premise. He actually concludes that females find different things funny.

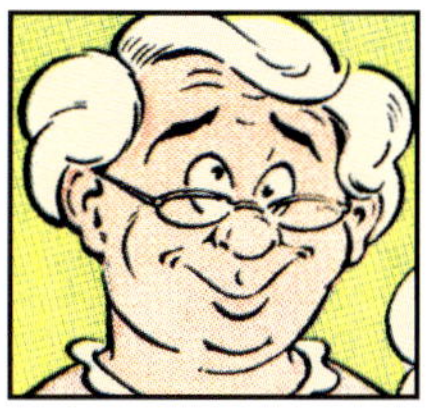

March 27, 1955. Page 86. **"Dave Grindaway" (1 of 4).** **Dave Grindaway** is very loosely inspired by **Dave Garroway**, a big enough period TV star that **Daisy Mae** thought he might be "th' most impawtint man on earth" (3/28/54). Here **Grindaway** is a documentary filmmaker who inadvertently discovers that **Li'l Abner** is "a great natural comic."

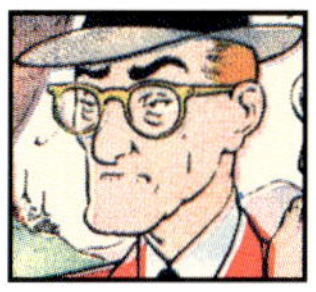

April 3, 1955. Page 87. **"Moving Mountains" (2 of 4).** **Dave Grindaway's** landlady, **Mary Workhorse**, is a dead ringer for competing strip character and busybody **Mary Worth**. See volume 2 of this series for **Capp's** harsh "Mary Worm" parody, one that sparked a professional "feud" and national publicity in 1957. The *Medic* show that the despairing director considers his starvation a suitable subject for was an innovative if short-lived medical program, the first to show a baby's birth. The cigar-chomping and guffawing TV executive is a **Capp** self-caricature. **Li'l Abner's** paltry $22.50 a week draw as a TV star is the same as his "ideel" **Fearless Fosdick's** perennial detective salary. $22.50, like many elements in "Li'l Abner," also had a hidden meaning. It was the exact salary that his original mentor and then lifelong enemy **Ham Fisher** paid **Al Capp** to ghost "Joe Palooka" in 1933. Every time **Capp** mentioned the paltry salary of $22.50 a week in his strip he hoped that **Ham Fisher** would squirm from guilt.

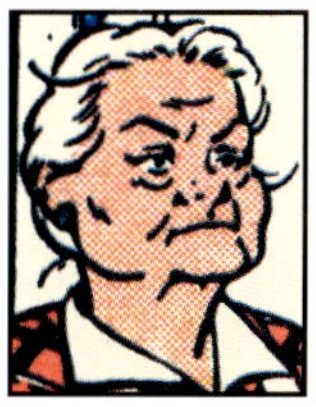

April 10, 1955. Page 88. **"The I Love Daisy Show" (3 of 4).** Eighteen years before PBS's groundbreaking documentary *American Family*, in which the Loud family was subjected to lengthy camera surveillance, and eons before the calculated cinéma vérité of *The Osbornes* and **Anna Nicole Smith, Li'l Abner** and **Daisy Mae's** "natural" on-air performances break ground first. The name *I Love Daisy* is an obvious riff on the enormously popular *I Love Lucy*.

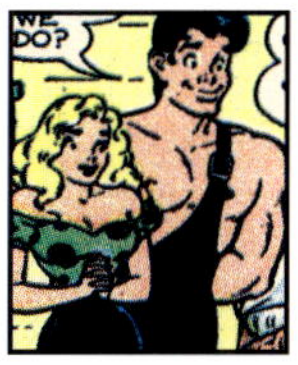
DO?

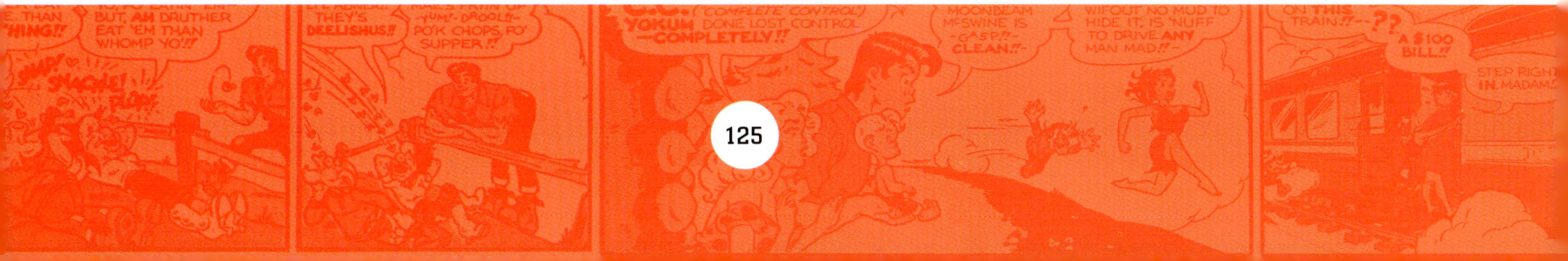
BUT, AH DRUTHER EAT 'EM THAN WHOMP YO'!!
THEY'S DEELISHUS!!
POK CHOPS FO' SUPPER!!
YOKUM DONE LOST CONTROL —COMPLETELY!!
WIFOUT NO MUD TO HIDE IT, IS 'NUFF TO DRIVE ANY MAN MAD!!
A $100 BILL!!

April 17, 1955. Page 89. "Sass All Folks!" (4 of 4). *The George Gobel Show* was a fixture on NBC and CBS from 1954-1960.

April 24, 1955. Page 90. "Luigi Lasagna" (1 of 2). Critics complained that "Li'l Abner" was a racy strip. Now *this* is a racy strip.

May 1, 1955. Page 91. "Back to Normal" (2 of 2). The only Italian words the average American understands here are the names of actresses **Gina Lollobrigida** and **Sylvana Mangano**.

May 8, 1955. Page 92. "The Old Pidgeon Drop" (1 of 5). Hollywood actor **Walter Pidgeon** was approaching the end of his career in 1954. His fan base at this point would be on the matronly side (i.e. **Mammy Yokum**).

May 15, 1955. Page 93. "She May Not be a Knock-Out, But..." (2 of 5). Popular TV stars **Jackie Gleason** and **Audrey Meadows** (**Ralph** and **Alice Kramden** on *The Honeymooners*) make ringside cameo appearances in panels 2 and 3.

May 22, 1955. Page 94. "Voodoo Hoodoo" (3 of 5).

May 29, 1955. Page 95. "Tuning in Channel Hex" (4 of 5).

June 5, 1955. Page 96. "Onappealin' Curvy Figger" (5 of 5).

June 12, 1955. Page 97. "Pappy and The Great Depression" (1 of 1). This self-contained Sunday is in the tradition of **Pappy Yokum's** other tall tales, all of which are reinterpreted by **Mammy**. (See also 7/18 and 7/25/54).

June 19, 1955. Page 98. "Trailer Trash Sisters" (1 of 4). **Cary Grunt's** name, though clearly no other attribute, is inspired by class actor **Cary Grant**. Seven-

foot-tall "**Tiny**" **Yokum** was introduced the previous year (September 1954) in the daily "Li'l Abner" continuity, in the same episode in which **Frank Frazetta** made his debut as an **Al Capp** assistant. **Tiny's** sudden and implausible appearance as **Li'l Abner's** full-grown brother was explained away with the same cartoon logic that got **Capp** out of some other tough plot predicaments. **Mammy** had somehow "forgotten" that she had given birth to **Tiny** fifteen and a half years earlier. In truth, with **Li'l Abner** now married, **Capp** needed an eligible young male to restore romantic tension in the strip and to take **Abner's** place in the annual Sadie Hawkins Day races. "Peanuts" cartoonist **Charles Schulz**, called the marriage of **Abner** and **Daisy** "the biggest mistake ever made in comic strip history... and *Li'l Abner* was one of the great comic strips of all time." **Al Capp**, **Schulz** added, "tried to return to it with the brother, which didn't work because the brother never had the appeal of **Li'l Abner**."

Like other key "Li'l Abner" cast members, **Tiny's** appearance dramatically evolved, but his change occurred much more quickly than the others. When first introduced he had a bulbous Yokum nose. But **Capp**, evidently determining that **Tiny** needed to be more attractive to the fair sex, moved fast. On December 2, 1954, less than three months after his debut, Tiny was in an auto accident requiring plastic surgery. Appropriately, the cosmetic surgeon was portrayed by **Al Capp** himself. This is **Tiny's** Sunday debut.

June 26, 1955. Page 99. "The Web Closes" (2 of 4). Admit it: you didn't know that Dogpatch had a Board of Health.

July 3, 1955. Page 100. "The Code o' th' Hills" (3 of 4).

July 10, 1955. Page 101. "Tiny's Wedding Day?" (4 of 4). **Marryin' Sam** operates a decidedly seasonal business. The great bulk of his weddings are performed in November, on **Sadie Hawkins Day**, the sanctioned holiday whereby Dogpatch's slow-footed bachelors are legally dragged kicking and screaming to the altar. But every once in a while **Sam** lucks out when "The Code o' th' Hills" is enforced (essentially a code phrase for a shotgun wedding).

July 17, 1955. Page 102. "Cousin Weakeyes Pays a Visit" (1 of 1). **Cousin Weakeye's** feline pet, **Milton Catnip**, is named after **Al Capp's** fellow cartoonist and close friend **Milton Caniff** ("Terry and the Pirates," "Steve Canyon"). **Capp** and **Caniff** met at the Associated Press in April 1932 when both were lowly staff artists. When **Capp** quit drawing the staid syndicated panel "Mister Gilfeather," the AP appointed **Caniff** to take his place. Soon afterward both made indelible impacts in their field and on the culture.

Milton Caniff (L) nose-to-nose with his friend Al Capp.

July 24, 1955. Page 103. "Our Rightful Heritage" (1 of 3). Dogpatch's native Americans are generally as lazy as their redneck neighbors. But absentee **Senator Jack S. Phogbound**, here in virtually indistinguishable gas-bag form, is the unintentional inspiration for Indian rebellion. When we last saw **Phogbound** (4/18/54) he was also "working" in France. The phrase "Un-American Activities," sadly, is not a **Capp** invention. It refers to the actual, if notorious, House Un-American Activities Committee (HUAC).

July 31, 1955. Page 104. "March on Washington" (2 of 3). Note that many of the Indians wear convenient bull's-eye targets as part of their war paint and attire.

August 7, 1955. Page 105. "Massacre Postponed" (3 of 3).

August 14, 1955. Page 106. "Comics' Bad Influence" (1 of 1). "Do Comic Strip Characters Influence American Youth?" The glaring headline comes from the fervent anti-comics crusade spearheaded by **Dr. Fredric Wertham**. The psychiatrist and author of *Seduction of the Innocent* argued that comic books had a depraved influence on young readers, leading directly to juvenile delinquency. **Al Capp** firmly and consistently stood up to this widespread movement in his cartoons, writings and speeches. Here **Capp** cleverly undercuts

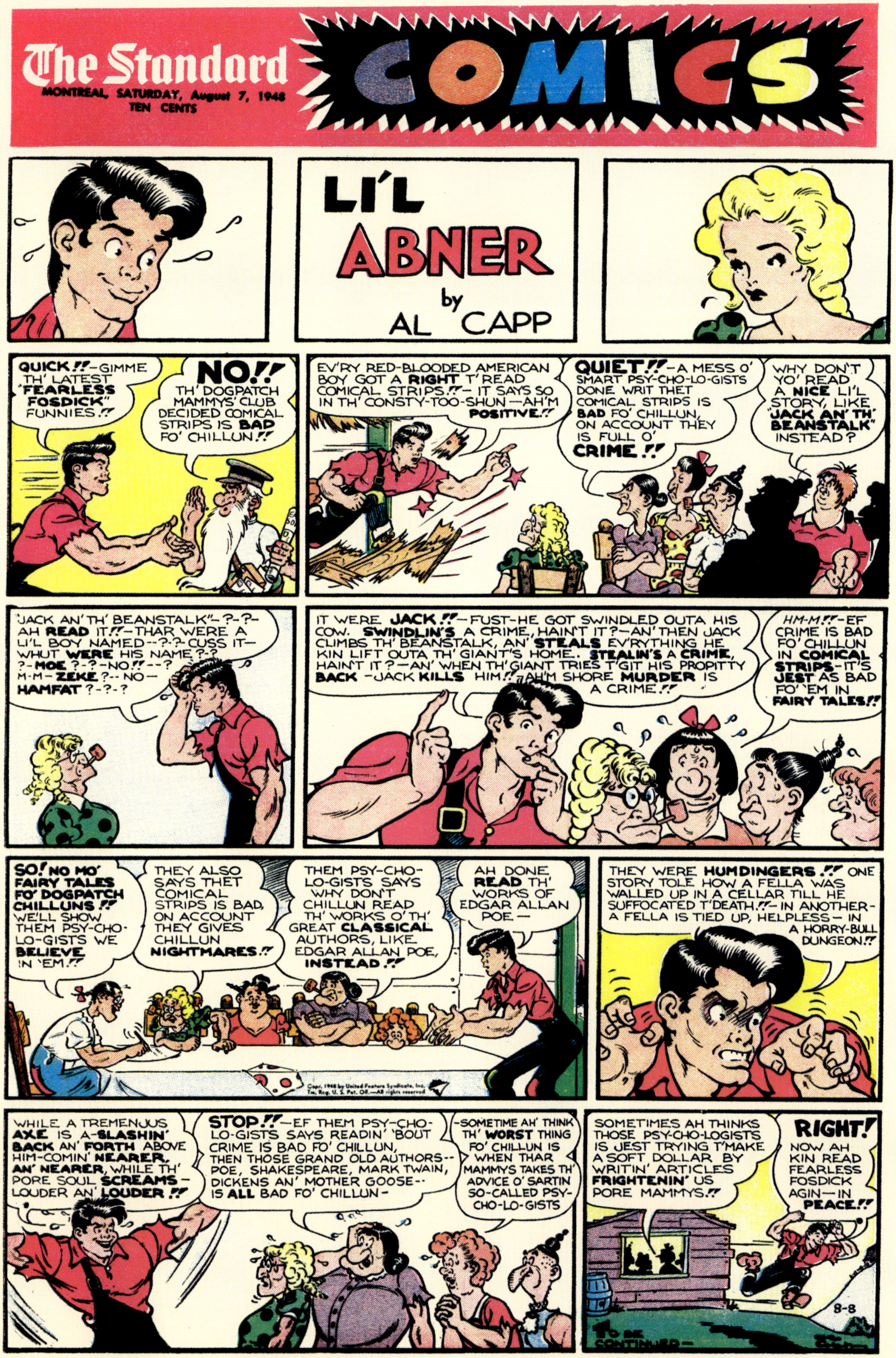
The Standard
MONTREAL, SATURDAY, August 7, 1948
TEN CENTS
COMICS
LI'L ABNER by AL CAPP
QUICK!!–GIMME TH' LATEST "FEARLESS FOSDICK" FUNNIES.!!
NO!! TH' DOGPATCH MAMMYS' CLUB DECIDED COMICAL STRIPS IS BAD FO' CHILLUN!!
EV'RY RED-BLOODED AMERICAN BOY GOT A RIGHT T' READ COMICAL STRIPS.!!–IT SAYS SO IN TH' CONSTY-TOO-SHUN–AH'M POSITIVE.!!
QUIET!!–A MESS O' SMART PSY-CHO-LO-GISTS DONE WRIT THET COMICAL STRIPS IS BAD FO' CHILLUN, ON ACCOUNT THEY IS FULL O' CRIME.!!
WHY DON'T YO' READ A NICE LI'L STORY, LIKE "JACK AN' TH' BEANSTALK" INSTEAD?
"JACK AN' TH' BEANSTALK"–?-?-AH READ IT!!–THAR WERE A LI'L BOY NAMED--?-?-CUSS IT–WHUT WERE HIS NAME?-?-MOE?-?-NO!!--?-M-M–ZEKE?--NO–HAMFAT?-?-?
IT WERE JACK!!–FUST–HE GOT SWINDLED OUTA HIS COW. SWINDLIN'S A CRIME, HAIN'T IT?–AN' THEN JACK CLIMBS TH' BEANSTALK, AN' STEALS EV'RYTHING HE KIN LIFT OUTA TH' GIANT'S HOME. STEALIN'S A CRIME, HAIN'T IT?–AN' WHEN TH' GIANT TRIES T'GIT HIS PROPITTY BACK–JACK KILLS HIM!!–AH'M SHORE MURDER IS A CRIME.!!
HM-M!!–EF CRIME IS BAD FO' CHILLUN IN COMICAL STRIPS–IT'S JEST AS BAD FO' 'EM IN FAIRY TALES!!
SO! NO MO' FAIRY TALES FO' DOGPATCH CHILLUNS!! WE'LL SHOW THEM PSY-CHO-LO-GISTS WE BELIEVE IN 'EM!!
THEY ALSO SAYS THET COMICAL STRIPS IS BAD, ON ACCOUNT THEY GIVES CHILLUN NIGHTMARES.!!
THEM PSY-CHO-LO-GISTS SAYS WHY DON'T CHILLUN READ TH' WORKS O' TH' GREAT CLASSICAL AUTHORS, LIKE EDGAR ALLAN POE, INSTEAD.!!
AH DONE READ TH' WORKS OF EDGAR ALLAN POE–
Copr. 1948 by United Feature Syndicate, Inc. Tm. Reg. U.S. Pat. Off.—All rights reserved
THEY WERE HUMDINGERS.!! ONE STORY TOLE HOW A FELLA WAS WALLED UP IN A CELLAR TILL HE SUFFOCATED T'DEATH!!–IN ANOTHER–A FELLA IS TIED UP, HELPLESS–IN A HORRY-BULL DUNGEON!!
WHILE A TREMENJUS AXE IS A-SLASHIN' BACK AN' FORTH ABOVE HIM–COMIN' NEARER, AN' NEARER, WHILE TH' PORE SOUL SCREAMS–LOUDER AN' LOUDER!!
STOP!!–EF THEM PSY-CHO-LO-GISTS SAYS READIN' 'BOUT CRIME IS BAD FO' CHILLUN, THEN THOSE GRAND OLD AUTHORS--POE, SHAKESPEARE, MARK TWAIN, DICKENS AN' MOTHER GOOSE--IS ALL BAD FO' CHILLUN–
–SOMETIME AH' THINK TH' WORST THING FO' CHILLUN IS WHEN THAR MAMMYS TAKES TH' ADVICE O' SARTIN SO-CALLED PSY-CHO-LO-GISTS
SOMETIMES AH THINKS THOSE PSY-CHO-LOGISTS IS JEST TRYING T'MAKE A SOFT DOLLAR BY WRITIN' ARTICLES FRIGHTENIN' US PORE MAMMYS.!!
RIGHT! NOW AH KIN READ FEARLESS FOSDICK AGIN–IN PEACE.!!
8-8
TO BE CONTINUED–

Comic book industry nemesis Dr. Fredric Wertham was tweaked in the August 7, 1955 Sunday annotated at left. But as this Sunday from several years earlier demonstrates, Al Capp had begun counter attacking comics critics such as Wertham much earlier.

Wertham's premise. The father of a teenager in 1955, **Capp** was also acutely aware that every generation rejects whatever style its parents embrace. Ironically, the hairstyle inspired by **Nightmare Alice** is back in fashion today. On the previous page is the Sunday "Li'l Abner" from August 7, 1948. It is another early example of **Al Capp's** staunch defense of First Amendment rights as they pertain to comic books and strips, under strong attack from Parent-Teacher groups (as shown here) and the infamous **Dr. Wertham** (the "psy-cho-lo-gist" referred to).

August 21, 1955. Page 107. **"I Know Joe!" (1 of 3).**

August 28, 1955. Page 108. **"The Magic Words" (2 of 3).**

September 4, 1955. Page 109. **"The Trooth Comes Out" (3 of 3).** Short reader's memories aside, it seems odd that someone as creative as **Al Capp** would prominently

utilize two different women named **"Joe"** in such quick succession (see the May 22—"Who is **Joe**?"—to June 5, 1955 Sundays).

September 11, 1955. Page 110. **"The Comedian's Secret" (1 of 1).** The TV comic who recycles **Pappy Yokum's** jokes is none other than **Milton Berle** a.k.a. **Mister Television**. One of **Berle's** shticks was that he "stole" his jokes from others. Fifteen years earlier **Berle** was the titular producer and co-credited songwriter for the low budget 1940 *Li'l Abner* film. Note that television sets were a rare commodity in America only a few years earlier, but by 1955 even a donkey stable in Dogpatch has one!

September 18, 1955. Page 111. **"The Genny-russ Millyunaire" (1 of 1).** A television comedian makes a guest appearance in "Li'l Abner" for a second consecutive Sunday. This time it's **Jack Benny**. One of the cornerstones of his humor is that he is a skinflint. Of course the irony is that by Dogpatch standards, **Benny's** nickel tip appears uncommonly generous.

September 25, 1955. Page 112. **"The Monstrosaurus Egg" (1 of 2).**

October 2, 1955. Page 113. **"An Expensive Dinner" (2 of 2).** Statuesque Indian Princess **Raving Dove** makes her second trip to the nation's capitol in two months, and **Lonesome Polecat** and **Hairless Joe** reprise their traveling dinosaur show from a year earlier.

October 9, 1955. Page 114. **"The Cornpone Confusion" (1 of 2).** Readers in 1955 would recognize **Pappy's** words in panel three as being lyrics from "The Sunny Side of the Street." For more on the fertile **Cornpone** family and the plethora of bare buttocks that accompany them see the 3/6/55 footnote.

October 16, 1955. Page 115. **"Blood Will Allus Tell" (2 of 2).** Honest Abe's first words were "p'ok chop," so regular readers instantly appreciate the bottom tier visual gag.

October 23, 1955. Page 116. **"The Time Capsule" (1 of 5).**

October 30, 1955. Page 117. **"Li'l Abner Declared Dead!" (2 of 5).** The desperate sort-of-widowed **Daisy Mae** appeals to the most "important people" she can think of. Senator **Jack S. Phogbound** is a fictional Dogpatch regular. Backwoodsman, congressman, and Alamo hero **Davy Crockett** was selling millions of coonskin caps for **Walt Disney** in 1955. Actor **John Wayne** needs no footnote, but he coincidentally portrayed **Crockett** five years after this mention. **Lawrence Spivak** was a TV producer. Singer **Nelson Eddy** was **Daisy's** first guess as "th' most impawtint man in the world" in the 3/28/54 Sunday. "The ever-popular" **Mae Busch** was an early film star who frequently appeared with **Laurel & Hardy**. **G. David Schine** was a controversial aide to commie-baiting Senator **Joe McCarthy** and his sub-committee counsel **Roy Cohn**. America's highest-ranking female officer **Oveta Culp Hobby** also served as Dwight Eisenhower's Secretary of Health, Education, and Welfare.

Robert Q. Lewis was a TV game show host. *Just Plain Bill* was a long-running radio soap opera. Presidential candidate **Alf Landon** lost to **Franklin D. Roosevelt** in the landslide 1936 election.

Montgomery Ward head **Sewell Avery** made headlines battling organized labor and FDR. **Farouk** was an international playboy, Egypt's last reigning king, and another "most impawtint" candidate (3/28/54). **Sonny Tufts** was such a bad actor that *The Golden Turkey Awards* created a special category for "The Worst Performance by Sonny Tufts." Singer and humorist **Tennessee Ernie Ford** had his own TV show in 1955. Cartoonist and **Capp** chum **Milton Caniff** is frequently alluded to in "Li'l Abner." Another cartoonist **Walt** ("Pogo") and actress **Grace** are linked only by their common last name, **Kelly**.

November 6, 1955. Page 118. **"Bargain fo' Bachelors" (3 of 5).**

November 13, 1955. Page 119. **"Mr. Perfect" (4 of 5).**

November 20, 1955. Page 120. **"Kickapoo Joy Juice to the Rescue" (5 of 5).** Eleven years after original publication, a *Li'l Abner* TV pilot was produced, based on this 5-part "Time Capsule" episode. In both plots **Li'l Abner** is locked inside a time capsule and declared legally dead by bewildered bureaucrats. Here the governor unveils the capsule. **Senator Jack S. Phogbound** has the honor in the 1966 pilot.

In this strip **Abner** is sealed for 10,000 years; it's a mere 1,000 on the small screen. The handsome stranger in the pilot is named **Henry Cabbage Cod** (see 11/14/54) and he doesn't use Kickapoo Joy Juice. The main twist is that the television version has **Daisy Mae** trapped with **Li'l Abner**, with both released by the handsome outsider. Abner keeps Daisy in both versions, *natcherly*. **Cod** is portrayed by **Robert Reed**. Three years later, **Reed** landed his career role as the father on *The Brady Bunch*. Other cast members: A not very brawny **Sammy Jackson** plays **Li'l Abner**; **Jeannine Riley** is **Daisy Mae**; **Judy Canova** portrays Mammy (without pipe or hat); **Jerry Lester** is **Pappy** (without a goatee!); **Dave Barry** plays **Phogbound**; and a convincing **Larry D. Mann** takes on **Marryin' Sam**.

The next story, encompassing six episodes, will run in Volume 2.